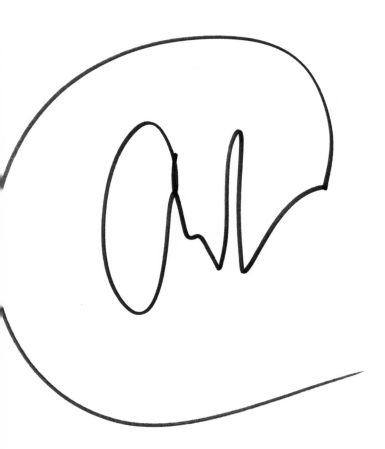

Better Together

Also by Christine Riccio

Again, but Better

Better Together

CHRISTINE RICCIO

WEDNESDAY BOOKS
NEW YORK

First published in the United States by Wednesday Books, an imprint of St. Martin's Publishing Group

BETTER TOGETHER. Copyright © 2021 by Christine Riccio. All rights reserved. Printed in the United States of America. For information, address St. Martin's Publishing Group, 120 Broadway, New York, NY 10271.

www.wednesdaybooks.com

Library of Congress Cataloging-in-Publication Data

Names: Riccio, Christine, 1990– author.
Title: Better together / Christine Riccio.
Description: First edition. | New York : Wednesday Books, 2021.
Identifiers: LCCN 2021002131 | ISBN 9781250760067 (hardcover) |
    ISBN 9781250760074 (ebook)
Classification: LCC PS3618.I279 B48 2021 | DDC 813/.6—dc23
LC record available at https://lccn.loc.gov/2021002131

Our books may be purchased in bulk for promotional, educational, or business use. Please contact your local bookseller or the Macmillan Corporate and Premium Sales Department at 1-800-221-7945, extension 5442, or by email at MacmillanSpecialMarkets@macmillan.com.

First Edition: 2021

10 9 8 7 6 5 4 3 2 1

For my siblings. Love yous.

PART 1

Rediscovering

1. Angst

I'm almost done living on pause.

Mom and I aren't *pause* people. We're a 1.5-speed household on our least productive day. We're always moving.

Productivity is an itch, one that most likely stems from Mom and her fervor for the *keys to success*. She doesn't reference them in our current day-to-day, but she spouted them incessantly through my preteen years. The *keys to success* include but are not limited to: goal setting, passion, preparation, discipline, perseverance, and luck. I've taken them all to heart. Preparation is my favorite key. The rest are fine. They're respectable, but preparation soothes my soul. If you don't regularly prepare to utilize your time efficiently, your goals just get further and further away.

I've been preparing for a ballet career my entire life. I'm always en route to the next practice, getting ready for the next performance, training harder, honing my craft. I crave the *chasse* prep before a leap. I like to be over the floor, not on it. I live for moments of perfect weightlessness—where I'm propelled into flight by nothing but my own strength and will.

I've spent the last twelve weeks shackled by gravity. This injury has been an unexpected hiccup. But it's a hiccup that's almost over.

I'm restless as the doctor brings us into his office. I stare at a small clock

3

set in a marbled piece of stone on the man's desk and try not to squirm in his burgundy fabric-covered chairs. It's slightly painful to squirm.

I've written down all the questions I have for him. There's only one that really matters: *When can I get back to work?* I need to unpause.

Ballet and I have been in a committed relationship since I could speak in full sentences. She's been my rock for as long as I can remember. We've never spent this much time apart. I'm tired of abstract healing timelines. I need an exact back-to-dance date I can circle on the calendar. I'm counting on it.

Mom sits in the chair next to me with her hands folded carefully over her crossed legs. Watching her continue to run on 1.5 speed while I've been stuck on pause has made this experience exponentially more frustrating.

We've been at this appointment for an hour now. The doctor ran me through a bunch of tedious movement tests. Bend over, stand up, walk this way, move like that. He asked fifty questions about my daily pain levels. He's examined the MRI. But he hasn't shared anything of substance throughout the entirety of the checkup!

I tap my foot against the chair leg as he slowly shuffles through the paperwork on his desk. This suspense is unbearable.

"So when can I get back to work?" I finally blurt.

He takes a breath. "You're still sleeping on the floor, correct?"

I swallow. "I mean, yes, but it's helping. I'm healing. It's not as bad. I *can* sleep now. The whole night. I've been sleeping without interruption for at least a week."

He breaks eye contact. Clears his throat. Scratches his balding head. Folds his hands together.

My heartbeat ticks up. Longer? How much longer?

"I'm very sorry, Miss Maza. I thought this was clear after our initial appointment. There's no going back to your previous lifestyle with this injury."

I scoff, pulling on my first smile of the last ninety-three days. "What? No, I'm healing. Of course I'm going back."

We sit in silence for ten seconds before he speaks again. "Back injuries are tricky. Something like this doesn't ever really fully heal. You're probably going to have to deal with chronic back pain for the rest of your life. What we can do is manage it with the right sort of physical therapy, yoga . . ."

I shake my head. This is laughable. *He's delusional.* This doctor is wrong. So wrong. He doesn't know me. He doesn't know how I'm healing.

I interrupt him. "No. No. I'm going to heal. I'm young, I'm only eighteen!"

He shakes head slowly. "I know this is a big life change for you. Lots of my patients find that swimming is a great replacement sport that won't put such intense pressure on your injury. I'd recommend giving it a try. Going back to ballet is going to make this worse. You could lose feeling in your f—"

"No." I'm still shaking my head. *Life change? Swimming?* I throw up my hands for him to stop because *he doesn't know.*

He's still talking. *Intercourse this.* He can't tell me no. He doesn't understand that I can't quit. I can't. This isn't a big life change—this is my *life.*

My mother is saying thank you and goodbye. She puts her arm around me, leads me out. I glare at her. *Why isn't she saying anything to him? Why isn't she fighting this with me?*

Tears start down my cheeks as we arrive at the passenger side of Mom's Toyota.

"You're going to be okay." We've been driving for five minutes and that's her opening line.

No. I'm *not* going to be okay. I have a fifteen-year plan. Prove myself. Join Mom on Broadway. We're going to be magnificent together. I've barely started! I've only performed in New York! I'm supposed to go everywhere! Work my way around the world and back!

Nothing is okay. This can't be a permanent hiatus. I don't do hiatuses in the first place! I'm consistent. I'm dedicated. I'm all the keys to success! I'm committed to *all of them*!

"Siri, it could be much worse, and I'm so grateful that for all intents and purposes, you're going to be fine."

That comment hurts more than I expect it to. I can't bring myself to be grateful. How can she say that? I can't break up with ballet! I'm not good enough at anything else.

My chest is convulsing. I'm trying to stay quiet, but I can't quite rein in the sound of my pent-up sobs.

"Siri, take a deep breath, get ahold of yourself."

Mom can't stand it when I get like this. *Sensitive.* I watch as her knuckles whiten against the steering wheel.

When I was a kid and emotions got the better of me, Mom would go out of her way to spend time together. We'd cook things. We'd watch one of the many dance shows cramming our DVR. Learn the routines together. I don't think she was ever comfortable with my tears, but at least she tried to make things better. Now she powers down.

We don't speak again until we're home.

"You're going to find a new dream," Mom says as she drops her purse on a chair. I still at the edge of the kitchen as she heads toward the stove. The celebratory *back-to-dance-date-appointment* cranberry granola bars I made earlier are sitting there mocking me now.

"What'd you make today?" Mom says as she pulls away the tinfoil over them.

Why isn't she more upset about this?

I fell in love with ballet watching Mom soar across stages on invisible wings, watching her spin for eternities. Like she was barely human. I don't know how many different times I've daydreamed about taking the stage with her. About the day she'd ask me to be in one of her shows. To even audition for one.

"You've never broken up with your dream, no matter how excrement it made things," I respond belatedly to her first comment.

Mom twists away from the food, her face pinched, skin pulled taut by her tight ballet bun. "Life throws boulders in your path. It threw them in mine. Not the same ones, but they still fell, and I had to find a way to get around them."

I try not to sigh dramatically, and fail. We stare at each other.

Mom doesn't like to share much, but Papa and I are close, and he's filled me in on her childhood. My nana died when Mom was too young to know her. Papa raised Mom alone. Mom had to put herself through college on part-time jobs, scholarships, and loans because Papa couldn't afford to send her to the fancy art school she wanted to go to.

But she's probably referring to my *greedy, selfish, abandoning jerk-and-a-half father* who left us when I was four.

Unless she means me? Am I a boulder?

I walk past Mom, through the kitchen, and into the living room where I settle flat on my back on the carpet. As of late, I usually spend about thirty minutes per day in this spot, staring up at the fake family portrait hanging above the fireplace.

Mom's face appears, hovering over me. Her amber eyes sear into mine. "What are you doing?" she says flatly.

I stare past her at the ceiling, opting not to respond. Mom's not usually here for this part of my post-injury routine. She's only around right now because she had to take off work early to drive me to that horrible appointment.

Mom takes a step, so she's standing beside my torso, looking down at me.

"I don't know if you forgot"—she folds her arms across her chest—"but you leave tomorrow for that Rediscover Yourself retreat we looked at a few weeks ago. I think it's going to be really good for you, especially now."

Not this again. I close my eyes, freeing some fresh tears. They slip sideways, toward my ears.

Mom's been pushing me to sign up for a random forest retreat in Colorado curated for people who feel like they've *lost their way.* We clicked around their website last month. I wasn't into it, but I humored her by agreeing to consider it.

"I've changed my mind. I don't want to go," I say quietly.

Mom shakes her head. "No, this is the whole reason we decided it was a good idea. You need to get out of here. Recenter yourself."

"We decided it was a good idea because of Bran, Mom, not because of this. I don't want to go anymore."

Mom steps back and sits on the living room couch. "It was partly due to what happened with your terrible ex-boyfriend, but we both know it was mostly because of your injury. You said you don't want to go back to therapy, so you'll go to the retreat. I've already paid and filled out your paperwork."

I jut up from the floor into a sitting position. "What?! You filled—Mom! I'm eighteen. Don't do excrement like that without telling me! You've mandatorily ultimatum-ed me without even presenting the options! What the underworld?"

"This is going to be a good thing." Mom's voice goes monotone. Powering down again. "It's only seven days."

"*Mom*, sitting around a campfire and singing top-forties music with strangers sounds like a literal nightmare right now!"

"I highly doubt you'll be singing music around a campfire at a Rediscover Yourself retreat. You saw the site. You'll be chatting with other people who are feeling lost, hurt—the things you're feeling."

Heat flashes through me. It takes everything I have not to scream. I yank the AirPods from my sweatshirt pocket, stuff them in my ears, and press play before reassuming my horizontal position along the floor.

My mother leaves the room. Good.

"Bury a Friend" blasts in my ears as I glare up at the portrait over the fireplace. It's almost six years old now. Mom looks beautiful with her long hair draped over her shoulder. Her handsome now-ex-boyfriend and my ex-kind-of-stepdad George stands next to her smiling. The middle school versions of his son, Gill, and I are sitting in front of the two of them, looking adequately awkward. We look like a perfect, happy family.

I loved envisioning us that way. I loved feeling like I had a family.

Before them, it was just me and Mom, and of course Papa. When George and Gill came into our lives, I thought we were locked in together forever. But Mom and George never married. So, when they broke up a month ago, the tentative family dynamic I'd been clinging to for the last seven years dissolved in a matter of days. This picture is a lie now.

George is wonderful. It'd been . . . a relief to imagine him as my dad. I can't keep doing that if he and my mom aren't together. It's weird.

My actual dad hasn't reached out since he left us for California. I google him once a month to keep up with his work; so we have a one-sided, distant, sort of stalkerish relationship.

I switch Billie Eilish's album out for the fury of my new favorite metal band, White Chapel, close my swollen eyes, and do my very best to disappear into the floor.

2. Angst and the Journey

SIRI
August 27, Thursday
New Jersey

Mom can't take me to the airport for my Colorado flight because a dancer got sick and she has to go into work early.

I flop the spoon around in my Special K and glare down at the Rediscover Yourself retreat pamphlet she shoved in my face last night. The brochure is covered in pictures of women of all ages participating in various outdoor activities, smiling their faces off. *No one is that happy.* Would it kill a marketing team to put a pensive person on a pamphlet?

I sit with my butt on the very edge of a plastic subway seat, back ramrod straight, suitcase tucked between my legs, en route to JFK. I'm staring at a partially defaced ad for one of my mom's favorite plays, *Mamma Mia!,* and mentally critiquing the irritatingly upbeat-looking actors.

Mom's "new normal" is blowing me off. It's why I spent the last five days reminding her about the doctor's appointment we went to yesterday. The woman's always, *always* headed to meet with her dancers. She's tirelessly rehearsing for the opening of a new musical she's choreographing called *Jean's Not Green.*

It's great. I'm happy for her.

But also, I'm not. Because I have to do things like bring myself to the airport via subway for a retreat I didn't sign up for.

A sigh escapes my lips.

I sigh too much probably. I know Mom doesn't like it.

White Chapel roars through my AirPods as the plane takes off. Metal works like that suction-tube straw thing the dentist sticks in your mouth to funnel out the drool when they're working on your teeth. You stick it in your ears, and it drains out the rage.

I managed to score a window seat for this flight, but I forgot to pack a book. I've been devouring poetry books these last couple of months because melodramatic metaphors about life have proven a worthy injury distraction.

Mom doesn't like poetry. Too dramatic. Poetry and I have that in common.

I've always been dramatic. I used to refuse food when I was upset as a child. I had an infamous imaginary friend from the age of one to five. I went through a phase where I refused to wear anything but white sneakers outside of dance, and I'd cry hysterically when they weren't immaculate. I was weird. But I wasn't *always mad* at *everything* like I am now. The day everything fell apart three months ago, I tripped into this anger ditch, and I can't seem to find my way out. I'm already pretty unlikable. I need to be alone too often. I'm too quiet. I'm too rigid. I like to be too early. And now I've got this hating-everything-thing happening. I hate it.

It'd be really nice to be chipper, or at least chipperish. It'd be nice if this place could help get me to chipperish. And if the meditation or whatever we'll be doing jogged a new life path idea, that would be ideal.

Right now, the future feels like a black hole. A dark, costume-less, stale abyss of heaving gravity where Mom can't help me.

I pull out the dumb brochure again and turn on my little overhead plane light.

———

It seems that a bunch of other women headed to this retreat and I have coordinated flights to Denver today, so that we can all be shuttled to the grounds together. I've positioned myself in the back left corner of the third bench in the Rediscover Yourself van we're all loaded into.

A cute dark-skinned girl with braids and mesmerizing eyes is sitting next to me. She's probably around my age. When I feel her look in my direction five minutes into the ride, I nervously pull out my brochure again to avoid speaking. The thing is looking pretty worn now, like I've been hoarding it in the top drawer of my nightstand for ten years.

The other girls and women are chatting with the super cheerful lady driving us. She has a ridiculous New York accent.

I tune in to what she's saying for a moment. *We believe yoga can play a huge part in recovering—*" And I tune back out. *Yoga.* Yoga is for people too damaged to do the activities they actually want to do.

A dull pain throbs in my low back and snakes down both my thighs. Yoga is for me now.

I pull up my hood and turn toward the window. The saddest part of all this is I need this retreat to work. I literally need to rediscover myself. What am I supposed to do now? I had enough trouble with this question during what I thought was a temporary recovery period. Now my goals are obsolete. I'm temporarily stuck . . . permanently on pause. That doesn't make sense, but it's true.

Mom has been little to no help on the issue. Little, because she gifted me a credit card so I can order groceries to the house and make things while I've been out of work.

I stick my hands in my sweatshirt pocket and fiddle with my AirPods, debating whether or not to pop them in again. I've become fairly dependent on angry music to get me through the day. It's part of my routine. Wake up, breakfast with Mom, pop in my AirPods as she leaves me in our now George-less house so I don't fall into a spiral of anguish, flip through the latest of Mom's old recipe books, and choose my next subject.

Cooking has become my number one distraction during these lonely times. My Instagram has taken a harsh turn. It's now full of mediocre food photography. There hasn't been anything else worth posting about. I need this retreat.

I hate that.

I need a new direction and I hate that.

I need all the ridiculous, uplifting clichés to find me and pull me out of this pit.

3. A Girl Is Mildly Traumatized

JAMIE
August 26, Wednesday
California

"Next up tonight, we have a charming young comedian. You've seen her around, she works tickets outside the club—James George Federov!"

The crowd cheers mildly as I skip my way to center stage and stop in front of the mic. Ten minutes. I have an entire ten minutes.

I shake out my limbs, feeling more tense than usual.

I've got this. I've fucking got this. "Hey hey hey, I'm Jamie George Federov!"

Adrenaline spikes through me as I take the mic off the stand. "You've definitely never heard of me. I'm but the humble semi-only child of a Hollywood producer."

The crowd chuckles.

"Yeah, my Dad's a producer." I throw on a haughty accent. "He fancies himself an *auteur*." I nod to the crowd. "For those of you who are unfamiliar, that's film slang for pretentious white man."

I pull on a smug grin. "My father, the *auteur*. I owe him so much—most notably my charmingly dickish Hollywood nature." I smile up at the ceiling. "Thanks, Dad." More mild laughter.

"My dad, he's a youthful, pretentious soul . . ." I sigh wistfully. "If I were to guesstimate, I'd say fifteen. He's a pretentious fifteen-year-old boy in a

13

forty-year-old's body." I wander to the right side of the stage. "I'd say I'm like a slightly frumpy forty-year-old in a"—I look down at myself in my red corduroy overalls—"twelve-year-old's body?"

Laughter.

I wander to the left edge of the stage. "I was carded trying to see the most recent *Titanic* re-release in theaters a couple weeks back.

"That film is PG-13 for boobs! I'm almost twenty-one, I have two real, physical, grew-them-myself boobs. But apparently"—I point to my head—"this face screams *not yet worthy of seeing Kate Winslet naked*." I catch a handful of snorts from the front row and smirk down at them.

"My pretentious dad, of course, has the latest iPhone. What is it, the iPhone 23H or something? It has a face reader. You all probably have it too; you live on Earth.

"And Dad and I, we share a similar facial structure. These knife-edge, scary cheekbones here"—I circle around the area vigorously with my pointer finger—"these are from him. When I have shades on—which is always, we live in LA—and I hold his phone to my face, the thing unlocks."

Someone in the crowd gasps.

"Yes, gasp! Exactly the reaction I wanted, *the scandal*! FEAR ME, FATHER, WE'RE INTERCHANGEABLE. Prepare to be hacked!" I laugh maniacally, before abruptly settling down.

"What does that mean, you guys? I'm legitimately concerned. Does my face look close enough to a forty-something-year-old man's or does my forty-something-year-old father look a lot like a twenty-year-old girl?

"He gets Botox regularly, so it has to be the latter, right?

"Man, if it were the other way around, I'd be hitting those PG-13 movies hard." I stop pacing and stare down the crowd. "Every day. No ID needed. Just walking on in like a real grown-up with real boobs, questioned by *no one*. Hit me with some Winslet nudes," I growl.

Lots of chuckles. So far, so good.

"You know what blows the whole *I'm youthful* charade for Dad though—Twitter." I bob my head around. "I mean, firstly, the fact that he even has a Twitter at all." Someone snorts.

"But more obviously, the fact that the dude has no idea how to wield it.

He's like a bird with a laptop. There's so much potential there, but all it decides to do is shit on the keys."

Mild, quiet laughs.

"This is a real live tweet he sent out to thousands of followers last week." I clear my throat and deepen my voice. "'There's nothing like a high-quality sandwich. Amirite. Yum.'" I raise my brows and glance around, looking for a smile. I don't find any. "He's really letting down the auteur community with that one."

A distant chuckle.

Okay, not hitting. Next.

Someone coughs.

Shit.

What's the next bit?

"Yeah, Father couldn't be more Twitter basic if he tried."

That is not the next bit.

My heart beats a little harder. I smile out at the now stone-faced audience. *Fuck.* I take a breath, trying to find the next line of my set.

I can only remember the joke I cut from the old five-minute lineup a couple of gigs ago. "What would you do with three hundred thousand Twitter followers? Take a poll about which chair to buy for your office? Because that's how Dad does it in the Federov household." I speak too quickly, without rhythm or pause.

No laughs. My mouth is dry.

"I've never actually been on Twitter myself. I am a forty-something-year-old man at heart." You could hear a pin drop in here.

What a mediocre nothing joke! *Stop talking about Twitter!*

"My dad spends more time on Twitter than he does with me, so I'm thinking of making an account. Slipping into them DMs and asking for a pony," I blurt.

One person guffaws in the back. Dear lord.

Get back to the set.

I lick my lips and stare out into the darkness.

Come on. SAY SOMETHING. Anything.

I can't remember my act.

The sound of my breathing is overwhelming. People start to mutter in the crowd.

I can't lose control of the crowd.

I glance around some more.

How long have I been silent?

This is so bad. The muttering turns into noise.

What is wrong with me?

I open my mouth. *Come on!* Even when I bomb, I bomb speaking! *SPEAK.*

"Twitter," my voice cracks.

"We don't give a shit about Twitter!" someone shouts.

Shut up about fucking Twitter!

"Get off the stage!" someone jeers.

I brace my hands and the mic against my thighs, gasping. Why can't I breathe? I can save this, if I skip to the next bit. *If I can remember anything other than my damn name and the word Twitter!*

"You're not your dad, get off," someone groans.

I gag as something surges from inside my gut, out my mouth, and all over the front of the stage. Maybe off the stage.

"Something" is the remnants of the pepperoni pizza I had for dinner.

Someone gags in the audience. I look into the spotlight. I can save this. *Talk about throw up.*

The crowd boos and yells. I stare at them.

There are so many jokes about vomit! Why can't I think of any?

I hear someone else throw up in the crowd.

Oh god. The manager's walking out toward me. I stumble awkwardly as he takes my arm and guides me off stage. The crowd cheers as a man with a mop glides into view.

"No!" I jolt upright in bed, panting.

My alarm clock is blaring the *Men in Black* theme. Bits of my hair are plastered to my cheek. Shit. I run a hand over my face and blow out a hard breath.

I've been reliving that disaster in my sleep every night for the past week and it's fucking horrifying every time. I silence the alarm clock with a slap. Why did I set that again?

I pitch forward as someone pounds on the door.

"Jesus Christ!"

"Up?" Grams shouts.

Double shit. I glance back at the time. Grams wanted to go to brunch; we're supposed to leave in fifteen minutes.

"Up!" I throw off my sweaty sheets and head for the shower.

I scramble downstairs eighteen minutes later, fully expecting to meet Grams in her car halfway down the driveway. She isn't one to wait patiently when I'm running late; she's always gunning the engine so we can take off the second my ass hits the seat. She's got sass and I love her for it.

I stop short on the bottom step as I catch sight of Grams standing behind the kitchen table.

"Morning, granddaughter." She smiles enthusiastically. Not her usual reaction to my tardiness. *Suspicious.* Her white-blond hair is pulled back into a low bun at the nape of her neck, and she's wearing a Grams standard—a purple, blue, and white ascot with a white blouse and slacks.

The kitchen table's decked out: French toast, a bowl of balled fruits, bacon, and sausage.

I blink at her, "What is all this? Are you posing for a cooking portrait?"

She tilts her head. "Sure, get your damn easel out. I can't stand here all day."

I skeptically make my way over. "Is this a *you were evicted* homemade pity breakfast?"

Grams steps out of portrait mode and takes her seat at the head of the table. "Excuse me, I wanted to share an early homemade meal with my granddaughter to celebrate her moving back home. Is that a crime?"

I raise my brow, studying her carefully. "It's suspicious."

She serves me an intimidating single brow raise of her own.

I grin. "But it doth look delicious. Thank you, Grams."

There's paperwork waiting next to my place setting. *Great.* I nod toward the printout. "What's that? New demands from dear old Dad?"

Of course, he's too busy to be here and enforce his own decrees. *This is definitely a pity breakfast.*

Grams sighs and motions me to sit. "Nothing new, you're all moved back in. It's time to start following through on his contract."

The guttural despair of all-consuming failure slithers through me. I shove it down. I got out of this house once. I'll save enough money and take on enough work to get my ass out again.

I waggle my eyebrows and start loading my plate. "Lay it on me."

Grams spoons a heap of balled fruit onto her plate. "You have to decide today about the first clause."

Ah yes, the first clause, mandated therapy. *A healthy mind equals a healthy career.* I'm to: *Schedule a weekly appointment with Dr. Ronnie* (one of Dad's many exes) *or sign up for that retreat your grandmother's been talking about.*

Grams serves me a spoonful of fruit without asking. "Weekly therapy with Ronnie or should we get you locked in at Rediscover Yourself? That one starts tomorrow. We'll have to get you scheduled on a flight, but you could knock this clause out in seven days and be done with it. Just fill out the paperwork." She taps the sheet on the table between us.

What a time to be alive.

I pull the paper closer and grab the pen Grams left next to it.

REDISCOVER YOURSELF, with us!—PREP SHEET

What do you want?

"*What do you want?*" I scoff. "What kind of question is that?"

Grams doesn't look up as she cuts up a slice of French toast. "It's a straightforward one, granddaughter. I think you can handle it," she snarks.

I click the pen.

What do you want?
To be a successful stand-up comedian and travel the world performing.

To write and perform the perfect set.

Duck Waterfall to score an audition for a weekly spot at QCZ

To not live in my father's house.

To never become my father.

What's preventing you from getting there?
My inability to deliver a perfect set.

How can we work on moving past this block in your path?
. . . If I knew I wouldn't be fucking coming, would I ?

I fold the paper in half and push it back toward Grams. "Locked and loaded. Don't read it."

With a satisfied grin, Grams plucks the paper from the table and drops it in the purse sitting on the floor next to her feet. "Great! I'll get it sorted. I think I can get you in to get your hair fixed this afternoon as well?" she proposes.

I roll out my neck. "Can we hold off on that one?" *Forever, preferably.*

She nods, picking up her still steaming cup of tea. "I'll see what I can do, but your father wants it done soon. I'm proud of you, granddaughter."

I force a laugh. "Proud of my failure to launch?"

I take a swig of my pre-poured orange juice waiting for her to take the bait and change the subject.

Grams shakes her head, grinning. "Don't get me started on that movie."

I smirk. "Hey, that's some of McConaughey's best work."

Grams sticks a piece of watermelon with a fork and points it in my direction. "No, Jamie, I'm proud of you as a human. You're trying, you're getting there, you'll relaunch."

4. A Girl Is Off to Colorado, Apparently

JAMIE
August 27, Thursday Afternoon
California

A pleasant, gentle knock sounds behind me. I turn to find Dawn leaning against the doorjamb in hot pink jeans, light pink crop top, and matching pink leather jacket.

"You texted?" she greets sarcastically.

I watch from my closet as she flops sideways onto my girly peach-pink canopy bed.

"Hey hey hey! Lady Torres," I yell from among the clothes.

She throws on a brief English accent. "Well met, Lady Federov, what doth I ask is up?"

We did a scene together in terrible old English accents last month, and we've been slipping random nonsense into our everyday exchanges ever since.

"I shalst haveth some news. My dad-slash-Grams thinks I should go to this off the grid Rediscover Yourself yoga bullshit retreat."

"A yoga bullshit retreat." Dawn laughs from the bed. Her head's hanging upside down off the edge now. Her shiny dark hair dances in the light. "Why?"

Ah, why? Dawn doesn't know about the therapy clause in Dad's contract. I've shared selectively.

I was kicked out of my apartment for being two days late on rent. I haven't booked an acting gig in months. I'm questioning everything I ever thought I could do because I completely humiliated myself on stage at the Laugh Drop—not just a historic comedy club, but also, you know, my place of work. Oh yeah, and I'm broke. I'm game to escape reality for a week.

I yank another plaid shirt from a hanger in my closet. "It's for people who are feeling lost, and it's in Colorado, and I leave tomorrow."

Dawn jackknifes upward. "Wait, what? What do you mean, *tomorrow?*" Her hair resettles around her heart-shaped face. "Jamie, you're going to Colorado?"

I shoot her a grin. "Why do you think I'm packing?"

"I thought you were picking out an outfit!"

"Nope, packing." I throw the pile of shirts draped over my arm out into the room. It lands in a muffled clump on my ancient fuzzy pink carpet.

"What about Duck Waterfall? We have practice tomorrow. How long will you be gone? I have an anatomy exam next week, Jame. I was counting on you taking lead."

Cultivating our improv team, Duck Waterfall, was a great idea, and through hours of practices and coaching, our little comedy group has bloomed into something really promising. It's been a strangely rewarding, hilarious journey. But to make all this progress happen, over the past year I've had to scale back hours at both my side jobs (hustling tickets for the Laugh Drop and teaching kiddies beginner hip-hop), turn down multiple auditions for practices, and consistently pitch in for biweekly coaching sessions with outside talent. One could say Duck Waterfall played the leading role in my financial demise.

"You can handle one week of Duck Waterfall practice. I'll be back next Thursday." I shrug. "And if you can't, just cancel it. It's only two practices."

Dawn shoots me a flabbergasted look. "Jamie, we're finally starting to really find our groove as a team. I'm not canceling practice."

I exit the closet, drop to my knees, pull open my bottom dresser drawer, and start transferring underwear into the orange backpack I have open at the foot of my bed.

Dawn rolls to her stomach and rests her chin on her hand. "Can you tell me what is going on with you this week? You've been off. Sidebar: I'm appalled you keep your underwear in the bottom drawer."

"Nothing's going on." I pull open a new drawer and focus on the disarray of socks inside.

"Jame. I know you had a stand-up gig last week. I know you must have bombed. Can we just talk about it? Would you please just let me come to a damn gig?"

I treat Dawn to a hard stare from my position on the floor. She pulls her legs up under her and stares right back from the high ground of the bed.

"No, thanks. I'm fine." I return to the drawer.

I've been performing a five-minute version of my set at open mics around the area for the last six months, but I've yet to do it in front of anyone I care about—or know.

I'm not ready. The set's not there yet. I don't want them to come out and see a mediocre comedian (especially after what happened last week). I want them to see someone worth seeing.

Only Dad, Grams, and Dawn even know I've been performing.

It's impossible to talk about pursuing stand-up without people snap judging everything about you. I don't want people to think *I think* I'm funny. I want them to think I'm funny on their own. And I don't want them to doubt me because I'm a woman. Or because I'm young. Or because it's a long-shot career that doesn't usually pan out. That's what happens when people you know watch you perform while you're still working on your exceptionally subjective, finicky craft. If they don't laugh, if they catch a bad go, if you don't shine like a perfect star, you're forever tainted in their eyes. Forever unfunny. Forever incapable of your farfetched goal.

"Jamie. You're obviously not fine."

My eyes flit up to Dawn's. "I need a whole new set, D. The plan is to milk the retreat for material. I'm betting I meet at least three screwballs with broken relationships and distorted senses of reality to dissect." I reach for the pile of clothes I chucked from the closet and stuff them into the backpack as well.

"Jame, if you let me hear your current set, we could workshop it! I can help. *I'm betting* you already have some good material."

I plaster on a smile and chuck a handful of mismatched socks up at Dawn. They rain down around her. "It's all good. I've got it under control."

She sighs and throws one back at me.

"With the eviction thing and moving back in here . . . Grams thinks I need to get away for a few days to figure out my shit . . ." I shrug nonchalantly. "Maybe she's on to something."

Dawn exhales a resigned breath. "Well, I for one, am glad you're back in this house. It's nice having you next door again."

I grin at her. "That is a fabulous perk." I shove everything down and attempt to zip the backpack.

Dawn shifts to hang her legs off the bed near my spot on the ground. "Have you told Aaron you're leaving for a week?"

"Why would I have told Aaron?"

"Did you already drop him?"

I scoff. "I never picked him up."

She shoots me a sad smile. "I love you, and I support your random whimsical lifestyle, but, Jamie, you can't sleep with people on Duck Waterfall and never call them again. It's gonna mess with our dynamic. He thinks you're dating. He talked my ear off about you after last week's practice. You have to call him."

I pull the top half of my hair up and tie it into a little foof on my head. "Maybe you should take a leaf from my tree and ask out Mona."

"A leaf from your tree? I'm not dating someone on the team."

I grin excitedly. "Fine, you should download Tunder or Hunge or whatever people are using while I'm gone, and then regale me with the dating stories when I return!"

Dawn rolls her head and executes a comedic teenage groan.

"You and Danielle broke up like ten years ago."

Danielle was subtly insulting Dawn and picking away at her self-esteem during the eight months they were together. I didn't find out until after the fact, and I'm still furious with that woman.

"Ten months," Dawn corrects.

"Same thing."

"It's really not, and like I said, I have a test this week. I don't have time. Call Aaron."

Breakups are fascinating. Sad, but fascinating. I've found, more often than not, they fall into one of five relationship-ending categories:

a) partner cheated
b) partner was a secret asshole
c) partner had commitment issues
d) partners drifted apart
e) partners disagreed on something fundamentally important

I've always wondered where my own parents would sort. My money's on a) Dad cheated. Considering his romantic track record, I think it's a fair bet. Dawn's Danielle sorts into b) secret asshole. I don't participate in relationships, but from Aaron's point of view this is probably going to sort under c).

I snatch my phone off the dresser, find Aaron Duckwaterfall in my contact list, and press send. Holding the phone to my ear, I pivot to widen my eyes at Dawn. She shoots me a withering look.

"Jamie?" Aaron's voice picks up on the other end.

"Hey, Aaron, I'm just calling to let you know we're not dating. You're cool, but we're just friends. Don't make it weird. See you next week at practice!"

"What? I thought, wait, is practice cancel—"

I hang up the phone.

Dawn *tsks.* "That was fucking brutal."

"We hung out alone once!"

She hops off the bed. "Get ready to treat me to an *I'm leaving you to run the team alone without any notice* dessert from a place on my Instagramable list."

I shoot my BFF a prizewinning smile. "You got it, dude."

5. Angst and Socializing

I can pinpoint the precise moment my metaphorical ball of life-yarn rolled off a cliff six months ago.

"Will you come with me?" My voice went up an octave as I ended the monologue I'd rehearsed. Reciting it for Bran made me feel like popcorn was exploding behind my sternum.

It's nerve-racking to buy tickets on the presumption that you'll have someone to go to an event with. But when I got those concert tickets, I had a best friend and a boyfriend. I had people in my life that weren't blood-related that voluntarily hung out with me. Two people that could potentially be my plus-one.

George's son, Gill, was technically around too, but he was away at college. We never bonded to the point where we did things together outside the house. We're mutually antisocial so if you put the two of us alone in a room together, the result is resounding silence.

Bran and I were in the dressing room. He slid his arm into a black windbreaker and looked down at me with a neutral expression. I tried to swallow down my anxiety. *Why wouldn't he come with me? He's my boyfriend.* If he invited me to a concert to see his new favorite band, I'd obviously go!

Bran smiled as he hoisted his bag up on his shoulder. I grinned back, the

25

popcorn in my chest easing. Then he said, "It's not my thing. Ask Celia, I'm sure she'll go."

That was it, that was the pivot point.

Those tickets ruined my life. If I hadn't bought those tickets, maybe he would never have seen me as some devil music–worshiping freak and things wouldn't have changed and everything wouldn't have fallen apart.

Once you start seeing someone in a new light that you're not a fan of, it's hard to go back to seeing them in the bright shiny light you started out with.

It's hard to know which parts of me will dim that light for people. I know now that my new music taste is one of them.

"Siri Martine?" Donya asks.

I blink back to the present, refocusing on the dirt under my feet. Excrement. I've been zoning out. I've spent the majority of the last twenty-four hours zoning out.

Yesterday I made it to the retreat. *Yesterday.* It's already been almost a day. I signed up for activities. I was assigned a cabin. I ate food. Slept. Woke. I went to group yoga this morning, and I'm currently in a group therapy session that thinks it's being inconspicuous by calling itself *Group Chat.*

Yoga increased my pain level earlier. Yoga! The healing activity for damaged people!

I'm sitting in my chair like there's a sword tied up against my spine because any sort of slouching is painful. It's been this way for months, but it's more prominent now post–disastrous yoga session.

"It's Siri," I correct quietly.

I'm doing my best not to let any rampant anger leak out in front of these innocent strangers, but it's coiling in my chest, rearing to strike. *I should be able to do yoga!*

"What was that?" Donya urges.

Donya's our "leader," aka group counselor. She's also the yogi who taught the class earlier. She's got light brown skin and long, curly dark hair pulled up into a tight high ponytail. Probably in her late thirties. She's a licensed therapist *and* a certified yoga instructor. Apparently, yoga and meditation are what got her through the anxiety she experienced through college and graduate school.

Seven of us retreaters, plus her, sit in a circle of folding chairs on the beachy dirt alongside a giant lake in the wilderness. The sun streams down on us. My jet-black braid drinks in its warmth, and the heat coalesces into a river against my back that I can feel through the fabric of my light athletic sweatshirt.

"It's just Siri." I try to project my voice without sounding irritated.

"How's your first day of the retreat thus far, Siri?" She projects a kindness into her words that prompts me to slowly meet her eyes.

"I'm frustrated thus far."

Donya nods. "I think a lot of us came here feeling frustrated with one thing or another. Can you elaborate?"

I clear my throat. "I can't elaborate." No one wants to hear me elaborate. Elaborating would consist of my extremely uncreative list of new things I've been irritated by since arriving: my dirty log cabin, the public bathrooms, the yoga class, the fact I haven't been able to listen to music for the last nine hours.

We have to be entirely off the grid here! I had to hand over my iPhone at registration, so I can't check my socials. I can't obsessively pick apart what Bran and Celia have posted today. That's another activity I've engaged in these past three months. Cooking, poetry, metal, posting food pictures, and stalking Bran and Celia on Instagram.

It's funny how much more alone you are without a phone. I thought I was alone back in my mother's house without Gill and George. But I had internet there. I had music. I was somewhat connected. Six hours into my first full day away, and I'm probably back on the path to hallucinating companionship.

It's only been twenty-four hours and I miss Mom's kitchen. I miss the oven chirps that call me over when the built-in timer goes off.

Donya tilts her head sympathetically. "Okay, how about you share with us why you thought to come do something like this in the first place?"

Why I thought?

I shake my head. "No, thank you."

Donya presses her lips together and moves on to coaxing words from the girl next to me. I yank up the hood of my Adidas sweatshirt and glare out at the lake. There's a small cabin down closer to the water with four canoes propped up against it. That must be where fishing classes will be tomorrow. Being alone in a boat on the water actually sounds kind of nice.

This session goes painfully slowly as I avoid participating at all costs. When Donya finally dismisses us, I stand from my folding chair and stalk down the dirt trail toward my cabin. I concentrate on the ground to avoid eye contact with any retreaters and kick at small rocks every few feet along the way.

I become so engrossed in my rock kicking that I'm completely unprepared when I'm forced sideways by an oncoming mass of flesh that must be a person.

My brain kicks into overdrive as it happens. Alarms spring up through my legs. I can't afford to fall right now. Falling isn't just falling anymore. Any weird fall can backpedal my healing progress. Any fall can end up being excruciating. *Falling isn't allowed.*

I stumble sideways off the trail into some grass, giving in to the momentum of the collision instead of trying to fight it, and re-right myself vertically as a pile of neon green papers flop to the ground near my feet. A guy drops into my line of sight.

"You have to watch where you're going!" I scold instinctively.

A brown-skinned boy, slightly older than I am, with styled dark hair, looks up at me. "Sorry! Just getting ready for classes to start and I wasn't paying enough attention."

I drop my hood self-consciously and kneel to help him gather his papers. When I lean forward, a bolt of pain shoots down my back. I try not to wince. *Move slowly.*

"Sorry, it's okay, I wasn't . . . either," I tell him guiltily without making eye contact.

"You must be one of our new students. Will I see you at fishing tomorrow?" His voice brims with carefree cheer. It irritates me.

It's weird how the people who work here refer to us as students. Yes, I'm eighteen and could be a student, but some of the women here are middle-aged. I gather up the last of the papers and shove them his way. He takes the stack from me as I answer, "Um, yeah."

"What's your name?"

I pull my hood back up over my braid and start hiking toward the cabins again. "Siri."

"Like an iPhone?"

Original. I keep walking.

The bottle of anti-bac I carry on me at all times is running low after a mere twenty-four hours because I can't wash my hands at will in this cabin. It's a six-minute walk from here to the "public cleansing" building.

At home I've been showering sometimes twice a day because it helps with the pain. Yesterday I opted not to use the shower at all because I got here after sunset. The retreat leader let us use her bathroom before she showed us all to our separate cabins. Once I was safe inside my space, there was no way I was leaving, alone, in the dark, partially naked, to locate the public cleansing building.

I found it this morning in the daylight to use the sink and toilet before our activities. Now it's been almost forty-eight hours since my skin has seen hot water. I'm gross. It's time.

I'm in my white sneakers, carrying flip-flops and a shower caddy my mother insisted I bring, as I make my way down the trail that cuts along the outer ring of this valley. It's lit with tiny lights every few feet along the ground.

The air is warm enough that I can get away with wearing a towel to min-imize the number of items I'll have to find a place for while I'm in there. I've inspected the showers. There's one hook per stall. What's anyone supposed to do with anything more than a towel when there's only one hook?

My shoulders sag in relief when I push open the door and find the build-ing entirely devoid of people. *Hallelujah.* I step onto the tiny black-and-white tiles that cover the floor and take two minutes to clean my sneakers off in the sink before turning toward the showers. There's a handful of them along the wall. I shuffle into one of middle stalls and pull the thin white cloth curtain closed behind me. I hang my towel, find a dry place for my sneakers, and squat down to carefully arrange my soaps on the floor. Then I spin the dial all the way up.

An involuntarily noise of relief escapes my lips as the water warms and runs down my back. Soaks through my hair.

You know what I don't hate—being clean. I love to be clean. It's very hard to stay clean in a waterless cabin in the middle of the woods.

I bask in the heat longer than usual. Eventually someone else comes into the bathroom. They shower and get out of the shower, in the time that I'm still in the shower. Another shower starts.

When two people, presumably at the sinks, start talking, I decide it's time to wrap things up. I'm too aware of their presence mere feet away to continue comfortably loitering naked under a meager stream of water behind this thin sheet of cloth. I reluctantly wind back the faucet.

"Looking forward to hearing your story," I hear someone say as I towel off.

I scoff quietly. These people are already forming friendships, and I've yet to look one person in the eye. Someone leaves the building. It's quiet other than the sound of a single shower still running. Time to bolt.

I knot the towel over my chest and prep my belongings, scooping them up into one hand and holding my sneakers in the other. I angle my eyes at the ground, and in one fluid motion I whip open the curtain—and ram right into another human being.

You've got to be kidding me.

My flip-flops are soaking. The floor is wet. I chuck everything into the air. Sneakers and toiletries go flying. I can't fall.

But the girl who bumped into me is toppling forward *onto me* and I can't support her. Gravity's going to win. I strain to hold onto the shower curtain, but it yanks downward with all the resistance of a paper towel. My feet slip out. I'm going down.

"HOLY FUCKING BUCKET SHITBALLS JESUS CHRIST MARY JOSEPH," the stranger belts.

I twist desperately toward the floor. My elbow takes the brunt of the impact. I'm so anxious, I can't even really feel it. All I can hear for a millisecond is my heart. Then part of the girl smashes into my stomach and the air is ripped from my body. I gasp as she lands awkwardly onto my chest, pinning my shoulder down against the cold, definitely gross, floor tiles. When

30

I inhale, I can't avoid her hair. It's wild and neon orange and it smells like airplane. I squeeze my eyes closed. *I was clean.*

My hair is caught under my armpit, yanking my chin up at a weird angle. I can't get in a full breath. The girl pushes up off of me after a decade.

I inhale deeply, pulling my hands up over my face to hide the tears forming in eyes.

"You can stop screaming now," she says.

Am I screaming?

I'm screaming. I stop. Pain pulses down my legs.

"Dude, are you okay?"

My arm is pried away from my face as the girl inspects my elbow. I glance over at it. The skin's all scraped off.

"Your elbow's all cut up," she comments.

We finally make eye contact.

And then she starts screaming.

6. A Girl Is Here for the Introspection

JAMIE
August 28, Friday Evening
Colorado

This just in: I love Terry, the early-thirty-something-year-old white lady with a New York accent and wild dark curls who owns this retreat. She picked me up from the Denver airport and we chatted the whole way here. She runs this Colorado retreat during the summer, and the rest of the year she's an elementary school art teacher, which is fabulously weird. She's engaged to a dude back in New York, and she laughed me off when I told her long distance was a death sentence. We're gonna be friends.

I follow her through the grass to a registration table set up in front of the cabin she parked us next to. The little square house is built up on six-foot risers with a set of steps leading to a front door.

Terry settles herself in the registration table chair and offers me a friendly smile. "Jamie, I really love your hair."

I snort and ruffle my permed, grown-out, neon orange frizz ball. "Wow, unpopular opinion, thanks, Terr! The fam hates it."

My roots are dark brown now and the orange starts around my ears. It's a look. It clashes with the red overalls I'm wearing today. I love a good color clash.

Terry laughs. "I'm sure they don't hate it."

They do.

I take stock of the area as Terry organizes some papers. The registration cabin is at the edge of a valley surrounded by towering trees. Across the way, the land swells upward into a hill, and atop that hill snakes a line of small, boxy cabins.

Alas, my new home.

"You have your cell?" Terry asks. She pulls out a lockbox and yanks a key necklace over her head while I fish my phone from my pocket. I offer it to her as she unlocks the box.

Terry dubiously eyes my old-fashioned, non-smart, baby blue slide-up phone with an iPodesque click wheel like it's a stick of dynamite.

I raise my eyebrows. "What?"

"What is that?"

"It's my phone."

Her warm demeanor dims. "We have a strict no-phone policy here, James. Is this really your phone?"

"Terry, go ahead and make a call. It's my phone."

She plucks it from my palm and screws around, sliding the buttons open and closed. Her face contorts. "What is this, like the Chocolate?"

I clap my hands. "Good eye! I like to stay behind on the latest tech."

"Okay . . ." She drops my phone into the lockbox and replaces the lid before handing me a clipboard with a pen dangling from a balled metal string. "Sign up for five activities and one group chat. During your open time, you're free to wander, hike, stargaze, visit the cafeteria, journal, come talk to me, whatever soothes your mind. Down by the cafeteria there are six different trails, all with different mantras and philosophical ideas to ponder during your hikes."

I bob my head in approval. "Do you have a favorite?"

"I love peace, but luck is probably my favorite. It's happy haunted."

A smile jumps up my cheeks. *Fabulously weird.* "What the fuck is happy haunted?"

Terry shrugs. "It's haunting in a happy way."

I head bob a couple more times, holding her eyes as I snatch the pen dangling from the clipboard. "I love it."

ACTIVITIES
1) Meditation by the Lake
2) Yoga
3) Rock climbing—FULL
4) Group Chat A
5) Slacklining
6) Group Chat B
7) Fishing
8) Cooking
9) Fire Choir

I scribble down fishing and slacklining. "So all the other retreaters are here?"

"We prefer to refer to our fellows as students."

"Students of what?"

"Life," she says simply.

I frown. "Okay, I dig it." I pick three more activities and hand her back the clipboard. "So, we have the rest of our time . . . to fill ourselves, out here in the nothing?"

"Yep, there's no shortage of ways to occupy your time and find introspection." She hands me a plain brown journal from a pile on the table. "Here's a new slate for your thoughts. You should put in a new entry every day.

"Activities are over for today, the sun will be setting in the next hour. You'll receive a schedule later under your door." She smiles. "For now, go get settled in cabin ten." She holds out an old brass key that I pluck from her palm.

"Grand." I spin to face the fifteen or so tiny cabins looming up on the hill. They're across the grass clearing, about two hundred yards away, tucked under a swath of trees.

There's a lake down a little trail that starts a few feet behind Terry and her registration table. She grins and points to her left. "Feel free to follow this trail, it leads down to the lake and back up to the student cabins."

"Aces."

The world is so much greener outside of Los Angeles and New York. I've gotten used to being the blip of color within a constant gray palette. The dirt path I'm on is lined with bright, saturated green wilderness. Up ahead a lake shimmers golden with the dying light of our beloved ball of fire. A small cabin with canoes propped up against it sits a little ways from the waterline. I've never been in a canoe.

I skip my way down to the long wooden boats, toss my bag on a patch of grass, and glance around before tugging at the boat farthest from the water. It's heavy, but I heave until the thing groans and slides sideways off the side of the tiny house. I leap out of the way, leaving it free to slam bottom-first into the soft dirt. A small boom echoes as it clashes against the ground.

"Look at you." I grin at it, snatch up my pack, and take a seat on the bench inside, looking out at the water. *Let the introspection begin.* "Really, why canoe on the water when you can have the same experience from the safety of land?"

"Excuse me?"

"Gah!" I whip around.

An early-twenties, tall, brown-skinned dude with dark hair wearing a green REDISCOVER YOURSELF RETREAT T-shirt is standing behind my boat, holding a giant stack of lime green papers under his arm.

The guy's hot. Killer jawline. Big brown eyes. Great hair.

I turn back toward the water. "You're not excused. How dare you sneak up on a lady. I'm canoeing over here."

A moment passes before he adds, "You're not supposed to touch the canoes."

"I'll return it."

He ventures closer till he's standing slightly in front of me, beside the boat with his stack of papers.

I squint up at him. "What are you, the canoe police?"

"I teach the fishing class." I drop my gaze as he lifts a foot to step into the boat.

Instead of landing in the canoe, his sole gets caught on the rim. The guy fumbles and his whole collection of papers goes flying. They flutter around me and the surrounding area like oversized lime-green confetti as he drops horizontally across the boat. He catches himself in a push-up position, his muscly arms bracing against the dirt outside the opposite rim of the canoe.

After a moment, I slow clap from my front row seat. "Wow. You okay?"

"Crap." He rights himself and skitters around picking up the papers. "Crap, crap, crap."

I lean down and pick one up myself. *A Guide to Canoe Safety.*

1) Always wear a lifejacket
2) Never stand in a canoe away from shore
3) Carry a canoe whistle
4) Bring a rope to pull a swimmer to safety

I stop reading as the dude settles onto the boat bench across from me, re-sorting the pamphlets into a neat pile.

I raise a brow. "Is that how all the pros mount a canoe?"

He stares at me for a second. "Well, these aren't actually classic canoes. They're a weird canoe–row boat hybrid . . . technically. But they do the job. We call them canoes because they all say canoe along the side." He points to my left.

I nod. "Okay, I see. So what you're saying is you're used to the classic canoe mount technique and these slightly different canoe-boat hybrids are throwing you off your usual step-into-a-canoe flow. And thus, that fall was completely warranted."

The guy stares for another moment before bobbing his head in agreement.

I bend over the left edge of the boat. A snort blows out of me as I spot the word CANOE printed in large, faded, old-fashioned yellow bubble letters. I swing back upright, cackling at the joke potential.

Hot guy tilts his chin down, really hitting me hard with the full force of his fantastic bone structure. "I'm Zarar, Zarar Jafri. Did you just arrive?"

"Wow, full-naming it. I'm Jamie. James George Federov for long, apparently the last student of life to arrive this session."

He studies me. "Your eyes are . . . captivating."

I waggle my brows. "I see you're single." I shoot him a smile before standing up. "I'm not here for that, but it was great meeting ya, I'll see you in class." I step out of the boat and shove my bag over my shoulder. "Peace."

"Wait—"

I start toward the cabins. "Don't worry. I'll face this way so you don't trip over my eyes on the way out."

The words CABIN TEN are carved into the wood beside the flimsy screen door of my assigned house. I throw that open to get to the plain brown one behind it, and use my key to get inside.

Cabin ten is one room. There's a window on the far wall allowing a flood of gray decaying light to fall across the wooden floor. A single bunk is on the right wall with a desk underneath it where a bottom bunk would be. A small old-fashioned lamp with an on/off beaded string sits on the desk. A green yoga mat is unfurled across the floor along the left wall.

"Wow, roughing it." I chuck my bag near the yoga mat, take a seat at the desk, and exhale. "What now?"

I flip open the journal Terry gave me and click on a pen.

Really thought we'd have roommates. Looks like I'll have to leave the cabin in search of human interaction. =P

I close the notebook and stick my head outside. It's getting dark, but the trail along the cabins is lit up every five feet or so. All is quiet. I drag the desk chair out the door and set up camp outside for a bit.

It takes five minutes, but eventually we have liftoff. There's a girl headed in my direction, about a hundred feet down the trail with a towel and a shower caddy. I duck back into the room and emerge a minute later in flip-flops with a towel over my shoulder and a Ziploc full of shower tools just as she's approaching my new abode.

"Hey hey hey! I'm Jamie!" I skip onto the trail. The girl's eyes widen a bit as I fall into step beside her, but it looks like she'll tolerate my presence. She has dark skin and long braids tied back in a low ponytail. "How's it going?"

"It's going," she answers with a wry smile. "I'm Thalia."

"Nice to meet you." The trail we're on slopes downward to pass six more cabins en route to a lit-up rectangular building labeled CLEANSE & SHOWER. "Have you explored this Cleanse and Shower building yet?" I smile at her.

She chuckles. "I have. I got here yesterday."

"How'd the showers treatchya?" A mosquito lands on my arm as we close in on the building. I swat at it.

"As well as to be expected. Water pressure's low. Floors are kinda gross. Hot water gets just below what you'd optimally want. Feels like college." Thalia pulls ahead of me to the entrance. She wrenches open the metal door.

I follow her in. "Wouldn't know what that's like, never went."

She looks over her shoulder. "Lucky you, that's why I'm here."

Inside, there are two paths. To the right are four shower stalls and two sinks. To the left are four toilets and four sinks. There's a pale young woman with freckles and shoulder-length wet blond hair at a sink on the shower side. She's working through it with one of those wet brushes.

Thalia streamlines past Freckles to the shower farthest from the door and yanks the curtain shut behind her. Someone's already occupying the second shower and a cozy amount of steam mills about the room. I head over to the sinks.

"Hey hey hey! I'm Jamie!" I project my voice a bit so Freckles won't have trouble hearing me over the running water.

Her eyes slide to mine in the mirror. "Kelly."

"Why are you here, Kelly?" I shoot her a smile and wash my hands so I have something to do.

She rakes through a new section of hair before answering. "Things fell apart with my high school sweetheart."

"Ah, a breakup, do tell!"

Kelly frowns at me through the mirror. "Is that why you're here too?"

I push the lever down a couple of times on the hand towel dispenser. "Nah, I'm just quarter-life crisis-ing pretty hard." I turn to look her in the eye. "What happened with you and high school boyfriend?"

Kelly grimaces before grabbing the shower caddy by her feet. She stalks around me toward the exit.

"Okay, well, nice to meet you," I call. "See you tomorrow! Looking forward to hearing your story." The door claps shut behind her.

I hum to myself cheerfully. Maybe I can camp out in here a bit post-shower and paint my nails, meet a couple more people, before going back to my cabin of nothing. Thalia was cool, maybe we can hang out.

I spin toward the showers, inspecting the neon chipped polish currently on my fingers. I've taken two steps toward the empty third stall when the plastic curtain to my right is thrown open and someone bulldozes into me.

"HOLY—" I flail for purchase for a brief slow-motion moment, before we're both in free fall. "—FUCKING BUCKET SHITBALLS JESUS CHRIST MARY JOSEPH—UGHF." My profanity stream cuts off with a grunt as I semi-brace against the ground with one arm and slam into this poor girl's stomach. She screeches like a dying animal.

I push up off her gingerly. As I do, her pale arms fly up to cover her eyes. She's still emitting a high-pitched wailing sound.

"You can stop screaming!" I tell her.

The sound stops, but she doesn't lower her arms. Blood begins to bead around her elbow. This girl's only wearing a towel.

"Shit, dude, are you okay?" I ask hesitantly.

When she doesn't respond, I gently pull the injured arm away from her face to get a better look at it. There are multiple splotches where the skin is scraped off. "Your elbow's all cut up."

I look up to meet her eyes, and the girl's face knocks the wind out of me like a swift kick to the gut. I gag for a second before finding the air to belt out a scream of my own.

What the actual flippity fudge fork jibbit fuck?!

"Gah!" is all I manage to actually get out before hopping up from the floor and stumbling backward. "Siri?!"

The girl doesn't respond, just closes her eyes. Small rivulets of water flow down her cheeks. She's still lying flat on the ground like a corpse.

"Siri?!" I repeat.

I clear my throat from where I'm now gawking at her, six feet away, against the sinks. "Hello?"

My heart's thrashing so hard against my chest, I feel like it's going to bust through my rib cage like the alien in *Alien*.

"Hey, excuse me! I'm going to need you to acknowledge your name. Is it Siri?" I demand.

The girl sucks in a breath. "Yeah, what's it to you?" she croaks.

I brace an arm against the sink. "Can you get up?" I think I'm having a hot flash. When she doesn't move or respond, I step forward and offer her a shaky hand.

She's crying silently like a creepy child in a horror film. "Take my hand," I instruct.

Without making eye contact, she takes my hand and braces the injured arm against her towel. She slowly positions her feet directly under her torso before standing straight up in one fluid motion.

"Your face," I breathe.

She's still not looking at me. She might not have even heard me. Okay, she's hyperventilating. And staring at the floor.

"Are you okay?" I repeat anxiously.

Siri steps back into her shower stall and pulls the curtain closed.

A sputtering noise escapes my lips. "Are you shitting me right now?"

Her shower turns back on.

"Hey!" I complain.

My stomach heaves. *Not this again.* I lunge to throw up in the garbage next to the sink.

7. Angst and the Shower Girl

SIRI
August 28, Friday Evening
Colorado

I let the hot water dribble over my face before rinsing the blood from my elbow. I think that girl just threw up. Gross.

My lower back is throbbing. I rotate to let the water fall over it. It's throbbing, not shooting. At least there's that.

"Siri."

I startle a little behind the curtain. Why the hell is she standing so close? How does she know my name?

"Please stay away from me if you're ill," I scold. "Give me some space."

"Are you okay?" comes the voice.

"Yes. You can leave, I'm fine."

"I can't leave," she insists. "I'm . . . I need to make sure you're okay."

My forehead crinkles up. "Yes. You can. I said I'm fine," I assert firmly.

"I don't . . . do you not . . . don't you—" She fumbles her words.

"Spit it out, or get out of here! At least move away from the curtain!" I can see her shadow a foot away. There's a shuffle as she takes a step back.

I glance down for my soap, but there's nothing in the stall because I chucked all my toiletries when we fell. *Excrement.*

I blow out a shaky breath. "Miss, actually could you hand me my toiletries please? I need the soap."

Twenty seconds later a hand shoves through the gap alongside the curtain, holding my shower caddy. I leap out of sight and smack into the wall by accident.

"Ow," I whine involuntarily.

"Are you okay?" the girl asks again.

I snatch the shower caddy. "Yes, thank you, you can leave now!"

She's silent for a beat. "How hard did you hit your head?"

There's a weird protective note in her voice. I don't like it. I barely hit my head. I swallow, gazing nervously at her shadow.

What if she never leaves me alone? What if she takes me hostage and tries to kill me? Why else is she still here? I said I was fine. What if she has a weapon? What if she's going to assault me again? I'll have to go find Terry. I might have to run, but I can't run with my back like this. I'll have to walk-run like an un-oiled robot. Dear lord, I can see it now: banished from ballet, exiled to Colorado by mother, and murdered in bathroom by girl with grown-out neon orange airplane hair.

Maybe I can kick her. I can throw the shower caddy at her as a distraction.

I quickly wash and re-towel off. I repack my shower caddy and angle it to optimal throwing position in my right palm. Braced, I yank the curtain open with my left hand.

The girl's leaning over the sink. She turns to face me with something vertical looking in her hand. *Weapon?!*

I chuck the shower caddy with an involuntary "Ahhhh!" battle cry, and hobble-fast-walk toward the exit.

I hear my shower things crash into her and onto the floor as I throw open the door into the night. I don't stop until I reach my cabin, slam the door shut, and throw the dinky bolt lock into place.

8. ???

I drop the nail file back into my Ziploc bag. What the fuck just happened?

9. Angst and Fishing

SIRI
August 29, Saturday Morning
Colorado

The ground squishes slightly under my black Nikes as I pad out onto the soft dirt of the lake beach.

On the way over here, I stopped by Terry's cabin to report the girl from last night for a personal space violation. Fingers crossed we don't have to interact again.

The first fishing lesson of the retreat starts in ten minutes. I'm *not* looking forward to it.

Eight canoes are laid out along the beach and then there's a wider row boat in the spot closest to the lakeside cabin. The sun has risen over the water and the light is warm against my face.

The teacher is the guy who ran into me on the path yesterday. Awkward. He strides out from inside the cabin and instructs me to pick a boat.

I pick one close to the cabin and take a seat inside it. Maybe I'll find peace in fishing? Could fishing be my future? Canoeing?

Eh, definitely not. That's bound to cause more back issues.

I stare at my black laces. Anger skulks its way down my limbs like lava leisurely making its way down a mountain side. It's antsy and restless and slow-moving, and I don't know what to do with it.

All these years I've channeled my emotions into dance. Not having that option now, it's like I've lost an essential limb. I can't dance (or listen to my music) so I'm lost and extra emotional and angry, and the way to get through that is to dance it out and I can't dance it out, so I feel even more lost and emotional and angry.

Other retreaters start trickling into the area. There's an old lady who's here because her cat died; she takes the canoe to the left of mine. Come seven o'clock, the only canoe still open is the one to my right, closest to the wider rowboat.

The instructor introduces himself as Zarar. He starts the lesson with a rundown of canoe rules and a disclaimer that these aren't actual canoes, merely mislabeled canoe-like narrow row boats. This place is ridiculous. I pull on the ugly neon life jacket sitting along the bottom of the canoe as per his instruction.

The fishing crash course goes on for ten minutes before he tells us to push our non-canoes out into the water. We might get a little wet. I'm wearing leggings that are too tight to roll up, so that's unfortunate.

I get out of my boat, walk to the end farthest up the beach, brace myself against it, and push. My hands fall as a spike of pain jolts up my spine.

For a moment I consider asking for help. But I don't want to talk to Zarar, or anyone else, any more than absolutely necessary. I reposition myself, concentrating on keeping my core tight as I push forward. It takes a moment, but this time the boat moves forward an inch, and then another, carving a path through the sand.

The triumph of pain-free progress is unexpectedly rewarding. I follow Zarar's directions and shove until ninety percent of the canoe is in the water before climbing in. It dips slightly as I gingerly situate myself facing the land.

I did it! For a second, I think I feel a smile coming on, but the urge dissipates as I catch sight of neon orange hair bouncing toward the beach.

Creepy shower girl is sprinting toward the area. She's headed straight for me because the only empty boat is to my right. *Please don't talk to me.*

I frantically pick up my oars, drop them into place, and heave away from shore. I'm still a little grounded so the boat only moves a couple of inches. I push harder.

"Sier! Wait up!" Shower Girl screams as she closes in.

Sier? Like we're on a one-syllable basis?!

I look over at the other retreaters, all calmly mounting their now-floating boats. Gosh darn it.

She's gonna be here in literally a second! She's tying the top half of her bright orange deep brown ombré bird's nest into a fountain on the crown of her head as she runs. I press with everything I have into the dirt with the oars.

Come on boat, move!

With a thunk, I find open water. *YES!* I exhale a sigh of relief as the boat floats into the lake.

The girl stops short at the edge of the water where I pushed off.

"Dude, come on. I asked you to wait!" She's wearing the same tacky red overalls and pink crop T-shirt as yesterday. And a blue nose ring. Absolutely nothing matches. She's wearing yellow boots.

I glare at her as my boat drifts out into the open water.

Zarar calls to her from down the shoreline. "There's a canoe for you one down!" He starts walking in our direction.

Shower Girl glances at him—*and walks straight into the lake.*

Oh no.

"Hey! Stop!" Zarar calls out from the shore.

"What are you doing?" I yelp. I'm ten feet out.

"You weren't here for the lecture; you can't just get in the water!" Zarar says.

The girl wades farther in, yelling back to him, "I'm fine, Zarar. I've read the safety manual!" She yelps as the water level rises. "SHIT, THIS IS COLD! Shit, shit, shit!"

She climbs into my boat, right over the bow. Her hands brace against the edges and she steps in, landing in a crouch while I watch like a dumbfounded deer.

"What are you doing? Stop! Go get your own! Leave me alone!" I find myself shrieking as half the lake falls off of her with a freezing splash and settles into the bottom of the boat.

She grins as I scream at her, casually situating herself on the plank opposite of mine.

"Are you absolutely insane?" I spit. "Zarar is still yelling at you from the shore!"

She doesn't even turn around. She keeps smiling like she's amused. Like we're friends. "Then we should paddle out farther so we can't hear him." The momentum of her climbing in has sent us considerably farther out already.

I gape at her. Something about her is . . . unsettling. *Probably the blue nose ring.*

Now that she's so close, I can tell she's around my age. She doesn't look . . . threatening. The bits of her wavy shoulder-length hair that aren't splayed upward toward the heavens in the fountain are sticking out in every direction around her face.

We're drifting outward now with the current. Should I row us back? I glance over her shoulder at the beach. Zarar is watching, but he's no longer shouting.

I turn back to the girl. "I don't want you in my canoe. I'd like you to leave me alone. I reported you to Terry this morning."

Her lip curls back in a weird little snarl. "You reported me to Terry?"

"Yes, you violated my personal space."

Her eyes are kind of familiar.

She blinks. "Siri, you ran *into* me!"

I look away and cycle through a row. And then another, trying to suffocate the unexpected onslaught of anxiety rising in my chest. I focus on the burn in my shoulders. "I said I was fine and you didn't leave! I don't like talking to people. I wanted you to leave me alone and you didn't and it was weird and now you've hijacked my canoe!"

"Do you really not recognize me?" Her voice sounds raw.

I squint, pulling the oars through the water again because if I stop, I know the panic will get me. Why am I getting so anxious? I was angry before. She's just a girl. A girl with familiar eyes. And terrible fashion sense.

She looks confused, and sad. And then her eyes go blank. "Dude, we really need to talk." Her fingers fiddle with her overall clasps like she pushed the emotions from her face to her fingertips.

I study her eyes again. "How do you think we know each other?" I'm breathing heavily now, but I keep rowing. Row. Row. Row. "Is it dance? Do you dance?"

Her weird orange eyebrows furrow. She must have dyed them too. Or maybe she draws them in with a pencil? *Her eyes are almost the same gold color as my mom's.*

"How do you not recognize your own fucking sister?!"

10. A Girl Is Sampling Sisterhood

JAMIE
August 29, Saturday Morning
Colorado

Siri scoffs. "I don't have a sister."

Ouch. "Wow, hate to break it to you, but you do, it's me."

Siri's rowing like her life depends on it. I reach over and clasp my own hand over an oar. "Can you stop rowing for a second?"

Her hand flashes out and swats my knuckles. "Don't touch it!"

"Dude, ow." I reach out again and grab the oar anyway. She re-smacks my hand, but I hold firm. "Damn, you are violent." I lunge for the second oar with my other arm. This time, I put my hand right over hers.

"Don't touch me!" She yanks her palm away like she was electrocuted.

I take advantage of the distraction to disengage both oars and put them behind me. Siri glowers like a rabid dog.

She's sitting perfectly straight, her long, pitch-black braid trailing down to her waist. I know she was young, and it's been over a decade, but *come on.* We still look so alike. Being this close is like looking into a warped mirror. Her nose should have grown differently, or her cheekbones should be softer than my harsh ones, but we match. The only exceptional difference is a movie-staresque beauty mark above her lip.

It's uncomfortably trippy.

"Come on, Siri." I gesture up and down myself in frustration. "Jamie?! Ringing any bells?!"

I don't know how Siri could get any paler, it's already like she's never seen the light of day, but she does.

After an extended unbearable tense silence, she jerks her head back and forth. "You're not real," she hisses.

Excuse me?

My jaw hangs slightly ajar as I try to figure out what the hell to do with that. Siri scrunches her eyes shut and covers her ears. "Jamie is not real."

"Siri," I say stupidly.

She keeps her eyes closed. Repeats herself. "Not real, she's not real." Her voice gets lower, softer, until she's speaking to herself, under her breath. Saying the same damn thing. Over. And over and over.

I swallow and glance at the nothing around us. We're not close to any of the boats, so there's no one to make nervous sarcastic eye contact with. Is she having some sort of mental break?

"Could you not go full exorcist on me?" I ask.

This does nothing. She's chanting to herself like a madwoman. I reach forward, pull her hands from her ears, and throw them down to her sides. "Siri!"

She goes abruptly quiet, opens her eyes, and scowls—like I'm a demon, and not a twenty-year-old punk in red overalls who forgot to shower because she's been dreading this conversation for the last twelve hours.

I swallow. "Dude. I'm real. What the fuck?"

We stare at each other.

Without warning Siri jumps to her feet. "GET THE HELL OUT OF MY BOAT!"

The row boat–canoe shifts violently.

"Shit, Sier, sit dow—" Something smashes into my head as we hit the water.

11. Angst and Swimming

SIRI
August 29, Saturday Morning
Colorado

Cold water slaps across my face. Engulfs me. My heart pounds like a manic prisoner chained to a wall.

She isn't real. I'm having some sort of episode. *She isn't real.*

I frantically doggy paddle for the surface. Lake water laps against me as I spin in place, gasping and trying to catch my breath. *Please be gone.*

She's not gone. Her hair is flopped across her face. She's draped over the oars, floating motionless.

Okay. Let her go. You are strong. You don't need her.

Swim.

I only know I'm swimming because the shore is getting closer. I must be breathing because I'm not drowning. I'm still alive. I'm still moving.

She seemed so real. She ran into me. She made me fall. She helped me up.

I could have slipped myself. I'm really upset. This happens when I'm really upset. And alone. I can't stop the tears searing from my eyes. I don't know where they end and the lake begins. I can't feel my limbs.

But Zarar spoke to her. Zarar yelled at her.

I crawl up onto the dirt. My chest is heaving, I'm sucking in air, but my body won't register it. A blond girl who I've seen around is dragging her boat up onto the beach. She drops it and walks over. "Are you all right? I saw the canoe flip, that's why I turned back. Screw this if they flip on a dime like that," she calls.

I gasp and gasp. Her voice is so nonchalant. So oblivious to the violent panic exploding in my chest.

"Did you meet a Jamie?" I rasp.

"Did I meet a what?" she repeats harshly.

I'm lying in the sand, and she's directly over me now. She reaches out a hand as if to help me up. I get onto all fours. "Did you meet a girl named Jamie?"

"The jerk who ran out to your canoe with the hair? Yeah, she asked me about my breakup in the bathroom last night."

A strange wail escapes me, like a dying seal has taken up residence in my throat. I stumble to my feet and push past the blond girl.

"I don't understand what's going on. I don't understand." I'm babbling to myself as I hustle toward my cabin.

Am I really losing my mind? Have I made up the blond girl as well? Every time I heave a new breath, sobs erupt out of me. I'm freezing.

I need a shower. I'm covered in lake water and dirt. A shower will help. I need to be clean. I need to think. I need to calm down. I'm having a panic attack.

I haven't had a full-blown attack since I was little. Not like this at least. This is so much worse than I can ever remember.

But that's all this is. You're just going through a rough time. It's getting to you even more than you realized.

I've gotten through this before and I can do it again. I nod to myself over and over as I put one foot in front of the other down the trail. It's going to be fine.

I throw open the cabin door and strip down. My clothes splat against the wood as I chuck them haphazardly into the corner of the room, grab my towel, and glance around for my toiletries.

The oxygen wisps out of me again.

I left my shower toiletries in the bathroom last night. I don't have any toiletries. I head out onto the trail without them.

Jamie.

Don't think about it. Think about something else. Billie. Slipknot. Billie.

White Chapel. Ice cream. Orange Creamsicle ice cream. Jamie used to get orange Creamsicle ice cream.

There's no one else in the bathroom. I yank the shower curtain closed behind me and hang up my towel.

Jamie.

Jamie.

Jamie.

Jamie isn't real.

I turn the dial all the way to the left. Steaming water blazes down my spine.

Mom is real. Papa is real. I am real. I am going to be okay.

I can almost breathe.

Five minutes later I can definitely breathe.

The episode is going to pass. *You're fine. You're fine.* I'm fine. I'm fine.

12. Is a Girl Alive?

JAMIE
August 29, Saturday Morning
Colorado

My eyes hurt as I throw them open. My lungs burn as I gasp and cough for dear fucking life. I'm fucking freezing. The sun is blinding. What happened? Am I dead?

A figure leans forward shading my face. They come into focus slowly. Nice jawline. Great hair. *Ah, it's Zarar.*

"Jamie?"

My pupils slowly adjust to the shade he's providing. Wow, his voice was calm, but the dude's frantic, I can see it in his eyes. There's some sort of innate gentleness to them though. Mmm. They make my lips tip upward.

Oh whoa, his hands are on my chest.

"If you're looking for boob, you're gonna want to slide a couple inches to the left." Zarar yanks his hands off me as I cough. "Shit, I sound like an ancient chain-smoker. Am I on the floor?"

I think he might be blushing. "You're in my boat."

"Boat?" My brow tries to crease, but pain lances through my head. "Ah." I reach to touch the pain, but Zarar catches my hand on the way up. "What the hell happened?" I croak.

It all comes hurtling back the second I ask the question. Siri flipped the canoe. *Siri doesn't think I'm real?*

"Canoe," I blurt.

"Your canoe flipped." He carefully lowers my hand to my side.

"Where's Siri?!" I try to sit up, but Zarar gently pushes my shoulder down. The small movement leaves me feeling woozy.

"Give it a second. You almost drowned and you're bleeding. I have to grab the first aid kit."

"I almost drowned and I'm bleeding?" I parrot back, my brain muddy.

Zarar scoots around, carefully shifting things behind him.

"Siri is swimming back to shore," he says. He lifts his head up over the edge of the boat. "Never mind, she's stepping up onto the beach now. She seems to be okay." He sounds a little irritated.

Zarar returns to optimal hover position, holding a white box with a red cross on it. He shines in the sunlight. Beads of water cling to his face, like he just stepped out of a shower. A drop falls onto my nose as he pushes some of my hair away from my forehead.

"Why are you drenched?" My voice sounds a little better. Zarar pulls some sort of thing out of the kit and puts it on some sort of cloth and lowers it to my forehead.

"Ow, Jesus Christ." I wince. "Is my forehead alive?"

"You're going to be okay. I'm going to bandage this up, and I'll walkie Terry. She's going to get a doctor out here to help you. She has an on-call person; they should be here within the hour. Don't worry, I've been trained for situations like this."

Situations like this?

"I'm fine," I grind out. Whatever he put on the injury is burning above my left eyebrow. "Right as rain now that I've got someone who's trained for situations like this in my corner."

Zarar proceeds to fuss over whatever monstrosity has ailed my head.

The puzzle pieces are slowly coming together here. "Did you . . . have to jump in the water? Did I actually drown? Am I living a dramatic moment from a Hallmark film?"

"You were floating facedown over the oars."

"What about Siri?" I insist.

His two fingers gently squeeze my forehead skin together as he does something with a tube of something in his other hand. "Siri swam past me as I was rowing out to get to your canoe. She didn't respond when I called out to her, but she was wearing a life jacket and she didn't look hurt, just rattled.

"She left you here unconscious. It's unacceptable. I'll have to have a word with her. I have to eventually have a word with you too. You've both violated so many safety rules, and I'll have to suspend your canoe privileges for at least forty-eight hours." His hands retreat from my vicinity for a moment. They return with a jumbo bandage.

Really not looking forward to the big mirror reveal back on land.

Zarar delicately removes the packaging and places the thing on my face.

I reach up and touch it before catching his eye. "How hot do I look now on a scale of one to ten?"

Zarar clears his throat. "How do you feel, Jamie?"

"Like I want to get the hell out of these freezing clothes."

Zarar picks up a walkie and brings it to his mouth without breaking eye contact with me. I don't think I've ever seen one of those up close. "Terry, we have a code seven, call the doctor, please."

The device crackles and then Terry's Long Island voice comes through. "Roger that, heading to the phone as we speak."

He lowers the device, and ever so quietly says, "I'm glad you're okay."

"Roger that, over and out," I mumble back as he settles himself onto a boat plank and begins to row.

Terry meets us at the shore. "Oh my gawd, what happened? You look like a murder victim, are you okay?!"

I blink from the bottom of the boat. "Always nice to hear." From my vantage point I can see Terry, Zarar, and the sky.

Terry waves her hands around. "Don't answer that. Z will fill me in. He's going to take you to my cabin and we'll get you sorted. I'm going to go find Siri. We'll meet at my place." She exits view.

Siri's not here? Zarar extends his arms and bends toward me.

"What are you—" I start. He squats down and scoops me up like I weigh ten pounds. "Gah!"

Pain rockets through my cranium with the movement. I reach up, pressing my palms into the sides of my head. My clothes pull downward on my legs. They're heavy and full of the lake.

Slowly, Zarar starts walking us up the path through the forest to Terry's cabin.

I let my head loll back and watch the trees go by.

"Are you really carrying me right now, or am I hallucinating and you've wrapped me up in one of those mummy blankets and I'm being pulled behind you in a wagon?"

Zarar looks down at me. "I'm really carrying you."

I close my eyes for a moment. "It's kinda hot, but I don't like it."

"Do you think you can walk to Terry's?" He comes to a stop and lowers me feet first.

"Yes," I say resiliently as he sets me down.

Immediately my knees buckle. Zarar's arm loops around my back.

"Has gravity doubled or is that just me?"

Zarar tilts his head to meet my gaze. "As far as I can gauge, gravity has remained constant."

"That's cool, good for gravity." I lean into him heavily as I drag one foot in front of the other. He smells like the lake and the forest.

My head feels like it's split above my eyebrow. "So, real talk, Zarar, how many women have you dropped your pamphlets in front of during your stint as fishing instructor?"

Zarar stops walking and takes a hasty step away. I list sideways, unable to stay upright sans human support wall.

"Well, it was nice knowing you," I inform him as I droop down to a knee.

A second later I'm up again, his hand supporting my torso. "Sorry! You took me off guard, I don't— How do you—? Did you see me with that Kelly girl on the trail?"

I pat his pec with my free hand, a lazy grin slipping up my cheek. "Jenga. And it all comes down." I snort. "Relax, man. I did not, but I wish I did. Is that like, your signature move? Take a little tumble, give a graceful peek at the guns on the way up? Has it worked? Because it's terrible. I need to know how many times you've succeeded."

"It's not a move," he states defensively as we start to hobble forward again. "It's hard to explain. I have this idea in my head, and this summer I've been trying to make it into a reality."

We're surrounded by green now. The newly risen sun has dialed up the saturation big time. Can't appreciate it because pain is overwhelming. "Do tell," I grind out. "Distract me, young sir."

"I'm older than you."

"How do you know?"

"How old are you?"

I glare up at him. "How dare you ask that of a lady."

"I'm twenty-three," he shares.

I nod. "Twenty."

We mull over this information for a moment as we make sluggish progress. Then I press him again. "Tell me about your pamphlets. At this rate we'll make it to Terry's by tomorrow, so you have about sixteen hours to get through the story. That's four hours more than the average audiobook, so I think you'll be able to squeeze it in."

He glances down at me. I feel it rather than see it.

"You're going to laugh at me."

I raise my eyebrows. *Holy hell, that hurts.* I stumble, and he tightens his grip, pulling me upward against him.

I seethe out a breath. "Yeah, probably. Tell me the story."

It takes Zarar thirty seconds to muster his courage, but he does.

"Last year I got out of my second dating app relationship. It didn't work out, but during that time, it was so boring to respond we met on Tunder to any and everyone who asked how we met. I really want a story for my grandkids. And out here we're off the grid, so I figured it would be the ideal time to go for it."

It's easier than usual not to mock him because, well, my head really hurts.

"I really want to meet someone in . . . a meet-cute way. Like people used to do before the internet."

I clear my throat. One foot. Next foot. "Are you telling me that you running into women with pamphlets has been some desperate attempt to orchestrate a meet-cute with someone hopefully willing to go out with you? Is that the fun story you're looking for?"

"When you say it like that, it sounds . . . bad. Everyone reacts differently. It's not like I'm orchestrating conversations."

I shake my head. "That is the absolute dumbest thing I've ever heard. Stop doing it."

"It's not that dumb."

"It is," I huff. "Meet-cutes have to happen naturally—that's why they're cute." I crane my head to look up at him. It hurts, but he's got a good face, so it's worth it. "Have any of these women even come off the slightest bit receptive?"

"No." He exhales a contemplative breath. "But it's a way to not be awkward during first conversations because you're too focused on the fallen stuff. Things just flow naturally, and when you think about it, it's not so different from swiping right."

"It is *so different* from swiping right. When you swipe right, you only match if the lass swipes right as well."

He tilts his head. "I guess you're right."

"I know I'm right." I poke gently at his shoulder.

"Would you go out with me?" Zarar asks quietly.

A laugh racks through me. I glance back up at his sweet open face. "No."

He pouts for a moment. "Could you not laugh?"

"No."

"I'm finding that your honesty is making me more attracted to you," he says seriously.

I cackle. It sounds shallow and broken. "I'm finding that you're weird," I cough out. That's when my knees give way again, and Zarar has to re-prop me upright.

Five minutes of agonizingly slow walking later, we make it to Terry's cabin. My head hurts an obnoxious amount, and I'm pretty sure I'm bleeding again because the bandage feels wet against my forehead. Zarar keeps glancing at me in fear, like the end is nigh. All he's mumbled since my knees buckled is the phrase *We're almost there, you're going to be okay* on repeat. This is the second time a human has gone on repeat in front of me today, and I can't say I'm enjoying it.

At the foot of Terry's steps, Zarar scoops me up again. And then he's setting me down on the soft fabric of a comfy-looking worn-in couch in a room plastered with . . . framed children's art? Terry. Art teacher.

"Don't close your eyes," Zarar says suddenly.

I didn't even realize I had closed them. I open them groggily. "Wow, I can't believe I managed to nod off. You've been engaging me in such scintillating conversation this last leg of the trip."

"I'm sorry, I'm worried. I think I should change your bandage. The doctor should be here soon, but maybe not soon enough."

"Maybe not soon enough?" I blink and it takes conscious effort to open my eyes again. "Where'd that dude go who wouldn't shut up about how okay I'm going to be ten seconds ago?"

He mashes his lips together.

I nod. "Go ahead and change it then, stud."

"Your jokes are getting less and less interesting. I think it's correlating directly with your loss of blood."

I glare at him, my eyes feeling heavy. "Wow, burn. Get your shit together then and fix me, sweetheart."

Zarar gently begins to pull at my current bandage. He's holding his breath, trying not to cause me any additional pain. "Za-rawr," I slur.

He drops his hands in fear. "Did I hurt you?"

"No. Just get it off. Do it already."

He positions one hand on the Band-Aid and the other comes up to carefully cradle my chin. My chin tingles.

That's when the door bursts open. We both startle—Zarar drops my chin, accidentally ripping off the Band-Aid.

"MOTHER FUCKER BALLS BASKET," I scream as my forehead explodes with pain.

13. Angst and All-Consuming Confusion

Zarar and Doctor Mariana find me lying in the fetal position on my yoga mat.

My brain is still short-circuiting. I need something to do with myself. I need a kitchen. I need a recipe. I need to chop something. I need my music.

Zarar says Jamie has a mild concussion and five stitches on her forehead. *Jamie is here.*

Jamie is a living, breathing person. She's resting at Terry's.

Clearly, I'm not the only one who can see her. So that only leaves two other possibilities and neither makes logical sense. The first is that everyone in my life has lied to me for as long as I can remember, and the second is Jamie is a ghost.

I can't entertain the first option so I have to entertain option two: ghost.

I'm very lost. My future is nothing. It makes sense that a guardian angel would send me a ghost like in *A Christmas Carol* to help me turn things around. Maybe she's the Ghost of End of Summer Present. The Ghost of Present Failure. The Ghost of Chronic Injuries.

Doctor Mariana thinks I'm fine, just experiencing some shock. She says I should take it easy for the rest of the day and get back to regularly scheduled activities tomorrow. I don't tell her about my nonimaginary imaginary friend.

I nod and thank her as she scribbles some notes down on a pad. Zarar's analyzing me from his spot near the door, like there's a riddle etched across my face.

I'm not going to find peace of any kind until I work up the energy to confront the ghost.

Please be a ghost. A ghost that's taken physical form. A weird physical ghost. Maybe my new career path could be ghosts.

14. A Girl Is Clammy

JAMIE
August 29, Saturday Evening
Colorado

They're screaming again.

This time I kind of knew the fight was coming. It's going to be their last one. Dad promised. We're leaving. He promised it'd be just the two of us. He promised I'd get to be an actress and I would never have to go to ballet again. Ballet has way too many rules. I don't want to wear pink. I don't want a tutu. I don't want to dance to classical music and point my toes. Dad said when we leave, we'll be free to do whatever we want.

Siri strolls into my room as I'm shoving clothes into my dance bag. The sight of her makes me bristle with irritation. She's gotten so annoying this year.

Somehow, we look almost exactly alike. I'm two years older than her, and no one can tell! She's four. *She's a baby.*

We're not Siri and Jamie anymore. People call us the "twins." We're not twins. I'm older. I came first. We're not the same.

Siri's skinny arms fall by her sides. "What are you doing, Jamie?"

I keep my voice cool. "Leaving."

"What do you mean, leaving? Can I come? Where are we going?" Four-year-old Siri exhales the questions in a cheerful frantic rush.

I yank open my drawer and dump everything into my dance bag. I don't answer Siri. I don't want her to come.

I run to my closet and start ripping things off their hangers, making a mess. A mess I know is going to make Mom mad. Mom is in love with Broadway and doesn't care what that means for the rest of us. Mom is obsessed with ballet. Siri is already somehow good enough to join my ballet class. So, Mom's obsessed with Siri too.

"We have dance today. Will you be back before then? Should I pack too?" Siri asks hopefully.

Her mouth hangs open, her lips forming a tiny O. I shove my clothes down to make more room. "No, Siri, you shouldn't pack."

Her lips start to wobble, like they've caught on to what's happening before she's worked it all out. "Are you going to Papa's?" she asks. "I'd like to come too, please."

"Me and Dad are leaving. We're going to live in Hollywood. Mom's holding us back."

"You're leaving? . . . I'm not invited?"

I zip my bag. It snags on a pair of socks right at the end, but I throw it onto my shoulder anyway. "Do you even want to come?" I spit at her.

She stares at me for a moment. "Can we wait till after dance?"

I toss my hands up. "You don't get it. I hate ballet. I hate it here. I hate you copying everything I do. I want to go, that doesn't mean you have to come. Get your own brain, Siri!" I shove past as tears begin to flow down her cheeks. I speed downstairs toward the screaming.

"You leave this family, then NEVER FUCKING COME BACK! I never want to see you again, you selfish, greedy asshole! Don't come crawling around in a couple of days asking to talk this through! Go live with your STUCK-UP BITCH of a mother!"

"I'm so done, Mara!"

I stop short on the bottom step. They're right up in each other's faces between the table and the kitchen counter. A moment later I feel the air shift as Siri stops right behind me. Our parents both turn to look at us at once.

"Girls," Mom breathes, falling into a kitchen chair like the weight of the world has collapsed onto her shoulders.

Dad looks at me. "Are you ready, Jame?"

"What do you mean is she ready? Grier, no. Don't you dare," Mom shoots at him. Her eyes fall to my bag and her expression softens. "Honey, are you ready for dance early?"

I walk over to Dad's side. "I'm leaving with Dad. Mom, I don't want to live with you anymore."

The color drains from Mom's cheeks. They go gray like someone turned off the light behind her face.

"She's coming with me," Dad answers forcefully. He looks over at Siri. "Goodbye, sweetie."

My eyes shift to Siri, who's staring at Mom.

"Mommy." The word dribbles out of my sister, waterlogged and desperate.

Dad heads toward the door. I turn my back on Mom and Siri. We head into the garage. I slide into Dad's back seat. He turns on the car and pushes the button to open the garage behind us.

As his car starts up, Mom's face appears at the side door, her expression dead as she presses the garage door button up on the wall.

The giant mechanism shudders for a moment and then starts to close on us. Dad throws the car into reverse, stepping on the gas. I'm screaming as I slam back against the seat. The car roof screeches against the closing door. We're going to die. We're going to be crushed.

But then we're in the driveway, zooming backward away from the house and into the street.

That's when Siri emerges, running from the front door. Sprinting for the car in her pink leotard with a thin satin skirt wrapped around her tiny waist. Screaming for us to wait in her little four-year-old voice. I watch her through the back window. Mom comes sprinting wildly after her, screeching for her to stop. Siri's fast.

Mom catches her in the middle of the road and scoops her up. Siri is kicking and crying and wailing . . .

I jolt awake on Terry's couch, sweating. I haven't relived that day via nightmare in years. It still feels fresh. Vivid. Every stupid six-year-old Jamie thought is so clear. I hated our ballet teacher for calling us the Fedorovs. Like we weren't two separate people.

I remember thinking that if I stuck around, I would become one of the Fedorovs to everyone. Then Siri's sister. And eventually no one. And I couldn't stand the thought of being no one.

I'm pretty sure that makes me a giant dick.

I snuggle back into the knit couch pillow and close my eyes again. Terry's been in and out, every hour, bringing me food, and testing my brain function with random questions about my favorite things. I've been prescribed Tylenol with a side of ice, and I'm to be woken up every hour for the next twelve hours, so I'll be sleeping here at Terry's.

When the door creaks open again I wiggle deeper into the couch, focusing on the crackling sound of Terry's fire. She lit it sometime between check-ins.

"Time to get up, Jamie," Terry says as she walks past.

I hear her sit down in the sofa chair next to the couch, and I take my sweet time, stretching like a child before sliding up the edge and lazily opening my eyes.

"BAH!" I bang against the armrest and immediately wrench a hand up to my forehead. Someone's glaring at me from the chair a foot away, and it's not Terry. Siri's sitting there like a nightmare incarnate, silently watching me with saucer-wide eyes, in a black sweatshirt with her hood up like a scary nun.

"I'm going to let you two talk alone before I join you," Terry says from down the hall.

After the stitches earlier, I explained away the whole incident in the vaguest of terms. She thinks: *Siri and I go way back, and we had a mild disagreement in the canoe.*

I turn back to Siri. Her eyes are completely bloodshot.

"Jesus Christ, blink. You're gonna go blind, Sier."

She flinches as I say her name.

"Are you okay?" I ask. "I have a gazillion questions for you."

She remains silent.

"For real. Are you not going to speak? First the weird shower attack, then you flip the boat and leave me drowning in the lake. And now you're what, the girl from *The Ring*? Are you trying to kill me?"

"Are you a ghost." She says this like it's a statement, not a question.

I glance over my shoulder and back at her.

"Is there a specter behind me that you're speaking with?"

Her brows descend menacingly. "I'm talking to you."

"I'm not a ghost. I'm your sister." I enunciate each word like she's hard of hearing.

Siri lets go of a guttural scream.

"What the hell, Siri?!" I lean as far from her as possible on this tiny blip of a couch.

Terry comes rushing in. Siri drops her face into her hands, folding forward with a straight back like she's made of wood.

"Are you okay? What happened?" Terry demands.

I keep my eyes trained on my sister. The girl's folded in on herself like a lawn chair.

"Siri's feral, it's fine."

Terry seats herself between us. "Girls. Clearly something's going on here."

I grin. "Girls? Terry, come on, you're like two years older than me."

"Jamie, I'm thirty-two. I'm twelve years older than you," Terry corrects.

I wink at Terry. "Wow, fast math, that's impressive."

Siri unfolds back into a human posture. "Could you not talk to our retreat leader that way?" she snaps.

"Could you not act like a scary movie caricature?" I ask sweetly.

Her brows descend with a vengeance. "You're such a gluteus maximus trench."

I throw a hand over my heart. "Thank you, you're a hot air balloon."

"What does that mean?!"

"Were we not calling each other random shit?"

"Ladies!" Terry yells over us. Siri tenses.

I turn to the retreat leader. "What's up, Terr?"

Her head slowly swivels back and forth between the two of us. "Wait a minute."

"Hey, Siri, set a timer for a minute," I tell the room.

Siri shakes her head from her perch.

"Are you two twins?" Terry asks, her voice strained.

15. Angst and Older Sisters

Jamie's eyes light up. "Ooh, Astute Terr, you're so perceptive."

"We're not twins," I respond curtly. Jamie is infuriating. And derisive. And rude. My skin feels hot and taut, and I want to scream and keel over and cry. I've literally already done all of these things in the last ten minutes. You'd think I'd have gotten it out of my system.

I have to keep it together in front of Terry. But how do you keep functioning when the dream you've been building since you could think catches fire and burns down to nothing, and you learn that your mother brainwashed you, and you find yourself stuck in isolation with a sister who apparently threw you away.

Jamie gestures to me. "She's right, Terr. We're not twins, just sisters with similar faces. Oh, the joy of being but two short years apart." She folds her hands in her lap. "We haven't seen each other in fourteen years because our parents hate each other, but we've both found ourselves at your retreat here in the middle of nowhere. I've been trying to reconnect, but she doesn't seem to think that I exist, which is frankly horrifying." Jamie meets my eyes.

My tears are back. I haven't been able to staunch them for any considerable amount of time since this morning. Maybe my new life path is to become the first living, breathing human fountain.

Jamie shakes her head, confusion clouding her features. "Siri. Why are you crying? What the hell is going on?"

Terry and Jamie study me expectantly.

"I'm crying," I huff, "because I spent three years trying to get over the loss of my imaginary friend, *Jamie*. I was in therapy most of my prepubescent life.

"I spent years trying to figure out how I could have imagined up a human being who lived in my house. A human being who I thought my friends and parents talked to. Who I went to dance with. Years coming to terms with the fact that I was legitimately delusional. Because Mom said you were never *real*.

"Jamie left the same day Dad did. She was a manifestation of my subconscious that I created to keep me company when I was a child because my parents were so tied up in their own drama. *And she's not real.* That's what Mom's reiterated to me a hundred times." My voice is quaking now. "*So if you are in fact Jamie,* the only two blood family members I know have lied to me my entire life. And you, my sister, abandoned me and never looked back."

16. A Girl Has Been Caught Off Guard

JAMIE
August 29, Saturday Evening
Colorado

Well, shit.

I feel a little like I'm falling. Maybe it's my mild concussion. I pull my legs up and hug them to my chest.

Abandoned.

I've locked that word away. Buried it under the floorboards of my dad's Beverly Hills home along with everything else from my previous life. I keep it away. I keep myself isolated. I don't use the internet. I don't see them. I don't hear about them. I don't talk about them.

But my mother told my little sister that I wasn't real. That's worse than what I've done.

I stare at Siri. Siri's staring at the floor. She can barely look at me.

I haven't heard from Mom in fourteen years. I shouldn't care about anything she does. Why am I having, like, an allergic reaction to this information? Why does it feel like my insides are fissuring?

"I need some air," Siri tells the floor.

I shake my head and fumble off the couch. "No, if anyone needs air, it's me. I'm the one who just learned they're fucking imaginary."

"You curse too much," Siri snaps.

"Jamie, be careful, slow movements," Terry says.

I wave her off, shove open the door, and shuffle out into the night.

It's cold without a sweatshirt, but I need the chill right now. My senses feel dull and foggy. I've been in and out of sleep all day, and it's left me feeling completely disoriented. It must be at least eight because the sun has set. It's still bright enough that I can follow the path that leads through the forest to the lake.

I stumble off the trail where the canoe cabin hugs the water and clamber up to it. The wood is freezing against my fingers as I shove a pseudo-canoe off the wall. There's a muffled boom as it smashes into the dirt. I step into the grounded boat and slump down onto the plank, hugging my arms across my chest.

Moonlight dances across the lake in a calm silver path.

I don't even know what my mother looks like now, because I've boycotted social media my entire life. In my mind she's a snapshot, frozen at twenty-seven, staring down at me, her mouth tight, her bun tighter. When I close my eyes, I can see her long, straight, dark brown hair. The way it would curl as one giant piece at night when she took out her bobby pins and tucked us into bed. Siri and I have *her* hair and *her* eyes.

She erased me.

I pull an oar off the side of the cabin and return to my spot in the boat. I row lightly into the ground, digging up the soft dirt.

I'm a skeleton in my mother's closet. And Terry knows about it.

"Canoe thief."

I twist around, throwing some dirt with my oar in the process. It hits Zarar across the knees.

Oof. I moved too quickly. I let go of the oar and grip the sides of my head, trying to press the angry tendrils of pain away. "Hey, teach," I grumble. "How's it cracking?"

Zarar pads over and takes a seat on the plank across from me.

"You're not supposed to touch the canoes."

I look up at him, one hand still on my head. Where I expect to find a smug expression, all I see is concern. He's in a dark sweatshirt with the Rediscover Yourself logo imprinted across it.

"Do you have any siblings?" I ask.

He blinks. "Yes, and in all seriousness, your canoe privileges are suspended."

I drop my hand and look him straight in the eyes. He's so calm, and unusually self-assured for someone who asked me out a couple of hours ago and got bluntly rejected.

"I was also serious about your eyes yesterday," he says quietly.

I sit back. "How many times do you plan to hit on me this week? It's fine, I just want to be prepared."

Zarar shrugs. "I like you."

I study him. "What kind of siblings do you have, Zarar?"

"I have an older brother. Are you upset?" he asks, tilting his head suddenly.

I blink a couple of times and stretch my jaw up and down to loosen my face. "No."

"You're upset," he says.

"I'm great," I insist.

"How are you feeling?"

"Great!" I blow out a breath. "What's up with you, Zarar? What's your deal, why do you work here? Why do you smell like the color green? Feel free to answer chronologically."

Zarar relaxes his posture. "I'm an accountant, but I've been trying out a bunch of new career paths, not sure what will stick. I'm looking for my passion. I don't know . . . I've been around trees a lot? I don't think you're okay. Does it have to do with Siri?"

I narrow my eyes at him.

"Are you two twins?" He continues, "I didn't catch the resemblance until today, seeing both your hair slicked back away from your faces."

I stand up.

"You're not supposed to stand in the canoe," he says.

I sit back down. "If I ever get my hands on some paint I'm making this a Bucket. You can teach Bucketing. Ask your students to choose and mount their Buckets. You're gonna have to print new pamphlets, *A Guide to Bucket Safety.*"

Zarar's concerned expression doesn't waver. He holds my eyes. I swallow and stare back, my smile melting after a few seconds of silence.

"Zarar, Siri and I haven't seen each—"

"Jamie?" Terry's voice calls out. I clamp my mouth shut and leap back up. Stumble out of the fake canoe. Terry's by the trees, at the edge of the path. "Jamie, you're strictly forbidden from those canoes right now. Please come back to the cabin."

I start trekking her way. "Already en route, Terr."

"Sleep well, Jamie," Zarar says quietly. I don't look back.

What the hell was that? I was so close to . . . venting. I almost sat down and spilled my entire sob story like a sad whiny asshole to a dude I met twenty-four hours ago. I felt it all cresting in the back of my throat like a tidal wave. I don't need to burden others with my issues. They're mine.

17. Angst and Flashbacks

SIRI
August 29, Saturday Evening
Colorado

Confirmation of Jamie's existence has slammed a finger down on the rewind button in my mind. I have to rethink everything anyone's ever said to me.

Mom lied about the existence of a sibling. I've spent so much of my life thinking something was wrong with me! Worrying about my brain! And those worries rippled out into obsessing over every aspect of my health.

I only have broken memories of Jamie. How she looked like me, what she sounded like. I remember I wanted to be just like her. And then she was gone.

The door to Terry's cabin slams open.

"We're back!" Jamie sings in an irritatingly cheery voice. "Terry says it's time to bond." She looks over her shoulder at Terry. "Are we making friendship bracelets? I make a mean friendship bracelet."

The two of them settle back onto the love seat. I find myself staring at Jamie's clothes. She's wearing a pair of gray sweats and a gray sweatshirt. I was too distracted before to notice. She looks like Danny Zuko when he goes through his jock phase in *Grease*.

My stomach lurches as she catches me leering. "Admiring my ensemble?" Jamie asks.

"No," I answer hastily.

"I was mandatorily re-clothed with Terry's scraps." Jamie puckers her lips.

"Danny Zuko but make it fashion . . . Terr, you've got my overalls going in your secret washing machine, correct?"

Did both of us watch *Grease* together with Mom? Was it not just the two of us? Did the three of us dance to choreography from "We Go Together" in front of the TV?

I can't believe I have to do this again. Question every memory. Reprocess. I already did this to get rid of her.

"I think maybe you two would benefit from private sessions with Donya during your stay," Terry proposes.

"Who's Donya?" Jamie asks.

"She's our licensed counselor here," Terry explains.

I remember Jamie braiding my hair. She knew how to do all these weird fancy braids. At six.

"We can handle this ourselves," Jamie insists.

Six-year-old Jamie was silly. We would laugh together about nothing because Jamie could make anything funny.

Terry looks at her hands. "I don't think Siri's comfortable with that."

I don't know what I'm comfortable with. How does one move forward from here? My imaginary friend is actually my sister.

"I need music," I blurt.

Terry bites her lip. "Siri, I'm sorry, but I don't have any music in here."

"Come on, Terr. Can't she borrow her phone for like an hour?" Jamie urges.

Jamie wants me to have my music? Does she know how much I need it? Jamie would always let me have the last red ice pop in the freezer even though we both liked it best. That fit well into Mom's imaginary friend trajectory.

I lock eyes with Terry. "How am I supposed to know if I'm comfortable with any of this without *my music*?!"

Excrement, I yelled at Terry. I glance nervously from her to Jamie. Jamie's wearing the same startled, guilty look she had when I screamed earlier. "Sier . . ." she starts, then trails off.

My anger is doing its pulsing thing. This happens sometimes; it feels like I have a second heartbeat for my rage. I feel like a pot that's bubbling over with no one around to turn down the gas.

Jamie always came into my room when my parents were fighting. She'd put a *SpongeBob SquarePants* video into the VHS under my little TV, and we'd climb under the covers and watch. She'd make it really loud to drown out the war raging downstairs.

"I'm going to set up a daily appointment with Donya for the two of you." Terry scribbles in a notebook she picked up off her tiny coffee table.

"Terr, we don't need Donya," Jamie insists.

Terry puts down her pen. "I'm setting up a standing appointment with Donya for an hour every day for the next five days. If you attend the appointments, you can skip your group chat sessions." Terry pages through her planner. "She has a slot after lunch every day at one o'clock. Let's plan for that, and we can have her host you both in here."

"Sier, don't you think we can handle this on our own?" Jamie says.

Jamie knew I existed, and she went on living like I didn't.

"Sier, can you hear me? Let's channel our feelings into a hike! We can do it bright and early, tomorrow morning, eight a.m.?"

"James, you can't hike right now, you're mildly concussed." Terry sounds exasperated. Jamie is exasperating.

"Siri, please acknowledge that you can hear us," Jamie says.

I get up and stride toward the door. I don't remember the walk to my cabin, but I got here. I lie on my yoga mat with my feet up in the air to try to stifle my anxious heart.

18. A Girl Is Trying to Reconnect

JAMIE
August 30, Sunday Morning
Colorado

Siri blows me off for the hike I pleaded for last night. I wait by the trails till 8:18 a.m. before giving up and wandering down to the small dock next to the canoe cabin. Zarar is there in his green Rediscover Yourself T-shirt and black shorts, hunched over the edge with his feet dangling and a fishing pole gripped in his hands.

The wood strains and squeaks under my feet as I approach. "How goes it, Zarar?"

He looks up, squinting in the light. "Fishing," he explains.

I plop down next to him. "Classic Zarar."

"Shouldn't you be resting?"

"Eh, I'm fine. I rested all yesterday."

I watch his eyes travel to my gauze square. "You wear bandages well."

I smirk at him. "Thanks, Zarar. I'm flattered."

"You can call me Z if you want."

My smirk morphs into a smile. "I'll take you up on that from time to time, but I love your full name."

He holds my gaze for a long moment before nodding. "So you're feeling better?"

I nod. "I'm hindered in the eyebrow raising department, but indeed, my general well-being has improved since yesterday."

"Good. I'm really glad."

I glance down at the dark water sparkling below my feet. I've yet to hear Zarar laugh at anything I've said. Tough cookie to crack in the humor department.

I swing my legs back and forth under the dock. "Do you like your parents, Z?"

"I love my parents." He bobs his fishing pole up and down and reels it in slightly.

"Well, that's built in."

Zarar lifts one shoulder and lets it drop. "I kind of want to be just like them. They moved here from Pakistan as college students back in the eighties and found each other at school . . . They really love each other, and they're perpetual optimists. They live and parent to the beat of their own drum: they've worked hard to foster a dynamic where we can all be super open together. My brother and I are big fans." He smiles. It's a sweet, subtle, close-lipped thing.

"Do you like your brother?" I ask.

He leans away. "What kind of question is that?"

I chuckle. "What do you mean? It's a regular question!"

"I love my brother. His name's Javed. He's my best friend. We lived together in New York for four years while I was getting my accounting degree and he was teaching at Pace."

"You don't live together anymore? Did it go horribly wrong?"

He bobs his fishing pole up and down again. "No, he's getting married, so he and his fiancée got their own place."

I fiddle with my overall buckles. "Damn, so what, you have a picture-perfect family life?"

"Nothing's perfect, but . . ." He shrugs. "I guess they're pretty good . . . I quit my job back in January because I was miserable, and they've been surprisingly supportive about it. My parents have always put more stress on the fact that their goal is for us to be experts in our field, rather than stressing a specific field they want us to be educated in, which is nice. My brother's still deciding; he's a legitimate scholar at this point. He has a PhD and he's working on his law degree."

"Wow." I take a second to process this. "Hold up, so you're not an accountant at all anymore?"

"I told you I'm trying out a bunch of new career paths," he says calmly.

"Yeah, you did," I say thoughtfully. "I guess I was distracted and haven't really taken a second to think about how that would work. What have you done so far?"

Zarar reels in his line again and casts it back out. "I was an accountant after I graduated, then a personal trainer and a lifeguard, and now I'm teaching fishing and slacklining out here."

I slump forward a bit. "Wow. That's rad."

He resituates himself next to me, shifting so he can make eye contact. "Can I rewind?"

"Rewind away."

"Am I to infer from this conversation that you don't like your sister?"

I swing my legs under the dock a few more times.

"I don't really know my sister. Right now, she's making it difficult to . . . connect at all. I don't know if I like her, but I for sure love her. It's built into my DNA or something."

Zarar studies me, processing this. "You're talking about her like she just came out of the womb and you haven't gotten used to her existence yet," he says.

I suck on a tooth. "Yeah well, I haven't seen her since I was six, so we're not exactly used to being around each other." What am I doing?

He blinks at me a couple of times. "Sorry, explain this again."

19. Angst and Reprocessing

Jamie's late for our appointment with Donya.

She shows up on the doorstep at 1:04, frazzled and breathless like she sprinted here. I'm agitated and she's barely walked into the room.

Why is it so hard for people to get somewhere at an appointed time?

Jamie's wearing another pair of overalls today. Navy blue ones paired with a red plaid shirt. Like she's cosplaying Old McDonald.

"Hey hey hey, I'm Jamie!" She smiles at Donya and shakes her hand. Her hair is tied up in a poofy fountain again, and there's a two-by-two-inch piece of gauze taped above her left eye.

"Thanks for fitting us into your schedule." She continues, "How's the day treating ya? I see you're wearing a wedding ring, how's that going?" I bristle from my spot on the couch.

What kind of question is that?

After a minute or so of humoring invasive relationship inquiries from Jamie, Donya swishes out of the room with a promise to be right back.

Jamie flops onto the love seat next to me. "Hey hey hey, you." She grins and pulls her feet up underneath her. Then puts them down on the floor, then pulls one up and sits on it.

I frown. "Why do you feel the need to say 'hey' three separate times?"

Jamie shrugs. "I enjoy the word 'hey' in a cluster of three."

I glance at her outfit again. "Do you not own normal pants?"

She snorts. "What are normal pants?"

"Doing your hair like that makes you look like a five-year-old."

"That youth serum Grams got me must be working."

Grams? Who's Grams? She's so calm. And self-assured. It's annoying. I roll my eyes and blow out a sigh.

Jamie grins at me. "You really have a way with that."

"With what?" I snap.

"You've mastered the execution of the perfect eye-roll-dramatic-sigh combo."

I glare at her.

She claps. "Oh my gosh, wow. Consider auditioning for a role on the CW. Excellent work."

Donya returns with a platter of tea-related ingredients, mugs, and a kettle. She takes a seat in the solo chair, and we begin.

20. A Girl Is a Little Disoriented

Donya and Siri are discussing our mother. I nod along now as Siri talks about the lifelong aspiration she's had to travel the world as a ballerina. I mechanically take another sip of tea.

I'm losing my shit over here. I know 100 percent of my focus needs to be on reconnecting with Siri right now, but I'm spiraling out about Zarar. It happened. I sat there with him and spilled my whole life story. We got up, we had lunch together, and I told him everything. I broke my own fucking rule. *My shit is mine. I can handle it myself.*

But there I was blabbering on. For like hours. To Zarar! He listened and nodded empathetically until I saw the time and bolted off to Terry's cabin for this appointment.

My brand-new hot fishing instructor friend who gently hits on me every other hour and runs into girls with pamphlets knows more about me now than my own sister does. Dawn doesn't even know the full reason why I'm here. She doesn't know about my massive bomb. She doesn't know about Siri.

Zarar knows I left my mother and sister and haven't spoken to them in over a decade. I want to slump over a table and drop my head into a plate of food. My privacy filter is on the fritz. Who knows what I might say in here.

I glance up at Terry's clock over the fireplace. We only have twenty-five minutes left. *I can stay quiet for another twenty-five minutes.*

Donya gathers her hands together. "I think the first thing we should work on is helping you and Jamie gain a better understanding of each other. You share common ground. Let's try to find it."

"How?" Siri asks eagerly.

"Pull out your notebooks," Donya instructs. "We're going to do a writing exercise."

Aces, Donya, what a beautiful idea.

"I want you both to close your eyes. Imagine a miracle is bestowed upon you overnight, to make everything in your life wonderful."

My head falls sideways. Interesting writing prompt.

"Let the different aspects of the miracle reveal themselves to you. They'll come up from the darkness. Explore the differences between this new day you're imagining, and now."

She lets us sit in silence for a stretch of thirty seconds. "Okay, open your eyes. Write down your miracle, detailing all the things you found that were different."

I click my pen, eager to get this shit out of my brain before it spews out of my mouth.

21. Angst and Hypothetical Miracles

SIRI
August 30, Sunday Afternoon
Colorado

"Just about done?" Donya says after twenty minutes.

I close my notebook and look up. "Yes." I've been done for about five minutes. Jamie's got her tongue tucked between her teeth like she's deep in concentration, writing a novel.

"Done. Damn, Don, that was fun." Jamie smiles and closes her journal. She glances up at the old-fashioned clock over the fireplace. "Thanks for a great session. I can feel the tension release in my bones."

Donya laughs. "We're almost there, but not quite yet. We're going to finish this exercise."

Jamie's smile falters. It's oddly satisfying to see her look uncomfortable.

"Open back to your miracle pieces, please." I open my notebook obediently. "We're going to read them aloud," she explains.

I should have seen that coming.

"Siri, would you like to go first?" She smiles at me kindly.

I nod. Either I can feel ill about this for the ten minutes leading up to my turn, or I can get it over with now and relax while Jamie's going. I've done enough of these random therapy exercises over the years to know as dumb as they feel, they kind of help.

22. A Girl Is Not Doing That

JAMIE
August 30, Sunday Afternoon
Colorado

Read them aloud?

Siri just accepted Donya's invitation to go first. What the hell? There was no disclaimer beforehand.

Why did I take this exercise seriously? Rookie mistake. I could have easily made this a comedy piece.

Siri clears her throat, and I watch in horror as she begins.

"If I was granted a miracle to fix my life overnight, so much would change . . . it's honestly hard to decide where to start. Things went wrong so long ago. Everything's so screwed up, even a miracle could only fix so much." Her voice is quaking. She takes a deep breath to even it out.

"I guess the first thing I would notice upon waking is being pain-free. My back would be healed. I would go back to my ballet company after this retreat and rise to the potential I've been building brick by brick my entire life. I'd feel like I have a purpose again."

Her back? What's wrong with her back?

"My mom wouldn't have messed things up with George . . ." She trails off for a moment. "If my life were fixed overnight, my greedy, selfish jerk-and-a-half dad would call."

I stifle a snort.

"There are no phones around here, but he'd find a way to get in touch with Terry, and he'd figure out how to get out here, and he'd come and get me. No matter what he had on his agenda. My dad would come for me, and bring me back to California so we could get to know each other. And I'd get a break from my mom, and time away to figure out how I move forward.

"Once I got to California, my dad would apologize for all the birthdays he wasn't around for. He'd apologize for deciding not to be my dad. He'd tell me how wrong he was to leave me.

"He'd ask about the last fourteen years. He'd want to hear the highs and the lows. He'd ask to see my winning solo routines, and I'd pull them up on Instagram. He'd be my father again.

"My sister and I would know each other. We'd know each other's lives instead of being strangers. We'd all be a family instead of a handful of people who can't stand to be in the same room. I know some families *are* just people together for the holidays who can't stand one another, but at least they're trying. My family gave up. We just stopped one day. I want to be a family that tries."

Siri closes her notebook and looks at me. Silent tears dribble down her face.

Donya's wearing a proud smile. "That was beautiful, Siri. Thank you for sharing. We're going to dig a little deeper into what you touched on. Jamie, let's hear yours first, and then you can both go back to your cabins, ruminate on what we talked about, and tomorrow we'll start connecting the threads." She looks at me and nods encouragingly.

Siri's gaze drifts to the closed notebook on my lap.

"Siri, I—"

"Jamie," Donya interjects. "It's okay. You don't need to respond right now. Just read yours."

I look back at Donya. "Um, I'm sorry, but I don't want to read mine."

Donya nods patiently. "I think Siri would really love to hear yours."

I shake my head. "It's too personal."

Siri blinks at me in disbelief. "Are you intercoursing kidding? Read yours, Jamie."

I shift to face her head on and widen my eyes, "I'm sorry. Did you just use 'intercoursing' as a stand-in for the f-word?"

"I don't use vulgar language. *Read your essay.*"

"So you replaced fucking with the technical term?" I snicker.

Siri's seething. Her face looks like a tomato.

"If you won't read it," she spits, "I will."

Siri snatches the journal off my lap.

"Oh my god!" The words fly out of me in a pitch yet unknown to human-kind. I grab hold of the other side of it and yank back. "Siri!"

Siri holds strong.

"Girls." Donya tries to catch our attention, but we've locked in on each other and there's nothing she can do that's going to make me let go of this book. I pull with all I have, bracing my foot in the crease between the couch cushions.

"Siri, this is my writing, it's my decision!"

She tugs it farther in her direction. "You have to finish the exercise!" she screams.

My heart is in my throat. "Dude, what the fuck, let it go!"

Siri suddenly slinks sideways off the couch into a standing position, yank-ing with an impressive amount of force that annihilates my grip on the edge of the journal. Just like that, she's glided across the room with it.

"SIRI!"

"GIRLS!" Donya's eyes are wide from her spot on the sofa. Siri freezes with the notebook held aloft. She's breathing heavily. Tears are still stream-ing down her cheeks.

I'm full-on standing on the damn couch. "Siri, if you really want to get to know each other, you won't open that notebook."

Siri's voice scrapes up her tear-laden throat. "If you wanted to work through this and be sisters, you would read it to me. That's a fact. You would read it, Jamie! The universe went through the trouble of bringing us back together, and you still don't want to talk to me?!"

I dig deep for my calm voice. "This isn't me not talking to you; this is me not sharing a journal entry about the most vulnerable aspects of my life, haphazardly, after knowing each other for twenty hours."

"You're a selfish jerk! Just like him." She chucks the notebook at me. I catch it awkwardly against my chest.

"And you're a bundle of joy," I tell her with a grim smile.

"This isn't a joke!" Siri screeches. She grabs her notebook, strides out the door, and slams it shut behind her.

I turn to Donya, who's holding a hand to her heart.

"We'll be fine," I tell her.

Her forehead creases in concern. "I can stay a little longer."

I shake my head. "Nah, I deserved that. I'm fine. Thanks for your time."

Donya nods. "You're very welcome. I'll be here tomorrow at one."

I trek out of the cabin and down the steps. Siri's fifty feet ahead of me, crossing the valley. I follow at a slower pace.

I wish I could call Dawn. She's great at this calming, making-people-feel-safe shit. She would know what to do. Or I wish I could talk to Grams. Or ask my mom why she would plant these seeds in Siri.

What the hell was Dad thinking? How could he let me think this was okay? That it was fine to start again completely fresh, without them?

In her little miracle, this girl who can't stand to be in the same room as me for more than an hour without screaming basically proposed a future where she comes to live with me, Grams, and Dad.

Dad, whose response to my eviction was not *What happened?* or *Are you okay?* He simply stated, *You're welcome to move back home if you sign my nine-point live-in contract.*

I signed an official printed list of stipulations before he let me "walk of shame" back up to my childhood room. Stipulation one was the therapy clause. Stipulation two is to *fix my look*. Sometime in the next month I have to dye my hair blond "for my own good," because that's how I'm going to "book more acting jobs and get my career on track."

He's . . . always been like this. Can we go to a One Direction concert? *We can go to a concert if you want to see Bruce Springsteen.* Can I go to this *New Moon* convention? *We can go to Ice and Fire Con.* It's been so long since I've really thought about the day we left New York.

That was messed up. Every decision he made feels disgusting now.

What kind of asshole convinces his six-year-old that she should leave her mother and sister to fly across the country with him and start a new Hollywood life because they're holding her back?

I watch as Siri veers off at the edge of the valley where the trail picks up in front of the student cabins. She heads to one four doors down from mine.

And Mom. She told my sister I was *imaginary.* I've had zero new set ideas because I can't go an hour without thinking about it. There's an angst bubble building in me that I can't moonwalk away from.

Siri's drama is contagious. If I wake up tomorrow with the urge to dress funeral casual, I'm gonna lose it—

I freeze mid-stride in the valley as *an idea* slaps into me so hard, I legitimately take a step back. I stare into the distance, letting the concept settle and solidify.

The potential comedy. The potential catharsis.

If I set it up right, if I pitch it correctly, I can make it happen.

Excitement scorches through me.

It will no doubt make for a spectacular new set.

23. Angst and Fire Choir

I open the cabin door to find my white sneakers and toiletries waiting on the ground. I glance around. Did Jamie leave them?

There's a folded piece of paper in one of the shoes. I yank it out and open it feverishly, my heart pounding—it has to be her miracle. She does want to bond! She's opening the door!

Let's chat at Fire Choir! See you at 8!

Ugh. It's not the miracle. I stuff the paper into my sweatshirt pocket.

As angry as I am at Jamie for . . . leaving with Dad and deleting me from her life, I want her *to want* me to be in it now. I want to be angry at her, but I want her *to want* to work it out. I want to hang out and get to know each other.

I want a sister.

Terry's hosting Fire Choir. She's strumming a guitar and the ten other retreaters around me are passionately singing along to a stripped-down version of the My Chemical Romance song "Welcome to the Black Parade."

We're all seated on big logs around a fire pit conveniently located at the heart of the valley between the retreater cabins and Terry's place. There are marshmallows and sticks and all the other ingredients one might use to make a s'more. One by one, we're supposed to suggest a song for Terry to play, and then explain why said song means something to us. She called it a team-building exercise. Or team bonding? Fun building? I don't know.

I got here five minutes early and now it's eight minutes past the hour. *Where is Jamie?* All of the cabins have wooden clocks on the walls. All of the main buildings have clocks somewhere mounted on the outside! They could not make it easier to be on time!

"Boo!" Her voice is deafening in my right ear. I remain still, glaring into the flames, and raise my hand to give her the finger.

"Wow, so you won't use the f-word, but you'll give me the finger. You keep throwing curve balls at me, Sier," she says cheerily.

Jamie's already clutching a stick loaded up with three marshmallows. She squeezes herself between me and the cute girl I noticed yesterday—who I sat in the vicinity of but have yet to speak a word to. I still don't even know her name.

Now Jamie's talking to her like they're the best of friends. She calls her Thalia. How does she know her already?

Jamie turns back to me. "So you made it!" She lowers her stick over the bonfire. She's still wearing those stupid overalls with the red plaid shirt. I thought maybe she would have changed into something less embarrassing.

I fiddle with my braid. "Why do you insist on dressing like a farmer from the fifties?"

"Oh, I find them super hot." She shoots me a vexing smile.

I groan and turn back to the fire. "I'm here. What do you want?"

"Well, first I wanted to share a thing I noticed that we have in common during our session as a sort of olive branch for the miracle exercise fiasco."

I wait for her to share.

"Um, well, I too had aspirations to travel around the world for work, and I too am facing the very real possibility that—that's never going to happen for me."

I glare at her expectant expression.

Jamie gestures excitedly with her hands. "We have similar failed career aspirations—it's groundbreaking!"

What an extremely depressing thing to have in common.

When I don't respond, Jamie babbles on, "So yeah . . . Anyway, um, I know you kind of hate me, and you most likely came here to actually rediscover yourself in some way or another and I'm probably getting in the way of that."

Eerily accurate. All I've been able to think about the last few hours is Jamie. Her presence is quite literally ruining the point of the retreat. How am I supposed to figure out where I'm going next post-ballet if all I can do is think about the past?

"But—" Jamie continues, "I wanted to tell you I've had a sister-bonding idea that would involve some travel." She does a little shoulder dance like this should entice me.

I am a little enticed. I raise my brows.

"I need a second to finesse it." She smiles. "So, I figured I'll leave you alone for a couple of days while I do that. This way, we get some time to figure out our personal shit before we come together to figure out the family shit. And, when I have everything sorted, I shall present my fully formed sister-bonding plan! Does that sound like something you might possibly be interested in?"

"Welcome to the Black Parade" wraps up around us, and I hold off responding as the group goes quiet. Terry gets her next musical request from the blond girl, Kelly. She wants a song called "ME!" by Taylor Swift because it empowered her in some way, blah blah blah. Terry starts strumming. Retreaters start singing along with her. I turn back to Jamie.

Does that sound like something I might be interested in? she asked.

Yes. It sounds kind of perfect. I don't want to waste this retreat. I need to use it to find inner peace and all that excrement. I love the idea of a sister-bonding travel plan. Also, putting a pin in this for a few days would be an enormous relief.

I can't believe I'm about to agree with her assessment.

"I guess, yeah," I say reluctantly.

Jamie's overalls jingle as she executes a weird, goofy shimmy. "Fantastic!

Okay! Before we go on hiatus, can I ask you three questions for sister-bonding plan research?"

The group song surges around us. "Only if you let me ask you three questions too," I yell over them. The music dies abruptly mid-song.

My heart falls into my colon. We shouldn't have been talking.

Terry's staring at us with a flustered look in her eyes. Not just Terry, everyone.

"Why aren't the two of you participating? Is everything okay?" Terry asks.

Jamie pulls her stick of food from the fire. "Everything's fabulous. We're having an introspection moment, Terr."

I shoot Jamie a death look. The haphazard way she speaks to authority figures makes my stomach hurt. "Sorry, we'll move farther from the group," I offer.

"That's considerate of you. Thanks, Siri."

I jump off the log and hustle away. When I'm a good thirty feet from the fire circle I slowly lower myself onto the grass. My back groans as I slouch for a moment. I snap upright again.

Jamie sidles over belatedly.

"You're so rude to our instructors," I hiss as she collapses in a heap across from me. She sinks her teeth into a roasted marshmallow. It gets all over her face as she pulls away.

"Whut dud you tink of their rendition of 'Black Parade'?" She swallows. "I danced my way down here from the cleansing room."

It's work not to roll my eyes. "You have marshmallow all over your face."

"Cool, I think it really adds to my youthful glow."

"I don't like pop music. It grinds against my soul."

Jamie snorts and stuffs another bite into her mouth. "Offf curse you dan't," she says around the food. "Since when does MCR count as popular music? What music *do you* like? Wasn't your favorite album the *Annie* soundtrack when we were kids?" She asks each question without giving me a moment to answer and then looks up thoughtfully. "God, Mom was obsessed with Broadway soundtracks. I forgot about that."

Mom *is obsessed* with Broadway soundtracks, present tense. I start picking at the grass near my feet. "I'm into White Chapel now. And the only other artist I really follow is Billie Eilish."

Jamie purses her lips. "Billie Eilish is most definitely popular music."

I cross my arms. "Whatever, you can ask me your three questions if you let me ask you mine."

She shrugs. "Aces. Number one: Why are you here? Does it have something to do with your back?"

I sigh. "It's a long story."

"Oh well, fuck it then. I don't have time for a long story."

My heart drops.

Jamie snickers. "I'm kidding, Angst Lord. Spill it. What is it with everyone and long stories? I asked to hear the story. I want the story, long or short, it makes no difference." She nudges me in the arm with her elbow.

I shift away from her. "Don't touch me and don't call me Angst Lord."

She smirks. "It's a term of endearment."

"I don't like it."

Jamie winks at me.

"And I don't like winks," I tell her.

"Noted." She's now wearing an irritatingly impish grin. She throws her legs out into an impressive straddle (does she still dance?) and gnashes into her last marshmallow. "Hut me wid a storytyme."

I grab onto the strings dangling from my hoodie. "The story might sound stupid out loud. I've only ever told Mom and the doctors what happened, and when I did, I felt stupid."

She swipes marshmallow off her face with the back of her hand. "What happened?"

I release the laces on my sweatshirt and they spring back up toward my face. "A lot happened. I guess we can rewind all the way back to . . . I got accepted into a ballet company last August."

Jamie's eyes light up. "Hey, congrats on getting into a company! Not that I ever doubted you." She raises her sticky marshmallow hand for a high five.

Never doubted me. She didn't even know I was doing it. I glare at her hand and scoot a little farther away.

"Sorry." Jamie drops her arm. "Keep going."

"I met my best friend, Celia, last year, working with this company. I hadn't had a best friend in, ever . . . so it was nice. And then a couple of months later I got together with this guy in the company, Bran. My life got really busy and really great, really fast.

"There was this seven-month period where things felt like they were all finally clicking into place . . ." Jamie's watching me so intently, I stumble for a moment. I smooth the stray hairs that have escaped my braid.

"Um, Mom was getting super busy at home, dropping the ball on things a lot, but I didn't mind so much because I had them. I didn't have to be home.

"This one day I was early to practice. Well, I'm always early. But this particular day, I found Bran and Celia having sex in the dressing room."

I close my eyes, as the scene reconstructs itself in my mind. The betrayal that speared through me like a sword to the gut. The breakfast burrito–flavored vomit I spewed across the floor moments later. The apathetic silence from Bran and Celia when they looked up and saw me. The anger I've always harbored, electrifying, solidifying into a new visceral hatred that I have yet to successfully expel.

I open my eyes to find Jamie cringing in an almost comical fashion.

"Shit." She shakes her head and her hair floofs about in every direction. "Assholes."

I yank on my sweatshirt laces again.

"That wasn't that long," Jamie notes.

"I'm not done," I grumble. My hood is now a shrunken ball against my neck. My heart's beating too fast. I exhale slowly, counting to eight.

Jamie nods. "Take your time." She turns and gazes out at the bonfire where they're singing another pop tune.

I can tell this stupid story.

I close my eyes and try to ground myself. Focus on something other than the anxiety. The cold grass. The song. The group is singing . . . the weird original version of "Wrecking Ball" from a viral video back like nine years ago. It sounds ridiculous. What an ill-timed background song for my anguish. Who would request this version—

"I came into the dining *hall*!" Jamie screams right beside me. I jostle sideways, scowling at her.

"We're in the middle of something, could you not right now?"

"Sorry, it's one of my favorites. I was letting you take a breather. You ready to go on?"

I pull out a giant chunk of grass and shake my head no.

"I'll give you a sec. Be right back." She walks over toward the group.

I practice breathing exercises.

I'm feeling slightly better when Jamie returns five minutes later holding two sticks loaded with three marshmallows apiece.

24. A Girl Is Rapt with Attention

JAMIE
August 30, Sunday Evening
Colorado

Siri delicately bites a tiny blip off the top of her marshmallow, chews, swallows, and dives back into her story.

"I got these tickets for a Slipknot concert in the city back before I caught Bran cheating on me with Celia. I was hoping he'd come with me. But when I asked him, he didn't want to." Her voice wavers.

I fight the urge to reach out and rub her arm or something. She backs away like I have the plague whenever I make physical contact.

"So, I asked Celia to come, and she agreed. The morning I caught the two of them together . . . it was the day of the concert. I'd been looking forward to going for ages. I'd been obsessing over Slipknot for a while and seeing them live was going to be a whole experience. Metal concerts are different than pop. They get really wild . . . and I wanted that. I wanted to let all of the feelings in me explode out alongside the music."

Siri's eyes glaze over. Like she's forgotten I'm here. Like she's not even here.

"Their whole thing, catching them in the dressing room, the day of the concert, I mean . . . it was like they planned it for that day so Celia could get out of going. So of course, I had no one to go with. But I said, intercourse this, I'm going anyway."

"Assholes."

Siri shoots me a look.

"Sorry, go on."

"I went by myself and I had an amazing time. I *was* having an amazing time. I felt so . . . free. I was in the mosh pit and things were getting wild. The adrenaline rush was mind-blowing. We were all plowing into one another and it wasn't uncalled for, it was expected and encouraged. And people were crowd surfing. Before I knew it, I was too. It was incredible, and I was screaming along with the band."

25. Angst and Metal

SIRI
August 30, Sunday Evening
Colorado

I close my eyes, the soaring feeling returning in my chest. I was smiling so hard, my cheeks hurt. Screaming so hard, my throat burned. Drenched in sweat, mashed up against so many people—something that would normally drive me insane. But I didn't care.

"For a fleeting moment I was invincible." I swallow, staring out at the darkening horizon. "And then I was on the concrete.

"The strobe lights kept flashing and the band kept singing and the people kept jumping, and I couldn't move without bolts of pain searing through me. Time melted. A stretcher somehow made its way in and got me out of the pit.

"I had a concussion. I messed up my discs." The words come quickly now, pent up and desperate to see the light of day. "I can't listen to Slipknot anymore without having a panic attack. I was benched at the company for three months. I went to the doctor with Mom a couple days ago and he said I can no longer safely pursue a career in ballet. Or else I risk all sorts of more serious complications. And then Mom shipped me out here to Colorado.

"Everything I ever planned for my life is a moot point, and when I look ahead to the future, I see nothing. I am nothing.

"I was going to tour Europe. I was supposed to end up with Mom on Broadway . . ." I trail off in a gurgle of snot. "Now everything's ruined."

"Sier . . ." Jamie's golden eyes are full of empathy. "I'm so sorry."

We sit in silence for a few minutes while I try to stop crying and Jamie finishes her marshmallows. I yank some more grass from the ground. "My turn to ask you something."

"Shoot."

"What happened to you?"

Jamie shrugs.

I throw a chunk of grass at her. "Jamie, you have a backstory. You're a person, not a cartoon character."

She laughs. "What kind of shitty cartoons are you watching?"

I am the opposite of amused. "I just shared the worst day of my life, Jamie. Answer the question."

"I'm just having a hard time right now," she says casually.

I cross my arms. "Did you just get out of a relationship?"

"I don't do relationships."

I roll my eyes. "Are relationships too mainstream for you or something? That sounds so California."

Jamie snorts. "They take up a shitload of time and effort, and compromise. Compromise that slows you down on the way to wherever you really truly want to be. And they always end up breaking."

The wind kicks up, blowing into us sideways, making Jamie's hair flap over her face in every direction. It gets caught in her mouth and around her bandage. I cringe, but she laughs and fights the breeze with her hands like they're playing a game until it passes. Then she tucks two bunches of hair behind her ears and continues like nothing happened.

"I don't have that time to spare on heartache. I don't have any interest in compromise."

"That's selfish."

A shadow passes through her eyes.

"And stupid," I add.

"I don't think so." Jamie rips the elastic from her hair and starts retying the top layer.

"Do you have a best friend?"

"That I do have!" A smile flies back onto her face. "Dawn. We're soul sisters. She's the absolute best. We grew up together; she lives next door to Dad's house in LA."

I glance at my feet, trying to ignore the uncalled for flare of jealousy in my throat. "That's a relationship," I point out.

"Yeah. I mean, I don't do romantic relationships. I do friendship and all the other ships."

"Have you—" I start, but she interrupts me.

"Does Mother Dearest have a romantic someone?"

I blink at her. "She does. Did. They've been broken up for a month because Mom's been MIA with work twenty-four-seven, and we've all taken a back seat. His name is George. He's great. He and his son, Gill, moved in with us when I was twelve. Gill's a big nerd, but he's cool. George got an apartment in town recently, and Gill lives in Boston most of the year for college now."

Jamie plays with a stray curl near her ear. "So you all lived in . . . our house?"

"No, we moved closer to Papa—um, Mom's dad—in New Jersey after Dad left . . ." I trail off.

Another piece of my heart breaks as I realize—*We probably moved to a new house to help Mom really sell her Jamie deception, so there would be no physical places I would associate with her.*

We don't even . . . I've never seen any pictures pre-move.

Jamie clears her throat. "Hey, Sier, you're doing that weird hyperventilating thing you do."

I try to deepen my breathing. "Does Dad have someone?"

Jamie shakes her head. "Nah. He has lots of someones. They're in and out every couple of months."

"Do you ever think . . . that maybe Mom and Dad are meant to be together? That he's still in love with her out in California and . . . that's why he hasn't settled down?"

Jamie coughs out a cynical laugh. "*No.* Do you not remember all the fighting?"

I shake my head. I barely remember Dad. Quick flashes. His smile. I have no idea what he was like.

Greedy. Selfish. Abandoning.

Jamie studies me. "I mean, I was only six so I have weird choice memories. I remember this one day when Mom had an audition, and later that day we had our dress rehearsal for a recital or something. Dad was responsible for getting us ready. And Mom came home to find that *I had done your makeup.*" Jamie smiles to herself.

I wish I could remember.

"I drew all over your face with her lipstick. I thought it looked fabulous, but she got so mad. Dad thought it was hilarious. We were supposed to leave immediately, but Mom had to scrub it off before we could head out. We were in the kitchen and she was half scolding us, half chuckling. Dad was sitting at the table watching with a big smile. I felt guilty about it at first, but when everyone thought it was funny, I thought I had done something awesome.

"Then in the car on the way there, the energy between them changed. They argued the entire drive. It started in hushed voices, but grew to the crescendo it usually did . . . Dad was threatening to drive us home. Mom was screaming to let her out on the side of the highway . . ." She trails off. "It was always like that. Nothing fun came without some sort of blowback." Jamie's voice gets quiet. "Dad only talks about Mom now to lay down burns, drive home a negative comment, or offhandedly insult me." She looks down at her empty stick.

A fresh batch of tears wells up in my eyes. Because Mom hates Dad too. And I hate it. And I can't help but hate him with her. And I hate that we all hate each other. And there's nothing I can do about it.

I can't believe Dad took Jamie and Mom *let it happen.*

I want to love my family. I want to laugh and smile with them. I want to have people who love me unconditionally, who I trust and turn to when my emotions swallow me up. But the only person I've *really* trusted for a while now is Papa, and now that's ruined too. He was in on this Jamie lie.

I already thought Dad was a jerk. But how could Mom do this?

How could she do this to me? She's late and she's distracted and she's flaky for everything that isn't work, but she's an amazing choreographer, and an epic ballerina, and she's patient when I'm a gluteus maximus trench. She's weirdly obsessed with the Game of Thrones books and dresses me up every year and drags me along to the fan conference, and I make like I'm too cool for it, but I secretly love that she brings me with her and not George and Gill, *just me.*

How can she be the same person who let my sister be dragged across the country and then lied to me about her very existence? How can the woman who made watching *So You Think You Can Dance* every Thursday a religion be the same person who legitimately made me believe I couldn't trust my own mind?

I love her. I want to be her. *Wanted.* I wanted to be her.

I lower myself onto the grass and lie on my back. "I need to tap out, Jamie."

Jamie scoots closer. "I can see that. Good talk. I'll see you in a few days, sis." She grabs my white-sneakered foot and squeezes it before rolling to her feet. "Good luck with the rediscovering."

PART 2

Pitch and Switch

26. A Girl Is Playing the Long Game

JAMIE
September 3, Thursday Morning
Colorado

"I have to meet Siri in ten minutes."

I glance over at my hat and orange backpack sitting on the ground loaded with everything I'm gonna need for this upcoming sister hike. I've done everything I can to prep for my giant *sister-bonding-trip-plan-that-I-will-turn-into-a-new-comedy-set* pitch.

Zarar and I are perched next to each other on the slackline we've been playing around with in our free time. I didn't know what slacklining was till this past week. It's basically tightrope walking with much lower stakes—tie a three-inch-thick bungee-cord-like thing to two trees, three feet off the ground, and try to walk across it. Get fancy if you want to.

I've made an effort to keep things more surface level between us these past couple of days. It's weird hanging around someone who knows all my shit. Unnerving. Who knows when something I've let slip is going to come back around and be used against me. It'll be nice to be free of that. Zarar's really grown on me in a lot of dangerous ways. It's definitely time to pull the plug.

"Thanks for getting up super early for one last hang." I lean into his shoulder. "It was grand."

He shifts so he can really catch my eyes. "I wish we could spend more time together."

I grin. "You're so weirdly straightforward. I'll treasure the mems, Z. Slacklining, sitting by the fire, drowning and being brought back from the brink of death. Thanks for those."

He studies me quietly as we micro-bounce on this taut cord. "You're welcome."

"What's next for you, Zarar? What's the verdict on this job . . . park rangerdom? Is this for you or are you off to try a new profession?"

"It's not quite my passion. I'm off to try something new."

I brighten. "What's up next?"

"I'm going to test out the entertainment industry. I've got two part-time jobs lined up. I'll be dabbling in acting and producing."

Producing?

"Wow, acting and . . . producing what?" *Don't say movies.*

"Producing music. I've got an internship."

I blow out a tiny breath of relief. "Damn, I love how wide of a net you're casting with this passion quest."

He gives me the smallest of sideways smiles. "Thank you. I'm enjoying it."

I look over my shoulder in the direction of the cafeteria. "I have to head to the trails if I'm going to be on time for the top-secret sister mission I have to tackle before we all head off today." I twist back toward Zarar. "I guess this is peace out."

"Can you leave me your number?"

"Z, now I get to be the one that got away." I rise off the slackline to stand in front of him. "We can't ruin that, dude. I can't be the one who got away if we exchange numbers."

He shrugs. "Can't we be friends?"

"Trust me, it's more picturesque this way. Now we'll both always be able to look back on this week like, damn, what a time I had with that sexy-ass bombshell. If only we'd started dating! And simultaneously be able to live our normal lives and go on pursuing true happiness."

"True happiness . . ." He shakes his head. "Disagree, that doesn't feel more picturesque."

I sit back on the cord with him. "Okay, let's walk this through a little further, Zarar. If you go into acting next, maybe I see you on a poster years from now. And then I'll make sure to go to the premiere, because whoa, there's that guy I had this great little whirlwind with for those seven days at a random retreat in Colorado. And I'll get dressed up in fancy overalls and wait outside along the red carpet for you to arrive and our eyes will meet and we'll have this amazing reunion. You'll either be married with a family or divorced, and we'll either go for coffee and reconnect and agree to be friends, or have sex in a closet on our first date. The possibilities are endless. Isn't that exactly the brand of love story you're looking for?"

He holds my gaze, and I bob my chin knowingly as his eyes give him away. "Epic love stories take time, Z. They take dedication to time apart."

He raises his eyebrows. "What if that doesn't happen?"

I lean forward, grab his chin, and pull his face to mine. He melts into the kiss, running his hand up my neck as he deepens it. The guy tastes like fresh air.

I break away feeling deliciously floaty. "Then we'll always have that kiss." I hop off the bungee cord to grab my stuff.

He watches me pack my things with a distinctly bemused expression. It's so cute, I can't help laughing.

"Why are you laughing?"

"Because I like you." I throw my backpack over my shoulder and stand.

Zarar stays calmly seated on the cord. "You're still not going to give me your number?"

"We're playing the long game, Zarar." I pull on my hat and start off toward the cafeteria.

27. Angst and Hikes

SIRI
September 3, Thursday Morning
Colorado

I am not ready to go home yet.

I'm not prepared for the harsh reality of New Jersey. I'm not ready to face my lying mother tonight when the plane lands at Newark airport. I can't go back there right now! Not like this. Not while I'm still floundering. I've had an ample amount of alone time to try to find my new path these past three days. I've dutifully attended the standing appointment with Donya. (Jamie did not.) But I still haven't figured out the answer. I still don't know what's next.

I've landed on . . . a bit of a wild contingency plan. Instead of going home, I go back to California with Jamie for a bit, get to know her better, and pull myself together. She alluded to her plan including travel, so if that gets me out of New Jersey, great. If it doesn't, I'll convince her to take me home with her.

I shift my weight nervously from foot to foot as Jamie approaches the trails. She's four minutes late.

Please have a good plan.

"Hey hey hey!" Jamie shouts when she's within twenty feet.

Today she's wearing turquoise overalls with a rainbow tie-dye cropped T-shirt underneath. She still has a giant bandage secured over her left eye. And she's wearing a dumb floppy sun hat.

"Your hat is stupid," I yell.

She shoots me a cheery thumbs-up. "It's Terry's!"

"It's stupid. Why are you wearing it?" I shout.

She's closing in on me now. "Gotta protect my stupid face from the stupid sun. Have you heard of it?" She points to the sky.

I squint as she comes to a stop in front of me. "You haven't worn a hat this entire time, and today you've decided your face is too precious for the light?"

She grins harder. "Yep."

I open my mouth and close it.

Jamie inclines her head expectantly. "Is there another insult in there you want to let out?"

"No," I huff. Insulting her is exhausting. I switch gears. "Do you still have a sister-bonding plan that involves travel?"

Jamie steps past me toward the trails. "Indeed, grasshopper."

I follow after her. "Okay, because I truly cannot fathom seeing Mom right now. I can't get on a plane back to New Jersey. I can't, Jamie! Donya and I have been discussing the prospect of working in other areas of the dance world, but I can't imagine it. It hurts. It makes the gaping hole in my gut yawn open even wider than it already is. Donya tried to pitch me teaching ballet to little kids! First of all, I have no patience, and second of all, *I can't*. Ballet and I just broke up, I can't step back into her world. We also discussed costume design, and choreography—imagining holding those positions without actually being able to dance myself is mortifying. It's a nightmare situation, it's—"

Jamie spins around and I stop short six inches from her face. "This is the longest I've ever heard you speak without sighing, yelling, or rolling your eyes."

I frown. "You've known me for six days."

"And four years."

"They don't count," I say, falling into step behind her as she starts up again.

"Disagree."

We pause at a fork leading out to the trails. There's a signpost with six different colorful labeled arrows on it. Four of them point diagonally right (PEACE, SERENITY, TRANQUILITY, ENDURANCE) into the woods and two point left (PATIENCE and LUCK). We head left.

I clear my throat. "So, what's the sister-bonding plan? What are you thinking? Go to your house and hang there for a while? Rent a car and wander the country from there? Do a sister road trip together?"

Jamie snorts. "Sounds fun. How would you propose bankrolling that trip? I seem to recall you saying something to Donya about having a little bit of savings and then trailing off in a sad mumble."

I gnaw at my lip. "Doesn't my greedy, selfish jerk-and-a-half dad work in movies? Doesn't he have money?"

I stop walking as Jamie causally wanders off into the brush, crunching over branches and leaves. "Do you always refer to Dad with that cute little nickname?"

"Yes. Could he maybe pay for it? As like an *I'm sorry I abandoned you* gift?"

"I can't ask Dad to fund something like that," she says from the foliage.

I fiddle with the end of my braid. "Jamie, I think you're looking at this wrong. Mom and Dad kind of ruined our childhoods with their terrible family decision-making. Doesn't it seem reasonable to ask for a small sort of sisterly road trip recompense so we can make some nice memories and really get to know each other?"

Jamie bends at the waist, plunging her hand into what appears to be a pile of leaves. She pops back up, clutching a tall beefy stick.

I sigh. "What are you doing with that stick?"

She beams, making her way back to the trail with it. "Professional hikers use sticks, Sier. You want one?"

"No."

She holds it out like a trophy. "This is Jonas. We met over there in the mud. He's divorced." She places it down against the ground.

"You are so annoying." I step around her and start walking again. She strolls behind me, using the stick as a sort of hiking cane.

The trail branches off one more time. Diagonally left is PATIENCE and hard left is LUCK. The signs are decorated with cheesy little blurbs about the trails.

Jamie steps up next to me. "We're doing Luck. It's Terry's favorite," she says. "We're supposed to close our eyes for ten seconds and set our hike intentions before we head out." Jamie closes her eyes for a few beats, opens them, winks at me, and skips ahead down the path with Jonas.

"What did I say about winks?" I mumble.

I power walk after her, catching up as we come to an enormous, fallen moss-covered tree blocking the trail. Jamie throws herself over it and waits on the other side while I maneuver slowly so I don't upset my back.

"Tell me your plan," I demand as I carefully step off the trunk.

"Well," Jamie says, as the path becomes more uneven, "I'm gonna need to confront Mom about all this imaginary friend crap before I can enjoy . . . anything really. It's kind of eating me alive."

I narrow my eyes. You wouldn't know by looking at Jamie that she's being "eaten alive." I've yet to see her shed a single tear about all this.

The path's becoming increasingly rocky, so I have to be extra deliberate with my steps. "Um," I finally respond after three minutes of silence. "Okay, you can call her—"

"Yeah, I need to have that Mom confrontation in person," she says.

Is her plan to come home with me?

Jamie pulls ahead. I quicken my pace, trying to keep up with her. "Okay, fine, so what? You want to come back with me and then we'll leave for California after you talk to her? That's going to cost us more money. If we did that, I would wait outside because—"

Jamie pivots, and this time I'm so close, I crash right into her and wobble over the rocks. Her hand flashes out and snags my elbow, steadying me. "It's cute that you think making Dad pay for some sister road trip will be a satisfying form of payback." She pokes me and starts walking again. "But I'll tell you right now. He'd love to be able to throw some money at you and get us on his side. And you're forgetting about Mom. She gets off scot-free in that equation."

"I'm not going to talk to her for a while. That's not nothing," I say.

We step over a muddy creek. The dirt squishes around my white sneakers.

"Oh, the horror." Jamie eyes me wearily. "Didn't you insinuate that she's never around? How much do you talk in the first place?"

"We still live in the same house," I grumble.

I hate that our reunion has brought these horrible truths about our parents into sharp focus. The closer I look at what they've done, the worse it gets.

"Funding a road trip isn't going to inconvenience either of our parents." Jamie twirls Jonas like a giant baton.

I stop walking and cross my arms. "What is your plan, Jamie? Spit it out already."

She stops a few feet down the trail with a hand on her hip. "Okay, but please promise to hold all judgment till after I finish the pitch."

I roll my eyes. "I'll try."

There's a bunch of fallen trees and brush along the edge of the path up ahead. I shadow Jamie as she stalks toward a giant log, plants Jonas in the ground, and takes a seat on it. I stop in front of her, a few feet away.

"Okay, tell me," I prompt when she doesn't immediately begin.

"Okay," she starts. "Here's the condensed version: I think we should switch places."

She waits, watching me carefully. I blink at her. "Um, sorry . . . *what*?"

Jamie crosses her legs and nods. "I think we've been presented with a rare golden opportunity to mess with our parents, and I, for one, can't bear the thought of letting it slip through our fingers." Excitement leaks into her eyes. "Dad had no idea you would be here, or he wouldn't have suggested I come. So as far as I can tell, they have no idea we've reconnected." She purses her lips. "Do you think Mom had any idea I'd be here?"

I slowly shake my head. *No.* She would never send me here if she knew her secret was about to blow up in her face.

Jamie nods. "Okay, hear me out. I'm thinking, we go home in each other's place so we can each confront our respective estranged parents, have the difficult, emotionally charged conversations we need to have so we can move forward from all their drama, and gain a better understanding of ourselves, blah blah blah blah. BUT to make this more interesting, and dare I say fun"—she grins—"we do it with a little twist."

She pauses for dramatic effect.

I roll my eyes. ". . . Explain."

Jamie smirks. "I think we should play dress-up. So, at a glance, when we first arrive, they won't know we've switched, and we can catch them completely off guard.

"That plot twist, landmine moment of parental dread when they realize we've switched, that'll be something we can treasure for the *rest of eternity,* Sier. It'll be a landmine moment to own all landmine moments!"

She starts gesticulating. "And I'm thinking after being switched for five days, we trick them into meeting up at the same place on day six, and then we can pitch them your *I'm sorry sister road trip* thing together in front of them both!"

"This way when we do head off on that little road trip, we do it with some closure on all this traumatic parental bullshit."

I gawk at her for a few long moments before I pivot and walk farther down the trail. *Jamie's asking me to participate in wild, mischievous sibling shenanigans.*

Jamie catches up to me three seconds later. "We'd get five days to talk and get to know our other parents alone—I'll have time to work through all this imaginary shit with Mom. And you can stay in Cali with Dad and Grams and work through the whole abandoning ordeal." *Go to California . . . without her?*

I walk a little faster, but Jamie keeps pace.

"Oh, and I figure after the landmine moment when they're all like, *WHOA—you're not my usual daughter, why are you here,* we tell Mother and Father respectively that the two of us have plans to switch back to living with our normal parent after two weeks, so they don't suspect the whole *tricking them into meeting up in the same place after five days* thing."

I come to a stop, and close my eyes, trying to process all this. When I open them again, Jamie's standing directly in front of me. "What do you think?" She beams.

I think . . . I'd get to avoid going back to New Jersey. "What's a landmine moment?" I ask.

She grins and bounces on her heels. "A mind-blowing moment! With great tea comes great revelatory-spillage responsibility!"

"What exactly do you mean by play dress-up?"

"Well, we don't want to give them any big easy tells, so we switch all our possessions and clothes, that's easy. But appearance-wise, I take out my nose ring, draw on your nifty posh beauty mark, dye my hair black, and we cut yours to match my length."

I throw a protective hand over my braid. *I can't cut my hair that short. I need to be able to get it into a bun for da . . . nnnce.*

No, I don't.

Jamie is literally quaking with enthusiasm.

"Before you ask," she continues, "I already secured scissors and hair dye from Terry. Sier, our faces are already so similar, hair tweaks are going to make us much more difficult to tell apart at a glance. Nobody's going to be expecting their estranged daughter of fourteen years to come crawling back home pretending to be their current, present live-in daughter!"

An unexpected bead of excitement begins to pulse in my gut. I tromp farther up the trail.

Jamie catches me again, walking at my side. "Doesn't it sound like a great way to bond? Take a few days, freak out the guardians, see how the other sister lives, confront some emotional trauma, come back together for hangs?"

It does.

It would be nice to meet Dad by myself rather than alongside the daughter he already knows.

"Really, what do we have to lose?" Jamie nudges.

The answer hits harder than I'd like.

Nothing. I literally have nothing to lose.

"I wrote up a whole detailed outline for you!"

My eyes snap to Jamie's. She smiles triumphantly. "I knew you'd love an outline. Gimme a sec, lemme add something."

My heart balloons a bit. *How did she know I'd love an outline?*

PARENT CONFRONTATION TRAP BREAKDOWN

Objectives: Meet estranged parent, exact mild comedic revenge through gotcha switcheroo mischief, & confront/work through their parental failures & persuade them to make up for their misdeeds with sister-bonding road trip funds/blessing!

How to accomplish: Switch places. Impersonate until the landmine moment, & confront. On day 6 lure parents to mutual spot (Vegas?) for final mutual confrontation via catfishing maneuvers!

Preparations:
- *Look more physically alike*
- *Trade physical possessions, and take each other's flights home*

Intel to dig for:
- *How did parents meet? Dad always just says Thrones.*
- *Why and how did they decide to rip us apart the way they did, and what split them so hard?*

Rules
- *Email updates to each other once a day: Siri will email Jamie before bed in California, Jamie will respond in the morning East Coast time*
- *Each sister must prep catfish project to herd parents to Vegas, starting immediately upon arrival*

28. A Girl Thinks This Pitch Is Going Well

JAMIE
September 3, Thursday Morning
Colorado

This hike has taken an exhilarating turn.

The trail we've been walking literally leads to the door of a weird, creepy, abandoned, *windowless* cabin. *Prime.*

And I'm fairly certain Siri is seriously considering my pitch.

On the "front lawn" of said creepy log cabin is a stone bench. That's our current place of residence. We've been sitting here through ten riveting minutes of silence. Siri's studying the outline I gave her like it holds the key to immortality.

I'm itching to check out the inside of this house. And trying really hard not to prod Siri for a response. I thought I was desperate before all this when I signed that damn contract to move back in with my dad, but begging my younger sister to switch places with me so I can briefly impersonate her and fulfill some weird revenge fantasy to then use in a comedy set? That's desperate. This is *desperate.*

All these years there's been a part of me that's felt guilty for leaving my mom. It's why I never bring her up. Or look her up on socials. Or have socials at all. But I didn't leave, *she let me go.* Like I was an old favorite sweater that no longer sparked joy.

I need to do this.

I glance over at Siri for the hundredth time in the last ten minutes. She's no longer studying the outline, she's staring at me.

"Four days," she says.

I blink. "What?"

"Let's do four days and we switch back the fifth day."

I put a hand to my heart. "Holy baloney bucket, are you saying yes, we can do this?" I wink at her. "See what I did there, de-vulgared for ya."

"Four days, and then we come back together and ask for the trip," she insists seriously.

Pure elation fills my chest. *Oh my god.* "I'm good with four days!"

Siri shudders on the end of the bench. "Okay."

I hop to my feet. "Okay? Holy shit, YES!" I do a weird impromptu jig. "Thank you! Sier! Ah! This is just ace of aces! Thank you!"

Siri fiddles with her braid.

I throw my hands and feet out in a star jump. "WE ARE GONNA PULL A FULL-ON MISCHIEVOUS *PARENT TRAP*! THIS IS EVERYTHING."

29. Angst and Saying Yes

I said yes.

Yes, to meeting my dad. Yes, to bonding with my sister. To California alone. To more time away from Mom. Yes, to more adventure.

I'm really excited about saying yes. It's been a while. Donya would approve . . . I think?

"We should cut your hair now!" Jamie cheers from where she's dancing in the grass twenty feet away. She comes bounding back in my direction.

My muscles tense. "Right now?"

Jamie dashes over to her pack. "It'll be way less of a mess to chop it out here." She emerges with a pair of scissors and stalks behind me to the back of the bench.

My heart thumps uncomfortably as I rotate to face her. "Do you even know what you're doing?"

She smiles, holding the scissors aloft. "Do I really look like someone who hasn't cut their own hair before?"

I grimace up at the orange mound on her head.

She lowers the scissors. "Are we doing this, or are we not doing this?" she asks quietly.

I nod more to myself than to her. *Yes. I'm saying yes.* "Okay, we're doing this."

I'm shaking slightly as I rotate back around. Jamie removes my hair tie and starts unwinding my braid.

"I'm going to need to be distracted," I tell her.

She snorts. "Sure thing, go ahead and ask me one of the many questions you have about my mysterious life."

I rub at my forearms, trying to concentrate on anything but the feel of Jamie gathering my hair into a ponytail at the nape of my neck. She tilts my head forward.

"What's going on with you and Zarar?" I blurt. "I've seen you two around all week. Are you finally doing a relationship?"

"Ah, Zarar! He's hot, right?" I can feel her working the scissors over the ponytail. I have a lot of hair; it's not going to be a quick snip. She's going to have to saw through that thing.

I squeeze my eyes shut. "Just keep talking."

"Zarar and I are a snow-globe relationship—my favorite kind." I can hear the smile in Jamie's voice—and the scissors hacking into my hair.

"What the intercourse is a snow-globe relationship?"

"It's the temporary, lovely kind with no complications that lasts a couple of days, or a week, tops, where two people with chemistry have a damn nice time together, and then part ways.

"When it's over you get to keep that moment in time, that sliver of new relationship glory, in a snow globe in your brain. It's rose-tinted and happy, basically flawless.

"Both parties know nothing's going to come out of the ship long-term, but you let what's going to happen in your window happen. Afterward you have all the adorable, beginnings-of-a-relationship moments to look back on when you want to. They're cemented in the snow globe, no bad memories to retroactively taint or shit on them because you parted amicably and never looked back.

"He's asked me out thrice now, despite my consistent rejections." She chuckles wistfully before suddenly emitting a gleeful dramatic gasp.

My stomach plummets. "What happened?!" I fold forward away from her, frantically grabbing for my hair.

It's gone. It ends right above my shoulders. I spin to look over the back of the bench. My two-foot-long ponytail is lying in the grass like a dead animal. I squish my hands up against my cheeks. "Oh my goodness."

Jamie comes around the front, gently taking my shoulders. "Don't look. You're fine. Let me fix it. It needs to be styled."

Hiccups pop out of me as she begins to pull, compare, and snip at the strands of hair around my face.

"Do you not like Zarar"—*hiccup*—"enough to keep talking to him after this?" I ask.

"That would ruin it, Sier. Number one rule of snow-globe relationships: Don't mess with the globe. It'll break and become a pile of moldy shit."

Twenty minutes later, Jamie swishes onto the bench next to me, smiling. "You look amazing."

I reach up and run my fingers through my hair. They hit my shoulders so quickly, it's disorienting. But I'm no longer anxious about it. My earlier nerves have, surprisingly, morphed into a mild, pleasant . . . buzz.

I am hesitantly excited about our pending shenanigans. It's kind of cool that Jamie's going to dye her hair black now, and we're going to match. The idea of us matching, I don't know, it feels so sweet and fuzzy. This whole adventure might help us turn into . . . real sisters.

"Can we head back now?" I ask in the most neutral tone I can muster. I don't want to give her the satisfaction of sounding eager.

"Yeah." Jamie grins. "After we check out the cabin!"

And, there goes my buzz.

I look over at the cabin. "Yeah, no. We're not going in there."

"Terry says this trail is happy haunted. We get up here and it spills into a creepy old log cabin? We have to check it out."

"I'm not checking that out. It could be old and collapse, Jamie."

Jamie leaps off the bench and jogs the thirty feet up to the door.

"Do not go in there!" I yell as she kicks out at the flimsy-looking wood. There's an unexpected scraping noise as her boot makes contact.

"Gah!" Jamie whines and nurses her foot. The door opens ever so slightly before closing again.

She glances at me over her shoulder. "Damn, that's a heavy door." Jamie takes a few steps toward me before pivoting and charging the door again. This time she plows torso-first into it with a groan of exertion. It opens about forty-five degrees. She slips inside and disappears into the house.

"Jamie!"

The door closes behind her. What the *intercourse?*

"Jamie!" I screech again.

After thirty seconds of silence I slide off the bench and wander over to the door. The weightlessness of my new short hair throws me for a moment. It feels . . . weirdly good. Light.

"Jamie!" I yell from directly outside the door. "Come out. Please. This place could be rotted through! Or have asbestos!"

She doesn't answer.

"Great." I glare for another ten seconds before pushing into the door myself. The wood feels hard and cold, like concrete. I have to dig my sneakers into the dirt to get it to open and then use my upper body strength to make enough space to slither inside.

It's dark when the door closes, and then a light clicks on overhead. I don't see Jamie.

"Boo!" She leaps out from behind me.

I go still. "Could you not?"

She laughs and comes to stand beside me. "Glorious, right?"

The cabin is one room, much like our retreat cabins. Across the floor on the far wall is a giant old-fashioned chest: the kind you see on TV holding overflowing bouts of treasure or a dead body. An old wooden rocking chair moves almost imperceptibly in the far corner. A lone light bulb dangles from the center of the ceiling and the wood floor is covered in debris. Leaves, sticks, dust. Gross.

"It bears a striking resemblance to the studio apartment I was evicted from last month." Jamie smiles at me.

I turn to meet her eyes. "You were evicted?"

"You think I voluntarily live with Dad?"

"I don't . . . you never—" I turn my attention back to the floor. "I don't know. Can we leave now?"

Jamie nods. "In a minute. I was waiting for you to come in so we could open that giant-ass chest together. What do you think is inside? Sandwiches? Rocks? Treasure? My hopes and dreams?"

I huff. "No."

"A puppy?" she asks in a childish voice.

"I think nothing. There's probably nothing in it."

She fearlessly throws herself onto the nasty floor and starts unlocking the six bolts that hold it closed.

"Jamie, I really don't like this—"

"Come sit next to me over here." She gestures to the area next to her.

With a groan, I walk over and carefully lower down to my knees. The floor is cold and hard, like the door.

She undoes the final buckle, glances at me, and throws open the top with a delighted flourish. I blow out a confused breath as it bangs against the wall.

The chest is empty with the exception of a small, bright blue wrapped box with a gold note taped atop it like a card. Jamie reaches for it, but I swat at her hand.

"Jamie, that's not ours!"

She takes me about as seriously as a two-year-old child, laughing and waving me off.

"Relax, Sier." She reaches for it again, leaning forward so her entire upper body is inside the chest. She makes contact with it and screams.

"Jamie!" I scream, reflexively grabbing at her waist like she's falling head-first into a pit.

Jamie falls backward cackling, the box clutched in her hands.

I drop my hands and scurry away. "Gluteus maximus trench," I huff. "That could be a weapon of mass destruction. Or a deadly virus. Or—"

Jamie gives me a flat look. "It's a present, Sier." She places the box on the floor and pulls off the note. It comes up easy, like a Post-it. The message on it is handwritten and small. Jamie hunches over the gold parchment, her eyebrows furrowing as she reads.

"What the fuck?" she mumbles.

Curiosity gets the best of me. I scoot in to read it with her. Jamie brings it even closer to her face so I have to lean on top of her arm to see it.

> *Walk with ease in each other's shoes*
> *Let me help pull off the ruse*
> *We'll go four days and five long nights*
> *You may tell just one. they'll see the light*
> *Once you've discerned how your counterpart feels*
> *To come back to yourself*
> *Just share something real*
> *You must reunite upon fifth day*
> *Or in this state you're doomed to stay*

Jamie lets the note fall. I watch it flutter to the floor.

"Why does that sound relevant?" Jamie says quietly. She brings herself up into a frog squat and glances around the cabin. "Is someone here?" she shouts.

No one answers. Jamie reaches for the blue box.

"Don't touch it!" I yelp. "It does sound relevant! I think we should leave!" I stand.

Jamie glowers down at the gift, mumbling something to herself.

"Come on, Jamie, leave it," I urge.

She doesn't.

Jamie reaches down and yanks the top off the box. It emits a loud bang as it explodes.

30. A Girl Is on Her Ass

JAMIE
September 3, Thursday Morning
Colorado

I'm on my ass. My ears ring. I stick a finger in one of them and wiggle it back and forth like I've seen people getting up after an explosion do in movies.

What the hell just happened? All I can see are sparkles. We're in a smoky haze of glitter. We were, what, glitter bombed? We've been swallowed by a cloud of gold-and-silver shimmering smoke. It's all I can freaking see.

"Siri?" I yell. I inhale a cloud of gold flakes and proceed to cough my lungs out.

"Over here," Siri says from somewhere in my vicinity.

"Door!" I yell, choking on more shimmer. I swat at the air. It's taking so long to settle. Is there a smoke machine in that box? I slam into the wall. "Ow."

Siri's hand pats against my face. "That's my face," I huff.

I grope along the wall until my hands find metal.

"Pull," I instruct. My fingers clasp the rail along the back of the concrete-feeling log door. I feel Siri's fingers land on the rod next to mine. We pull.

It doesn't move at first, but I dig in with my feet and lean until the thing begins to budge. And then opens. The fresh air comes in with a rush.

Siri and I tumble out toward the grass, both of us locked in our own separate coughing fits. Terry's sun hat falls to the ground as I crumble to all fours, crawling away from the house, hacking up gold spit. I turn to watch Siri lower gently to her knees beside me.

Christ. She's completely covered in gold glitter. All I can discern of her features are her eyes and mouth. I raise my own hand in front of my face.

Holy . . . *it doesn't look real.* We look like horrifying sparkly versions of those street artists who pretend to be statues.

I brush at my arm with a finger. The shit falls to the ground like pixie dust. Next to me Siri's frantically swatting her arms and legs, trying to get it all off.

"What the underworld was that?" Siri gasps.

My voice wheezes out of me. "I guess we were played? Sidebar, really, you don't even say hell?"

"Played? What do you mean played?"

"I don't know. Terry says this trail is happy haunted. I'm assuming that's what . . . that was. Some sucker must be glitter bombed every session. She must have heard that we were taking this trail today. I told her a few days back that we were going to hike it. I bet she customized a note for us. Maybe?"

"What?! That sounds like an insurance nightmare." Siri stands, huffing and puffing. "There's no way that Terry tried to kill us via glitter!" Her eyes are exceptionally striking amid the glitter icing her skin. They're always a gold color, and now they weirdly match her body.

I get my feet under me and stand, brushing off my legs. "Not kill us—it's probably organic."

"It doesn't feel or taste organic. I think my lungs are chafed. I might need to go to the hospital."

I scoff. "We don't need to go to the hospital. That's a surefire way to ruin Plan Parental Confrontation before it's even begun."

We trudge back to the path, leaving a trail of gold behind us. Siri's shaking as she waiks, like a dog after a dip in the pool. "You had to open that stupid box."

"Terry would never do anything to hurt us." I hack out an extra nasty gob of shiny spit. "We're going to be fine. Let's go do my hair! You can put the crap in it!" We start down the hill.

Siri trots behind me. "You don't know we're going to be fine! What if we were just contaminated with some sort of scary plague explosion, Jamie?"

I walk backward for a moment. "Oh my god, you're right. I've heard about rare plague-starting viruses being delivered via glitter."

Siri's face folds into a grimace.

I pivot back around, smiling. "God forbid you laugh at something I say."

"Plagues aren't funny," she says behind me.

"I mean, there's something to be said for a glitter plague."

"No, there's not."

"I mean, yes, there is. I'm saying it right now."

31. Angst and Cellular Device Access

SIRI
September 3, Thursday Afternoon
Colorado

We're actually doing this.

I've showered multiple times, we've dyed Jamie's hair, and Terry's unlocking her cell phone safe.

Jamie's insistent on trading phones both for general "authenticity" and so we have each other's local contacts at the ready: *Siri, we have to go big or just go back to our regular homes.*

We're going big. I'm about to casually switch identities with my sister.

I'm going to get to know Jamie.

I'm going to get to know the rest of my family.

Jamie plaited her new dark hair into a headband braid. She's wearing a pair of my leggings and her red plaid button-up. She's eventually going to put one of my sweatshirts on, but she says she "wants to be in color for as long as possible before having to desaturate."

I feel silly in her red overalls and bright pink top. How does anyone take her seriously like this?

"Is there a reason you're dressed as each other? You are dressed as each other, right?" Terry asks as she places five cell phones on her coffee table. "The makeovers really threw me for a second," Terry continues slowly as she studies us, "but Jamie's nose ring gives it away."

129

"We're doing an experiment, Terr," Jamie explains. "You passed. You really know us."

My eyes snag on an ancient phone among the smartphones. It looks like it's from the mid-2000s. *Wow.* Probably the one old lady out here that was in our fishing class.

"Is that why you dyed your hair black?" Terry asks. "And you cut off your beautiful hair? Are you doing a weird twin cosplay thing?"

Jamie nods. "There you go, it's all coming together now. We're doing a"—she raises her hands to do air quotes—"twin cosplay."

Terry puts up her hands in surrender. "As long as you're getting along." She hands Jamie the ancient phone. "Here's your Chocolate. Have at it."

Jamie accepts it with a grin.

"No," I whisper to myself.

"Old Yeller and me, back together again." She pockets it.

I balk at her. "What the underworld? That's not your phone, right?" I can't be using an outdated relic. I need a real phone!

Terry hands me my own iPhone X. I cradle it possessively against my chest. I miss Instagram. I miss TikTok. Even Twitter.

Jamie smiles wildly. "Oh, it is my phone. We haven't been around technology so it hasn't really come up, but I hate it."

"You hate what?"

"Technology."

"What does that mean?"

"It means I don't have a smartphone."

"Oh my god."

"Don't worry, I'll introduce you to Gladys at the airport."

She named her cell phone. Just looking at that outdated slide-up thing makes me anxious. Am I really about to agree to a second week without a smartphone? I miss at least pretending I'm part of a social circle.

"Do you have Instagram?" I ask desperately.

Jamie shakes her head and grins. "Off the grid, baby, forever and always. I am but dust in the wind. I can't be tracked, I can't be found, you'll see me when you see me, and we can chat then like the humans do."

"Ew."

———

We load into Terry's car with two other retreaters. Jamie keeps up a steady stream of chitchat with them all. I take advantage of this precious time with my iPhone.

As soon as we have service, I'm scrolling through Instagram. It doesn't take long for quiet tears to make their way down my cheeks as I wind through videos of Celia and Bran dancing together. They're slowly getting less chaste on social media.

Five minutes into my stalking, someone shoves a tissue in my face. Jamie's golden irises pierce mine through the gap between the passenger seat and the door.

I take the tissue and blow my nose. Shimmer catches my eye. My snot glitters full of gold flecks. My hand shakes as I fold the tissue closed. *That's concerning.*

"What were you looking at, Sier?" Jamie asks, speaking through the space between the top of the seat and the headrest. It's mind-boggling seeing Jamie with dark hair and dark clothes. I was really doubting the probability of this makeover being convincing in any way, shape, or form, but she looks . . . like me. I almost feel guilty about it, like I leached away some of her free-spirited whimsy.

She's taken out the nose ring. She usually wears some bright-colored eyeshadow. She's only wearing mascara now. Like me.

"Instagram," I respond after an extended silence.

"What on Instagram?"

Heartache clangs down my esophagus. "Bran and Celia."

"Your ex-BFF and boyfriend?"

I nod.

"Why would you look at that?"

I train my eyes down at Jamie's heavy yellow boots. I'm wearing them. We're the same shoe size. "Because I like to keep track of what they're up to. I need to."

"Sier," Jamie whispers. "I know you're struggling with the idea of being smartphone-less, but—switching phones with me is going to be great. You don't need *Instagram*. It's not helping you. It's keeping you down. It's gonna feel freaking freeing to be in the real world and live completely for the moment. Not for the next picture. Not to prove anything to anyone who follows you. Not to wallow in hurtful shit."

I press my lips together. "Are you giving me sisterly advice?"

Jamie smiles through the gap. "Better late than never, eh?"

My mouth curves into a wet smile.

Jamie grins. "Holy fucking shit. You're smiling." She taps me lightly on the arm through the gap along the edge of the seat. "There's hope for you yet, Angst Lord."

32. Angst and Goodbyes

SIRI
September 3, Thursday Late Afternoon
Colorado

Eight hours ago, I was completely freaking out about going back to New Jersey, and now I'm about to commit identity fraud to go re-meet my dad.

"Wow, you go by Maza, not Federov?" Jamie frowns down at my ID as I follow her through the crowd toward airport security.

"Yeah, Mom's doing. She filed to have it changed along with hers when Dad left," I explain.

We're about to part ways. *Will we hug?* I don't like to touch people, but for some reason I want to hug. Families hug.

At least other families do. My family doesn't. We usually kind of just say goodbye and dash off in our separate directions.

But I'd like to be a family that hugs, and this feels like a good place to start.

Jamie's talking again, running down our plan one last time. I nod at what feel like the right moments, but all I can think about is hugging. Can you be a bad hugger if you don't hug people regularly?

"Okay, kiddo," she finishes as we stop in front of the roped-off queue. "I'm going to go through first since my flight is first. We should scatter our security journeys. Wait ten minutes and then go through, okay?"

I swallow hard and nod. This is wild. We're doing this.

I hope I don't disappoint her.

Jamie pokes my shoulder. "We've got this."

I nod again. "Okay."

She grins. "Aces. See you in five days."

I step forward, my arms slightly raised. She pivots and heads into the security queue before I can initiate any semblance of an actual embrace.

My stomach dips in embarrassment. We didn't say we love each other like sisters are supposed to either. Will we ever get to a point where we can casually say *Love you*? How do we do that?

After ten minutes I enter the security line. I'm nervous handing the agent Jamie's California driver's license, but they don't question it; they just wave me forward.

California, here I intercoursing come.

33. A Girl Is on a Plane

JAMIE
September 3, Thursday Evening
Colorado

I bounce on my heels as I'm herded down the jetway among the other pas-sengers, holding a plane ticket with Siri's name on it. I just realized I'm not going to get to talk to Dawn today. We have so much catching up to do. I'll have to call her when I get the all clear from Siri that she's past the landmine moment. Dawn will see through the makeover immediately.

I shuffle my way down the plane to row 17 seat A. Siri's a window person, not surprised. I pull out her iPhone and spend the next fifteen minutes typ-ing out a text that says, HAVE DAWN CALL ME WHEN SHE REALIZES YOU'RE THERE AND NOT ME SO I CAN EXPLAIN. THX. I hit send and deflate into the seat.

A young mom and a little boy climb into the spots next to me. We have a three-hour-and-forty-minute flight ahead, so I pull up Siri's hood and lean against the window. My eyes drift up to the thin, slightly curved, slightly puckered scar running perpendicular toward my left eyebrow in the faded window reflection. I finally took the bandage off today. It's still the angry pink color of a fresh wound. I fog up the glass with a pointed exhale and close my eyes.

34. Angst and the Middle Seat

SIRI
September 3, Thursday Evening
Colorado

I hate overalls.

I *strongly dislike* overalls.

I'm trying to stop hating things, step back, and assess how and why I actually feel certain ways. I told Donya how I hate the hate monster inside me, and we've been strategizing different ways to defeat or extract it—whichever metaphor feels more relevant. Strategy number one: Try to figure out why you hate the thing, and find something positive that counteracts the negative.

Overalls: As uncomfortable as they are, all these stupid pockets are coming in handy to hold stuff. Jamie's Chocolate in one, my new hand sanitizer in another, my ticket, my ChapStick. They're convenient.

I spent my final ten minutes at the gate stretching carefully in this unstretchable outfit to try to minimize the back pain I'm going to be in during this three-and-a-half-hour sitting fest. Donya taught me some lower-back yoga exercises. I did those at the gate as well. People were definitely judging me, but I'm past the point of caring.

When I arrive at row 19, an old man in the aisle seat gets up to let me by to seat E. As I step past him, he hacks up a nasty wet-sounding cough. I whip out my hand sanitizer.

When the plane finally roars to life, I'm squished between the sick old man and a guy who's six foot seven. I can't help but crave the safety of my big sweatshirts. I feel so exposed. I miss my hood. It's my own personal travel-sized cubby hole to hide in whenever I need to.

As we take off, I feel exhaustion setting in—an anxiety crash coming after a day full of chatting, hiking, and hair styling with Jamie.

I jolt awake as the plane rumbles.

The speakers crackle. "We're experiencing turbulence, please buckle your seat belts."

I don't even remember falling asleep.

My back aches, a low pulse travels down my legs. I need to get up.

I'm so groggy. I don't usually fall asleep on planes. I glance around with my limited range of middle seat movement. As I do, my bladder presses needily against my stomach. *Excrement.* I really need to get up.

The men next to me have nodded off as well. I hate asking people to get up.

I mean . . . I strongly dislike it because it's really annoying to annoy people. Especially if they're asleep. I don't know what the silver lining is to asking people to move on planes.

I tap at the touchscreen in front of me and open the flight map. A CGI globe opens and zooms slowly in on the West Coast of the United States. We're over Nevada. We still have an hour left on the flight.

My back pulses harder. The old man in the aisle seat's head is lolling to the left. I poke him and hold my breath.

He doesn't react.

Excrement, excrement. Now that I'm anxious, I have to pee twice as much. I press my lips together, calculating the path over him to the center aisle.

I should not risk climbing over him. I could fall and hurt myself more.

I glance around for a flight attendant. No one's in the vicinity to watch.

Well, I'm going to climb over him.

Jamie would do it.

Carefully, I unbuckle and hoist my feet onto the seat. Once I'm crouched in a ball, I rise as much as possible, slowly with my back straight, and step onto the empty left armrest on the ball of my left foot.

Please don't wake up.

I carefully raise my right foot, spin to the left 180 degrees, and place it on the armrest closest to the aisle, behind the man's bony age-spotted elbow.

Exhale.

Okay. Now I'm straddling him.

I lean to place my right hand on the far edge of his headrest, avoiding his hair, and spin back toward the seats in front of us, freeing my left foot and bringing it in close to my body as I bend my right leg to dismount into the aisle.

Holy poop! I did it! My heart beats unevenly in my chest. I almost want to raise my arms in triumph like a gymnast.

I giggle to myself as I reach the bathroom without getting in trouble. The plane rattles as I push in the vacant door and close it behind me. That was kind of fun.

I re-clasp the overalls, close the toilet, and flush before turning to the little sink to wash my hands. These airplane sinks always make things overly complicated. If the water would stay on for more than one second, I could do this efficiently.

I'm drying my hands when I catch sight of neon orange at my shoulder in the mirror. I glance up to take stock of my full reflection and do a double take before stumbling back into the flimsy bathroom wall. What the—?

"Jamie?!" I hiss.

Jamie is staring back at me in the mirror. Not me.

I clasp a hand over my mouth. So does Jamie. I scream behind my hand, it comes out muffled.

Oh my god. I'm seeing things. I squeeze my eyes shut. Maybe I'm dreaming. Maybe that's how I got away with hopping over a sleeping man.

I count to eight and recall five things that are on planes to resettle my brain. *Floppy seat belts. Poorly placed outlets. Disgusting bathrooms. Silver carts of hot food. Shades for the windows.*

I open my eyes again.

Jamie is still in the intercoursing mirror! But . . . *it's not* the Jamie with dark locks I said goodbye to. It's Jamie without a scar. Jamie with half-brown, half–neon orange, wild unkempt hair. Blue nose ring. Chipped nails. Jamie, the first time I saw her.

My breathing hitches. *No, do not have a panic attack here.*

I actually slap myself. "Wake up!" I yell at Jamie's reflection. The air shimmers with glitter. I growl at it, swatting the area near my face.

I showered twice earlier!

I fall close to the mirror and put my hands against it. Jamie's reflection follows. I step away and look down at myself. I pull my hair in front of my face. It's dark. My hair is black. Mirror me/Jamie is doing the same with her hair.

I hastily scrub my hands again and burst out of the bathroom. I need a flight attendant! I lock onto one on the left side of the plane, past the middle partition of seats.

"Excuse me!" I yelp, grabbing eye contact as the young man turns my way.

"How may I help you, ma'am? The captain still has the fasten seat belts light on. You should proceed to your seat."

"What color is my hair?" I ask awkwardly.

His forehead scrunches. He looks around at other passengers who are watching us.

I clear my throat, making eye contact with a bunch of randoms looking at me. "Please, sir, what color is my hair?" I say through some fresh tears.

"It's an ombré . . . brown and neon orange?" he answers hesitantly.

"I'd say it's more of a sunset orange," a teen boy tells me from a window seat on the left side of the plane. I'm definitely having a panic attack now.

Turbulence rattles through the plane again.

"Ma'am, you have to return to your seat," the flight attendant repeats.

I stagger to my row. Pain slithers around my back as I catch myself against people's seats.

The old man's still asleep in the aisle seat of my row. Without hesitating, I step up on the armrest.

139

"Ma'am! Please don't—"

I push up, step onto my own seat, and spin down carefully in one fluid motion. The man's still sleeping. I have to be dreaming. This doesn't feel like a dream, but I have to be dreaming. Maybe plane dreams are always like this. I buckle my seat belt, close my eyes, and count to a hundred.

35. A Girl Doesn't Understand Your Compliment

JAMIE
September 3, Thursday Evening
Somewhere over North America

Someone pokes me, but my eyes feel so heavy. *I'm sleeping here.*

"Ma'am, would you like something to drink?" someone asks. I'm poked again.

"Do you want a dwink?" squeaks a tiny voice. I open my eyes to see the child next to me has invaded my personal space. *Oh yeah, I'm on a damn plane.* I smile at him before pushing back my hood and glancing up at the flight attendant.

"Vodka tonic," I tell her.

"We're not serving alcohol." She smiles.

I grin sleepily and squint at the name tag on her chest. "I kid, Kathy. Can't you see I'm a youth? Orange juice, please."

The boy's mother in the aisle seat watches me.

"I love your hair," she says as the stewardess moves on. "Beautiful braid."

I smile slightly and touch the headband braid in my hair. "Thank you . . . cute kid, where'd you get him?"

She laughs. "Memorial Day sale at Macy's a few years back."

I nod appreciatively before turning back to my window. It's dark and the cloud cover is thick so all I can see are the lights along the wing of the plane.

There's an uncomfortable creeping panic in my gut. It intensifies as I catch the darkness of my hair in the almost imperceptible window reflection. I should be proud of the excellent job I did matching Siri's hair with mine, but when we stood in front of the mirror side by side in the public cleansing room today, looking like twins—it freaked me out. I did not like seeing her in my clothes.

This whole thing was my idea. I shouldn't be panicked!

This is all going to be amazing material. These past two weeks have been all sorts of tragic. Tragedy is comedy. You just have to let it ferment.

"I like your hair too!"

I twist back to grin at the five-year-old in the seat next to me.

"What's your name?" I ask.

"Ian!" he says.

Weird that these people are enjoying my braid so much. You can barely see it with the dark hair; it just all kind of blends together without the proper light.

"What do you like about it? I did the new color today and I'm not sure how I feel. What do you think?" I ask him seriously.

The boy shrugs. "I don't know. I like how long it is! It looks like horsie tail."

I pull an over-the-top confused expression. "Ian!" His mother chuckles in an embarrassed sort of way.

I laugh and point to my head. "This poof ball is eons away from that kind of glory."

"How long have you been growing it out?" his mother asks me.

"I, I mean, not long at all . . ."

"You're kidding me? You're just blessed? My hair stops at my collarbone. I used to try to grow it long in my college days, but it never happened for me."

I run a hand over my barely shoulder-length hair. *What the fuck is she talking about?*

"If you don't mind me asking, how do you keep it so healthy-looking? Even in the braid, it has this sheen that you don't see with hair that long."

I almost snort. *Okay, what?* "It's just shampoo and classic conditioner. The dandruff kind is great."

"Oh—"

I turn to the window and shift focus to my reflection. I can't really see much, just an outline. I move my head around awkwardly, sitting up and slouching, trying to get a better view of my hair. And . . . dear lord, it does look like I have thick, dark something running down the side of my head and over my shoulder . . .

I frantically feel myself up, searching for what I'm getting a glimpse of in the window, but there's nothing there but boob and shoulder. I spring from the seat and make eye contact with the mom. "Would you excuse me?"

I fumble my way to the back of the plane, ramming into seats, ping-ponging side to side because my motor functions seem to have lost their ability to human in my current panic.

The restroom door opens in its fold-away fashion and a middle-aged woman sidles out as I arrive. I leap in and slam the door shut. The automatic overhead light goes from neon green to bright yellow as I slide in the lock.

I spin to the mirror and immediately lean forward and slap my reflection with both my hands. There's a . . . there's a waist-length braid. The girl in the mirror has a braid. A fishtail braid. When I look down at myself, there is no braid. But she has a fishtail braid that falls all the way down to her waist! It dances over her right shoulder when I move. I paw at my shoulder-length hair, trying to grab hold of the thing.

There's nothing here!! And oh my Jesus, my reflection literally isn't me. It's Siri?! Siri is staring back at me.

But I just chopped Siri's hair! I watched it hit the ground. I went through it with the scissors I requested from Terry!

The girl in the mirror is fresh off the plane to Rediscover Yourself Siri.

"WHAT THE FUCK IS GOING ON?"

I smack the mirror again. Glitter flutters around my hands.

I remove my hands from the glass and bring them toward my face for examination. They're my hands. My gross nails. But in the mirror . . . they're neatly filed. Unpainted. Unblemished.

I smack the mirror again. More glitter flutters around my hand. "What *the fuck*?" I yell again.

My eyes are bulging so hard, they might just roll right out of my head. There's a knock at the door.

"Gah!" I fall awkwardly onto the airport toilet.

"Ma'am, are you all right in there?" someone asks.

"Fine!" I blurt. "I'm fine, privacy please!"

I hop off the toilet and smash my face up against the mirror again, fogging up the glass with my frantic breaths. I trace where the scar is on my forehead. I can feel it under my finger, but the pale girl in the mirror's skin is clear. I touch the spot where mirror me (Siri?) has a beauty mark. I smear it with my index finger. I inspect my finger pad and see the makeup on it, but in the mirror, nothing is smeared. Like I have a legit freaking Siri beauty mark.

I smack the mirror again. Glitter poofs around my hand like dust.

The.

The glitter.

The note.

Terry.

I push open the door to exit the stall.

Have I been magicked? Am I happy haunted?

"Are you done?" There's someone waiting out here to use the toilet.

"Uh-huh," I heave. Then I realize I have to pee and slam the door closed in their face. I flop onto the toilet again. Is magic real or am I having a very vivid dream?

I wash my hands and am suddenly struck with another thought. I pull up my sweatshirt and top to inspect the appendix-removal scar I have below my hip bone. When I look down at myself I see it. I see my stomach, my boobs. In the mirror . . . are not my boobs. And no scar. In the mirror is a ripped eight-pack. I drop my clothes back down. That's a teenage ballerina's stomach.

FUCK FLIPPITY JIBBITY FUCK.

I stumble out of the bathroom past the waiting passenger.

I don't even know what to do with myself right now. Am I wearing a Siri mirage?

My rowmates kindly get out again to let me slip in. I fall into the seat like a lifeless doll. There's a 50 percent chance I'm losing my mind.

36. Angst and LAX

I cut the entire bathroom line when I get off the plane and inhale breath after startled hysterical breath when I still see Jamie in the mirror.

I still look like Jamie.

I mean . . . I am Jamie when I look in the mirror and apparently to anyone who sees me?! I'm wearing a Jamie glamour. It looks like I'm literally in Jamie's body. Jamie with terrible hair and a blue nose ring.

I spend a few minutes awkwardly interrogating other bathroom-goers about my hair color and facial piercings. They all see Jamie.

What am I supposed to do with this? This isn't part of the plan!

I splash cold water on my face and pinch my arms in five different places. The only result is pain and a light dusting of gold glitter on my hands again. Like it was hiding in my pores. Does this have to do with the . . . glitter?

Outside the bathroom I tap my foot impatiently against the tile as Jamie's Chocolate takes its sweet time booting up. *Why does she use this?!* When it finally lands on the home screen, I frantically punch in my own phone number and press the green send button.

It goes straight to voicemail. She must still be on the plane.

"Jamie! Nine-one-one help, please call me as soon as you land!" I hang up and shove it back into the boob pocket of Jamie's overalls.

I walk in circles for ten minutes before doing the only thing I can think to do: join the stream of people headed toward baggage claim.

I'm about to meet Grams, or maybe my dad? And I'm wearing a weird projected Jamie skin. I know I'm dressed as Jamie, and the plan was to impersonate her for *the landmine moment,* but that was never going to last for more than a hot second. A minute! Five minutes tops! However long it took to get a hard look at my face! *Any parent would realize!*

And then I could be me, and spend these next four days learning what it would be like to live in California, and talking to Dad about these past fourteen years. I could pick his brain about what to do with my future!

If I'm *Jamie* on the outside, I won't be able to tell them I'm Siri without sounding legitimately insane. I hastily wipe at the tears dribbling down my cheeks as I pass the mouth where security spills into the terminal.

I call Jamie one more time, but it goes straight to voicemail.

How do I not melt down right now? What would Jamie do?

That answer comes immediately: Jamie would take it in stride and make it work for her. She's so good at that. Any insult I throw her way swings back around to me.

How do I do that with this? Am I supposed to just roll with it?

I guess I can do that. I can definitely do that until Jamie's plane lands and we figure this out.

Donya would urge me to ground myself in the moment. Take the situation one step at a time. At least that's the advice she gave about confronting Mom. Ground myself with a classic antianxiety exercise so I can gather my thoughts. Don't think ahead in what-ifs, just be present.

Jamie will call me when she lands.

Jamie said Grams would be the one picking me up from the airport. Apparently, Dad doesn't pick people up from anywhere. "It's part of his charm," she quipped. I still kind of hope he's here.

When I get to Jamie's room, I'm supposed to create a new email account to catfish Dad so we can get him to Vegas in five days. I can do that fine wearing a Jamie projection. In fact, I can do it more easily wearing a Jamie projection.

I'm going to be fine. This is fine. I step onto the escalator descending to ground level. Inhale a slow breath. Blow out a slow breath. Baggage claim rises before me.

I scan the few people waiting, looking for Grams. Jamie said she'd be wearing an ascot. My eyes snag on a beautiful Asian girl smiling at me. She's dressed in tight bright pink bell-bottom corduroy pants and a tight light pink T-shirt with matching platform sneakers.

Brilliant monochromatic outfit.

She throws her hand up in a regal wave. "Fucketh you, Lady Federov! Why dothen't you call me the second you landed?" she yells enthusiastically in a weird Shakespearean-sounding accent.

That has to be Dawn. Jamie's favorite person. I hope she likes me. Jamie texted while I was still in Denver to have Dawn call as soon as she realizes I'm not her.

My stomach does a front flip. *Will anyone ever realize that now?*

Dawn moves to stand at the bottom of the moving staircase. I'm still descending to ground level. *Could this escalator go any slower?* Her long dark hair is curled at the ends and it sways when she walks.

As I step onto solid ground, she embraces me in a tight hug. It's been months since I've hugged or been hugged by anyone, and it feels wonderful.

"I missed you so damn much," Dawn spurts. "You haven't called me all week!"

Dawn doesn't let go, so I wiggle my pinned arms up and wrap them around her to hug back. I inhale her hair. Her shampoo smells deliciously fruity. I should try to find a recipe that creatively utilizes fruit. I could look one up in the car . . . well, I can't on Jamie's phone, but as soon as I get to her computer—

Someone nudges my back and I realize we're in the way. We sidestep, still half embracing, before I finally step back.

My heart stutters. This girl is looking at me like I'm the coolest human to ever walk the earth. She's so attractive. How am I going to pretend to be Jamie around her? I can barely string together my own thoughts at the moment. She has dimples.

"Hello?" *Oh, she's shaking me.* "Jamie! Are you alive in there? Why aren't you speaking? Did you take a vow of silence? Was it my hug? Dude, what is wrong with you?"

Yeah, I can't do this.

"Uh, yes?" I reply belatedly.

Dawn narrows her eyes. "Did you volunteer to do divorce stand-up for the plane or something? Did you bomb on the plane?" She cocks her head sideways. "That doesn't sound right."

I stutter for the right words. I don't know what Jamie would say. She'd say something funny. Something random.

"The plane was cold," I tell her.

What the intercourse?

Dawn looks concerned.

"I really like your hair," I say. "And your outfit is like amazing, amazing. Top notch." What is it that Jamie says? "Aces!" I yell.

Dawn cocks an eyebrow. "Have you been drugged?"

I feel a sigh coming on. I hold it in. "Yes?"

Dawn presses her lips together before pivoting and slinging her arm casually around my neck. "Are we doing a bit?" She leads me toward the automatic doors. "Grams is circling the airport waiting for us, so we've gotta roll out."

An old blue Mercedes pulls up to the curb outside baggage claim. The passenger window zooms down to reveal a sophisticated-looking old woman on the driver's side. She's leaning over the center console dressed in black with a gold ascot around her neck.

"Hello, my beautiful wild granddaughter, it's great to have you back. Get the hell in here."

I blink at her. "Grams?"

She blinks back at me a couple of times . . . sarcastically. "Yes? Are you coming in?" She retreats back to her seat.

Dawn yanks open the back door and slides in like she's part of the family. I hesitate with my fingers on the handle.

Dawn leans forward over the center console. "Jame, you okay? Get in the car."

I get in.

As soon as my butt touches the seat, Grams puts the car into drive. I fumble for my seat belt.

"Granddaughter, I made you a hair appointment to fix your bird's nest. Your father got you an audition for something next week, and he's insisting you return to blond today as per your agreement."

Blond? Agreement?

Jamie's Chocolate comes to life in the pocket over my chest.

BZZZZZZZZZZZZZZZIT.

I go still as Grams pulls away from the curb. *BZZZZZZZZZZZIT.* Excrement. I can't have an absurd glitter glamour magic conversation with Jamie, in this car, with Grams and Dawn.

BZZZZZZZZZZIT.

"Are you going to get that or not?" Dawn leans up from the back seat.

"Um, not." I shrug.

"Who is it?" Grams asks.

BZZZZZZZZIT.

"A friend from the retreat. But we can talk later."

Grams shoots me a quick look. "You made a friend?"

Dawn falls back with a laugh. "Jamie always makes friends. It's her MO."

The ringing seems to have stopped. Thank the heavens.

"Anyone special, this friend?" Grams asks.

Jamie never answers questions she doesn't want to. How do I do that?

"Umm . . . special to who?" I throw back. *Wow.*

"To thy Queen of England perhaps?" Dawn jumps in to save me with her random Shakespeare accent.

My heart does a little wiggle. I channel Jamie the best I can. "I actually did meet Prince Harry. Nice chap, but married dudes aren't really . . . my speed." Oof.

We fall into silence.

BZZZZZZIT.

My hand flies up to clutch at my chest.

"I think Prince Harry needs you," Grams snarks.

BZZZZZZIT.

"Just pick it up, Jame, jeezus," Dawn pipes up from behind me.

BZZZZZZIT.

Fine. I snatch the thing from my pocket and slide it open like Jamie showed me at the airport.

"Hello . . . um, hey hey hey," I add belatedly. I feel Dawn lean forward to listen.

"Pail, what's your emergency because I, too, am experiencing a call-worthy event!" Jamie says quickly.

"Did Prince Harry just call you Pail?" Dawn pipes in. I lean away from her.

Jamie said we should use code names. I'm Pail and she's Bucket.

"Prince Harry, I can't really talk—"

Jamie interrupts me. "Prince Harry? Hm, weird, we look nothing alike, but he's cute. I'll take it." She puts on an accent. "Is this betta? Do thy think I'd be a better sister if I had an accent? I thought we agreed my name was Bucket."

"I have to call you back," I say abruptly.

"Hold up, we haven't exchanged emergencies!" she says.

"I'm in the car with Grams. Keep the phone on. I'll call you back." I slide the phone closed and drop it back into my pocket.

"Jame," Dawn says from the back seat. "Are you okay?"

"Yes." I look over at Grams. We're at a light and she's side-eyeing me. "I'm fine," I say.

Grams raises her brows. "Good, because your appointment is in twenty minutes and we're booking it to the salon."

My jaw falls open. "What? I can't right now."

"Dawn has volunteered to keep you company."

"Grams, I just got back."

"Jamie, you signed that contract. We put it off for a week; it's time to follow through," she says firmly.

What contract?!

BZZZZZIT. The phone buzzes with a text over my chest.

BZZZZZIT. I put my hand over it.

BZZZZZIT.

"Lady Federov, you got some spilling to do about whoever the hell is on the other side of that text." Dawn smirks at me in the rearview mirror.

37. A Girl Is Going to Implode if Siri Keeps Ignoring Her Calls

JAMIE
September 3, Thursday Evening
New Jersey

Siri *hung up* on me. I should have seen that coming. That girl will run away from an in-person conversation. She cannot be trusted with an end button.

My brain is cranking out glitter-based-magic-body-switching theories like no tomorrow, and I have no one to share them with. We definitely haven't switched bodies . . . I'm wearing, like . . . a Siri illusion which is so effing weird and way more confusing than your average *Freaky Friday* situation.

I've just returned from the bathroom where I thoroughly inspected myself. I scratched my skin and banged the mirror and slapped my legs, and little bouts of glitter floofed out of me and into the air every time.

I officially have a ghost braid that people can see, that doesn't actually exist.

Call me crazy, but I think we've been happy haunted. Maybe Terry's a wizard. Or the campground is a wizard. Or the Luck trail is a wizard. Something's a wizard, and it's dusted me with Siri's appearance.

This a whole new level of trip that I don't really know what to do with. *What if it never comes off?*

I've been trying to piece together the terrible poem that was on the box we found because surely that's the key to understanding this, but who knew there was going to be a test! I wasn't paying enough attention. Something about walking in each other's shoes? There was a thing about four days and five nights, so that's gotta be an expiration time on the dusting. It can't be permanent. I think there was also something in there about being doomed?

I roll Siri's carry-on to one of the pillars surrounding the baggage claim carousels in Newark Airport and take a seat.

Has Terry been glittered before? Did she have a riddle? Why didn't I pocket that thing?!

I glance down at Siri's iPhone. My mother is late and I'm trying not to take it personally. She was supposed to pick Siri up at baggage claim.

I settle in to send my sister a text. I have t9 on Gladys: an ancient typing technology from the olden days of 2004. I have a blackbelt in t9. Give me a flip phone, watch me type a thousand words a second.

But I'm slower than a dog texting on this damn iPhone. My fingers feel like giant clumsy marker tips.

Me: WHEN ARE YOU GOING TO CALL ME BACK

Me: CALL ME THE HELL BACK AS SOON AS HUMANLY POSSIBLE

Me: SERIOUSLY U CANT TEXT ME BACK?

That took me seven minutes. Three texts. Seven minutes.

I know Siri's in the car with Grams, but she can use the keypad. She could send me *something*.

I call her two more times for good measure. The first time she sends it to voicemail. The second time she picks it up for thirty seconds, but all I can hear is her talking to Grams in the car. I hear Dawn in the conversation too.

A nasty wave of jealousy careens through me at the thought of Siri hanging with Dawn without me. Dawn will figure out she's not me soon. I'm surprised she hasn't already—

Mother of crap. *Siri probably looks like me.* She's probably wearing a me mirage!

Why haven't I thought about this yet? What if they never realize it's not me! What if . . . they think I'm just different? *Why is this horrifying?*

A vertigo-like sensation hits me. I drop my head into my hands, cutting myself off from the lonely bustle of strangers roaming the airport.

This is not permanent, everyone will find out eventually. And this is comedy! Just like everything else! I can use this. In the end, this is funny. This is Netflix special–level drama.

This carousel area is starting to empty out. The mom and son who sat next to me are exiting through the sliding doors to the parking lot.

Siri's phone buzzes with a text.

Mom: Running late. Sry, be there in 15.

I fall into a pool of self-pity for a bit.

"I want my hair to be like that!" I look up to find a little girl being dragged along by the hand toward the exit. She's pointing unabashedly at me and staring. What is it with people and long hair? Calm down.

I roll out my neck, trying to clear my head.

Logically, this *Freaky Friday* dust can be used to execute a best-case re-venge-y Parent Confrontation Trap scenario. I mean, *logically* this is the best twist a mischievous bitch could ask for. Maybe the universe wants me to—

Siri's phone buzzes.

Mom: Pulling up outside door 6

It takes me a full thirty seconds to write back *coming* without typos.

My heart's beating in my mouth as I stand. Like at the front of my esophagus. I pull up my hood as the exit doors slide open.

The air bites with the chill of East Coast fall. I hug my arms across my chest.

The expansive sidewalk out here is thick with the foot traffic of travelers, calling out to their friends and loved ones. I navigate through them and step up to the curb. Siri said Mom drives a black Toyota RAV4 Hybrid. Unfortu-nately, it's dark and a black Toyota RAV4 Hybrid looks like every other car that's ever existed.

A horn blares. I jump three feet to my left as said black Toyota RAV4 pulls up right next to me. Frig. I clutch at my chest.

The passenger side window rolls down and there's my mother in the driver's seat. My father's arch nemesis, *Mara*.

"What was that?" she says anxiously. "You're not supposed to be jumping! I didn't mean to startle you; you don't usually get startled. Are you okay? I'm sorry, Siri."

I exhale a frenzied breath. *Get it together. Be Siri.*

I put my hand on the door and serve her an angry look.

She frowns. "Please don't do the silent staring thing. I said I was sorry."

I literally haven't seen this woman's face in over a decade. Her long brown hair is swept up in a perfect bun. Her eyes are heavier than I remember. She's thinner. Bonier, like all the youthful softness to her skin has been tightened and yanked hard across her frame. Her cheekbones are more pronounced. She's sharp like her personality.

I've been thinking that Siri and I have Mara's hair and eyes, but our father's sharp cheek bones and chiseled features. And we do, I think, but she's not soft anymore like I remember either. It's jarring.

"Are you going to get in the car? Are you in pain?" Mara enunciates every word like the female voice on a GPS.

I load in, hoist Siri's carry-on into the back, and buckle my seat belt silently. You can usually count on Siri to be silent.

"Feel good to be back?" she asks quietly as she pulls us away from the airport.

I don't respond, but god, the urge to immediately chat candidly with her about everything I've learned is like an itch I'm not allowed to scratch. I want to demand to know every tiny detail about what happened with Dad, and I want to know right now.

But if I want to milk this for the comedy, I have to hold my tongue. Play the long game. I could get so much more out of this landmine moment then I ever imagined. Hypothetically it might not come until . . . Siri and I reunite in Vegas. I could play mind games with this woman for four days.

I need to find a suitable way to distract myself through this drive so I don't ruin everything with my giant mouth.

I reach behind me and unzip the front pocket of Siri's carry-on where I stashed my notebook. I can write down my magic dust theories so I have them all on paper to run through with Siri later. I angle myself against the corner where the door and seat kiss.

Mara glances over. "What are you writing?" she asks in an overly polite, cheerful voice.

I flick my eyes to hers for a moment before dropping them back to the page. "A haiku about how hard it is to be your daughter."

Mara grinds her teeth together as the light turns. "You're clearly tired from your travels."

"I slept on the plane," I reply blankly. She grips the steering wheel harder.

"You'll be happy to hear I've been talking things through with George. We're planning a family reunion dinner with Gill on Saturday."

I think Siri will be happy to hear that. It's strange to hear Mara use the phrase "family reunion," knowing that it has nothing to do with me. She doesn't consider me family worth reunion-ing with.

I hold on to my silence for a bit. Mara looks tense, like I might pull out a sword and attack her at any moment. Like she's afraid of Siri. *Siri does have some anger issues.* Perhaps Mara lives in fear of her daughter finally untangling her disgusting web of lies.

"Are you getting back together?" I respond belatedly.

"We're working things through," she says.

"Good." This is good. I can have a lot of fun at this dinner.

"I was thinking you could make that delicious Greek casserole you made a few months ago. George and I loved it."

Casserole? My mouth pops open, but I close it quickly. "You got it, Mother."

I add this to the list of crap Siri and I have to work through on the phone later.

Mara pulls up to a small gray house on a dark, but quaint-looking, suburban street. She puts the Toyota into park and looks over at me.

"What?" I ask after ten more seconds of excruciating silence.

"I have to go back out," Mara says. Her hand is still on the gear stick.

Is she kidding me?

"I just got home, Mom." The word tastes like ash on my tongue. I, Jamie, am not ready to call her *Mom*.

"I picked you up a sandwich earlier, it's in the fridge. I'll be home around 11:30."

I execute a trademark Siri dramatic sigh, slip outside, and slam the door. Mara reverses and leaves me in the driveway.

Siri and I exchanged garage codes earlier. This is not the same garage I left out of with Dad. But it's a similar style. Similar size. I input the numbers (Siri's birthday) and head into the Maza household, completely unsupervised.

38. A Girl Has Never Been to Her Mom's House

JAMIE
September 3, Thursday Evening
New Jersey

Through the garage door I find myself in the little hallway to the kitchen that Siri quickly sketched out for me on a piece of notebook paper.

On the wall directly in front of me is a framed 8 × 10 black-and-white photo of my sister in a perfect leap. She's wearing a black tutu. Her toes are perfectly pointed. She's at least six feet off the ground. Her back leg is bent up, and she's arching her head toward it. Her toes are centimeters from her dark bun.

I move toward the kitchen. There's a white oval-shaped table on the left, and a nice U-shaped cooking area with a small white and gray marble island to my right.

Straight ahead, the kitchen opens into the living room. It's framed by a cream leather sectional. A sophisticated-looking gray House Stark blanket is draped over the back.

There are pictures on walls. One of Mom and young Siri together outside this house. Mom on stage with a cast of actors at the end of a show. There's a classic family portrait hanging over the fireplace. A slightly younger, rosy cheeked Mara stands next to a handsome dark-skinned man with circular black-rimmed glasses. That must be George. In front of them sits a young, maybe thirteen-year-old pale-ass Siri, and a cute dark-skinned boy around her age who looks a lot like George: he must be Gill.

I wander into the foyer where I find the front door and a staircase to the second floor. I kick off Siri's sneakers and head up.

More dance pictures of Siri line the wall going up the steps. The staircase empties in the middle of a narrow hallway with options to go left or right. Siri's and Gill's rooms are to the right, Mara's bedroom is to the left.

Pictures litter this hallway as well. I walk by middle school portraits of Siri and Gill. Siri's smiling like a total dweeb with braces. I pause, staring at all the frames along the wall. I don't exist here.

I should be in that family picture over the fireplace. I should know Gill and George. I should have been made a part of this.

I plant myself in front of the last picture before the door to Siri's room: preteen Siri and an old white man with gray hair and clear-rimmed glasses, wearing a collared shirt with a sweater vest, sitting on the front steps. Her papa.

My papa. I don't remember much about him from before. The way Siri talked about him, they're close—

"GAH!" An electric doorbell set to the tune of "Twinkle, Twinkle, Little Star" scares the shit out of me. Who the hell is here?

I abandon the picture. There's a vague outline of a man through the thin translucent window on the side of the front door.

A knock comes now. "Siri Martine, it's Papa! Your mother said she dropped you here and had to leave for work?"

I fumble down the stairs, taking them two at a time.

"Coming!" I lunge forward and pry open the door.

A second later I'm scooped into a hug by the same kind-faced pale old man from the hallway.

"Sweetheart, we missed you! Great to have you home."

"Hey, Papa," I return hesitantly. "It's late."

Seriously, it's ten o'clock. Isn't that late for old people? Grams is usually in bed by eleven.

He reaches down to where he's rested a large pink, orange, and white box. He holds it up in offering. "How about some checkers and donuts?"

39. Angst and Salons

SIRI
September 3, Thursday Evening
California

There is bleach in my hair.

Whatever's happening right now is very confusing. I watched as the stylist picked up chunks of Jamie's hair in the mirror, but I *felt her* picking up my hair. She commented on how strange the texture was as opposed to how it looked, and I sat here nonplussed.

Aluminum foil, bleach, and whatever other chemicals they use are all over my head. In my actual, carefully curated, healthy hair. Draining away the color and the nutrients and hydration. I can feel it. The acrid smell and sting of it is on *me*, not just the glamour. It's taking all my willpower not to cry.

The only choice I got to make here was the shade of blond, so I went with the gray variety.

What's going to happen when they take the foil off? Will the illusion hair still be neon orange? Am I going to turn into a lab experiment? Who the underworld knows!

The saving grace of this fiasco is that Dawn can tell I'm in major distress, and she's trying her best to calm me down. She's on the salon chair next to me, jabbering away about the week she's had. She filled me in on all sorts of "Duck Waterfall" news as the stylist mixed and slathered my head with gook.

Jamie has told me exactly nothing of Duck Waterfall. From what I've discerned, it has nothing to do with ducks or waterfalls. It sounds like a club they run together? Most of the recap went over my head. She talked about all the members—random gossip and scenes they did together. And then about some other groups with equally random names like Martian Candy and Golden Coattails. Maybe they're an acting club?

Jamie's *need to know before we switch* rundown included her garage code, a layout of her house, and the fact that Dawn lives next door. The more I listen to Dawn, the less I feel like I know about Jamie, and the more insecure I feel about this whole mess I've gotten myself into.

Apparently, I have a Duck Waterfall practice at Dawn's house tomorrow morning at 10:30.

In the past thirty seconds, the conversation has finally taken a welcome turn. Dawn took "my advice" and engaged in a first date extravaganza this past week despite an anatomy test, which she aced anyway. She went on four dates in the last seven days!

"Four dates in seven days?!" I exclaim. "How? What apps were you using? Did they go well? How lo—" I almost ask how long she's been single, but I stop myself mid-word and feign a coughing fit.

Why would Jamie tell Dawn to go on a bunch of dates? Did Dawn also recently get out of a relationship? Did she get cheated on too?

"She speaks!" Dawn chuckles. "Your extended silence has really been freaking me out. Seriously—absolutely no comment on all my Duck Waterfall gossip? Cynthia is pregnant, Jamie. With Josh's baby. Did you even know they were seeing each other? Two more of our eight members have slept together now," she states fiercely.

I hesitate, feeling like she caught me in a fib. "Um, no, I mean that was good stuff . . . but your dating life is way more exciting?"

Dawn stares at me for a long moment. This really feels like lying. My insides wriggle around uncomfortably.

She clears her throat. "I've been trying to figure out how to word this for a few weeks now, Jame. I need you to stop shutting me down and boomeranging the conversation when I try to be your best friend in any emotional capacity. When I'm done with this story, we have to talk about what's going on with you." She nervously rubs her hands over her thighs before looking back up at me. "I'm your best friend, and no matter what it is, no matter what's going on, I love you and I want to help. I'm never going to judge you. I want to be here for you, but if you never open the door, I can't. And eventually that door is going to come between us and . . . I don't want that to happen."

I have to grind my teeth together to keep my lips from wobbling. Jamie's so lucky to have a best friend who says stuff like this. She sounds like family. Like a true sister.

"Jamie, can you promise me, please?" She continues, "Tell me exactly what happened to make you go along with this whole retreat thing after I share my dating app saga? We don't have to do it here out in the open, but when we get back to your place, okay? And I'll give you full permission to milk any of these dates for set material." Dawn smiles knowingly.

How do I promise to tell her something I don't even know? How do I not promise her? How would I even go about telling her *I'm not actually Jamie?* When will I stop looking like Jamie?!

I do not have time to go down this mental rabbit hole right now.

"Okay," I whisper.

The tension ebbs from her face. "Thank the gods!" She chuckles. "Okay, hit me with the Q's I know you were compiling during that speech."

I try to grin smugly like Jamie does. "Well, for starters, what app were you using?"

"Pizza Perfect."

"Pizza Perfect?!" I squeak. "What? That's not a real thing."

"It really, really is. There's a dating app for pizza lovers. I just had to use the Google and thar she was!" Dawn pulls on an exaggerated English accent. "Prettie as a pictcha."

I snort. Note to self: Dawn loves pizza.

"The whole gimmick is pizza-related," she continues. "You put your favorite topping in your profile and then you grab pizza together for the first date."

"You had pizza four times last week?"

"Living my best pizza life, Jame." She leans back and puts her hands behind her head.

I wonder what her favorite topping is. I've never tried making pizza, but it can't be difficult. I've made way more complicated dishes. I'll google some recipes later.

"So how . . . did the dates go?" I ask. I want to ask more about pizza and her specific preferences, but Jamie has to be aware of that sort of information.

Dawn examines her fingertips (they're a pale pastel blue color). "Well, the first girl—"

Dawn likes girls!

"—was a gorgeous redhead, favorite topping, ham, which is fine, but something about the way she talked about people . . . it reminded me of Dani. And then she went and backhand complimented my nails.

"Can you believe that shit? I go through the trouble of painting my nails for a damn first date, and this woman has the gall to insult the paint job. Look at these!" She whips up her hands. The nails have been heavily coated with polish, and it's gathered and bunched in places. I can see a few fingerprints. I resist the urge to laugh, but I can't *not* smile. My heart knocks against my sternum. *Dawn is gorgeous and kind and genuine*—and Jamie's best friend in the universe, and I should not be thinking about her in any romantic sort of anything.

I swallow. "I think your nails are perfect. They look great. Look at mine." I hold up Jamie's shitty chipped nails.

"I swear to god, Jame, you're getting nail polish remover for your birthday."

I bark a laugh, unable to hold in my amusement at Jamie's expense.

"Okay," I prompt, "keep going, what about the other ones?"

"None of these stories are going to end well, so don't get too excited about anyone."

I smile.

She guffaws. "Why are you smiling, you asshole?"

I drop my grin immediately, *oh my god, what am I doing?* "Sorry, I mean, that must mean you've got some good stories."

She eyes me suspiciously for another long moment. "Really? You have nothing to say about this?" She sticks out her nails and parades them in my face.

"I like the color . . ."

She gives me stink-eye. "What's with you?"

What am I saying wrong here? I shrug.

"Really looking forward to the Jamie saga later. You're being weirder than usual." She recrosses her legs. "Okay, girl number two's name was Evian. Like the water. Favorite topping, pasta—on a pizza, Jame."

40. A Girl Appreciates a Donut

JAMIE
September 3, Thursday Evening
New Jersey

I snatch a jelly donut from the box and place it on a napkin. Papa and I have organized ourselves across from each other at the table, with a red-and-black checkerboard between us. Papa watches me curiously, like I'm an animal at the zoo.

"What?" I ask.

He raises his eyebrows. "Nothing," he says before lifting his plain-looking donut and dipping it into the decaf coffee he made himself.

I smother my pending comment, *It doesn't look like nothing,* and wait for Papa to lead the conversation. He lifts the donut and takes a bite of the saturated portion.

I grab my donut and take a giant bite where the jelly is falling out. Sugar scraps across my cheeks as raspberry heaven explodes in my mouth. I shoot Papa a closed-mouth smile with my mouth full.

He nods to me. "You move first."

I pick a piece and try not to litter the board with the sugar granules sticking to my hands. Papa quickly follows with his own move.

"So how are you doing? How was your retreat?" he opens.

I move my next piece. "It was nice. It's forced me to really take a step back

165

and examine my past to try to figure out what my future looks like without ballet."

He moves. "And what does it look like?"

I hop over one of his pieces. "Still murky, but I'm working on it."

"Do you want to go to school?" he asks.

LOL, hell no. "I don't know."

He jumps two of my pieces. "King me," he says.

I glare down at the board. "What just happened?"

It's 11:30 and Mara's still not home. I played conversation with Papa very Siri: brief responses and silence. We got through two games of checkers, he thoroughly kicked my ass. The man is a checkers savant.

I walk him to the door.

"If Mara's leaving you alone too often, I can always come over and keep you company." He makes his way down the front steps and turns to look me in the eye. "Remember that. You can call me if you need someone to talk to."

The look he gives me is conspiratorial, like he knows I know something we haven't spoken about knowing. I narrow my eyes at him. ". . . Okay."

"Love you," he says as he waves and turns to walk down the path.

I slam the door shut and call Siri again. She still doesn't pick up. What the hell is she doing?

I jog back upstairs, hang a right past the school portraits, and finally check out Siri's room.

The door itself has an artsy picture of ballet shoes nailed to a wall taped to it. When I head inside, I'm met with darkness.

It's still pretty dark when I flip on the lights. Her comforter is black. The shams are deep blue. The walls are painted a dark bluish-gray. There's a decent-sized window on the far wall, and on either side of it are framed posters, one of Billie Eilish and one that says SLIPKNOT.

Scattered about the darkness is ballet. There's a white pillow between her blue shams with black ballet slippers stitched across it. Under her window, lined up neatly along the wall, are *at least* ten pairs of old worn-out ballet shoes. Black ones, pink ones, tan ones, white pointe shoes dirtied with age, peach ones falling apart at the seams. It's a little dance shoe graveyard.

The whole room is like a physical manifestation of *Black Swan*. In the corner near Billie Eilish is a little black desk with a black laptop on it. There's a mirror over a chest of drawers to the left. Pictures from recitals or competitions throughout the years are stuck into its edges; there are so many unfortunate tutus I missed out on making fun of.

The door to Mara's room is slightly ajar. It creaks as I push it open. The first thing that catches my eye is the enormous lit-up bookcase stretching across the entirety of the right wall.

I snort. "Hot damn."

It's brimming with Game of Thrones books, all different editions, and various pieces of memorabilia: I see the three dragon eggs, Arya's Needle, the Red Lady's choker, Longclaw, a Valyrian steel dagger, a 3D mini-recreation of King's Landing. They're all placed meticulously among the books.

Looks like she's just as big a super fan as Dad.

There's a framed picture on one of the higher shelves. I step into the room, throw Siri's iPhone onto Mara's bed, and shuffle closer. In the picture Mara's wearing a long, elaborately braided red wig and a light blue dress. A young Siri's next to her, her hair tied back, wearing a loose, cream-colored tunic, long skirt-like wrap, and a brown leather belt. She's holding a wooden sword. The two of them are in front of a Winter Is Coming Con step-and-stop. Mara's smiling with her whole body, hugging what looks like a ten-year-old Siri against her side. Siri's smiling too, but smaller, a close-lipped grin that shows she's pleased to be the object of Mara's affections. It's adorable. Heartwarming even. It's so great that Siri got to have such nice times with Mom.

I reach up and slowly pull a red Game of Thrones book out from its place next to the frame. I drag it to the very edge of the shelf, take my finger off, and let it fall the ground. It thunks against the dark wood floor.

I glance back at the picture. Young me would have loved to spend a day like this with my mom. Cover me in armor. Glue on a beard. Scales. Make me a wolf. I would have been thrilled.

I pull another book and let it fall. And another. And another and another and another and another and another. They clunk and thump over one another. Snap and crack and I don't fucking know why this feels so good. I remove all the memorabilia and stick the pieces in various places around her room, all over the floor. I put the Red Lady's choker around my neck.

I stop short as Siri's phone buzzes from Mara's bed.

It's not Siri.

Mom: Going to be back late, working more stuff through with George. See you at breakfast tomorrow, hon.

Ah yes, their mother-daughter breakfasts. Siri said they religiously have breakfast together every morning at 8 a.m. before Mara heads off to work.

I shoot my sister a few more frantic texts before glancing around at the shit storm I've created. The floor is overrun with fallen tomes. The only thing left on Mara's Game of Thrones shrine is the picture.

I slap my hands against my thighs. "Okay, here we go."

Thirty minutes pass before I finish up and check the phone again. Siri still hasn't gotten back to me. I guffaw as my millionth call goes to voicemail. *Seriously?*

41. Angst and Jamie's Room

SIRI
September 3, Thursday Evening
California

Dawn follows me up to Jamie's room so I can deliver on my promise to share *what's going on with me.* My insides are wringing themselves out as I try to formulate a viable way out of this without hurting her feelings. I don't know what's going on with Jamie! She's been so vague about her life. I know nothing!

I come to a stop and linger for a few awkward moments outside Jamie's bedroom door. It's covered in glow-in-the-dark plastic stars.

"Are we going in?" Dawn asks behind me.

Guilt floods my chest as I turn to face her. "I'm not feeling well."

Her brows descend suspiciously. "What's wrong?"

"I'm really tired . . . and I haven't had dinner. Can we talk tomorrow?"

Disappointment swells in her pretty, dark eyes. "You're gonna blow me off, after leaving me hanging for seven days?"

I hate this. "I'm really sorry! I promise tomorrow I'll tell you everything!"

Dawn doesn't leave; she stares me down. "Why are your facial expressions so warped today?"

What? "What do you mean?"

"I mean, I've never seen you frown in that way. It's unsettling. What the hell is going on?"

I try to take a step back and hit the doorknob. On a cowardly impulse

169

I spin and slip into Jamie's room, closing the door slowly but surely in Dawn's face.

"Really? Wow." Her voice is much quieter through the door. Hurt.

I hate this. There is no silver lining to hurting Dawn. *I hate this!*

"I pinky promise tomorrow morning after practice, I'll make it up to you," I whisper-talk into the crack where the door meets the frame.

I listen to her footsteps as she retreats, and with a shaky exhale, I slide to the floor.

Jamie's Chocolate buzzes with another message. Her GODAMNIT CALL ME BACK texts have been coming in for hours, and I haven't been able to respond. I pull the phone out to catch the latest.

Jamie: Gave Mara's shrine a makeover.

I gasp as a picture loads underneath it. Mom's Game of Thrones books have been shuffled around and are now on the shelves backward, pages out. All her memorabilia have been repurposed in a sort of modern art fashion, spewed about the floor!

Mom is going to kill her. Every time she gets a new piece of memorabilia, we spend an hour reorganizing that shelf to perfectly display it!

Another buzz comes in.

Jamie: I'm an evil mastermind, I know.

There is too much going on right now.

I drop the phone and look around at Jamie's room. I'm sitting on a sparkly fluffy pink carpet that matches the peach canopy bed in the center of the space. A full-length gilded mirror leans against the wall directly across the way. Mirror Jamie stares back at me. The weird glamour magic adapted to the salon chemicals. Mirror Jamie's new hair bears a striking resemblance to Albert Einstein's.

I can't fully see how the bleach affected my actual hair as a whole, but I can look down and pull the strands in front of my face to confirm that they too now have a gray-blond hue.

Movie posters are scattered about Jamie's walls, a vintage one from *Grease*, one from *Shrek 2*, and a third from *Men in Black*. There's a white desk against the wall next to the bed. On top of it sits an ancient Mac desktop with orange accents from the mid-2000s. A groan escapes me.

That can't be her actual computer.

Ugh. I have to call Jamie. But I'm so tired.

There's a knock on the door behind me. I scurry away from it on all fours and stand to perch on the edge of the bed as Grams peeks in.

"Dawn left looking very upset, Jamie."

"I'm going to make it up to her," I say quietly.

She puts her hands on her hips. "Your father's home. He wants to talk to you, and we have to decide on dinner. Should I make something or do you want takeout?"

"I could help make something," I offer. Good god, let me cook something. I need to turn off my brain.

Grams's eyebrows raise. "You realize I mean food?"

I nod.

She stares at me for a moment before shrugging. "Okay, get your ass downstairs, let's food, and then let's *Runaway Bride*. It's been too long since we rom-com'd."

42. Angst and Dad

SIRI
September 3, Thursday Evening
California

It doesn't really hit me until I reach the bottom of the staircase and see him in the kitchen. *I'm about to meet my dad.* Sitting at a rustic-looking kitchen table, drinking from a cheesy Iron Throne–themed mug, and scrolling on his phone is my greedy, selfish, abandoning jerk-and-a-half father.

His hair is dark. He must dye it. He's wearing a button-up light blue shirt with khaki pants.

He glances up.

"Jame!" His voice sends a shock wave through me. It still sounds *familiar.*

"Hi," I whisper, like he's not twenty feet away.

"Welcome back!" He puts down his mug. "Come take a seat, kiddo."

Mom boycotts all of Dad's films.

I'm not a big movie person, but I watch his. He makes the kind you see at the Oscars. Jamie called them pretentious when I brought them up. They are pretentious, but that's part of why I like them. They're very particular. Three of his movies have been nominated for Best Picture over the past ten years. He's got another one in the works. It's about a dysfunctional father-daughter relationship.

I've been secretly hoping it was about me since I read about it. I had this stupid idea that he was going to use it as a way to reach out and rekindle a relationship.

That was before I knew about Jamie. The whole daydream is embarrassing now.

Dad looks down at his phone again as I make my way from the living room to the kitchen. The chair skids against the tile as I drag it out and sit down.

Maybe Jamie wouldn't sit down at all? I bet she'd do the opposite of what he asked. I stand back up and head toward the refrigerator. Grams is over here bustling about, gathering ingredients.

"How was your retreat?" Dad asks.

"Um, great. I worked on finding introspection," I say as I make an educated guess regarding what cabinet might hold the glasses, choose wrong, and get the plates. I find the glasses on my second try.

Dad puts down his phone and gives me his full attention as I move toward the water dispenser. "Your hair looks great," he says.

I press the water button. "Thanks."

"You know that gray-blond look is very in now in Hollywood. I'm telling you, you're going to book some jobs next week. Switch your outfit out for some jeans and a white shirt, and you're golden. I'm assuming you've spoken to Anya since you've been back?"

Who the underworld is Anya? Cold water overflows onto my hand.

I step back from the dispenser and shake out my fingers. "Uh-huh," I mumble as I start my return journey with an overflowing glass of water.

"I booked you a gig for Saturday, James," Dad boasts proudly.

I freeze mid-step as that registers. "Wait—a what, when?" The stupid water sloshes over my hand and splats to the floor.

He meets my eyes and grins in the same smug way Jamie does. "This Saturday! I know you think your old man is too busy for you, but I'm always watching."

What?

"Always watching what?" What does Jamie do? For some reason I've just been assuming acting! Did he book her an acting gig? I walk the eight extra feet to the table and sit down. Is Jamie in a band?

Dad chuckles at my expression.

"What kind of gig?!" I ask more forcefully.

He crosses his legs. "A twenty-minute set at a private barbecue Timothée Chalamet is holding this weekend for one of his friends."

"Timothée Chalamet?!" My arms swoop upward in shock, and water splashes across half my face and shoulder. "Excre-shit," I grumble.

Dad hops up and snags me a paper towel. "He's been cast in *Father Daughter* . . . did you forget? He's playing Caroline's love interest."

"Oh yeah . . ." I reply dumbly as he hands me the towel.

"He was looking for new up-and-coming young comedians, and I recommended you."

"You recommended *me*?"

Jamie's a comedian?

"I've snuck in and caught your set a couple of times these past few months, Jame," Dad says.

I can't handle this right now.

"I know I wasn't invited, but I've been keeping tabs on your progress . . ." he chatters on.

This is not how I wanted *meeting my dad* to go. I wanted him to run up and hug me, apologize profusely, and tell me he loves me. And yeah, I wasn't expecting that to happen to me right now, while wearing a Jamie illusion. But for some reason, I believed Jamie today when she said Dad was a big asshole. That he only cared about himself. But he's apparently been secretly going out of his way to watch Jamie perform?

Sounds like it's only me he doesn't care about.

And now Jamie's three thousand miles away, and she has a stand-up comedy gig for a celebrity barbecue in two days? She should have been here to get this news! She should be having this moment.

I STILL HAVEN'T TALKED TO JAMIE!

Grams interrupts whatever Dad's saying. "Hold up, Grier. Granddaughter, you said you'd help! Come over here and listen while you chop this, will you?"

I leap up gratefully and head to the counter. Grams trades my damp paper towel out for a knife and sets me in front of some garlic. I start at it immediately: crush, peel, chop, chop, chop. I focus on the satisfying staccato of the knife hitting the cutting board.

Dad's still talking. His chair pushes out from the table.

". . . Jame. I was at the Laugh Drop to watch your first go at ten minutes when you had your incident last week. It sounds like you've written a lot of content for a short set. You're doing great. You just have to tighten everything up. I took down some notes. I'll email them to you, and you should get back out there."

He took notes. On Jamie's stand-up? She had an incident?

I blink at Dad uselessly. "Okay."

He smiles and pokes me in the arm. "Great. I'll text you details. The gig doesn't pay, but it's going to be great publicity. This kid has millions of followers."

This kid. Like I don't already know of Timothée Chalamet. I've watched and loved *Call Me by Your Name*.

I continue chopping garlic. "Okay."

Dad's phone starts to ring. He picks it up and gives me a wave as he heads out of the room.

Chop, chop, chop. Excrement, excrement, excrement. In our original plan we're supposed to be switched till Tuesday. And if this glamour magic is related to that glitter explosion, which it has to be, that stupid riddle probably dictated how this works. It definitely said something about helping us pull off the ruse of walking in each other's shoes, which means that Jamie probably, most likely . . . looks like me right now. And I know that stupid poem said four days and five nights—the line is burned into my brain because I had just proposed that addendum to Jamie's plan not forty minutes before. And if the riddle timeline is real, then hypothetically, probably, most likely, we're stuck looking like each other for at least four more days, and even if Jamie flew back here to make the performance, I'll still, for all intents and purposes, *be her* on Saturday! And I can't be a comedian for Timothée Chalamet!

My knife hits the bare cutting board as I run out of garlic.

43. A Girl Can Rock a Catfish

Mara,

Your choreography work on Broadway these past two years has been outstanding and we'd love to offer you an opportunity in Las Vegas. We're bringing *Mean Girls* over to a new theater with a new sense of space. It needs a flashy Vegas-worthy choreography revamp. We're very interested in bringing you aboard.

We're meeting with two other choreographers this Tuesday at MGM here in Vegas. If you'd be interested in throwing your hat in the ring, please let us know.

Please get back to us as soon as possible and we'll schedule a call.

All the best,
Lara Thorpe
23 Publicity Inc.

I close the laptop and curl under Siri's dark covers, listening as Mara's footsteps make their way upstairs. This woman is creeping in scandalously late. I finished my catfish account and email draft ten minutes ago. I have it scheduled to send to Mara at 8 a.m.

I still haven't heard from Siri. If she doesn't call before I go to sleep, then fuck it, I'm just texting over my main talking points.

There's a light knock on the bedroom door. I have to restrain myself from yelling *What doth yonder want?* "What?"

Mara, cheeks flushed and hair down, appears in the doorframe. "You're still up. How are you doing?" she asks slowly. "You're back sleeping in the bed. That's great."

I pull on a close-lipped smile. "Uh-huh. I'm marvelous, Mother."

Mara sighs. "I'll see you in the morning for breakfast?"

"You got it, dude."

She narrows her eyes and retreats.

I listen as she walks to her room. Closes the door. Turns on the light. Screeches at the top of her lungs, "What the intercoursing excrement?!"

An evil smile crawls up my face. I watch the door for a few minutes, anticipating Mara's return, but she never shows up.

44. Angst and Rom-Coms

SIRI
September 3, Thursday 10:20 p.m.
California

Grams and I are forty-five minutes into *Runaway Bride* when I reach out and hit pause.

I've never seen this movie. We're watching the rise and fall of four different Julia Roberts almost-marriages, and I can't stop thinking about the questions Jamie had down on her outline. I know nothing about my parents' marriage. They got married so young, just like Julia Roberts's character in the first couple of weddings. How *did* Mom and Dad fall in love?

Grams looks over at me in the light of the television. "Your hair is intense," she says from her spot up against the edge of the couch. "Just like you."

I don't say anything.

"What's up? You going to press play?" She hugs her legs up onto the couch and curls them next her.

"I want to ask you a question."

"Ask, then. Julia's waiting." The way Grams talks already reminds me so much of Jamie: strangely guarded and cynical, but upbeat at the same time.

I smile at her. "This movie is making me think about Mom and Dad. I feel like I don't know anything about their relationship. How it started, why it ended. Do you know how they met?"

Grams's expression flatlines. She pulls her mug of tea from the coffee table and takes a sip before meeting my eyes again. "I've been dreading this question for years, Jame. I'm surprised it took you so long. I haven't volunteered this particular story because I'm not so proud of my part in everything that happened."

I reposition myself along the edge of the seat cushion where I can sit properly without slouching.

She pulls a blanket off the edge of the couch and tosses it onto her legs. "Your mother and I are both strong-willed women." She pauses. "I admire her in some ways, but I never embraced her as family. I villainized her. When my husband passed, I missed my son too much. I wanted him near me here in California, and your mother wanted to keep him in New York.

"I could have, should have, been nicer to her. But I encouraged Grier to move back here when he brought it up."

I frown. *Is it Grams's fault that Jamie and I were separated?*

She clears her throat. "Your parents fell for each other very quickly in their junior year of college. They were both involved in a play about that book series they're so obsessed with."

"Game of Thrones?"

She rolls her eyes and takes another sip of tea. "Your father called me up three months into their relationship and told me he was going to be staying in New York through the summer because your mother was interning for a Broadway production. At this point I had already secured him an internship with Paramount." Grams clacks her manicured nails against her mug. "He blew it off entirely. Lovesick idiot. Started working for a bank. I would never have thought . . ." She trails off, staring at her hands.

"His father and I had a clear vision for his future and . . . Well, it's strange being in love. I know you"—she raises air quotes—"'don't believe in romantic relationships.'" She lowers her hands. "But you'll stumble into love someday and see how real it is. How pliable it can make one's heart. I miss it."

I blink at her. That was specific in the vaguest of ways. "I— Are there pictures? Do you have pictures? Was there a wedding? They had to be married to have a divorce."

Before I even stop talking, Grams is shaking her head. "If there were pictures, I never got them. Your father was mad at me for a long stretch of their courtship. They had a small wedding on the East Coast that I wasn't invited to. I started to visit once your sister was born."

Grams abruptly reaches out and presses play on the remote. This is clearly still a touchy subject. Grams stares hard at the screen as Richard Gere interrogates another one of Julia's exes about eggs. Jamie's Gladys buzzes in my pocket with a text.

I slip the phone out. I have new messages from Jamie and Dawn. I tap open Dawn's first.

Dawn: Are you okay, Jamie?

Wow, she really is so sweet. I wonder if her outfit will be just as monochromatically wonderful tomorrow.

It takes forever for me to text back because you have to click every button on this phone multiple times to get the letter you want.

Me: Yes, Im sry 4 being obnoxious. Hope ur okay. Im so glad u were there w/ Grams to pick me up 2day. Excited to c u tomorrow <3

I actually am excited for tomorrow. I want to do something nice for her. I can't forget to google pizza recipes. I tap out of the thread and over to Jamie.

Bucket: SIS WAY 2 LEAVE ME HANGING FOR ALL OF ETERNITY. I've been happy haunted & I look like you. please confirm my theory that you've been glitter dusted to look like me.

Bucket: PRETTY SURE riddle was our instruction manual. It said something about being doomed if we don't reunite by day 5 so be sure to get ur vegas catfish rolling. I prepped my email for mom.

An immense sense of relief washes over me. It's overwhelmingly nice to know for sure that I'm not the only one experiencing this surreal glitter magic nonsense.

I finally text back.

Me: Agree bout theory. Will get catfish set up latr. Random, do u know Dawn's favorite pizza topping?

My phone buzzes back four minutes later.

Bucket: scuse me where the flibity jibbitif \k have u been! Dont u robot minimalist text me now! Daown enjoys quite a large varieety but her current favorite is broccoli, an unpopular but golden opinion. Why? // HOW AVE U STILLNUT CALLED ME??!!!111@

Me: busy with fam

Bucket: Mom question-how deepp does her Game of Thrones obsession run?

Me: When I was 10, I asked her 2 buy me the Twilight books. she said she had better idea—started reading me A Song of Ice and Fire aloud every night n censoring all the inappropriate parts.

Bucket: so like all the parts

Me: Have more to tell you, talk soon.

Bucket: DON'T U DARE TELK SOON ME U JUST GOAT HERE.

"Are we watching Julia be glorious or are you texting Dawn?" Grams snaps next to me as she pauses the TV again.

I fumble the phone and slip it back into my pocket. "I'm watching Julia be glorious. Julia is the sun. Praise Julia. Sorry, Julia."

45. A Girl Needs Adventure

JAMIE
September 4, Friday Morning
New Jersey

When Siri's iPhone alarm goes off at seven, I roll over and open her laptop. I cannot believe how hard I was blown off last night. *I better have an email waiting.*

Siri Maza <AskSiriAboutBallet11@gmail.com>   3:30 AM
to Jamie

Jamie, here's my first catfish email, I was maybe thinking I'm going to lure Dad to Vegas with . . . Mom? (obviously I made a new email, I'm not sending from asksiri)

<< Grier,

I know we promised a clean break, but I yearn for you in the depths of the night. I've been reliving the year we met. The play. The good times. Why did we feel the need to erase each other from our respective lives so completely? I miss you.

Love,
Mara >>

Thoughts? Also who's Anya? Also I have stuff to tell you about
Dad that you'll probably want to hear over the phone. I'll call you
tomorrow.

I send a quick reply back: Anya = agent. Catfish email is a go.

I'm dressed and downstairs by 7:50 for the daily Maza 8 a.m. mother-
daughter breakfast. Siri said they both usually eat Special K and fruit. The
fruit bowl is already on the table, so I do the honors and fish out the bowls
and the Special K—they really go all out here in New Jersey.

Mara saunters into the kitchen at 8:05. She eyes me wearily before sitting
down at the table.

"Good morning," she says politely. "Thanks for getting breakfast out."

"Thanks for taking the time out of your busy day to join me, Mother." I
pour my Special K and nab an apple from the fruit bowl.

Mara takes the box from me and pours her own bowl. "I'm sorry I
wasn't able to be here with you last night. You're obviously angry with
me."

"What makes you say that?" I ask.

She holds my eyes like she's trying to penetrate my soul. "Tell me more
about your retreat. I'm here now."

I chomp into my apple. "They had those Twilight books people love so
much in this little wooden library cabin, so I finally read them, and honestly,
way more enjoyable than Thrones." I swipe at some juice dribbling down my
face.

"Ugh." Mara's semi-open expression closes. She grabs a banana and puts
it in a bag next to her chair. "You never made it past *Clash of Kings*. Finish
the series and get back to me."

"Mom, a girl didn't make it past book two because a girl was exceedingly
bored."

Mara drops her spoon into her bowl. "A mom is not doing this with you.
You're looking for an argument and I'm not going to bite." She pushes away
from the table, picks up her bag, and heads toward the door.

"A mom!" I call out as she steps out into the garage.

She comes back in, one foot still holding the door open. "What?"

"Quick question before you head out to dance your troubles away: Does Dad give you money?"

She frowns. "Excuse me."

"Like in a divorce," I continue, "sometimes one of the parents gets alimony for the kid. Do you get that?"

She hesitates for a moment. "Why are you asking?"

I lift a shoulder. "You never talk about him. I don't know anything about your relationship."

She lets the door fall shut behind her with a light bang. "That's because he abandoned us, Siri."

"But does he pay it?"

"Yes, by law your father was required to send child support until you turned eighteen. You're almost nineteen now, so it stopped coming about a year ago."

"Do you know why he hasn't reached out to me?"

Mara's jaw tightens. "What's bringing this on?"

I take another bite of my apple. "We did a lot of self-reflecting at that retreat."

Mara shifts the bag onto her shoulder, her face scrunching. "I really can't talk about this right now. I have to go. I have rehearsals all day. I'll see you at nine." She slings the door back open and romps out into the garage.

I glance down at my soggy cereal. I guess this was an official divorce between us all. There must have been lawyers and everything. I toss my cereal into the sink.

I smirk as I catch the time on the microwave. It's only 8:20 a.m. I grab Siri's iPhone and dial my number. She picks up on the third ring.

"Are you kidding me?" Her voice is a raspy grumble on the other end of the line.

"So the regular phone function does work! Amazing! Good morning, dear sister, thanks for all the communication last night! Tell me, how doth you get to New York City from your house?"

"It's 5:21 a.m."

"But can you run me through the directions real quick?" I request cheerily.

"Uber. To the train station. Five minutes. Train runs to New York every thirty minutes. Google next time."

"I don't use the Google."

"Then hold down the button and ask Siri." The line goes dead.

Time to get out of this depressing house. A girl is no one here.

With an assist from Siri's precious Google, I find my way to the world-famous Central Park. Along the way I tried to strike up conversation with four different people because talking to strangers is one of the great joys of life. Three of them walked away from me, and one acted like they didn't hear me at all.

Cool, New York. If I wanted to spend time *alone* with my thoughts, I'd have spent the day in Mara's empty house.

Central Park is lush with the warm colors of real, live, not-a-movie-set fall. I walk the paths among lovers and business folk for a bit. I try to take a few selfies, but they're all weird and off-putting because I don't see myself in them. I see ghost-braid Siri me. *Bleh.*

I eventually settle in on a bench alongside the path, pull my notebook out of the backpack I found in Siri's closet, and open to a fresh page. It's time to start writing this elusive new ten-minute set. Yesterday was absolutely batshit. There's definitely material there.

I stare at the page and click my pen on and off ten times fast.

I guess first I have to figure out what the issues were with the original set. I've only performed the ten-minute version—well, half the ten-minute version—once, and that was at the Laugh Drop leading up to the big bomb, so it's hard to really gauge the audience reactions accurately. I've run the five-minute version at eight other open mic gigs.

The other performances weren't all bad. Some of them were even decent and got a good amount of laughs. I semi-bombed sometimes, but I always finished the set despite whatever degree of comedic self-annihilation was occurring in the moment. By performance eight, I was feeling pretty confident in my ability to take on ten minutes. *LOL.*

It's actually really hard to pinpoint where things start to drop off joke-wise in any given performance. What I take away from each imperfect gig is the silent moments. The absence of laughter. I don't remember what came before or after, but I vividly recall the stretching bouts of crippling loneliness that filled each elongated silence. Silence feels like failure. Failure turns me into mindless Jamie zombie spewing random nothing jokes in a desperate attempt to find my way to the end of the set.

There was so much silence during that Laugh Drop performance. Stomach-eviscerating silence.

I rap my pen back and forth against the page. Thirty minutes have passed and all I've written is *NEW SET.* I've been underlining it over and over again. I fling the notebook closed.

iPhone Siri proves surprisingly helpful in locating the New York QCZ (Quality Comedy Zealots) theater. I follow her robot directions to the near-est subway. I haven't been down in a subway station since I was a kid. All the weird smells, the metallic-ness of it all: It used to make me feel like I was boarding an alien spaceship. I loved it.

The subway car that pulls up is packed. Human asses and backs are pressed up against the windows, but the packed-ness is all part of the public transport experience, so I squeeze myself in, and attempt to cling to a pole at the center of the tram. A guy with his back pressed up against it is making it fairly impossible to get a decent grip.

"Excuse me, dude," I say as the doors close. "Kindest regards. Can you get off the pole?"

"Yeah, sorry." Pole Hog Guy hastily rotates toward me as the train jerks forward. I grasp at the precious open metal while he's mid–position change, and he seizes a spot millimeters above my fingers. I maneuver my head so I can properly look up and assess his face.

Shock stabs through me as I see that *he's Zarar.*

Pole Hog Guy is Zarar.

Zarar is standing inches away from me, looking off into the crowd.

As I'm having this darling revelation I do a double take, let go of the pole, and stumble into the people behind me as I'm thrown by the momentum of the train.

"Get off!" Someone shoves me right back. I fall into the metal post, inches from Zarar's neck. He finally glances down, and I watch in a weird panic as his eyes register my presence.

"What the hell are you doing here?!" I squawk.

Yeah, I don't say hello. Not hey. Not *Zarar question mark?* No. I screech out an accusatory statement like a dying chicken.

Zarar's face screws up in confusion. "Siri?"

Crap, I forgot. There's a lot going on right now.

"What am I doing . . . I live in New York," he says plainly. "I flew back from Colorado last night."

He's wearing black jeans, a burgundy T-shirt, and a leather jacket. *Damn it, I love a dude in a leather jacket.*

"I'm headed to my new job . . ." He squints at me. "Didn't you have shorter hair yesterday?"

"We didn't talk yesterday." Now I sound weirdly defensive.

"That doesn't mean I didn't see you around," he adds with a tinge of confusion.

I look up at his cozy brown eyes. "Dude." I gesture around limply with my free hand. "You were supposed to be gone, and I was supposed to be gone, and we were never going to see each other again."

Zarar's head tilts. "You sound like Jamie. What is it with you two and never wanting to see people again?"

I bark a laugh. It took him all of thirty seconds to sense that. "Do you want to know a secret?"

The train screeches to a stop and an onslaught of people floods out around us. He shrugs. ". . . Sure."

I wait for the doors to close. We rattle forward again.

"This is gonna sound weird," I start. ". . . I *am* Jamie." The second the word leaves my mouth, I have to sneeze. It's loud, it's obnoxious, and it's right in Zarar's face.

I smack a hand over my mouth. An *oof* sound escapes Zarar's lips as he stumbles back with closed eyes. He drifts sideways now that he's not holding the pole, and *oh eff,* his face is covered in a spattering of glitter.

"Shit, Z! I am so sorry. I did not feel that coming." I loose a sad little laugh as he wipes his face with his arm. When he blinks and looks up at me a moment later, his eyes bulge, and he pitches backward again, caching himself against a free vertical railing near the door.

I cock my head, smiling now. "What, is there a horrifying snot on my face?"

"What the—what . . . what happened?" he sputters.

"Yeah . . . I sneezed on you, I'm really sorry." An array of panicked emotions passes through his eyes. I walk over to where he's now leaning against the side of the train. "Dude, you're freaking me out a little."

Zarar's looking at me like I'm a new species of tree that just materialized out of thin air. "Are you okay?"

"What the hell just happened?" he bleats again.

"I mean, how else can I explain this . . . I sneezed. I got some shit on your face and I'm real sorry about it. It was very unsexy." I resist the urge to reach up and wipe at the glitter still spackled across his cheeks with my sweatshirt.

"What are you doing in New York?" he demands.

I huff a laugh. "Um, it's a long story—sorry, do you, are you referring to me as Jamie now? You actually believe I'm Jamie?"

Zarar's shaking his head. "Jamie, you were Siri with long hair, and you sneezed and now you're you. It was like a hologram blinked out. Your face changed and your hair evaporated!"

"What?!" My jaw flops open. "You're shitting me. I'm me again?!" I look down at myself.

Of course, I never saw Siri when I looked down, just me, and my newly darkened hair.

I am not prepared for how great it feels to know I look like myself again. I thought I was going to be stuck like that for at least four more days!

I laugh and clap my hands together. "Ah! This is great! Looking like Siri was getting real old, real fast."

Zarar shakes his head again. "You're going to have to explain this more.

Also, I saw that you dyed your hair this color yesterday, and I didn't get to ask you about that either."

"How many stops do you have left?"

"Four," he says.

"Fuck you," I blurt.

Shit, what is wrong with me right now?

"Excuse me?" he asks calmly.

"That's how many stops *I* have left."

His eyes crawl over me. "Do you have some sort of high-tech projector on you?"

I shake my head. "No. Okay. Sit down and buckle in for some loopy-ass weird."

"There are no seat belts; we're on a train. Should I hold on to the pole?"

I nod. "Hold on to the pole."

46. Angst and Improv Practice

SIRI
September 4, Friday Morning
California

I still look like Jamie.

This morning I woke up on the princess bed with pain roiling up and down my back. I found an orange sleeping bag in the closet, so I'll make a nice little floor bed for the rest of my stay.

I've showered the pain to a manageable level, and I'm now sitting in Jamie's hard plastic translucent pink chair next to the orange computer, rereading my catfish draft to Dad. Jamie said to send it, but looking at it now, in the light of day . . . it's making me nauseous. I close out of the draft and get dressed.

Duck Waterfall practice is in thirty minutes, and I'm trying not to be nervous about it. I sort through Jamie's collection of clothes, opting to pull on a pair of magenta overalls and a white off-the-shoulder fringed long-sleeved shirt. I'm excited to see Dawn and try to make up for yesterday, but I'm fairly worried about participating in a practice that I know absolutely nothing about.

No one's in the kitchen, so I set myself to fixing some breakfast. Grams keeps a stocked fridge. She has everything you need for an omelet, so I twirl my way around the room gathering ingredients: eggs, onion, tomato, frying pan, butter, salt, pepper, sliced ham. I also find broccoli in the fridge, which is an unexpected score. I lose myself in the chops and sizzles.

At 10:35 a.m. I'm outside Dawn's with two omelet bagel sandwiches wrapped in tin foil: ham and cheese for myself, broccoli and cheese for her. I'm about to remind myself to smile as I ring the doorbell, when I realize with a start that I'm already doing it! I'm smiling by accident! I can't remember the last time that happened. I smile wider because I'm so happy about it.

The door swings open. Dawn's wearing a blue crop tank today with high-waisted baby blue jeans and a baby blue belt and a baby blue headband. Her eyes have perfect winged eyeliner. She's barefoot and her toes are also painted blue.

"Jame," she says, surprised. "You're almost on time, what's happening?"

"What? I'm late. I'm five minutes late . . ." *I made sure to be late.*

"Well, practice actually starts at 10:45 so you're ten minutes early. Congrat-ulations, the retreat fundamentally altered your internal clock for the better."

I stare at her for a moment. She smiles. "Dude, you can come in . . ."

I nervously take a step inside. A few pairs of shoes are lined up near the door. I hastily bend over and struggle to remove Jamie's yellow boots without hurting my back, while juggling the two sandwiches. I end up flopped on the floor folded over my legs, frantically unlacing the boots with the tinfoil-covered food in my lap while Dawn watches skeptically with her hands on her hips.

"Are you drunk?" she asks as I finally stand up in a pair of Jamie's orange socks.

I shake my head and hold out her breakfast. "I made you an omelet bagel sandwich if you're hungry."

She squints at me. "You made me food? Homemade food? To eat?"

I shrug awkwardly. "Yes?"

"Don't forget to grab a pair of tsinelas if you need them," Dawn directs as two more Duck Waterfall members arrive. There's a whole basket of flip-flops by the door that she has ready for guests who aren't wearing socks.

There are eight of us here for the practice. They all greet me as Jamie, and a lot of them comment on how they like my new hair. I'm not introduced to anyone as they arrive because I supposedly know them.

One typical blond Californian-looking boy-man keeps sneaking glances my way and asking if we can talk after practice. I nod and smile. I think his name is Aaron? His flirtatious attention makes me think of Bran and Celia, and how I've been so distracted the last twelve hours I forgot to stalk their Instagrams on Jamie's ancient computer. It's kind of like I've entered a new dimension where they don't exist. It's nice.

Dawn gathers us all in a U formation. She looks over a few times like she's expecting me to do something. I try to say *Nah, you shine today* with my eyes.

She announces the word "Horn," and looks at me again.

The group repeats the word slowly. "Horn. Horn. Horn."

"Horn," I join in on the third horn. We sound like a scary cult.

Then people just start spewing random intercoursing words.

"Subway," a dark-skinned boy wearing a Dunder Mifflin shirt shouts.

"Meatball parm," a petite pale woman with spiky purple hair responds.

"Chemistry class," Aaron shouts. My eyes bounce from one team member to the next, trying to understand the pattern. Each time someone says a word, they hold eye contact with someone. Sometimes me. I try not to look as stupid as I feel. Everyone's constantly looking at each other to make eye contact instead of looking away to avoid it. *It's extremely intimidating.*

"Benjamin Franklin." A tall, white, skinny, freckled guy with a man-ponytail giggles.

"Benjamin Franklin working at Subway!" Aaron counters. He looks at me, seemingly for approval.

Dawn hops in. "The Founding Fathers founding Subway the sandwich company!" She says it with confidence. Authority.

"Yes!" the others chorus. "Yes!" I throw in belatedly, nodding along with their overeager enthusiasm. Some of them throw in commentary of what the Founding Fathers founding Subway would be like. It's a struggle to match their energy levels through the many layers of confusion fogging my comprehension.

Clearly, they're all following some sort of pattern, and I am not in the know.

"Horn!" Dawn starts again, her eyes searching mine now. *What the hell are we doing?!*

My eyes fall to her long perfectly styled tossed waves. "Hair model!" I shout blindly.

The woman with the purple hair pipes up, "Rapunzel!"

We play this weird game three times, and then everyone moves back against the wall of Dawn's spacious living room. I've never felt like more of a floundering idiot.

They're performing what feels like a choreographed act, and I haven't learned the steps. In sets of two, the team members get off the wall and start performing scenes loosely related to the phrases yelled out during the weird cult shouting game.

How do they know which ideas to use? How do they decide who should step off the wall and who stays here? Dawn keeps throwing me questioning looks. Maybe other members are too, but I don't notice them as much because my eyes follow Dawn around wherever she goes, and everything she says takes root in my mind and settles there and makes me like her more. It's subtle, but it's clear she's in control here. She's the team leader. When she says something, everyone takes it in. And when she speaks, it's always simultaneously thoughtful, spontaneous, and hilarious.

I wonder how Jamie is with these people. Is she commanding? Do they listen to her? She's probably usually the one to take the lead, judging by the way Dawn checks in with me every few minutes with her eyes. I hang against the wall throughout the "performance" until Dawn physically yanks me off and out onto the living room floor.

She puts on an English accent. "Yes, I'll have a six-inch redcoat with mustard and olives."

I look at her and back at the other teammates nervously.

"Hello?" Dawn says in a flustered British way.

I put on my own sad version of a British accent. "Um, I don't work here. I'm waiting for the manager because apparently they don't serve," I use air quotes, "'Lobsters' . . . I'm not a lobster, I'm clearly a human man." I gulp, staring nervously into Dawn's eyes.

Aaron jumps out off the wall. "Howdy, y'all, I'm the manager here. How can I help you folks?" He looks to Dawn. "Oh dang. George, you better get out here, we gotta another two. How many times I gotta tell y'all we don't serve no Brits?" The purple-haired woman comes into the scene, presumably to play George.

"Why not?" I ask, fake-annoyed.

"Taxation without representation," Aaron exclaims.

Dawn rolls her eyes. "It's been three hundred years, man. You won, make me a sandwich."

A smile breaks across my face, but I tamper it down, trying not to break "character." I let Dawn lead the scene and follow along. It's actually a little fun.

By the end of the Gerald (this is what Dawn calls the performance, I don't know why), it's apparent that the team is baffled by my behavior; they're all shooting me bewildered looks.

When practice is over, I sit with my head hung on the couch as everyone puts on their shoes and trickles out. I can feel the disappointment radiating off of each individual person as they say goodbye to me.

"I'm sorry," I tell them over and over. "I'm just having an off day."

These people must feed off Jamie like they feed off Dawn when she's performing. I'd imagine the team is much stronger when there are two powerhouses to bounce off of.

Nerves snap at my stomach as Dawn closes the door behind the last team member. She spins around with crossed arms and a stern expression.

"Okay, Jame, speak. What the hell is going on? The most active member of the team does nothing her first practice back? You didn't even join the group game? You looked like you've never seen a Gerald before, let alone performed in one!"

She heaves a weighty breath and runs her hands down her face. "I want to help you, but you're giving me nothing here. I've been holding this up on my own longer than just this past week. You've been drifting for a while now, letting me plan every practice, letting me lecture the people who aren't being team players, letting me call and scold the people who miss practice. I'm the one who hustles for potential auditions or gigs."

I stare at her from the couch, soaking up every last drop of secondhand shame.

"I know you're going through something," she continues, "but I can't keep this afloat by myself with no input or support! We need your energy. We need your loud unfiltered brain. We're supposed to be in this together." Her words are so passionate and full of hurt.

I frown, trying not to cry. Her eyebrows come down. "Where are you?" she asks, striding closer. "What are you doing with your face?"

I drop my head into my hands. Where do I even begin?

After a moment she reaches out and touches my arm. I look up to find her sitting on the couch with me. Her expression has softened. "Are you crying? Jesus, Jamie, I haven't seen you cry since you were nine."

And now I'm sobbing.

She puts her arm around me. "Jame. Talk to me," she says softly.

I lift my head and look into her pretty pitch-dark eyes with their perfect liner. "Dawn," I blubber, "I'm not Jamie. My name is Siri."

And then I slobber-sneeze in her face.

And holy intercourse, I snotted glitter all over her!

I am mortification incarnate. Dawn blinks and screams bloody murder, scrambling away from me. I keel over and cycle into a bout of hysterical sobs. When I look up, Dawn's glaring at me with a vase hoisted menacingly above her head.

"Who are you?" she yells. "And why did you look like Jamie? What have you done with her?! Are you a body snatcher? Am I being punked? Is Jamie in the next room? Is this like *Men in Black*? IS SOMEONE ELSE HERE WITH YOU?"

"What?" I mumble, looking around. "No!"

"Don't test me. I'm a green belt in karate and I know that's not that impressive, but I just decided to start a few years ago—don't think I can't do damage!"

"Please don't hurt me!" I yelp, throwing my hands up. "I don't have any belts! Some weird body-switch thing happened between me and Jamie!"

"Well, it's not happening anymore! Whatever weird spy technology you're using must have died! I knew that retreat was sketchy!"

We hold at a weird standoff for ten seconds, me with my hands up and Dawn with her vase, until something clicks in my brain.

"Wait . . . I don't look like her anymore?" I slowly stand.

There's a bathroom off the living room, and I robot-run in to look in the mirror, hope soaring in my chest. *Thank god! I can stop pretending with Dad and Grams and just be—*

My face drops when I still see blond-haired Jamie. A moment later Dawn appears in the doorframe, now holding the vase on her hip like it's a toddler. She scrutinizes my reflection.

"You kinda look like her . . . but your hair is way less damaged, you have no nose ring, and your face is different . . . You have a beauty mark. Are you taller? Who are you?"

Apparently, she can see the actual me, but I can't. A flash of anger sears over my skin as I meet her eyes through the mirror. "I'm the sister she abandoned fourteen years ago."

The vase slips from Dawn's fingers and crashes into pieces at her feet.

47. A Girl Fancies Zarar

JAMIE
September 4, Friday Afternoon
New York City

Zarar and I spill out of the train and start the hike up to ground level.

"So . . ." he starts, straightforward and even-toned as ever. "You're saying you've been using the last four days to prepare to switch places with your sister. And on the final day of the retreat, you encountered a magical glitter bomb, and later when you woke up on the plane to New Jersey, you were wearing Siri's reflection, but when you looked down at yourself, you saw yourself. And your theory is that happy haunted magic knew what you needed to make your farfetched Parent Confrontation Trap plan work, so it dusted you and Siri with mirage magic and now you're successfully living as her with your mom who you haven't seen in fourteen years, and you intend to use this week to mildly torture her?"

I'm wheezing, listening to him say it aloud. "Yep. I also intend to mine the experience for new set material. If I can't turn this into something amazing, then I truly am barking up the wrong career." I try not to think about the infuriatingly blank *New Set* page in my notebook . . . and fail.

Zarar purses his lips. "I don't know how to process the magic bit of all this."

"No shit. I don't know how to process the magic bit either, but here we be. You saw it with your own two lovely brown eyes."

"I don't think you're barking up the wrong career," he adds.

"Thanks, Z. We'll see."

When we finally hit street level, Zarar leads us off to the side of the subway entrance, and we come to a stop. I exhale a pre-goodbye breath. My hands automatically search for pockets along Siri's yoga pants and come up uncomfortably empty.

"Well, time for me to go my own way." I scrunch my shoulders to my ears.

"I loved running into you," Zarar says. The left end of his mouth turns up.

I beam and tolerate a cheesy-ass moment where we look at each other. It's always nice to have someone around who *you know* enjoys your company, but it's especially nice right now. In New York. Alone. Living in a house with my mother who pretends I don't exist.

"We're in the same city for at least three days," Zarar comments.

"Except we're not. I'm out in Jersey."

"Okay, we're on the same coast for the next three days," he corrects.

I nod. "We are."

"So, will you go out with me while you're here?" The edge of his mouth turns up again.

My heart pounds excitedly. I urge it to calm the fuck down.

"If we go out as friends," I tell him.

Z looks toward the sky, and lets his eyes fall back to mine. "Okay."

"Okay." We stare at each other for another moment.

Zarar feels like a lifeboat in a sea of distrust. I want him on my side. I want him to talk to when I need someone to talk to. To hang out with when I'm not working Parent Confrontation Trap bullshit. I need an ally over here.

"You're going to need my number, then," I snark.

"Finally."

I smile harder. "What's your number, Zarar?"

I punch it into Siri's iPhone and press send. He pulls his phone from his pocket and I snatch it from his hands. "Thank you."

I add myself as Your Friendly Neighborhood Jamie. It takes me an embarrassingly long time to do. One day I will conquer the intricate labyrinth that is the iPhone keypad.

Zarar takes the phone back from my outstretched hand. "Phone thief."

"That's what my coworkers call me."

"Do they?"

I grin. "No."

"One of my new jobs is having a rooftop thing Sunday night. Come with me?"

"A rooftop thing—how swanky."

"Is that a yes?"

I put a hand on his arm. "It's a yes, Z. Text me." I drop my hand and take a step in the direction of QCZ. "I'm this way."

His brows rise. "I'm that way too."

I serve him some side-eye as he continues to walk with me. "Are you stalking me or are you really this way?"

"I am really this way."

I grin at the ground, watching other feet go by ours. I'm wearing Siri's stark-white sneakers. She has three pairs of them in her closet. Zarar's wearing stylish black boots.

I glance up at him. "You've got mad style, Z."

He pulls a sort of bashful expression. "Thank you. One of the many things I enjoy is being well dressed."

I nod appreciatively and hang a left at the next corner. Zarar hangs it with me.

"Okay, I'm just a block farther this way," I explain.

Zarar stops, lightly taking my arm to stop me as well. "I'm also a block this way."

We're standing in front of a diner that looks like it's straight out of *Men in Black*.

I shoot him a suspicious look. "Where the hell, exactly, are you working?"

"QCZ theater," he says.

"Stop it. No, you're not."

"I am. Part-time. I'm working there three days a week, and three days a week at a music production company. Both are internships, but I get paid a bit." He shrugs. "I had my first session at the production company this morning. I just came from the studio."

I drop my head in my hands. "QCZ is where I'm heading, Zarar. Fuck."

He's quiet until I look up again. "Why do you say that like it's a bad thing?"

Ugh, because you don't actually want to spend this much time with me. I blow out an exaggerated breath and shake my head.

"It's not a bad thing. I'm a hoot." I loop my arm into his.

Zarar's mouth rises again.

"I'm planning to hit up this theater multiple times these next four days to catch as many shows as I can before heading back to the West Coast. Starting tonight."

"I'm working tickets."

"I need to study the schedule."

He gestures forward. "Shall we?"

I'm staring at the QCZ schedule posted next to the ticket window, but I'm having trouble taking it in, because what the hell were the chances that I'd run into Zarar on the subway and we'd be headed to the same exact destination?

He's zipping around the theater, talking to the manager and learning how things work and what his responsibilities will be. He's going to be taking the Improv 101 course they offer, for free, which is a pretty nice deal. I've been loitering here in the lobby for about fifteen minutes now. There's a 7 p.m. show tonight, like I thought. I'm sure Z can slip me in for free, which will be nice. *A girl isn't working right now and she's broke.*

There's a clatter as Zarar reappears behind the ticket booth. "You do comedy!" he says in greeting.

I bring up a close-lipped *I don't like that you know that* smile. "Yep. I do."

"The manager was just telling me that they do open mic night for stand-ups on Saturdays. I should sign you up for a ten-minute slot tomorrow so you can give it another go."

I shake my head. "I don't have my shit together yet."

He leans forward on the ticket counter. "What do you mean by that?"

"I haven't figured out where I went wrong with my set yet."

"How do you plan on figuring it out?"

I throw my hands up and let them fall to my sides. "I don't know, Zarar. I'm trying to figure *that* out."

"We can work on it together, tomorrow, beforehand. It'll help me learn more about comedy."

"I don't know if I want anyone else's opinions on it right now . . ." I trail off, letting my gaze wander down to my feet.

"Isn't the whole point of a comedy set to get a group of people's general opinion on your material?" he asks pointedly.

I narrow my eyes.

"Wouldn't it be beneficial to get the opinions of people you know, so you can better predict the crowd's opinion beforehand? And if you don't like the opinions of the people you know . . . can't you use said bad opinions to fuel the bits in your set?"

Why does that make sense?

"I thought you were doing a whole acting thing this quarter, not comedy."

Zarar tilts his head. "I'm taking a serious acting class too. I'm doing this full throttle. Improv class, acting class, working here, and because I couldn't arrange the timing perfectly, I'm also dabbling in music production these next four months. It works out because this job is evenings and that job is during the day. Acting class and improv class are only once a week."

Wow. I feel strangely proud of this guy I've known for seven days. "You're going to be a super busy dude. I don't think you have time to add workshopping my set to that schedule."

"It'll be the highlight of my schedule," he says. "I'm off tomorrow during the day. Also, I got you a ticket to the 7 p.m. show tonight. You can go get dinner and come back. I'll be here."

I take a beat to study the red-carpeted floor. He really isn't letting me deflect this, and I don't know how to deal with that.

I also . . . kind of like it.

"Z, one afternoon is hardly enough time to workshop a set."

"Jamie, you don't need time, you need a little push."

My head droops sideways toward my shoulder like a corpse in a zombie apocalypse. "I don't need a fucking push."

His mouth kicks up again. Why is that quarter smile so much sexier than a full one? "I misspoke. You don't need a push, you want a push."

I swallow hard, glaring at him now. "Did you already sign me up or something?"

He picks a clipboard up from somewhere behind the ticket window. "I'm doing it now."

"I have a dinner thing tomorrow with my mom."

His eyes flit up. "Your slot is at midnight."

Damn it. We stare at each other for a beat. "I might be able to fit it in." I pivot and tromp out the door feeling naked.

As I step outside, Siri's phone starts having a seizure in my backpack. I yank the bag off and fish it out. My own number glows across the screen.

"Pail?" I ask carefully.

"JAMIE?" Dawn's voice roars over the line with a powerful grace.

My throat squeezes shut. "Dawn?"

"You have a fucking sister?!" she booms.

Shit. I hobble to the nearest city bench. There's a woman sitting on one end of it, but I plop down anyway. "I'm sorry! I haven't talked about her to anyone, Dawn!"

Dawn is crying on the other end of the line. "I'm supposed to be your best friend, and instead of communicating in any clear way, after abandoning me without notice to run Duck Waterfall alone this week, you sent a stranger into my life to impersonate you."

She pauses, catching her breath.

"Can you see how messed up that is? There's a stranger in my house who you led me to believe was you. Do you know how much of a dick that makes you? You couldn't call me with a heads-up about your asinine plan?"

"Dawn, I—"

"Don't you dare tell me this was supposed to be funny."

"No, I—"

"I'm not ready to listen to you right now. I've been dishing my life out to a stranger for the last twenty-four hours!"

"She's not—"

"Nope sorry. I can't." The line goes dead.

I pull the phone down in front of my face. "Fuck!"

The woman on the other end of the bench shoots me a dirty look and walks away. I squeeze my eyes shut and punch the call back button.

"Hello?" comes Siri's quiet voice.

"I told you to let me tell Dawn! You were supposed to dial me and hand her the freaking phone."

"Sorry, Jamie—"

"Can you put Dawn back on? Are you still with her?"

"She . . ." There's a pause. "She doesn't want to talk to you right now. I'm sorry . . . this is awkward."

Dawn will always talk to me. We don't *not talk* to each other. She's the only person I know will always have my back. She's the only person who will call me out for being an ass and work through it on the spot instead of cutting me out—

I hang up as nausea roils through me. I put a hand over my mouth.

No! This isn't a thing I do now. Please no— I heave forward and toss my lunch all over Siri's freakishly white sneakers.

48. Angst and Empathy

Dawn and I have been sitting on her couch in silence for the last ten minutes.

"I'm really, really sorry for misleading you," I finally say. "I feel absolutely terrible."

Dawn slumps forward. "This is all so weird. I don't know how I'm supposed to react. I feel so stupid."

I shake my head adamantly. "You're not stupid. Remember how you aced that anatomy test and also went on four dates this week?"

She snorts.

"I've only known you for twenty-four hours, and I already think you're incredible."

"Uh-huh."

"I do! For starters, your baby blue eyeshadow and winged eyeliner are perfect."

Dawn rolls her eyes.

"They are," I insist.

She sighs. "My ex was a beauty guru. I was trained by an extremely judgmental professional."

"Oh." I press my lips together. "I'm sorry . . ."

We're silent for a moment.

"I don't really follow beauty gurus," I say quietly. "But I had a major crush on this one girl who was big on YouTube when I was in high school. I watched her tutorials religiously . . . and I didn't learn anything. It takes skill to acquire those eye makeup capabilities, not just a teacher."

Dawn studies me curiously. "Hm. It's so weird to see someone who's not Jamie . . . dressed like her." She sniffles. "It's really messing with my brain. If we're going to continue hanging out, I'm going to need you to be you."

I am genuinely shocked. "I—Wa—You want to keep hanging out with me?"

She shrugs. "I mean, I'd like to get to know my best friend's long-lost sister."

"I—I'd love that."

A muffled sob slips out of Dawn, and her face crumples in on itself again. I scoot over and pull her into a hug, the sweet scent of her hair tickling my nose.

"I'm sorry." I hold on to her for an extra moment before pulling away.

"You know," Dawn says as she swipes away her tears, "Jamie's not a hugger. We high-five when she wants to get across the sentiment of a hug."

My mouth pops open. "I'm so sorry—"

She waves me off. "No, it's fine. It was a great hug; I'm just sharing."

I frown. "I guess that's why I was straight up shut down at the airport when I kind of raised my arms."

Dawn nods. "She's a strange one."

I laugh. "Tell me about it."

Dawn is still watching me carefully, like she's afraid I'll shape-shift again into yet another stranger. It's making me hyperaware of my movements.

"You laugh different. Some of your facial features are freakishly similar. But you use them differently. It's unsettling." Dawn shakes her head, her eyes clearing and refocusing on mine. "I don't want to seem rude, but . . . I think I have to kick you out. I need some time to process all this. Would you mind giving me some time alone?"

I leap up from the couch. "Of course, I'm sorry, I didn't mean to overstay my welcome."

Dawn shakes her head. "It's okay, Siri. I wasn't lying, I'm down to hang out. But I just had a huge fight with Jamie and—"

"You need a second. I get it. I completely get it." I hustle toward the door and start pulling on Jamie's yellow boots.

"We can hang later. If you want . . . and you can fill me in on all the ludicrous details of what just happened."

I nod like an overeager intern. "Okay. Yes, I'd like that. Thanks, Dawn. You're like . . . really cool."

She nods once. "I know I am, thank you."

I make my way up to Jamie's room and carefully lie on her bed, feeling jittery and excited. Dawn wants to get to know *me*.

I jolt back upright. I never told Jamie about the Timothée Chalamet gig. *It's tomorrow.*

I draft out a text and hesitate with my finger over the send button.

Me: Bucket, huge news, call me ASAP.

What if Jamie asks me to switch back?

I'm not ready to go back yet, and based on my reflection right now, I'm pretty sure I still look like her to everyone other than Dawn.

A bell goes off in my brain: *Tell just one, they'll see the light.*

That's a line from the poem. That's what happened! Which means we still have three more days with the glamour magic.

And Jamie can't be Jamie tomorrow. So sending this text without a plan is going to cause unneeded Jamie panic.

I backspace the text and climb over to the computer where my email draft to Dad is still waiting to go out. I BCC Jamie and press send. *At least I did that.*

No one appears to be home downstairs so I head into the kitchen and take out a bunch of ingredients from a recipe I looked up last night on the computer.

As I'm sleuthing around thinking about Jamie, Timothée Chalamet, and Dawn, an idea strikes. I send Dawn a quick text.

Me: I'm so sorry! I know you said you needed space, I don't mean to be a clingy annoying person, but I kind of have an SOS. Can you possibly come over for dinner tonight? No one's here. I'm cooking!

She responds quickly.

Dawn: Can you cook it over here?

49. A Girl Is Questioning Everything

JAMIE
September 4, Friday Night
New Jersey

The train back to Jersey jangles wildly past another stop. Earlier I chucked Siri's scary white shoes and bought myself some red boots with our mom's credit card that Siri has permission to use for groceries and emergencies.

'Twas a vomit emergency.

Whilst shopping, I received three more compliments on my "gorgeous long hair." It would appear that Zarar is the only one who can see through the damn mirage magic.

I grabbed sustenance and headed back to QCZ for the 7 p.m. show. It was fun, but I had trouble actually enjoying it knowing that Dawn was over in California wanting nothing to do with me.

This group, Metal Spacerat, really stood out tonight. One of their scenes really wasn't hitting, and they had to continue it three more times—that's how an improv Gerald works. It was failing, no one was laughing, but they doubled down, kept on it, and toward the end of the second iteration of the scene, they found a groove, and it got good. They worked together, found the funny, and saved the beat.

I know how to do this. I've been in loads of failing scenes. I've doubled down a million times over: but I do it knowing my team is up there with me to back me up, and offer whatever support I need in the moment.

It's so different being up there alone with a microphone, with no one but yourself to count on.

Zarar's point about being able to utilize feedback, good or bad, irrelevant or relevant, to enhance the set was . . . a really good one. And his comment about feedback in general was annoyingly accurate.

I've been so worried about how people will perceive me personally, as someone who's trying to pursue stand-up, that I haven't been gauging the idea of feedback . . . logically.

What would Dawn have thought if she saw me bomb at the Laugh Drop? Would she really have left thinking *Jamie is an unfunny loser who should never perform again?*

What would it have been like if I had her there in the audience? Would it feel like I was there with my team? Like my support was just in a different area of the room?

Have I wasted a shitload of time thinking about this the wrong way?

Dawn has great taste. If any portion of the set wasn't working, she'd probably help me find my footing with it *just like she does when she's on stage with me.*

I pull out Siri's cell and dial Dawn. It goes straight to voicemail after one ring.

A horrible gutless feeling washes through me. That kind you get when you're a kid and you lose track of your parent in a public place. How do I fix this if she won't talk to me? This doesn't happen with us!

I tap through some missed texts from my mother. She checked in around two to tell me she'll be home around eleven. I never responded so there's a string of follow-up texts throughout the rest of the afternoon and evening.

It's 11:16 when Mara opens the door from the garage to the kitchen and flips on the light.

I'm sitting at the table, staring at her with my hands folded.

"Ah!" Mara falls sideways into the wall with a hand to her chest.

I keep my features neutral. Somber. Still. I beat her home, and I've been prepped here to scare her for forty-five minutes.

Leave a girl alone in the dark at a table for thirty minutes, waiting to freak out her mother, and she'll be exhausted. Leave her for forty-five minutes, and she'll start to actually feel like a serial killer.

"What on earth are you doing down here with the lights off?!"

"Sitting."

"In the dark?!"

I let the silence stretch for a beat. "I've been seeing Jamie again," I whisper.

"Ja—" A look of terror crosses Mara's face. "Wha—" She takes a nervous breath. "When, where? Was she the, the same as before?"

"No." I tilt my head. "Older. I saw her in my room next to the bed this morning, and then again an hour ago in the living room. She seems upset."

Mara seats herself at the table, bag still slung across her chest. She runs her fingers up the back of her head, tracing the hair into her bun as if a strand had fallen out of place. "You didn't mention that this morning."

I raise my shoulders a millimeter, executing the smallest shrug of all time. "I wasn't sure how to bring it up. I know it upsets you."

Her eyes dart around. "Okay, we'll make an appointment with your old therapist."

I catch her flighty pupils. "Do you hate Jamie?"

Mara stands from the table nervously. "Where were you today?"

Wow. Completely disregard the question. I push out of my seat. "Space, trying out the whole astronaut thing as a potential career option."

Once I'm back in Siri's room I pull out her iPhone. I have a new text waiting.

Zarar: These shows are fun

Me: They're the most fun. We get a bad rep on mainstream media, but you'll never have as much fun as you do at a good improv show

Zarar: I thought you did stand-up?

Me: I want to do stand-up, but I do-do improv ;-) My team is called Duck Waterfall. Much more fun to be up there with people you love than up there alone

Zarar: I'd love to see Duck Waterfall someday and meet these people you love

Me: They're pretty great. If you're ever in LA.

Zarar: I'm looking forward to seeing you tomorrow

I smile at the phone. This dude is such a cheeseball.

Me: We doing lunch?

Zarar: Meet me outside the diner next to QCZ?

Me: You got it, dude. I'm kinda really glad you're out here in the tri-state area with me.

The phone bubbles next to his name as he types a response.

Zarar: I live here, you're the one who's out here with me. I'm glad you have a nonsensical sense of humor and decided it would be great comedy to try to avenge you and your sister's lack of bond through a weird Parent Trap-like plot that's definitely going to fall apart. It's a little rash but it's something you needed to do. You dive headfirst into life and I admire that. I'm glad you happened to run into me along the way. More to add to our epic story. I still like you, James Federov. I'm not going anywhere.

I blink at his essay, my heart dancing around pointlessly in my chest. How does he say things like this with absolutely no regard for how embarrassing it sounds?

The phone chimes again before I can send a response.

A new text from Papa? He texts?

Papa: How are you doing, Siri? Want to come over for a game of chess?

As far as I can tell, Papa is Siri's best and only friend. It makes me want to give those bitches at the ballet company a piece of my mind.

The phone pings again. Another text. This one from George?

George: Siri, I heard you've been having a hard time since you got back. I'm looking forward to spending some time with you and your mom at dinner on Friday. She told me you're making that Greek casserole we all loved. You're really becoming quite the chef. I'm proud of you. I hope you know if you want to talk, I'm always here.

I tap out of the message stream. What the hell? Did Mara send out an SOS or something?

The phone pings again. This one from Gill, the cute, nerdy, pre-law, unofficial stepbrother.

Gill: Hey, Siri, it's been too long. I heard we're having dinner later this week though. How are you doing?

Mara needs to grow some balls and come talk to me herself. I tap out and call Dawn again. When it goes to voicemail, I chuck the phone to the end of the bed.

A second later I crawl over, retrieve it, and reopen my thread with Zarar. I hate spending so much time staring at this thing, but I'm starting to understand why Siri feels so attached.

I draft out a needy text that I would normally never send.

Me: I'm in the midst of some family drama. Want to dissect it with me?

I send it. A moment later Zarar calls.

"What's going on?" he asks.

I roll off the side of the bed and curl up on the floor to give him the latest.

50. Angst and Pizza Hangs

Dawn answers the door, no longer dressed, but wearing a robe covered in a pattern of yellow ducks and pajamas like she's showered and gotten ready for bed since we last talked. Her pajamas are color coordinated, a faded baby yellow color. Her hair is pushed back in a matching headband. She's not wearing any makeup. She still looks gorgeous.

"Hi!" I squeak. "Thanks for inviting me."

"Long time no see," she says quietly as I step into the house and shove off the yellow boots. I didn't lace them up this time. "What's all that?" She points to my bags.

"Oh, ingredients for dinner."

"What are we having?"

"Homemade pizza?" I say hesitantly.

A sad, breathy laugh falls out of her.

"Do you not want . . . I thought you—"

"No, no, that's great, okay." We head through the living room. "Is there really a big SOS, or were you overwhelmed with a desperate need to share the full scoop re: body snatcher–gate?"

We round the corner into a lovely pink and white kitchen. It's like a clean, pristine lady cave.

213

"Um, there is an SOS, but I can also tell you about . . . body snatcher–gate." I put the groceries on the gray marble island at the center of the area and glance around. "Do you have parents?"

Dawn circles the island so she's standing across from me. "Yeah, my mom's at work. It's just the two of us." She ducks down, opens a cabinet, and returns holding a bottle of wine and two glasses.

"Oh." I start unloading ingredients, eyeing the wine. *Wine feels romantic.* "Should we make her a pizza too?"

Dawn shakes her head. "She was called into the hospital for emergency reconstructive surgery; she won't be home till late."

"Oh, whoa. Does she get called in for stuff like that a lot?" I start rummaging through Dawn's cabinets and grabbing different cooking tools as I come across them. I find some wax paper and spread a large piece over the counter.

Dawn watches me for a second, her mouth flipping up in a small smile. "Um, yeah, every so often. She's a plastic surgeon so she does the majority of her surgeries during business hours, but she gets called in whenever there's an emergency that requires her skill set. She's doing facial reconstructive surgery for someone who was in a car accident."

My mouth falls open. "Holy excrement. That's intense."

Dawn nods. "Yeah, she's kind of a badass." She uncorks the wine and starts pouring it out.

"Is holy excrement like holy shit?" Dawn asks as she fills a second glass.

I busy my hands measuring ingredients. "Um yeah, my mom has a thing with bad words, she uses . . . other words instead and has ever since I can remember. I guess I'm more comfortable saying them than the actual curses."

I glance up nervously and find Dawn biting her lip. It momentarily pulls all my focus.

"That is absolutely fucking adorable," she says.

My cheeks burn, and I reflexively reach up to cover my face with my hand. In doing so I get flour all over my forehead. *Excrement.* "My mom's a nerd," I mumble, subtly swiping at my face.

Dawn leans forward across the counter. "Do you have a replacement for the f-word?"

214

I dump warm water and instant yeast into the mixing bowl. "Intercourse," I say to the bowl.

Rich, deep laughter bubbles out of Dawn. It's one of those laughs that's so fun, you can't help but join in. I giggle with her. I guess it is kind of funny.

Dawn is beaming at me now. "I'm using that from now on, your mom's an intercourse-ing comedic genius, Siri. Do you say"—she puts on an angry voice—"*Intercourse you*."

My face heats as I nod through a bout of silent laughter. "Yeah," I admit.

"Do you just yell *INTERCOURSE* when something really shit happens?"

I have to consciously stop myself from hunching over as my abs convulse so I don't hurt my back. "Sometimes," I breathe quietly.

Dawn pushes the second wine glass across the counter to me. "Wow, this is the best thing I've heard all week. When something's really great do you ever just scream"—she stands up out of her seat and holds her glass up in the air—"INTERCOURSE, YEAH!"

I shake my head now, tears of laughter building in my eyes.

"It's so sex positive!" Dawn bursts.

We're both howling. When I regain my composure, I start kneading the dough, now sporting a grin I can't quite manage to tame.

Dawn watches me across the table. "You look so different now compared to earlier—in a good way." She points at me with her wine glass.

I've changed into the most "me" outfit I could find: a white sleeveless shirt and black yoga pants Jamie had in the back of her closet.

I shrug, trying not to look too flattered, but I'm secretly stupidly excited that she thinks so. "I tried to dress more like myself."

She raises a shoulder. "It's not just that. You look more comfortable."

My smile widens. I focus on pushing this giggly energy into kneading the dough.

"Do you not like wine?" Dawn asks after a moment. I glance up at my untouched wine glass.

"I've never actually dabbled in wine or alcohol at all because I'm an athlete . . ."

Her expression warps into a knowing smile. "Ah, that makes sense."

I pull over the garlic and crush into it. "What makes sense?"

"That you're an athlete. You look like one. You have really nice arms."

Okay, I'm definitely blushing now. I concentrate on not chopping off my fingers. "Thanks. Um, I was a ballerina up until a few months ago. I was recently injured, and I, well, I won't be able to go back."

We're quiet for a beat, listening to my knife hit the cutting board. *Way to dampen the mood.*

"I'm sorry, that sounds really shit," Dawn says.

"It is," I say without looking up from the knife.

Dawn slips off her stool and comes over to my side of the counter. She pulls out another knife and a second cutting board. "What can I chop to help?"

"Um, if you want to do these." I push over the bowls of toppings I prepared.

She sizes up the food thoughtfully. "While we chop . . . could you possibly walk me through the saga of what happened with you and Jamie? Like, start at the beginning. Wait, how old are you? Older or younger?"

I huff a little laugh. "I'll be nineteen in two months."

She nods. "Slightly younger, cool. How the hell did this switcheroo *excrement* happen?"

As we slice basil, tomatoes, mushrooms, spinach, olives, and broccoli, I tell Dawn everything that's gone down between Jamie, my parents, and me. Everything except the bit about my mom telling me Jamie was imaginary. I'm scared to portray her in such a negative light. I want Dawn to think I was raised by a decent person. Because Mom is a decent person. She cares, she's just terrible at showing it. The more I think about her, the more I'm determined to believe she was forced to make the decisions she did.

Dawn listens, empathizing at all the right bits. Her attentiveness is such a stark contradiction to Jamie, who I felt itching to interject and ask things at every turn of any story I shared with her. Dawn doesn't even butt in during the off-the-wall magic parts, which is extremely impressive. Toward the end of my tale, as I'm stirring the homemade sauce over the stove, I start crying. I've been trying really hard not to, but who was I kidding. I'm a human fountain; this was inevitable.

"It's completely reasonable for you to be upset. Jamie's pushed all this on you in a way that didn't really leave you with much of a choice," Dawn reassures me. She grabs my dangling non-sauce-stirring hand for a moment and squeezes it gently before letting go.

How did someone as abrasive as Jamie manage to lock down the nicest human in the world as a best friend?

I turn the stove on low. "So the SOS . . . last night, when I got here, I found out this amazing news from my dad about Jamie. And I still haven't told her."

"Because you're mad at her," Dawn fills in with a smile. She nods to the pot. "How much longer we got on that?"

I put the top on the sauce. "It's done, but it's gonna be thirty more minutes before we can roll the dough and put the pizza together."

"Okay, want to sit down?"

We pad over to the kitchen table. Dawn brings my untouched wine over with her own. She shifts her chair toward mine and holds her glass aloft. "To Jamie, for bringing this hang together."

I pick up my glass. "To Jamie." Dawn takes a sip of hers and watches me expectantly.

I brave a small sip and immediately spit it back into the glass, sticking my tongue out and closing my right eye in a weird spasm. "Oh wow, Dawn, that's disgusting."

Dawn's laughing. "Thank you. I'll treasure that hot take forever."

"So, this news my dad shared."

She nods. "Yeah?"

"Um." I swirl the wine for a moment before meeting Dawn's eyes. "My dad booked Jamie a stand-up gig at a party Timothée Chalamet is throwing tomorrow. And Jamie and I aren't switching back till Tuesday. Do you think we could go on as Duck Waterfall?"

Dawn's face goes slack. Her brain takes five seconds to reboot before she explodes into action, rising abruptly from the kitchen chair.

"Are you kidding me? A gig at Timothée Chalamet's house?! Siri! We need to get you into improv express training right now if we're going to perform for Timothée fucking intercoursing Chalamet tomorrow! Cancel all your plans."

I snort. "I don't have any plans."

She glances at the clock. "We still have twenty minutes before pizza rolling, let's go upstairs. I have to get dressed if we're going to be working tonight. I can't teach in a robe! Timothée Chalamet! Get up, hurry!"

Dawn's in her closet. I'm waiting on her pastel rainbow-striped comforter. Her room is amazing. Each wall is painted a different pastel color and she's decorated them with artsy pictures of ice cream. Coming in here was like walking into a dream cloud.

Dawn gave me her iPhone to play with while she gets dressed, so I spend a second scrolling through Bran and Celia's Instagram feeds. I stop on Celia's newest picture. Bran and Celia selfie-ing at the top of the Empire State Building. Bran is kissing Celia, and Celia's eyes are slightly open, looking sideways at the camera.

Having my own adorable kissy picture has always been a sort of stupid dream of mine. When Bran and I started dating I thought: *I'm finally going to get the picture!* I've imagined it as a sort of rite of passage for a new couple— the kissing post! But we never took one. I was always too self-conscious to ask. Now here they are on Instagram, doing my picture without me.

Dawn comes up over my shoulder to see what I'm staring at. "Wow, could his nose be any more basic? I mean come on, Ken and Henry Cavill wore it best, find your own look."

A laugh blows out of me. Dawn sits next to me on the edge of the bed.

"Am I right in assuming one of those humans is an ex?"

I hand her back the phone. "How'd you know?"

She grins. "You had resting ex-stalking face."

I shake my head, smiling. "That's not a thing."

"It totally is, I know it well." She taps out of Instagram. "Um, before we go any further with our improv express prep, I think you have to call Jamie and tell her about her dad and the gig." Dawn presses her lips together. "It's the right thing to do. She has to know. And if he said anything else about her comedy stuff, and how he got the gig for her, she needs to know that too."

I frown down at her rainbow bedspread. My hand has started nervously marking out a ballet combo over the comforter. "Yeah, okay . . . heads-up, I might start crying again."

I look back up and Dawn smiles at me. "That's fine, you're a gorgeous crier."

I scoff at that, but my heart eats it up.

Dawn's changed into a fantastic Creamsicle orange outfit that Jamie would probably love since she's obsessed with orange. And Creamsicles.

"I don't know how Jamie cries," Dawn continues, "but I'm going to assume she doesn't look cute because she refuses to ever do it."

57. A Girl Is Taking All the Calls

JAMIE
September 4, Friday Night
New Jersey

I'm lying on the floor near Siri's window, becoming one with the dead shoes as Zarar gives me a play-by-play of the 11 p.m. improv show over the phone.

I pull the thing away from my ear as call waiting beeps in. "Siri's calling me."

"You should pick it up."

"I'll see you tomorrow."

"Okay, good luck."

I swipe up on Siri's call. "Pail," I greet.

"Hi."

"What's up, Angst Lord? You sound distraught." I climb back up to her bed and flop onto my stomach.

"I have to tell you something."

"What have you ruined now?" I ask cheerfully. Guttural breathing comes over the line.

"Crap, are you crying?" I groan.

"I don't like you being mad at me."

"Don't worry about me being mad at you—" There's a murmuring on the

220

other end of the line. "Are you with Dawn right now?" I ask, anger lightly coating my words.

More murmuring. I stand up off the bed, needing to pace.

"Are you two hanging out? Put her on, Siri."

"She doesn't want to talk to you, Jamie. She's just helping me out."

"Helping you out?" I repeat in disbelief. "She's helping you—the imposter—out, and she won't talk to me?"

"Jamie, come on, this isn't about Dawn."

I blow out an indignant sigh. "Fine. What's up?"

There's a pause on Siri's end.

"I . . . your dad—" Siri sucks in a breath.

"—did something dickish? Dad had a threesome? Dad never showed up for dinner? Dad tried to cook and burned down the kitchen? Feel free to stop me when I get it. Dad's decided he wants to go to space? Dad bought a monkey? Dad's dating Cameron Dia—"

Siri finally interrupts, "Dad was at your latest comedy gig."

My mouth clamps shut.

"The one right before the retreat," she says quickly. "The one that I think made you decide to go, right?"

"How?" My voice has thinned.

"I don't know . . ."

How the hell did he even know where I was gigging? Spies? Little birds? Does he know the owner or something? I clear my throat. "Are you telling me my father took the time to come out to one of my gigs, and it happened to be the most embarrassing night of my life?"

Wow, Grier's going to reinforce the fact that I can't do this. I can already hear it. I can see him laying down the next stipulation, amending his contract. Stop chasing something you're not equipped to succeed in.

"Jamie?" Siri's voice is in my ear. "Jamie? Hello?! Did you hear what I said?"

"Yeah, Dad was at my big bomb." I try to make my voice sound light. Sounding light is one of my specialties.

I try to concentrate on Siri's voice, but I can't stop imagining all the things my father's going to spew to crush this dream entirely the next time I see him. He might have already said them to Siri.

"Have you heard a word I said in the last two minutes?" Siri yelps.

My surroundings blur as another wave of horror hits. *"Oh god."* I lean a hand against the blue wall. My dad watched a set that was almost entirely about him.

"Jamie! Are you hearing me? Dad said you were great and he has notes! Dad said you were great! *Dad said you were great, Jamie.* Is this getting through your incessant frantic mumbling?!"

My head snaps up. "Wait, what?"

"He said you were great, you just needed to tighten it up, and he has notes in his phone or something for you."

"No, he didn't. Are you fucking with me?"

"Are you having a panic attack? Go get a drink of water. I'm not 'fucking' with you. He's so confident in your stand-up abilities that he booked you a gig."

I choke on air and proceed to have a coughing fit.

"Jamie, seriously, water."

"No, he didn't. What do you mean he booked me a gig? What gig?" I wheeze, sprinting out of Siri's room to the bathroom. I flip on the sink and crane my head down to drink from the faucet.

"Well, um," she starts. I shut the spout off so I can hear her. My mouth's overflowing with water that I'm now trying to choke down.

"He booked you a twenty-minute set for a private barbecue Timothée Chalamet is throwing."

I full-on projectile spit all over the bathroom mirror.

52. Angst and Good/Bad News

I think Jamie's legitimately choking on the other end of the line.

"Jamie! Get water! What's happening?"

"FRICK!" she screams. I turn the phone volume down. "FUCK FRICK-ITY JIBBIT FLIP." And then, "HE BOOKED ME FOR TIMOTHÉE CHALAMET?!"

"Yes," I tell her nervously.

"NO."

"Yes."

"He didn't."

"Um . . . But he did," I tell her.

"No no."

"Yes, he did."

"When?!" she breathes.

"Saturday."

"Saturday when?"

"This Saturday."

There's a long silence.

"Not tomorrow," she whispers.

I look up at Dawn who's lending me a *gah, it's going to be okay* expression.

223

"We have to switch back," Jamie finally says.

My throat tightens uncomfortably. I take her off speaker and bring the phone to my ear.

"No, we shouldn't. It'll ruin our whole plan; we've only been switched for a day. Don't worry, I'm figuring this out."

"Figuring this out?! Sier, this is my career. Are you shitting me?"

Nerves gather in my gut. "Jamie, I promise I will not ruin your career. Think about what switching back right now would entail logistically—you would have to get on a flight first thing tomorrow, and you still wouldn't be able to make it. The performance is at two p.m.! And a flight would cost hundreds of dollars that you don't have, and it would ruin all our confrontation plans. I'm sure you have a whole slew of things planned with Mom that you haven't gotten to yet. Plus, you're forgetting that you don't look like you."

Jamie groans on the other end of the line. ". . . I, I mean, this is unbelievable. I can't believe this is happening."

I get up from my perch on Dawn's bed and wander into her hallway. "Jamie," I whisper, "I'm going along with your landmine moment confrontation plan. I've sent that evil catfish email, I've mentally made my peace with what we're doing, and now we have to see it through. You still haven't confronted Mom, and I haven't confronted Dad. Right? We haven't gotten out of this the most important things we wanted from it."

I pause to let her retort. She stays silent.

"I won't let you down. I have a plan. That's what I'm working on with Dawn."

"I don't look like you to Zarar," Jamie says suddenly. "Maybe if I tell other people I'm Jamie, I'll poof back to myself in front of them too."

I huff a short laugh. "Oh, and that won't be distracting at a barbecue—you individually pulling each guest aside and scarring them by exploding into a different person before their eyes. That's not plausible."

Jamie doesn't respond.

"Wait, Zarar is there with you?"

"I ran into him in New York yesterday. Have you told anyone else?"

"No . . . just Dawn. She can see me, and I'm pretty sure this correlates with a line in the riddle."

"Which line?"

"*Tell just one, they'll see the light,*" I say. "We've both told one person."

"I"—she stumbles—"can't believe this is happening."

"Jamie—"

The line goes dead.

53. Angst and Preparation

The dough is ready. I'm working it flat while Dawn gives me a light-speed improv rundown.

Dawn snaps her fingers in front of my face. I refocus on her words.

"Siri. Try to stay present. The last team member just texted back—we're all good to perform tomorrow at two. You can take a less active role and we'll pull it off, but you need to get the fundamentals down."

I look up from the dough. "Sorry, I'm anxious, but I'm trying to listen, I promise."

Turns out I was right: Improv isn't freeform like I previously imagined. There's a pattern to it, a dance that all the performers know the outline to. They fill in the gaps as they go along.

I add the homemade sauce to the pie as Dawn finishes her thought and leans her elbows on the table. She watches me for a quiet moment.

"I never realized making a pizza was a yearlong event," she comments cheekily.

I grin, littering it with all sorts of goodies: olives, tomatoes, basil, mushrooms, broccoli, and of course cheese.

"Just adding the final touches. I'm sorry. I didn't completely register the time it would take when I read the recipe. I just wanted to make you a pizza," I answer quietly.

She smiles. "That was very kind of you. I appreciate it."

I put the last mushroom on and smile back at her for an extended moment. Then I get nervous about the silence and the extended moment and Jamie, so I pick up the pizza and shove it into the oven. Twenty more minutes and we can finally eat.

"So," I ask, "how did you get so good at improv? Do you want to do stand-up too?"

Dawn vacates her stool at the island and comes over to where I'm now carefully moving things into the sink. "Can I help with this?" she asks.

I wave her off. "No, I like to do dishes; it's soothing." I flip on the water and dig into the sink.

Dawn props herself up and sits on the counter right next to the faucet. "I teach a 101 and 201 course at QCZ in West Hollywood. I want to be a comedy writer. I've written a bunch of spec scripts for some of the big sitcoms, and I've got a couple of pilots I've written these past four years. Haven't sold anything though."

My mouth pops open as I'm scrubbing the sauce pot.

"That's so cool. What sitcoms?" For a second, I try to imagine being a writer. But I can't. I need something I can go to every day. I want structured hours of focus.

Dawn looks down at her knees instead of my face. "The first one I did was for *Modern Family*. That show's done, but I loved that spec script. I have one for *The Big Bang Theory*. Also, over. I have one for *Young Sheldon*, one for *Grown-ish*." She shrugs. "I'll keep trying. One day I'll make my way in. For now I'm working QCZ, captaining Duck Waterfall . . . and doing pre-nursing courses part-time to keep my mom happy. We're Filipino and basically my entire family is in the medical field. There's a lot of pressure from all sides to take my career in that direction."

I look up from my sudsy measuring cups. "Does your mom not like all the comedy stuff?"

Dawn leans her head side to side. "She definitely isn't big on the comedy writer idea, but we've had this argument out multiple times over the years now and settled on a compromise."

I nod, setting things to dry on the rack next to the sink. "You must have a packed schedule."

She hunches forward slightly, shrugging. "I've made it work by scheduling classes all on one day of the week and leaving the other days open for work, practice, and studying. Jamie and I make a great team with Duck Waterfall . . . when it fits her whimsy."

Dawn's expression falls. She's putting up a happy front, but she's still upset.

"Do you need another hug?" I ask quietly.

She laughs. "Sure, I would love one." She hops off the counter in front of me, and I embrace her like my life depends on it for a good four seconds before letting go.

She grins and fiddles with her hands for a moment. "Okay! We have ten more minutes before we eat, let's run through the Gerald structure again."

I pay an excrement load of attention this go around. I won't let Jamie down.

The information spills out of Dawn so easily, like she lives and breathes the stuff.

The name of the game is saying yes to your team apparently and supporting their choices. And paying attention. I'm supposed to make dramatic choices. *I can do that.*

And be okay with failing. *I don't know about that one.*

"If we fail, it's as a team," she stresses. "It's no one person's fault, and when we go down, we go down hard. We don't abandon beats, we work to find the funny and turn it around, and if we can't, then fuck that, people will forget about it in less than twenty-four hours. We'll perform again, we'll get over it. The only way you can really fail a scene is by abandoning your teammates." She finishes the sentence as the pizza timer starts to ding.

As I rise to turn it off, Dawn reaches out and touches my arm. She catches my eyes with her dark, endless ones. She has actual ocean eyes. I sit back down.

"Once you relinquish the need to control what's happening around you and accept the present, you start to see a path forward . . ." She clears her throat, drops her hand, and smiles. "I think subbing for Jamie in a last-minute celebrity improv performance is exactly what you need right now."

My arm is tingling where she touched it. "How so?"

She shrugs. "Well, from what you've told me, it seems like your brain is so caught up in what you can't do, you can't see what *you can*."

I gaze at her wearily. "Is that like a Dumbledore quote or something?"

"No . . ." Dawn tilts her head. "It's just a truth."

I move to free the pizza. "Why are you so wise?"

At the table Dawn shrugs and mockingly throws her nose up in the air. "I don't know. I'm a smarty pants. I can't help it."

An unacceptably embarrassing giggle flows out of me. I try to cover it with the squeak of the oven door.

"Failure's all about perception," she continues. "You didn't fail at ballet, Siri. You had a successful career and were forced to retire early."

A sarcastic huff falls out of me as I carefully place my pizza masterpiece on the stove. Dawn comes over to admire it with me.

She bumps me with her hip, and I look away from the pizza to meet her playful gaze. "Huff all you want. From my point of view, you're a ballet legend. Pro by age eighteen? Going professional ever at a sport is huge." She shrugs. "You got paid to dance. You made your favorite thing your job. That's the dream."

Goose bumps rush up my arms. Dawn's perfect hair has fallen ever so slightly into her face, and before I can overthink it, I reach out and push it behind her ear.

She blinks and steps back, staring down at the pizza. "Well, this looks delicious. Let's frickin' eat, shall we?"

It's late when I finally go back to Jamie's house. Improv structure and rules are cycling through my brain. That's all Dawn wanted to talk about the rest of the night.

The lights are off in the house, so Grams must be asleep. I haven't seen my father since before dinner last night. Does he even live here?

I'm changing into a pair of neon green pajamas from Jamie's closet when Gladys rings. It's 11:40 here. Almost 3 a.m. in New Jersey.

"Hello?" I whisper.

"You have to cancel the gig," Jamie says quietly. Her voice still holds the same panicked quaver from earlier. I don't think she's okay. What's Mom doing to her over there?

"No, we've figured it out. Duck Waterfall is going to perform. I'm going to participate the barest amount possible, and it's going to be great for your team, because they're going to kill it! You don't have to worry."

Jamie exhales an audible breath. "Okay." She hangs up.

54. A Girl Needs to Do Better

JAMIE
September 5, Saturday Morning
New Jersey

Lara,

Thank you for reaching out with this opportunity, it's truly an honor
to be considered. I'm available for a call today any time before 7pm.
Looking forward to hearing more details.

All the best,
Mara Maza

Good deal. I shoot her a thrilled email back explaining that I'll call her
today at 4:30. There's no new email from Siri in the morning.

Siri,

Hope the plan works. I'll be confirming Mom's catfish today with a
fake phone call from a British talent manger. I'll let you know when
she gets a plane ticket.

P.S. Can you get Dad to send those notes so I can read them? Thank you!

—Bucket

I pause mid-bite of Special K as Mara tornados into the kitchen at 8:15, grabbing things from the fridge and stuffing them into her bag. She pulls a granola bar from the pantry, rips the wrapper, and yanks off a bite before meeting my eyes.

"Sorry, I'm running late, have to get to rehearsals so I won't be able to sit down."

"Avoiding me?" I ask.

"If anything you're avoiding me, Siri Martine." She fills her water bottle at the refrigerator.

"I'm right here."

She screws the top onto her water canteen. "Don't pretend you didn't see my texts yesterday." Before I can respond, Mara yanks open the garage door and leaves.

The iPhone buzzes with a text.

Mom: I'll see you for dinner tonight. Still on for Greek casserole?

I almost roll my eyes, but I catch myself. This woman is turning me into Siri.

Me: Yep.

Mom: You have an 11 am appt with Dr. Sparrow on Sunday. See you at 8.

Ten minutes later, the doorbell rings. I peek into the foyer to find Papa looking in through the fogged side window. He waves.

I unbolt the front door and throw it open.

Papa's standing outside with his hands in his pockets. He shrugs. "I think we need to talk, sweetheart."

The two of us sit down at the table.

"What's up, Papa?" I ask. "I have an appointment in the city at twelve."

"It's 8:30. I think you're fine." He folds his hands.

"Does Mom just beep you the second she's in distress or something?"

232

Papa sits back. "Your mother and I talk. I'm her father. She's been calling more often since you got back. She's worried about you. You haven't cooked or baked anything since you returned. Over the summer, you were channeling your emotions into an activity. Now you're disappearing, holing yourself up in your room, defacing your mother's bookcase."

I guffaw. "That can hardly be considered defacing. I moved the books around, Papa. Mom is completely overreacting."

How often is Siri fooling around in the kitchen with food? I've been here less than forty-eight hours.

"Your mother notices more than you give her credit for. As do I." He raises his fluffy gray eyebrows.

I execute a Siri sigh–eye roll combo. "Enlighten me, Papa."

"You're not wearing your white sneakers."

I glance down at my new red boots. Ugh. "I spilled something on them."

"Don't you have three pairs?"

"I'm changing it up."

"You picked up a jelly donut instead of the ridiculous one with the sprinkles and strawberry icing that you pick up every single time I bring them over. There's no music on. You don't have headphones in your ears. You're acting out in strange ways, like you're trying on an entirely new personality. Does it have to do with something that happened at the retreat? You can tell me."

I make a flustered noise and smack the table with my hands. "How could I possibly tell you anything? You're like an extension of Mom. She's using you to talk to me like her personal puppet because she's too chicken-*excrement*"—I put unneeded emphasis on the ridiculous non-curse—"to have any sort of meaningful talk with me herself."

Papa shakes his head. "I love your mother, Siri, but that doesn't mean I can't keep a secret. I am here. I love you too."

I know this man loves Siri, but I can't . . . trust him. He's complicit in my deletion from their life.

"Did Mom tell you I'm seeing Jamie again?" I ask plainly.

Papa pushes his lips together, and his expression evens out. Guarded. "Are you . . . ?" He looks down at me over his glasses. "Really?"

I shake my head in disbelief. "I'm out of here." I grab my bag and plow out the door without looking back.

It's a fifteen-minute walk to the train station. I don't feel like calling an Uber, so I set off down the road at a brisk pace.

This man who supposedly loves Siri, and should by default care about me, went along with Mara's plan to completely write me out of her life. And now he has the audacity to question whether or not *I'm lying*?!

I stop short at the corner. My chest is tight. I slow down, moving with one hand at my throat, and one holding my hip, staring at the sidewalk.

You're looking at this too personally. This can be funny. You just need to find your angle and put it into perspective. What is my angle?

I make my feet keep moving.

55. A Girl Is on Time for Once

JAMIE
September 5, Saturday Afternoon
New York City

"Tell me exactly what happened during your infamous stand-up performance," Zarar requests as we stride down the sidewalk.

When I walked up to the diner exactly on time, Z was already there, leaning against it in his stylish leather jacket. Instead of going inside, we started down the block.

We cross an intersection. "Didn't I tell you about this already at Rediscover?"

"No, you told me *it happened* and it shook the very foundations of your confidence, but you didn't say *what* exactly happened."

I make a move to shove my hands into my overall pockets and am again thrown to find only the smooth vacant emptiness of Siri's black leggings. "What happened was I choked, forgot my set, stood on stage for a solid one hundred twenty seconds of awkward silence, threw up, got booed, was still convinced I could find *some* way to save it, and had to get escorted off by the manager, who I vaguely know because, *surprise,* I work there."

Next to me, Zarar coughs a chuckle. I snap my gaze over to him as we navigate down another block.

"Zarar. Did you just laugh?" I ask, astounded. "You haven't laughed in my presence since I met you."

He coughs another chuckle. "I'm sorry, I don't really laugh."

"You don't really laugh?" I say in disbelief. "I think you just did."

"Well, I don't find many things laugh-out-loud funny. I think it makes people uncomfortable. I have a theory that it's why none of the romantic endeavors I've embarked on this past year and a half have worked out. I had a girlfriend in high school, but we had known each other for years so she knew it was a weird thing of mine."

"Wow." I start cackling to myself.

"Are you laughing because you think I'm funny?" Zarar asks sweetly.

I glance up at him. "You are the most unfunny, and I find it hilarious. I'm going to need more details here. How often exactly do you laugh out loud?"

"I'd say almost never. Maybe once every few months."

"Zarar, you just laughed twice. Did you exhaust your quota for the next half a year?"

He shrugs, his eyes shining with a new excited light that I haven't yet gotten to witness. "I don't know. It's not an exact science. It's kind of like getting to the center of a Tootsie Pop, there's too many licks to keep count."

I snort as we hang a right. "That is the most irrelevant metaphor I've ever heard. Do explain, Z."

"I don't think it's irrelevant. The licks are the times I think something's funny and I don't laugh, the Tootsie Roll is the laugh."

"Profound." I smile at him. "This is why I like you."

"Because of my metaphors? I'm fairly sure this is the first time I've made one in conversation with you."

"Because you're a Tootsie Pop in the bag of shitty candy. Isn't that what we're all looking for?"

He slides his eyes down to me. "I'm only looking at you."

"Oh, man." I stop moving, roll out my neck, and quell my smile into a neutral smirk. "You are such a loser."

As we start walking again, Zarar reaches out and casually takes my hand. My stomach shrinks up into a ball.

I shake my fingers out of his. "I don't do hand-holding, Z. Intimacy in public is nauseating."

He eyes me sideways as we cross another intersection. "How cool one must be to find hand-holding nauseating." I snicker, my fondness for him doubling in the span of five seconds.

He points enthusiastically to a food truck on the next corner. "I figured we could eat there. They make a mean grilled cheese."

I laugh, taking in the You Think You're Feta Than Me? Gourmet Grilled Cheeses truck down the street: There's a cartoon of two mobster-looking guys in suits and top hats holding grilled cheese sandwiches with a dialogue bubble that says *"Oh, cheese"* painted along the side.

Zarar leads us (myself and our grilled cheeses—I got the Leave Me Provolone, he got a Grilleroni) over to a small, picturesque square of a park among the skyscrapers.

"Bryant Park," he says by way of explanation as we arrive up against a giant, chest-high, gray stone balustrade lining the far end of this little green oasis. The ledge along the top is wide enough to sit on, but definitely not what anyone would define as easily accessible. He places our sandwiches on the ledge and hops up next to them.

"Way to help the lady breach the wall," I tell him.

"I knew you'd want to handle it yourself," he says.

I grin at him for a moment before bracing my arms against the ledge and popping up next to him. Zarar hands me my grilled meatball parm, and I pull my legs up pretzel style so I can shift sideways to face him.

He picks up what's essentially a grilled macaroni and cheese sandwich, takes a bite, and closes his eyes, savoring it.

I arch the eyebrow under my scar. It doesn't hurt anymore, but it does have a weird stretched prickly sensation. "That good, huh?"

He nods and swallows. "That good. Your scar is starting to look badass," Zarar says. I touch it self-consciously. It's been super weird not being able to see it myself. "It looks great on you."

I swallow, feeling that compliment unusually hard. *Who the hell compliments a face scar?*

I take a bite of my own specialty grilled cheese. Z watches expectantly. I try not to laugh at his expression while I chew and weigh the taste. "It's pretty damn good."

He nods happily. "So, is your set super dark like your sense of humor?" he asks, prepping his overflowing sandwich for another bite.

"Who says my sense of humor is dark?"

"Plan Parent Confrontation Trap."

I glance up at the sky thoughtfully. "Huh, touché."

I watch him take another bite of the Grilleroni. It sparks a memory. "Hey, my mom used to make us a weird grilled cheese sandwich like that . . . with like, brie-based macaroni and cheese and apple slices on bread. It was my favorite. Dang, it was so good. And so weird."

The side of his mouth kicks up. "You should do your set for me right now."

I chew a second bite of meatball parm grilled cheese. "I mean, first we're going to workshop it."

"This is how we workshop it—you perform it."

I make a *pfft* noise, and set down my sandwich. "We're in a park. I can't do it here."

"Why not?"

I laugh. "Z, I don't think you're really comprehending the scope of the humiliation I experienced the last time I performed this set. *I threw up on stage.*"

He cough-laughs again.

Not gonna lie, it's really satisfying hearing him laugh, even if it's at my expense.

"Why is that so funny to you?" I demand.

His eyes widen. "I really couldn't tell you. It's just funny."

"It's really not funny," I tell him.

"Then why are you smiling," he says.

"Because."

"You should do your set for me," he repeats.

The sun peeks out from behind the clouds and beams down through the trees, sprinkling his face with light. I take a mental picture and file it away for when this inevitably falls apart.

"I can't do it here," I insist.

Zarar purses his lips and stares me down. "You're procrastinating. You want to do it. I can see it in your face."

I blink at him, feeling strangely exposed and pleased at the same time. How the hell does he know that? I rip off another bite of sandwich before digging my notebook out from my backpack.

"I don't usually do my set for people I know."

Z slides sideways so he can dangle one leg off each side of the ledge and face me head on. "I know you don't, yet, but you probably should. It'll be good practice. And, big perk, I don't laugh, so there's nothing to distract you."

I eye him warily. How weird is it that I'm this attracted to a guy who doesn't laugh (except apparently at my saddest, most insecure moment of shame).

"I'm usually distracted by silence."

His eyes widen. "Ah, so it'll help to practice with a person who is silent. And it will help me learn about comedy and timing. That's a big part of why I took the job at QCZ. Actors need a good sense of comedic timing in addition to their dramatic talents; you have to have range to be the next Shah Rukh Khan."

"Who's that?"

Zarar shoots me a look of disbelief. "You've never heard of Shah Rukh Khan? The king of Bollywood? He's one of the most famous actors in the world. Like more famous than Tom Cruise. Shah Rukh Khan can do everything: zany comedies, family dramas, tragic love stories—sometimes all three in the same movie."

"Shit. I'm gonna have to look him up. Is Tom Cruise like the crux of international fame?"

Zarar stares me down with his quarter smile, refusing to tolerate my bullshit. "I'm ready for the set whenever you are."

I glance around. People are walking by and eating lunch at outdoor tables around us.

"Just here on this ledge? I have to be standing up. It's called stand-up." I imagine myself standing up on the path beside the ledge, telling jokes about my dad. It's nauseating.

Z talks out of the side of his mouth. "You could easily stand if you wanted to. But, it'll be good practice to be able to do it sitting down. It shouldn't be dependent on standing. You should be able to do it in any position."

Hmm. He's right. I drop my gaze to the ledge and exhale a long breath, a smile growing across my face as I let my brain sink into performance mode.

Well, here goes everything. I meet Zarar's excited eyes.

"Hey hey hey, I'm Jamie. Your friendly neighborhood Hollywood kid trying to lead a normal life." I pause. "And by normal, I of course mean—making it big, this is Hollywood."

His lip goes up on one end. I glance around as if I'm talking to a larger audience.

"As a kid growing up in Hollywood, I haven't really experienced much *normal.*" I glance down at my booted feet. "What is a normal life *really?* Is it living within walking distance of a SoulCycle? Is it Botox? There's a place called MyBotox less than a mile from my house. I walk past it on my way to the local coffee shop.

"It's great branding, MyBotox. Casual. Like I already own it. Like we're friends. MyBotox. Kind of like *iPhone,* every actor's favorite pronoun next to the thing they want—a phone. But applied to Botox.

"I can't help but think to myself when I pass it, like, is that really what Botox users are looking for? A friendly open relationship?" I pause, perusing this concept. "Cuz that's not the impression I've gotten. You hear these celebrities in interviews: *my dog, my kids, my fancy accent couch*—I don't think I've ever heard them mention Botox.

"Botox is like the uncomfortably crude uncle you hide in the closet at important gatherings. No one introduces you to their Botox. It's their deep dark secret friend they pretend they don't know at parties. No one is coming up to you like 'Oh my god, do you love my face, meet my Botox. She's really great, right next to the coffee shop, we hang out all the time.'

"They should maybe rebrand with something like 'Not Botox.' *Get your Botox now and get out. Don't worry, you were never here.*

"Do you know who gets Botox regularly?" I pause. "That's right, ladies and gentlemen, it's my big shot Hollywood producer dad.

"My dad, he's only forty-three, but like, it's totally normal because we live in Hollywood. My grams gets Botox. My dead ancestors get Botox. My friend's mom. My dog.

"Kidding, I don't have a dog. But you know what I'm saying. It's part of our culture in La La Land. In New Jersey, you know it's Gym-Tan-Laundry—GTL. In LA it's PTSB. Personal Trainer-Starbucks-Botox. It's normal, it's how we do.

"Ah, *normalcy*." I smile fondly.

I rock on into my social media bit. And I keep going.

I let everything I've got spill out, and Zarar vaguely smiles and nods. It's been so long since I just did the set—all of the content I've written—completely on my own terms, with my own rhythm, without any distraction from an audience.

The absence of laughter leaves me room to imagine, to feel, to think straight, to really fall into my own words.

I keep going until I get to the end.

It all feels so low stakes that I never stumble.

I just get there. I arrive. I go from point A to point B without hitting one snag in the road and it feels . . . amazing.

I tell Zarar *he's been a great audience, thanks for coming out, good night* and slump forward in relief.

56. Angst and Emails

I've woken to both a text and email from my father.

Dad: Meet me in the kitchen at 11:30, Jame. I've got the address and details for the gig today

The email is a reply to my catfish.

Mara,

What's brought this on? Were you drunk?

—Grier

I don't know what I expected him to say. Not this. This aligns more with the greedy, selfish, abandoning jerk-and-a-half persona I've been conditioned to expect. I mash my lips together and type a response.

Grier,

I've been having trouble with Siri lately and it's been making me question whether we made the right decision splitting the girls up. Maybe we should have co-parented. What do you think?

—Mara

Send. I have an email from Jamie too. I can tell from the lack of detail she's not exactly happy with me. I can't let her down today.

I pull up YouTube, open a White Chapel playlist, and blast it as I get ready.

57. A Girl Gets Feedback

JAMIE
September 5, Saturday Afternoon
New York City

"You've now been silent for three straight minutes, Zarar. Talk to me. I'm feeling uncomfortably vulnerable."

"I liked it," he says simply.

I sit up straighter. "You did?"

"You should lose the Pinterest bit."

"So you didn't like it," I clarify.

Zarar tilts his head to the side. "It's clear you don't know anything about Pinterest, so it's not funny enough to stay, but I liked a lot of it. The Twitter story landed well."

I mash my lips together. "Okay . . ."

"The car phone/cell phone bit takes too long."

I exhale. "Harsh, but keep going."

"Does your dad really get Botox?"

I wiggle out of my backpack to grab a pen. "Uh yeah, everyone does."

"Strange."

"You'd be surprised. More people over here do it than you'd think. You just don't notice till you know what to look for."

My hand flies around the bottom of the backpack, without settling on a pen. "Crap."

"Maybe take out the side tangent about Bluetooth, it's a little overdone," Zarar continues slowly.

"Halt, I need to find a pen to take all this down."

"You can keep the millennial bit," Zarar adds as I continue to tear apart my backpack.

I glance up at him. "Oh, I can? Thanks."

"I thought I was a millennial," he says thoughtfully. Zarar puts his hand atop my frantic backpack-searching arm to get my attention.

I look up at him. "Congratulations, you didn't make the cut."

"You can take down notes on Siri's iPhone if you want," he says.

I scrunch up my forehead, feeling the scar crunch. "Do I look like the kind of person who can type on an iPhone?"

Zarar blinks. ". . . Yes."

I stand up to full height on the ledge. "Hark! I require ink and quill, you fool! Is there a Staples around here somewhere?"

Zarar leans back on his arms to hold eye contact. "There's a Duane Reade down the block."

I hop off the ledge, landing lightly on the sandy dirt walkway. "Take me there, kind sir!"

Zarar joins me in a jaunt toward the sidewalk. I shake out my limbs. Left-over *I'm doing my set* adrenaline-spiked nerves are hurtling through me and coalescing into an airy triumphant joy. I can't wait to jot down these notes and put them into effect!

I'm excited to try Dawn again on the train home and hope to god she picks up so I can get her opinion too! I still have a couple of hours to edit what I'm going to perform!

As soon as we hit the sidewalk, we're in view of a Duane Reade.

I bound into a cheerful skip. "Hurry, Zarar!" I call behind me. "I have to catch the four p.m. train home to prank call my mom and cook a terrible dinner!"

He jogs to catch up to me. "That's three hours away. I think we'll manage." He spoke out of the left side of his mouth again. *Why is that so sexy?!*

58. Angst and Expectations

SIRI
September 5, Saturday Morning
California

I dress in the Jamie-est of outfits today. Bright yellow off-the-shoulder crop top under bright orange overalls I found in her closet. Yellow eyeshadow accents. Yellow boots, and a little darker than neutral shade of pink lipstick. She's counting on me, and Dad's counting on me. He's the one who put Jamie up for this. I can't embarrass either of them.

I've spent the morning running through the lessons Dawn gave me last night in my head. I keep hearing the last thing she said before I left: *Try to start at least one of the scenes tomorrow, okay? You can do it. That's all you'll have to do, start at least one scene. We'll be there with you every moment making it work.*

Dawn's counting on me too. Say yes. Make dramatic choices. Never give up on a scene.

I can do this. I nod at the Jamie in the mirror, grab Gladys, and head downstairs to face my dad. My back barely aches at all right now. Good omen. That's a good omen.

I'm shivering as I walk through the living room, anxiety humming through me in the most literal sense. I haven't told Dad that I'm doing the gig with Duck Waterfall. I have no idea how he's going to react or what his opinions on Jamie's improv team are. The plan is to spring it on everyone there and hope for the best.

He's waiting at the kitchen table with a cup of coffee and his phone again; that seems to be his natural stance.

I'm trying really hard not to let preconceived bias from my mother make me judgmental of his every move. I mean, he's already proved me wrong. I know he's rooting for Jamie. That's something a good dad does. He set this up. He's going to come and watch like he's been doing with her comedy all along. That's a good dad.

But looking at him right now, I'm having trouble seeing the dad I want to see. I see that insensitive email that was in my catfish inbox addressed to Mom this morning.

I stick my shaky hands into Jamie's overall pockets. Today he's wearing a white button-up collared shirt with a pair of blue slacks.

"Hey, Dad," I say as I approach the table. "Morning."

He looks up, taking in my appearance. "Hey, Jame! Wow, going colorful for your performance, huh? You feeling ready?"

Instead of taking a seat at the table, I head toward the fridge. "Yep! I don't know if you were planning on going together, but Dawn's picking me up early and we're going to prep beforehand."

I get to work making myself a brunch omelet to try to calm my rising nerves. I pull out the eggs and grab a frying pan from the cabinet.

Dad puts down his phone and gives me his full attention as I spin toward the island with a bowl to crack the eggs in.

"Whoa, Jame." He smiles. "Whatchya doing there?"

"Making an omelet," I say cooly. "I haven't eaten."

He chuckles from the table before wandering over as I start whisking the eggs. "Should I call the fire department?"

I shoot him a tight-lipped smile. "I think I'll make it out alive, but thank you . . . I've been cooking with Grams," I add by way of explanation as I snatch out the butter, salt, and pepper and put them on the island. "What did you need to tell me about the gig?" I ask.

"Well—" he starts but stops as I pivot back to the fridge, looking for more. I find some spinach and cheese to add to my ingredient pile. I throw some olive oil in the frying pan and turn on the burner before turning back to face my father.

"Well," he starts again. "So, I'm not actually going to make it to Tim's barbecue today. Hopefully I can make it to the next one."

I feel my lips flop open.

"But he says to just wait along the left side of the house when you get there, and at two, someone will come take you around back when they're ready for you." He picks his cell back up. "I'm forwarding you the address now." Gladys buzzes in my pocket.

I stare at him. The oil sizzles behind me.

My dad, who set this up for Jamie, can't come. Who went out of his way to watch Jamie perform. That dad is now going to bail the one time he might get to see me do anything.

"Why can't you come?" I ask. I grab the whipped eggs, pivot, drop them into the skillet, and pivot back to him.

"I'm sorry, kiddo, you know how it is. I have a thing."

I stick my hands in my pockets, wrapping my fists around the material in there. "A work thing or a lady thing?"

He grins. "A both thing."

I try to plaster on a smile, but I know I'm grimacing as I bob my head. Anger is pulsing over my skin. I spin around again, adding the ingredients to my omelet a little too late. "Because you're a greedy, selfish, jerk-and-a-half abandoner," I mumble accusingly to the skillet as I work the eggs with a spatula.

"Say that again?" Dad says behind me. I freeze, staring at the food.

No . . . I didn't say that loud enough for him to hear me over the eggs.

"Nothing," I say. I make myself unfreeze and move the eggs around.

Dad walks around the island, stopping right next to me. I keep staring down at the eggs, mushing them around with the spatula so they're no longer an omelet, just a blob of scrambled nothing.

"Did someone call me that to you?" he asks. "Have you been in touch with your mother?"

All the levity has drained from his voice. I look up at him, my eyes wide, and shake my head.

"I've told you how manipulative that woman is. She's already trying to turn you against me. You know I'm always here for you. I'm the one who's been supporting you for the last fourteen years. Caring for you, housing you, providing for you. I love you. Don't let that bitch—"

I flinch like he hit me.

"Sorry." He closes his eyes. "Don't let that woman get to you."

I turn off the stove and wander to the cabinet for a plate, carrying the skillet along with me.

"She hasn't done anything," I mumble. "I haven't talked to her in over a decade." Tears are in my voice, but thank god not yet in my eyes.

I intercoursed up.

Dad's pacing toward the table and now back up toward the island, shaking his head. "Don't lie to me, Jamie George."

"I'm not lying," I whisper in the kitchen corner, uselessly holding a plate and a hot skillet full of egg and spinach.

My father sighs, sounding exhausted. "You're lying and we both know it, so just give it a rest. Did she email you too?"

I close my eyes, needing a second to myself to sort through how to respond. I finally decide on, "She emailed you?"

"What did she say?" he demands quietly.

"Nothing, we didn't talk!"

He shakes his head for an endless ten seconds. "I can't hang out with you if you're going to lie to my face."

My shoulders shoot up, my face warping into an expression of pure confusion. "We're not hanging out!"

"Why do you think I'm in here right now?" he yells.

My insides quake as I search for the right words to hit back with.

That catfish I sent is never going to work now. I've ruined it. How the hell am I going to get him to Vegas on Tuesday?

I let my shoulders drop, knowing tears are just seconds away. "You know what. Just go, Dad."

He stares me down. "I'm your father. I love you. I am doing my absolute best. Do not let *her* tell you any different." He shifts his weight from one foot to the other. "I know you'll do great today. You don't need me there to tell you that." He grabs his jacket off a kitchen chair and stalks toward his office in the other wing of the house.

I drop the skillet on the stove, run to the bathroom, put my face in the hand towel, and scream.

I haul breaths in and heave them out, trying to smother the firestorm in my chest. I roll some toilet paper around my hand and blot my eyes, trying to preserve my Jamie makeup.

The girl in the mirror is not okay.

But she's going to pull it together.

I do the re-centering exercise Donya had me doing every session at Rediscover Yourself: I name five things in the room. Gladys buzzes in my pocket.

Dawn: Hey hey! HAPPY DUCK WATERFALL PERFORMANCE DAY! I'm in the driveway!

It's better if Dad doesn't come today anyway.

59. A Girl Is on the Train Again

JAMIE
September 5, Saturday Afternoon
New York City

I am effervescent on this train back to Jersey. Hope is thrumming through me as I flip through Zarar's commentary. *Notes are invigorating!*

Dawn is a comedic genius. She has a more understated style, but her instincts are impeccable. I need her input ASAP! I need all opinions on deck to make this the best it can be. I need to tape myself. Why have I never taped myself performing? Why haven't I been doing this the entire time?

I text Zarar.

Me: I'm a dumb.

Zarar: You're the smartest dumb though.

Me: K

Zarar: Our text conversations are so thought provoking. You are a true master of the English language.

Me: coo thx

Zarar: I'm very honored to be the first person you know to have heard your complete set. You'll rock it tonight. You can always sit down on stage if that feels safer in the moment.

Me: IT'S CALLED STAND-UP, ZARAR.

Zarar: You could be the sit-down stand-up.

Me: you are the most unfunny

Zarar: =D

I glance up at the current stop. I have a handful more before I get off. It's 3:07 p.m., if I get on the phone with Dawn now, I can do my set and be discussing it by the time I jump in an Uber and ride to the grocery store. I cross myself like I've seen religious people do when they pray and dial Dawn's number.

It rings! It's been going straight to voicemail, but it's ringing!

"Hello?"

Elation surges through me. "Dawn?!"

"Jamie, is everything okay?" It's not Dawn. That's Siri's voice.

"What the hell are you doing on Dawn's phone?"

"We're on the way to the barbecue. Is everything okay?"

"Can I talk to her, please?"

"Um." There's some mumbling. "She's driving. Maybe try her later?"

I sigh. "Fine, quick question, you remember those brie-and-apple macaroni-and-cheese sandwiches Mom used to make us?"

"Ew, I've seen Mom make that every once in a blue moon for herself. Why would you put macaroni on a sandwich. We used to eat those?"

"They were only my favorite."

"Weird."

I hang up.

60. Angst and a Barbecue

SIRI
September 5, Saturday Afternoon
California

Grams comes out of the woodwork, wishing me luck as I frantically *whoosh* out of the house with a Rubbermaid full of eggs and a fork.

It's a relief to step out the door. It's so bright! The palm trees sway in the light breeze as I make my way down the driveway to Dawn's waiting mint-green Prius.

There's a giant painted DUCK WATERFALL poster crammed in the back seat. I pull open the passenger door and slide in carefully, settling the food on my lap.

"Wow, did you make that?" I ask her, gesturing to the art project. It looks really good. And really her. It's all pastels.

She giggles. "Yep, stayed up most of the night doing it."

"Did you sleep?" I ask anxiously.

She looks as perfect as usual. Her outfit is mint green like her car. Her loose curls fall in a cascade over her shoulders. She's wearing mint-green overalls. I've never seen *her* wear overalls. Together we . . . look like a team.

"Only for like a second because I'm so damn excited." She smiles her dimply adorable grin. It lights a baby flame in my chest.

Smiling back at her is an unstoppable instinct.

253

She taps her phone on the dash and opens Google maps. "We shall now be led to our Chalamet destiny!"

I rattle off the address as she types it in. A moment later, she's put us in reverse and backed us out of Dad's fancy driveway. She switches back to drive, reaches over the center console, grabs my hand, and squeezes it. "We're about to perform for the kid from *Call Me by Your Name,* Siri!!" She drums her palms against the steering wheel.

I laugh at her blatant excitement. "I know! It's one of the only novels I've ever read myself and loved."

I watch as Dawn catches her full bottom lip in her teeth. "It's the book that got me looking at books again after only reading scripts for years on end." She glances over at me. "I can lend you a few other LGBT romances I loved if you're interested?"

My cheeks burn at the prospect of sharing romance books with Dawn.

I nod from the passenger side. "That would be really cool . . . The only other . . . novel-y books I've read outside of school are Game of Thrones, which I was force-fed by my mother repeatedly throughout my teen years."

"Sounds familiar," she says softly.

The car is suddenly filled with what I recognize as the theme song from *The Office.* I only know the tune because Papa watches that show sometimes when I'm around. Maybe I should watch it.

Google Maps is replaced by an incoming call on Dawn's phone.

It's not someone in her phone book. But I recognize those digits.

"That's my number. That's Jamie," I say quietly.

"You want to pick it up?"

"Um, sure?" I reach to swipe in the call.

Dawn and I have been practicing the weird opening pattern game the team does and starting scenes together for thirty minutes on the grass along the side of the house where we're performing when the other members of Duck Waterfall start to show up.

As long as Dawn is in the scene with me up there today, I know things are going to be okay. She makes anything into something worth exploring. My stupidest idea can be warped into something hilarious within thirty seconds.

I just have to start one scene. I have to hold on to one good idea from the weird idea-generating section of the performance and initiate a scene based off of it. I can do it. *I can do this.*

People are chatting and laughing farther back behind the giant house at the barbecue.

Once the team has arrived, Dawn leads us in some warm-up games. They involve a lot of making eye contact, spouting nonsensical phrases, and dancing. Somewhere along the way, being silly with these relative strangers, my shaky-nauseous nerves shift into the adrenaline-pumping, happy-making, performance kind that engulf me before a routine.

These are all really nice people and they're so confident in us! We're all chatting in the aftermath of our last warm-up when someone taps me on the shoulder. I almost stop breathing when I turn around to find Timothée Chalamet himself.

"Timothée Chalamet," I blurt.

"You must be Jamie! Your dad talks about you all the time. It's great to meet you." Timothée Chalamet holds out his hand.

I nod and smile stupidly before reaching out to take his hand.

Try to be like Jamie.

"Hey hey hey, great to meet you," I say. "Are you ready for us?"

"Yeah, um, are you all doing stand-up? There's a lot of you."

I smile nervously. "We're doing an improv performance. This is my crew, Duck Waterfall."

He laughs. "Okay, Duck Waterfall. Fantastic. Come with me and I'll announce you. We have a little makeshift stage area set up."

Timothée Chalamet leads us out into the heart of his barbecue. There have to be at least forty people lingering about around a pool and a bar area. The entire backyard is framed by an assortment of trees that provide a sense of privacy. At the forefront of the different socializing areas is a small, raised dais and that's where Timothée leads us. There's a microphone standing at the front of it.

He walks right up to it. "Okay, next up in the entertainment department tonight we have the next big improv comedy team, DUCK WATER-FALLLLL." He shouts our name like an announcer, like we're super high in demand and people requested we be there. Aaron sets down the sign Dawn made along the front of the stage.

There's a smattering of applause before Dawn takes the mic.

"Hey, y'all!" She rouses the crowd with her socializing powers. More people look up from their conversations to assess us. "We're an improv comedy team and we're gonna do a little long-form improv for you. Don't be frightened; it's gonna be a fucking hoot. We're called Duck Waterfall. We feed off the pain of our insecure childhoods. Somebody shout out the name of something you loved when you were a kid."

"FRUIT ROLL-UPS."

"DRAGONS."

"FLIP-FLOPS."

"FLIP-FLOPS?" Dawn says, aghast. "What did flip-flops do to lose your trust in adulthood, kind sir?"

"They hurt my feet," the twenty-something shouts over his beer.

"Ah, they hurt him," she repeats dramatically. "Due cause to end any relationship. Okay! We're going with flip-flops."

We huddle up into our little acapella shape and start the pattern game, and my heart is beating so fast as Dawn repeats *flip-flops* and everyone else repeats it with her, turning to lock eyes with a different person with each word.

"FLIP. FLOPS. FLIP. FLOPS. FLIP-FLOPS." Dawn catches my eye and winks.

I close my eyes as random words start being rattled off. *Please let me remember a phrase and successfully turn it into something funny.*

61. A Girl Does Family Dinner

JAMIE
September 5, Saturday Evening
New Jersey

At 4:30, I called my mother from a restricted number as Lara Thorpe, the talent agent. In a posh British accent, I talked her through when, where, and what her fake interview will be like in Vegas. Not to toot my horn too hard, but I killed it. She was so enthused! I answered all her questions. She said she'd be securing her travel immediately. She'll be emailing over her receipts so we can "reimburse" her.

I googled the Greek casserole recipe—it was a three-page essay with a thousand ingredients that I would most definitely butcher, so I've made some changes to the menu.

This kitchen smells amazing: like warm brie, apples, and chicken soup. I bought four cans of Campbell's chicken noodle and tossed them into a pot to have as a side along with our brie, macaroni, and apple grilled cheese sandwiches. I've got tango music playing off Siri's iPhone through the Bluetooth speakers. George, Gill, and Mara should be here any minute.

I'm coming at Mara hard today. I'm going to push for answers with Gill and George here to keep her honest. An hour ago, I raided her closet for an outfit and stumbled into her cosplay collection. I selected a dark V-neck blue dress and cape paired with brown pants worn by the Mother of Dragons.

"Ah, you're all here!" Mara swoons as she walks in. "Am I late?" She smiles at George and Gill already at the table. I let them in a few minutes ago, and they've been very nice. Both men have politely ignored my ensemble.

"Only by seven minutes, Mother!" I cheer.

I've ladled some soup into the bowls I put out, and I'm now hovering near the stove in front of my platter of food.

Mara's eyes bulge as she takes me in. "Jesus, Siri! What are you wearing? Is that my Dany costume?"

I scrunch my nose in a mocking smile and grab the tinfoil-covered plate of hot grilled sandwiches. "I wanted to wear something I knew you would really love."

Gill chuckles from the table. Mara lets me off with an irritated look. She wants peace tonight.

I place the serving plate in the center of the table as they make small talk about how they're doing today.

"Dinner smells . . . different than I expected," Mom says from her seat next to mine. "Did you—"

I pull off the tinfoil. "That's because it's gonna be better than expected." I grab a sandwich with a pair of tongs and carefully place it onto Mara's plate.

Her brows come down. "Wow, this isn't what we discussed, Siri. I thought—"

I serve a sandwich to George. "The idea came to me last night when I was trying to sleep, around three a.m., and hallucinating Jamie in the corner of the room. She said this recipe was her favorite and is one of your favorites too? So, I thought I would give it a go."

I place a sandwich on Gill's plate. Father and son look uncomfortable.

Mara's face has gone gray. Yahtzee. I've hit a nerve. *Speak, Mara. Acknowledge Jamie. Acknowledge me.*

She sucks in a deep breath and lets it out slowly before opening her mouth. "Okay, I haven't had this in a while . . . Looks great, honey." She lifts the sandwich and takes a bite.

Something in me cracks as she brushes me off for what feels like the hundredth time. How much weird Jamie shit do I have to lay out for her to get what I'm putting down? For her to open up in the slightest? Does she really think she can just hide me from Siri forever?!

George is trying to catch Mara's eye and make sure she's okay. I serve myself and flop into the seat across from Gill.

The sandwich is actually pretty tasty. Who knew I could make a meal. After a few bites I raise my fingers and perform a little chef's kiss. "Wow, I am good."

Gill catches my eye. "You're going to see that doctor again to help with the weird hallucinating thing happening, right?"

"Right." I give him finger guns as I chew. "Tomorrow."

Mara sucks a tooth before getting up. She pulls a bottle of red wine out of a cabinet and brings it to the table to uncork it. "So, how was everyone's day?"

"I had a successful presentation at work." George perks up.

"I got a very interesting email—" Mara says at the same time.

The wine bottle pops open as she beams at George. "That's fantastic!" She hurries to the cabinet, grabs three glasses, and divides them up among herself, George, and Gill.

I tilt my head, eyeing her hard. "Excuse me," I say politely. "I don't get a glass and Gill does?"

"Gill's in college, sweetheart . . ." Her voice trails off.

My eyebrows are practically floating over my head. The nerve of this woman. "He's twenty, Mother."

She concedes and grabs one for me. We're all silent as she pours a small amount of red wine into each glass.

"What kind of email?" George forces out cheerfully in Mara's direction.

I grin with my wine glass held aloft. "Yeah, Mom, tell us about your exciting life."

Mara's smile goes in and out like a flickering bulb. She lets it settle before looking up at George. "I'm wanted to choreograph a *Mean Girls* production in Vegas!"

George's hopeful grin wavers. "Oh my . . . goodness, wow, congratulations, when did this come through? Are you, um—" He sets his wine glass down, his expression going pensive. Instead of finishing his thought, he picks up his sandwich and takes a bite.

There's another silence.

"This is actually really good, Sier," Gill says across the way.

I nod. "Thank you, sir."

"It wouldn't mean moving there," Mara explains. "It'd be a month or so, and then I'd be back . . . probably. I'm going to go to the interview and hear them out. Nothing's for sure yet."

George's forehead lines become more prominent. "When's the interview?"

"This Tuesday—"

"This Tuesday, as in three days from now?" George cuts in. "Is the interview over the phone?"

"Um, I had a preliminary phone interview today and the main one, it's—" Mara stutters. "It's in Vegas."

George blinks at her. "You, you bought a ticket and said you would go without even . . . telling me about it? This is exactly what I'm talking about, Mara. You don't treat me like a partner, you—" He snaps his mouth shut.

"George, I haven't gone yet. I'm telling you now—"

George shakes his head, staring down at his meal.

"Siri, why don't you tell us how things have been with you since your big retreat? Where did you go today?" Mom says with false enthusiasm. "You've been leaving the house from morning till night since you've gotten back from Colorado. Where have you been going?"

I aggressively scoop some soup. It flops right off the spoon. "How would you know that, Mom? You're out all day."

"You've been going into the city," she says. "What are you up to there?"

I take a giant bite of macaroni sandwich. "Why would you think that?" I say around the food.

"Can you not chew like a cow, and speak independently of your food?"

Gill's eyes ping between the two of us.

Bits of pasta spray from my mouth as I respond sweetly, "Can you tell me how you would have the slightest idea of my whereabouts?"

My mother grimaces as she takes another swig of wine. "I would have the slightest idea," she says with forced kindness, "because after the incident this year when I didn't hear from you and you were hurt—I didn't know where you were till the hospital called me! I turned on the parent tracker in your phone for my own peace of mind."

I process that for a moment, nodding and smiling, before turning to grin at George and Gill. "Wow, what a complete and utter lack of respect for my privacy. Wouldn't you agree, Gill? George?"

"Uh." Gill looks down at his food without comment. George has a silent conversation with Mara through the power of sight.

After a moment, Mara speaks down to her barely touched sandwich. "Siri Martine, I am not mad you're out all day. I know you're an adult. I'm just curious, what have you been up to?"

I take a sip of my wine. "If you must know, I joined a *Twilight* cult and quickly rose to the head position. We're plotting the takedown of all other pop culture phenomena and the re-rise of our lord and savior, Edward Cullen. Maybe you'd like to come to a meeting?"

Mara's strained smile falls away. She refills her wine glass.

"A cult?" George asks in disbelief.

"Yeah, we meet every day downtown," I explain casually.

"And do what?" George cocks his head to the side.

"Burn Game of Thrones books."

Mom locks eyes with me. "Stop it, Siri."

"I'm kidding, Ma. We just worship vampires."

There's another extremely uncomfortable pause as George shares a look with Mara. I shrug at Gill.

Mara responds on a thirty-second delay. "It will be nice to check in with Dr. Sparrow tomorrow."

I widen my eyes. "Yep."

"You're planning on going, correct?" she clarifies.

"I've said I was going to go multiple times now, Mother. Should I get up and do a cheer about how excited I am about the appointment?"

She meets my bluff. "You're not usually one for cheers, but if that'll make you happy."

I gesture toward Gill and George. "I'm happy just eating with these two wonderful guys; that cheer would be for your enjoyment."

She bites into her sandwich and we all fall, once again, into uncomfortable silence.

I shove my last bite of grilled cheese down and stand. "Well, as much fun as this has been, I have somewhere else to be."

Mara's eyes pierce mine. "Don't you dare leave this table, Siri."

"Sorry, Mom, cult thing, can't get out of it." I grab one of the spare sandwiches off the serving plate and place it in a Rubbermaid I left out on the island. "Taking this to go!" I turn to wink at her over my shoulder. "And I'll be turning my phone off!"

I snatch the backpack I left near the front door and escape into the night.

62. A Girl Is Braving Another Open Mic

JAMIE
September 5, Saturday Evening
New Jersey

I forgot to grab a jacket. I'll have to make do with this Daenerys Targaryen cloak. Luckily, I had the foresight to steal a red lipstick from my mother's bathroom earlier. I do my best to apply it now with a compact as the train rumbles into the city. I don't want people thinking I'm doing a *Game of Thrones* bit for open mic, and red lipstick plus my Siri-dark hair is a hard left from Dany's look.

I told Mara I was turning off my phone, but I haven't been able to actually do it. I haven't heard from Dawn. I dial her again as I step outside onto Eighth Avenue.

This is the last chance I'm going to have to get her thoughts on my set before I stand up in front of people again and possibly confirm or deny my ability to do comedy. I leave her a message: "Dawn, please, please, please pick up. I miss you so much and I need to talk to you tonight, please."

I try her four more times before I drop the phone in my backpack.

Zarar meets me at the entrance to QCZ. "Whoa, is this a . . . comedy costume?"

I shake my head. "No, I attempted a parent confrontation thing during dinner."

"Ah." He nods. "How'd it go?"

I pull on a smile. "Okay. I brought you something." I pull my pack to the side and yank out the brie, macaroni, and apple sandwich I salvaged. "A Grilleroni with a twist if you get hungry."

The left edge of his lip goes up. He takes the Rubbermaid carefully, like I've presented him with a sacred gem. "Thank you, Jamie."

I shrug. "Hope you like it. Pop it in the microwave."

"Will do." He tucks it under his arm. "You look upset."

I shake my head vigorously and smile harder, my cheek muscles hurting. "I'm not upset. I'm great. Where can I wait till it's time to do this thing?"

He puts a hand on my back and leads me past the line of people waiting outside, into the tiny theater, through a door, all the way back to their very tiny, very full green room.

"I have to work, but I'll be back when it's almost time," Zarar says.

I nod and shoo him away before taking a seat in one of the folding chairs scattered about. I pull out Siri's iPhone. I'm becoming addicted to this thing and I don't like it.

I suck in a sharp breath. I missed a text.

Dawn: Can't talk today, Jamie. Need a little more time. Siri will call you later and fill you in on how everything went.

I stare at it for an unknown length of time. I completely forgot about the barbecue. It has to be over. Why the hell hasn't Siri called me already?

It must have gone poorly.

Did my dinner go poorly?

I didn't get around to asking Mara about Dad. I wanted to corner her. The key questions, the key statements I wanted to spew in front of George and Gill didn't come out of me. I got too caught up in the moment, pushing Mara's buttons. *She's so good at pressing mine.*

I run a hand down my face and groan when it comes away covered in red smudges. Fuck me.

At 11:45 Zarar walks in to find me with my head in my hands. Half the people who were here earlier are gone. Zarar sits in the folding chair next to me.

"What's going on?" he asks.

I look up at him, revealing the flattering red lipstick stains streaking from my lips down my chin. "This is."

Zarar snorts.

I shake my head. "Are you kidding me?"

"You still look beautiful," he says through the side of his mouth.

I glare up at him through my lashes. "I know. I'll make it work."

"What's really up?" he asks.

I groan. "I don't know. I didn't push enough on Mara today . . . on the topics that really mattered, and the aftertaste of failure is pretty shit."

"Do you want a piece of gum?" Zarar asks.

I smirk at him. "Shut up."

"Your food was really good."

I nod. "Thanks."

"You can ask her the questions when you get back," he says.

I can. But it won't be the same. I glance at the phone clutched in my hand.

"This just feels wrong." I voice the thought without context.

This is going to be my first time performing in front of an audience where someone I know and care about is in the crowd (excluding my father who I didn't know was there so that doesn't count). And that person isn't going to be Dawn who's been at my side supporting everything I've done over the past ten years.

Zarar pulls his folding chair around so that it's directly across from mine. "You're working yourself into a nerve tornado."

I scoff. "Yeah, join me in here, won't you? You're way too level-headed. I'm not ready to get back on a stage yet. I've barfed in emotionally charged moments twice since this happened, Z! I can't have that happen again."

"Jamie, you've done variations of this set so many times, and we combed through every joke this afternoon. You were already ready."

I shake my head. "I've only done five-minute versions of this set many times! I've done ten minutes once, and it blew . . . literal chunks. Everything's different in front of a crowd!"

"Just look at me, then."

"I can't just look at you. I have to interact with the audience."

Zarar takes my hand in his. I let him. My arm's a limp fish between us.

"You are hard-wired to perform. It's part of your personality. You're going to pull off this comedy thing. It's just a matter of when. You have another shot to practice right now. That's all this is. You're going to have to do hundreds of practice gigs before you're ready for a big gig. Start knocking out the practice gigs now. Get back on the horse. You're going to get back on it eventually. I know you will. You're as persistent as I am, just in a different way."

I shift my eyes from the crook of my arm to his pupils. How does he know these things that I need to hear and manage to say them in the most precise and calming way?

"Okay," I huff. "You're so rational and annoying."

He nods. "Okay."

"Glad that's settled."

"You're on in ten minutes."

I stare at a yellow stain on the concrete floor. I'm praying to the universe that Dawn decides to defy her text and call me, all the way up till the second Z pops his head back into the green room and says, "You're on, canoe thief."

I follow him to the edge of the stage on shaky legs and watch him take the aisle seat of the front row.

How many times has Dawn asked to come to a gig? Asked to hear the act? Asked just to see my notes—and I've turned her down.

I was afraid of what she might suggest, and if her suggestions would be better than what I had originally written and therefore prove that I'm not good enough on my own.

"Our next performer is doing ten minutes of stand-up for us. Jamie Federov." The announcer claps politely with the audience and clears the stage.

I swallow, smile, and step out toward the microphone.

The spotlight hits me and everything else goes dark. For a second, it's just me and the light and the pressure of its attention. Then the front row slowly comes back into focus. Zarar nods at me, the side of his lip kicked up.

I pick up the mic. "Hey hey hey, my name's Jamie Federov! Your friendly neighborhood vampire." There are some scattered huffs. No gasps of horror or surprise though, so I must not magically flicker back into myself. The Siri mirage glitter dust magic is holding for the masses.

"Excuse the mess." I make circles around my chin area with my finger. "I've been waiting backstage for two hours and I got hungry." A few chuckles. "They don't feed open mic-ers, you guys. I have to feed myself."

I wander to one side of the stage and drop a hand on my hip. "I don't know how much you know about vampires. We're just people like you who've had a little nip and tuck done to prevent us from aging and allow us to live as youths forever until the end of time.

"It's really not a big deal, it's kind of like Botox, but with much less upkeep. You only have to go once."

Some people chuckle, some shift uncomfortably.

"I'm kidding, you guys. I'm not a vampire. I'm just a gal from LA who smeared her lipstick. You're only allowed in there if you can play a teenager on a CW show . . . I'll have to go vampire eventually. But I'm only twenty, I can hold off, like, ten more years."

I start talking about the quirks of living in LA. About my father and my quest for his attention. People are laughing. I bring it back to Botox. I start my Twitter bit. I'm probably six minutes in when I glance at Zarar again, and there in the aisle seat of the front row I see him mouthing the words along with me. My brain fumbles to a full stop on the word millennial.

How many spec scripts of Dawn's have I read and given feedback on?

At least six.

She values my opinion and I have never shown her how much I value hers.

I'm a terrible friend. And here I am without her, proving that again. I've chosen bros before hoes. I'm human scum. I'm . . . not talking.

I gaze out at the audience. The light. The silence.

The pounding of my heart is all I can hear. It's all I can feel. Count. Think.

I stride off the stage.

Zarar walks me back to the train station. It's freezing and he's offered his leather jacket, but that's my least favorite trope and there's zero chance that

I'm going to participate. Zarar isn't going to be cold because I didn't plan my outfit accordingly.

He's been telling me how great I was and highlighting the bits that hit the hardest with the audience, and it would all be fabulous and dandy if it were actually true. But I didn't finish the set. I froze and my brain completely blipped.

I was a joke. And not the good kind. Maybe that's what I am in the broader sense.

A professional can handle their shit. Put their personal life aside for their performance. They make their emotions work for them, not the other way around.

Zarar was there to see me flop.

"You didn't flop," he says suddenly. As if he'd read my mind.

"Excuse me?"

"Jamie, there was no blowing of literal chunks. You were doing great and you got spooked, but it's probably because of what happened last time you performed. You'll keep trying until your brain moves past it."

I start walking faster. "Zarar, there were no chunks because I ran off stage before it had a chance to get worse. This was proof that the Laugh Drop wasn't a fluke. I have some sort of performance anxiety or stage fright or whatever sad, stupid brain thing you want to call it. Everything I like to do has some performance aspect to it! This could get worse, Z, and leak into my all other shit. I'm fucked."

"I think you're being too hard on yourself." Zarar puts his hand on my back and rubs the space between my shoulders. It feels nice. Also couple-y.

I shake his hand off. He drops it, and we keep walking side by side without comment.

"I have a performance coming up for my acting class next week," Zarar says casually. "I've been pretty good at the other jobs I've dabbled in leading up to this, but I don't know about this one. You have to have major balls to get up on a stage in front of an audience at all, Jamie, but to go up there by yourself: That's really difficult, and you do it with ease."

"Your improv class is already performing?" I eye him sideways.

"Nope, the regular acting class. We've been split into groups and every week there's a little show where each group puts on a five-minute scene."

"Dude, you have so much on your plate right now."

He shrugs like it isn't a big deal. "Trying to get as much done as efficiently as possible. I like being busy."

"When's your performance?"

"Next Saturday at the Bluetail Theater."

I blow out a resigned breath. "I'm sorry I won't be here to see it. How's the music production internship going?"

He nods enthusiastically. "Really good. The guy I'm working with is great; he walks me through everything he's doing and lets me help out in whatever ways I can. We're working on a new EP for this singer-songwriter that has a decent following on YouTube."

I jut out my lip and nod approvingly. "That sounds cool. You're in the recording room with the dude and the singer?"

Zarar's side grin is back as big as I've ever seen it. "I am. It's kind of awesome."

"How'd you get this killer internship?"

"Knew somebody who knew somebody who knew somebody. The guy I'm working with actually went to school with my brother; they were in a band together way back when." He purses his lips. "I come from a very friendly, curious group of chatty people."

"Your family sounds fun." I come to a stop as we reach the train station.

"They are." He cocks his head to the side for a moment. "You should come over and meet them before you leave."

I open and close my mouth a few times, smiling at his blatant lack of awareness as to how couple-y this would seem. Or maybe he is extremely aware and that's why he's asking.

Honestly, at this point, what does it even matter? I'm leaving on Tuesday. He knows I'm leaving on Tuesday. We're going out on a damn date tomorrow.

I shrug. "I'd love to meet your family."

"We're doing a family dinner thing Monday night," he says.

"Um, cool, that's perfect."

"Shall we meet here at five tomorrow for my rooftop work thing?" he asks.

"Sounds good."

We look at each other for a moment. Zarar reaches forward to hug me, and I instinctively step away.

"Sorry," I explain quickly. "I don't do hugs."

I sprint up the steps into the station. The more time I spend on this coast, the clearer it becomes that I'm failing. I'm failing in every mainstream sense of the word: career, home, love life, friends, family. My career is going backward, I no longer have an apartment, I'm dating someone too pure for this world that I promised I wouldn't, I hurt my best friend, and I have a mom who actively doesn't want me.

I don't know how to fix any of this shit. I'm terrible at feelings. All I've ever done is tell myself I'm stronger than emotions. I can choose what I feel.

I really thought I had that superpower.

I don't bother to sneak into Mara's house quietly when I get back at one thirty. I have questions. I need the damn answers. I slam the door shut when I come in from the garage.

Mara's not in the kitchen.

She's not in the living room.

Her bedroom door is closed.

"Mom?" I throw open the door. The bed is made. The Game of Thrones shrine is reorganized. Mara isn't here.

"Mom!" I yell. I stomp back across the hall and collapse onto Siri's gray carpet with a flustered roar.

Is this how Siri is feeling? Has been feeling? Like she's slipped down an Alice in Wonderland *pit and she can't stop falling because there's nothing to grab on to?*

Why hasn't she called me?

When is Dawn going to let me apologize?

Fuck this. I pull Siri's stupid iPhone from my bag. This time I actually do turn it off.

63. Angst and Ice Cream

The second Dawn and I get into her car and close the doors, we start screeching like little girls.

"THAT JUST HAPPENED!" Dawn yells.

"THAT JUST HAPPENED!" I confirm.

"INTERCOURSE YEAH!"

The afternoon has been a blur of anticipation, joy, shared glances, and hysterical laughter. Euphoric energy is ricocheting through my bloodstream! I feel like I can do anything. I can be anything. I want to tackle the world.

Dawn's all dimples and teeth, smiling like we won the lottery, drumming her hands on the steering wheel. "You fucking did it, Siri! You nailed it! And you've never done this before! Ahh! We need to celebrate with some damn good pizza and ice cream. And that is not to say your homemade pizza wasn't delicious because I loved it, but we don't have time for that shit."

Dawn turns on the car and puts us in drive as I cackle in the seat next to her. *Cackle.* I can feel the amount of laughter I've done today in my abs. I've never experienced that before in my life.

"I haven't shared this with you yet, because it's weird, but I have to now for background. I'm a pizza-grammer," she says.

"You're a what?" I ask, amused as all heck.

"I have a pizza Instagram where I post pizza pictures weekly along with a review out of five stars, and I do a monthly ice cream 'gram. So I make a point to hit every pizza place I can in the general Los Angeles area. I'm currently on a quest to find chicken adobo pizza, and taste all the pretentious ice cream flavors of the land. I've gotten to know a lot of great places—there's a magical combination of ice cream and pizza in Santa Monica, and that is where we're going."

I think my insides are exploding. "I'm obsessed with your Instagram already. What's your handle? I'm so excited to follow you!"

Dawn beams at the windshield. "It's pizzapizzadawn. I have a thousand followers." She tosses her amazing hair, putting on a silly French accent. "Someday I'll be a famous pizza-grammer with access to all ze hottest, most exclusive pizza joints."

"My Instagram is actually food-based too."

"What?"

I nod. "It used to be a lot of dance stuff, but now it's all the dishes I've tried to cook over the past three months. Amateur photography at its finest."

"Siri— Oh my god, I want to full name you but I don't know your full name."

"It's Siri Martine Maza."

"Siri Martine Maza!" Dawn bites her lip and it makes me feel things.

I swallow hard, glancing out the window so she doesn't see my face going red.

"I'm gonna need to see that Instagram, stat," she says seriously.

"My handle's not as good for branding," I tell her as we turn out of the residential area and onto a major street.

"Spill it."

"AskSiriAboutBallet11."

Dawn bursts into laughter. "I can't wait till we get there, so I can stalk the shit out of you."

I don't know if it's my crush talking, but I feel like I'm flirting with Dawn. I don't know if I've ever felt so happy and carefree and like . . . how do I describe today? I feel like sunlight is beaming through me and all my insides are bouncing around with unbridled energy. I want to hold on to it forever. Capture it in a bottle for the next time "happy" feels impossible, so I have it in case of emergency.

Dawn yanks her phone out of the cupholder. "Should we put on some tunes and jam?"

"I'd love to jam."

"Pick your poison." She holds her phone up so it unlocks and hands it to me.

I pull up one of my favorites on her Spotify—"Bad Guy"—and click play. The beat immediately starts pumping through Dawn's speakers.

"Yes!" She cranks it up, head banging to the beat. When Billie starts to sing, Dawn screams the lyrics with her.

A grin the size of a life-ending meteor smashes onto my face. It only takes me a second to join in, screaming along with her.

We hit a red light at *DUH*. The beat drops and we're shouting and flailing and catching each other's eye. The light turns green, and we jet off, laughing.

The song slows and gets sexy. I close my eyes, letting the rhythm move through me. I tap my thighs lightly. Left then right then left then right (another thing Donya was having me do every day at Rediscover last week to try to hold on to good moments, tap them in).

When the song ends, Dawn turns down the stereo. "Amazing album."

I stare at her for a moment and nod. "The best."

"Siri," Dawn starts, her tone more grounded now. "Why did you agree to do this switch? Like I get it—she's really convincing and you can get swept up in a Jamie adventure, and you're mad at your mom, but there must have been something you wanted out of it too. What's your big incentive here? Is there something other than getting to know Grier?"

"I . . . need to figure out where I go next. My future felt . . . feels like an empty soul-sucking abyss without ballet. I didn't want to go back home without a new direction."

"So you're in the market for a new dream job?"

I shrug. "I guess. It sounds fun when you put it that way."

"I can help with that. I'm great at pitching ideas. When I think of a career path, do you want me to throw it at you?" Kindness and humor twirl through her words. We slow to a stop at another red light.

Dawn looks over at me. "Your smile is like stunning," she says. "You're usually stunning, you look like an old Hollywood movie star from the fifties. But I haven't seen you smile-smile, with your whole face, yet, and it's like . . . wow."

My heart's still dancing to "Bad Guy" in my chest. I look down at my hands. "Any pitches are more than welcome."

"I've already got one. Scale of one to ten, how do you feel about becoming a food influencer?"

I chuckle. "Three."

"Wow, harsh. Okay, I see you. I'll keep on it."

The light turns green.

"It's weird," Dawn starts. "At first this all freaked me out to the tenth degree because I thought you were some creepy Jamie clone . . . I mean the projection magic that made you look exactly like her is batshit. I'm just going to ignore the fact that that's a thing because . . ." She holds out a hand and waves it around frantically. "Nope, I can't."

"Anyway," Dawn continues slowly, almost like she's thinking aloud rather than speaking to me. "The more we hang out, the less you remind me of Jamie. You're taller and willowy-er and you move so differently. You have this grace that's almost inhuman. You don't walk, you . . . glide, like they try to make Sandra Bullock do in *Miss Congeniality*.

"Your skin is so milky, your eyebrows are completely different, they're wonderful, by the way, bold as hell with your new gray-blond hair. Your nails are super clean. And you're like buff as hell." Dawn swallows.

I look down at my knees, feeling like an electric switch has flipped on under my skin. That's a lot of noticing. Almost like how I've been noticing, except reverse. I feel so noticed by the kindest, most beautiful girl in the universe.

"And I mean, that's just on the outside," she adds quickly. "From the first moment you got here, you were completely different in demeanor and personality. You are completely the opposite end of the spectrum . . . and . . ."

She trails off and clears her throat. "The place is coming up. We're only like a block away so I'm going to take this spot."

I don't know what she was going to say there, but it didn't feel negative.

Dawn steps back onto the sidewalk to admire the building. I step back with her.

"What do you think?" She joyfully throws her hands in the direction of the door. The place is very minimalist-looking, very . . . white with plants and vines as decor and a select neon sign that says ULOR'S GOURMET ICE CREAM.

"I think that's one LA-looking ice cream place." I giggle.

She gasps and carefully bumps me with her side. "This place is everything. Give her a chance, Ms. Maza."

A giddy buzz zips through me. "Aren't we going to get pizza?"

"Yeah." She grins without moving.

"Now?" I ask.

She shakes her head. "No way, we're going here first."

"Isn't that like . . . against the rules?"

"There are no rules, Siri. Let go of your restrictive dystopian ice cream mindset!"

"But we haven't really had lunch or dinner," I explain.

Dawn serves me a hard look. "Ice cream is lunch."

I hold back a smile, slipping my hands in my overall pockets. "Okay. Are we going in or do they like, throw the cones at us from the door?"

Dawn purses her lips, concealing a wicked grin. I can see it in her eyes as she looks me up and down.

The inside of Ulor's is as hipster as the outside. Their logo is a line drawing of an ice cream cone, and they have flavors like balsamic blueberry date, honeysuckle raspberry, and lemon zest birthday flan. They actually have a flavor called chocolate chip cricket mint. There are crickets in one of their flavors!

I've never tried cricket. I'm kind of curious to know what they taste like, and how they might complement normal human food.

"Why are you looking at that one so hard? You are not getting ice cream with crickets in it."

I look over at Dawn and shrug playfully. "I don't know, I'm pondering it."

"Wow." She smiles and puts on a detective voice. "Are you some sort of ice cream adrenaline junkie?"

I grin. "Which are you going to get?"

"I don't know. I've tried all of these, but never that one"—she taps on the glass—"because, well, it sounds nasty."

I look back down at it. It's really just a twist on chocolate chip mint. The crickets are covered in chocolate so there's nothing to ogle at except the sign that pronounces it cricket-full.

"It matches your outfit." I shoot her a smile. "Do you want to get it together? Then you can say you've tried every flavor."

"What if we both don't like it?" Dawn reasons. "Maybe we should share two ice creams—you get the disgusting bug-filled one and I get a delicious flavor to act as our control."

Butterflies flurry to life in my stomach. "You're going to eat this with me, and I'm going to share yours?" I clarify.

"It seems the only viable solution. I need you to understand what makes this ice cream place extremely superior, and if that bug flavor isn't good, then you'll get the wrong impression. But the bug flavor will be an adventure, and if you don't get it now, we'll be missing out on all the fun of seeing you eat a bug."

"Okay."

"Let's get these pretty chocolate-dipped cones, we're definitely Instagramming this momentous occasion."

Out the back door of the ice cream parlor, there's a bit of a cliff overlooking what Dawn tells me is Santa Monica beach. We're sitting on top of one of four wooden tables with wooden benches, looking out at the view. Wind tousles Dawn's hair as we arrange ourselves next to each other with our feet resting on the bench.

Dawn does a maintenance lick of her ice cream, shaping it along the bottom so nothing falls off. She closes her eyes and savors it for a moment. "Exquisite."

She most definitely has pretentious taste in ice cream, and I am all for it.

"Are you going to try yours?" she asks, brows raising expectantly.

I lean forward and take a chunk off the top, mulling it over as I chew. A smile breaks across my face as I bite down on something crunchy.

"That'll be the cricket." Dawn smirks.

I swallow. "Tastes like mint chocolate chip with some nuts thrown in." I give the cone another lick for good measure. "It's actually pretty good."

Dawn lifts her shoulder with a smug grin and slips out her iPhone. "We have to take some pictures, or else our subjects are going to lose their shape."

"Do you want me to take some of you and your ice cream?" I ask.

"No, I want to take some of both of us with our ice cream, and get the logo on the back of the building in it with us." She grins. "Come lean in."

I scoot closer and tilt my head toward hers. She positions the ice cream up toward her face. When she raises the phone, a small gasp wisps out of me. I'm Jamie on the screen.

Dawn lowers the camera. "What's wrong?"

I shake my head, embarrassed. "Sorry, I, um . . . saw Jamie in the viewfinder."

I glance down at Jamie's yellow shoes. "It was just jarring. I've been seeing her in every reflective surface since I got here, but I haven't taken any pictures . . . It was particularly weird this time because I forgot in this moment that . . . I wasn't completely me, and am currently, mostly, invisible." I try to laugh, but the noise that comes out of me is depressing.

Dawn's expression sobers significantly as she shifts her whole self to study me head-on. "That has to be so disorienting." She puts down her phone and reaches out slowly. She runs her finger over my nose, my eyebrows, cheekbones, over the raised beauty mark above my lip. Chills race down my arms.

"You're inescapably visible to me," she says.

Her finger stops on my lip. She pushes down on it slightly and my body pulses in response.

I swallow as her hand falls away. We're so close. Her bent leg is pressed up against my thigh. I stay perfectly still, scared any sound or minuscule movement might give her reason to shift away. Dawn holds my eyes for a long moment.

I feel something fall onto my pants and look down. My cricket ice cream is dripping over my hand. "Excrement," I mumble.

"Oh no." Dawn looks over at her own ice cream which is also starting to drip over onto her hand.

We take a second to do some ice cream maintenance.

"Come on, let's still take the picture," I urge. I want this picture no matter who I look like.

"Come closer," she directs me. I come even closer, wearing a close-lipped smile. Dawn looks like happiness incarnate on the screen with her mint-green outfit and pink honeysuckle raspberry ice cream. She raises her cone a little higher, trying to get the whole thing in the shot, and accidentally clocks me in the face as she takes the picture.

She gasps and lowers the phone. A pink splotch is dripping down from my cheekbone like runny paint.

"Oh my gosh. I'm so sorry, Siri."

I laugh and reach out, trying to lift her phone arm again. "Don't be sorry. Come on, get the shot."

Dawn smiles and lifts the phone. As she gets it back up to eye level, I bop her on the cheek with my ice cream. It's an exercise in facial control to keep my lips closed as Dawn gasps again.

Her face goes slack. "You did not just bop me with your bug-ass ice cream."

"I definitely did."

Mirth sparks in her dark eyes. She raises the camera. We look into it, cheek to cheek, with close-lipped smiles and ice cream running down our faces. Dawn snaps a bunch of options, slightly switching her pose and the angle of the phone to get the shop properly in the background.

A shimmery warmth is growing in me. I'm high on the performance, and her attention, and I'm suddenly seized with the strangest urge to lick the ice cream off her face. I turn my head and lick the green ice cream off her cheek.

It tastes like mint and joy.

Dawn stills. She lowers the iPhone once more. Slowly, with her gaze trained down, she turns her face to mine. We're almost nose to nose, and when she meets my eyes with her deep endless ones, I swear I see desire there. I lean forward the slightest bit and kiss her. Her cold lips are pillow soft and they taste like honey.

She kisses me back.

Dawn is kissing me back! It's gentle and slow and sweet, and it keeps going. And in this moment on this perfect afternoon, I feel like the wind has scooped us up and we're soaring around with a warm flurry of butterflies in a gentle tornado of bliss, and I never want to go back down to the cold hard ground where I was 24/7 before I came out to California.

When the kiss breaks, Dawn spends a long moment with her hand in my hair, studying me. Her fingers dance through the strands and it feels amazing.

"You hair is so . . . thick and heavy."

"I like you," I say immediately. "I think you're beautiful and the nicest human being I've maybe ever interacted with." I glance down at my hand which is now covered and dripping with cricket mint ice cream.

Dawn clasps her hand around my wrist, brings the dripping mess up to her mouth, and takes a giant bite. She cringes as she crunches down on the bugs, but her lips turn up in a smile as she finally swallows.

Her eyelashes flutter upward. "Today is evolving into one of those very rare perfect days."

I don't think I'm breathing. I blow out a pent-up breath. Yeah, I had stopped breathing. I nod.

Her eyebrows pull together. "The plan is for you to head back home to New York when these four days are over?"

I press my lips together and nod again.

"Then should we just go full carpe diem today and enjoy the shit out of it?"

It feels like there's a helicopter launch happening in my chest. "I would love to spend the rest of today carpe diem-ing with you."

"I'm gonna silence this." She pulls out her phone. "We can deal with non-perfect things tomorrow."

I pull out Gladys and do the same. I'll call Jamie to catch her up on the gig tonight when I get home.

"You still want to get pizza next?" I ask.

"We must! Amazing pizza place and then back to my house?" she suggests.

I beam at her. "Okay."

She grins. "But first, it's mandatory you try my ice cream because it's like a thousand times better than yours." She shoves her melty cone under my nose.

64. A Girl Needs a Break

Mara's Toyota is idling in the driveway when I walk outside. I don't know if she came home at all last night. She rapped on my door at 8 a.m. to let me know she'd be waiting to take me to my therapy appointment at 10:30.

Mara says nothing when I load into the car. We sit together in awkward silence for a decent stretch of the drive before she loses it.

"What has gotten into you?" she explodes out of nowhere. "What happened last night? How could you be so rude to Gill and George?" She sounds genuinely befuddled.

I almost laugh, but opt instead to exhale a long, exhausted sigh. "Are you ready to talk about my greedy, selfish, abandoning jerk-and-a-half dad yet? Because it's essential to my healing process."

Mara's face twists up, her mouth shrinking to a tiny angry pinpoint. "Why can't you just talk to me!"

I shake my head in frustration. "I'm sorry, what are we doing right now, clamming?"

"Clamming? Why would we ever be clamming?"

I groan and drop my head into my hands.

She merges onto the highway. "When I say I wish you would just talk to me, I mean talk to me *about you.*"

"This is about me! I need to know *about Dad*. That's part of me understanding *myself*. I need to have all the information in this equation to be able to settle my heart and move forward as a healthy human being."

I watch as her grip tightens around the steering wheel.

"Maybe you need an appointment with Captain Sparrow too," I suggest.

Mom's expression neutralizes. "You need to stop disrespecting me."

"Tell me why I haven't heard from my dad."

After four silent minutes, I reach out and slap on the radio.

A millisecond later, Mara reaches up and turns it off. "Your father and I decided it would be healthier for you to grow up in one place rather than be tossed around between us like an object we were sharing."

I blink at the road as endless clusters of evergreen trees go by. "You thought it would be healthier for me to . . . grow up completely devoid of a father?"

Mara rolls her eyes. "Come on, Siri, you have Papa and George."

"Yes, I have Papa, your dad, and George, your boyfriend, and they're great, but they're not my dad. The problem isn't what I have, Mom, it's the absence of him all together. The void where there should be some sort of information. Why hasn't he ever tried to get in touch with me? What made him so upset that after he left, he never wanted to talk to me again?"

Mara speeds up and gets into the fast lane. "It's part of our divorce agreement. He's not to contact you. He left. He made his choice. He didn't deserve you. That much emotional turmoil in your day-to-day isn't good for a kid. Children need a strong foundation, structure, and you can't get that when you're splitting your time on opposite ends of the country, Siri. You can't. He wasn't coming back here, and I wasn't putting you on a plane like an overnight package however many times a year."

"Doesn't Dad have the money to pay for that kind of travel?"

"That's not the point, Siri."

"He agreed to that?" I say quietly. Dad can be an ass, but that big of an ass?

"Yes, he agreed to it."

"So, you also agreed to it."

She blinks. "Yes. I did."

"He's not allowed to contact me for the rest of my life?" I clarify angrily.

"Till you're a legal adult." Siri is already a legal adult.

We fall into silence. What she's not saying is that she also agreed not to see me, Jamie. She agreed to drop me from her life without argument. It's been *almost three years since I turned eighteen.* But of course, she couldn't dare reach out and ruin her relationship with Siri by revealing her horrible, giant, chest-crushing lie.

I reach up and grab on to the weird handle all cars have along the rim, just for something to do.

"Were you that desperate to be free of him that you were willing to cut off his kid from the prospect of ever knowing her father?" I grind out.

I'm gripping the handle so tightly that it's digging into the skin of my hands.

Mara's mouth melts into a flat, skin-colored line. "Your father doesn't deserve to be a part of this family."

"What family? It's just me. And Papa when he's over. You're MIA all the time. Who are you to decide who I deserve in my family? You haven't even given me a choice! What makes him so terrible?"

"Have you forgotten"—she raises her voice—"that your father left us? I'd say that's pretty intercoursing terrible! He put himself before us!" Mara hits the blinker, making her way over to the exit lane.

"Haven't you been putting your career before George and me?"

"That's enough," Mara snaps. "Life is about balance; marriage is about compromise, not ultimatums."

I put my feet up on the dash. "Yeah, I don't think you've mastered that balance."

"We're not talking about this anymore."

I shrug half-heartedly. "I'm still talking about it. I'm going to keep talking about it until things start to make sense."

Dr. Sparrow is a nonstarter. I inform her that I lied about hallucinating my imaginary friend to piss off my mom, and we sit in silence for fifty minutes.

I take the train into the city three hours earlier than I need to so I can shop for a non-Siri, non-Mara outfit to wear to Zarar's swanky rooftop party. The pent-up anger I'm holding toward my mother is not doing her bank account any favors today. I've seen Zarar dress in the wild. The dude's got game. Hopefully Siri's credit card rights won't be rescinded when Mara gets the bill.

Within an hour, I manage to find the most amazing blazer of all time. I drop two hundred Mara dollars on a sparkly orange masterpiece with gold lightning bolts running down the side of each breast. It makes me feel like a fucking rock star. I wish I could actually see *myself* in the mirror, but even with Siri's pale reflection staring back at me, I'm not deterred.

I balance out the wild blazer with a sexy forty-dollar low-cut plain black jumpsuit I found at H&M. It's formfitting, so it looks more like a catsuit. Siri and I have different boobs. It fits her nicely in the mirror and a bigger size would look stupid. When I look down though, I can see it fits me a little less cleanly. The fact that only Zarar will be able to see my cleavage-y cleavage is giving me the best sort of hot flashes.

I stop in at CVS to grab the necessities before striding into the first bougie hotel I can find and setting up camp in their fancy restroom. I shave my legs over the sink. Spray the shit out of my hair despite the fact that all I can see in the mirror is Siri's stupid auto-generated braid. I fill my/Siri's eyebrows in dark and bold to match my dark hair, paint my eyelids a sparkly gold, add a heavy eyeliner, and leave a neutral lip.

When I'm done, the Siri in the mirror looks all wrong. I can almost see myself through the illusion.

At 5:05 p.m. I spot Zarar waiting on the corner in front of the train station a block away. He's wearing weathered dark jeans, a brown vest over a button-up white dress shirt, and a dark maroon leather jacket.

Damn. Fashion sense in a guy is a new kind of hot I've yet to appreciate in this life.

I feel like I'm living a slow-motion moment as I strut across the street, and for once I don't want to mock it. I want to live in it. For a few hours I want to forget about the shitty fail-nado that is my current life. Right now, I'm just a slow-motion bitch crossing the block to the handsome lad waiting on the other side of the street, and that's glorious.

65. Angst and Vulnerability

Grams texts me as Dawn is pulling us into her driveway. Dawn and I shared the most delicious melt-in-your-mouth deep dish pizza, and now we're going to hang out together. In her house. Alone.

I think Jamie texted Dawn at dinner. Dawn typed out a quick response and put her phone away because we're carpe diem-ing.

Grams: Sorry I've been busy, granddaughter. Let's cook dinner together again tomorrow night? Your father has promised to get his ass in the kitchen at 7pm. We'll do a family meal. Your choice of recipe.

Me: Sounds good, I'll start brainstorming what to make.

People want to hang out with me. People are actively asking to hang out with me.

"What's up? You're smiling like a goof," Dawn says as she unbuckles her seat belt.

"Nothing, my Grams wants to cook with me. I used to love cooking with my mom, but she's always busy now. I enjoy making stuff on my own, but it's fun to have company sometimes."

Dawn pushes her lips out in a silly contemplative duck face way, watching me. I unbuckle my seat belt self-consciously. "What?"

"You're so cute."

I beam at Dawn across the car console. "Want to help me pick out a recipe?"

"I'd be honored."

Dawn and I flip through a recipe book in her mom's kitchen. We're hip to hip and shoulder to shoulder. Our ice cream kiss flipped on some sort of magnetic switch between us. We haven't been more than a foot away from each other since we entered the house.

"What's chicken adobo?" I ask quietly as I draw my finger down the ingredients for a chicken saltimbocca recipe. I've been wanting to ask her since she mentioned it.

Dawn leans forward on the island and gazes up at me through her lashes. "It's this delicious Filipino dish. It's like sweet and salty and garlicky and tangy. It's so good."

My foot starts nervously drawing semicircles over the tile. "Well, if you don't find it in the wild . . . or even if you do, I'd love to try to make a chicken adobo pizza with you sometime."

Her lips break into a heart-stopping smile. "I'd love that."

I have to grin down at the recipe book to gather myself.

"What sparked this love of cooking?" she asks.

I shrug and flip the page. "I have anxiety, and I guess cooking brings me this sense of Zen. No matter how off-kilter I'm feeling, I can eventually get lost in ingredients and measurements and the precision of it all. Especially when I'm feeling like I've let everyone down and I don't know how to fix things . . . There's this sense of accomplishment I know I can get from conquering a recipe. I know I can do that. I know I can follow it perfectly and be proud of myself. And I love seeing people eat the food and enjoy it." I glance down at a pork chop recipe.

"How often do you feel like you're letting everyone down?" Dawn asks.

"Well . . . kind of all the time. I'm always letting someone down. I'm that person who's always on the outskirts of every relationship because I can never measure up to anyone's expectations." I swallow a lump in my throat. "The only person who I thought maybe would . . . who maybe thought that I was exceptional was my mom, and that was because of how I could dance. And now I can't dance. I'm just a shadow of a person who provides a perpetual stream of food in our house.

"Gill . . . my stepbrother, has been gone all summer and he doesn't text me because he has better things to do. My ex-boyfriend started dating my best friend because . . . I think I bored him. My . . . ex-best friend, Celia, is this vivacious, sassy, intense, unpredictable, spontaneous person, and I'm not like that. I don't know . . . I really, really wanted to make Jamie proud and pull off this Parent Confrontation Trap thing without a hitch, but I slipped up with our dad this morning, and I don't know how I'm going to fix it."

A single dramatic tear drips off my chin and onto the page. *That was way too heavy for our perfect day.* Excrement. No one likes a sad person.

Dawn's two cold hands reach out and pull my face toward hers. With her hands on my cheeks, she says, "I love how open you are. It's a beautiful trait, Siri."

I shake my head gently. "It's not. It makes my mom uncomfortable."

"It is. Don't argue with me. Your mother's discomfort is her issue, not yours. Having the courage to wear your heart on your sleeve is fucking beautiful."

I roll my eyes. She's still holding my face.

"Whatever you think you did that's ruined this psychotic plan Jamie has you wrapped up in is fixable. You can fix it. You're smart and you're resourceful, and you've got great hair."

I snort as she lets go of my face.

"What about cooking?" Dawn says suddenly like she's had an epiphany.

"What *about* cooking?" I flip to the next recipe in the book.

"Like cooking as a career path," she says.

I scrunch my eyebrows together. "Like professional cooking?"

Dawn puts a finger in between my eyebrows where my skin is scrunched up. "Yes, like professionally. You turned your other passion into a career. You can do it again."

"Is cooking a passion though?" I say. "I don't know anyone who's passionate about cooking."

"Are you for real? Who do you think is behind those doors in the back of every restaurant you've ever been to?"

I laugh, realizing how dumb I just sounded. *Wow.* "I don't know . . . it's not like something you physically train for and it's so . . . I've never thought of cooking as something people do for work, even though it clearly is."

Dawn taps away on her phone. "Think about it, woman. You are a food artist." She flips it around to reveal my Instagram feed and scrolls through all the posts from the last three months with her finger.

I roll my eyes. "No, I'm not."

"Um, if food tasting good and looking great is artistry, which it is, you are a food artist."

I flip to yet another recipe. "Dawn, can I ask you a super personal question?"

"You may."

I look up from the book. "Do you also have an . . . estranged dad?"

Dawn's chin tilts downward ever so slightly. "No, he died in a car crash when I was six."

I open and close my mouth. "Oh my, I'm sorry. I shouldn't have assumed." I frown down at the island.

Dawn pulls out a stool on the opposite side of the granite and sits. I close the recipe book and sit next to her.

"We kind of have that in common," she continues slowly. "We both lost our dads around the same time, and were raised by strong stubborn women." She smiles slightly. "They have a way of churning out more strong stubborn women."

"You *are* strong." I smile at her. "You're so self-assured and on top of things, your mom did a great job."

"Why, thank ya! I try." She uses a funny Southern accent and flips her hair.

I laugh. "I don't think anyone would ever describe me as strong," I say, looking at the knees of her mint-green overalls. They're pressed up against my own knees.

"Are you kidding? I feel like you haven't seen your arms." Dawn scoots closer, opening her knees so there's less space between us on our stools. She pushes my hair behind my ear. Her fingers trail down to my shoulder, and she slowly runs her hand down my arm. Shivers race through me.

"I don't mean physically strong," I explain quietly. "I mean, I'm like a delicate butterfly, the smallest mishap can send me spiraling into tears or anger." I take a deep breath. "I kind of left out a thing about Jamie and me and our parents."

Dawn looks up from my biceps to catch my eyes. "You don't have to tell me if you don't want to," she says softly, searching my gaze. She's taller, she's standing, she must have slid off the stool. My knees open to allow her closer.

"All that stuff you said about me being on top of things and self-assured," she says, "I've been working really hard on that. It didn't come naturally. I was really messed up just last year." Our faces have gotten unbearably close. "If you want to be, you can be. That's all it really comes down to."

I tap my forehead to hers. How did she go from kind to cute to sexy in a half a second?

"I feel like I'm in a really vivid daydream," I whisper, gazing into her eyes.

She lightly bumps her nose against mine and smiles. "Do you want it to continue?"

I nod ever so slightly. "I would like that."

Dawn closes the millimeter between our lips. Her hands trace down my sides until I'm standing with her. I slide my fingers up the back of her neck and into her hair. It's so soft. Her head falls into my palm with a shaky exhale. She reaches back, grabs my hand, and leads me up the staircase.

When we reach the landing, Dawn twirls me slowly and pushes me against the wall so our bodies are flush. I'm breathless as her mouth meets mine again. These kisses are harder. Eager. Intoxicating. Her hands find my skin through the open gaps in the orange overalls.

I grab across at her left bicep and pull, spinning us. A smile finds its way onto my lips as I execute the switch successfully, pinning her against the wall in my place. I'm rewarded with a mischievous grin.

"This is a top-tier daydream," I whisper.

We end up kissing on her bed. I don't know how we got here. All I want to do is kiss her forever. She tastes and smells wonderful and she's so soft and careful, but also not, at the same time. That doesn't make any sense.

It feels like a bubble machine flipped on inside me. I'm full of a floaty, wonderful, inexplicable lightness that I've never experienced while on the ground.

I'm lying on my stomach with a pillow under my hips and my chin resting on my hands. Dawn's sitting up, drawing shapes on my back with her finger. Billie Eilish plays quietly on her phone. It's getting late.

I twist around slowly, my overall strap falling off my shoulder as I shift onto my side and move the pillow away. "Today weirdly reminds me of something Jamie said last week."

Dawn flops leisurely onto the bed next to me and scoots a hand under her head. "Hmm, do tell."

"She was hanging out with this one guy throughout the whole retreat. And when I asked her about it, she said it was a snow-globe relationship. Which sounded, you know—"

She smiles. "Dumb?"

I nod. "Yeah. I could tell she liked him, so I asked her to elaborate." I swallow, getting lost for a second in the universe within Dawn's eyes.

"She said it's when two people who have chemistry and like each other find themselves in the same vicinity for a limited amount of time. Both members understand that there's kind of a time limit on whatever romance you might embark on, but you go ahead and build the foundations of a relationship anyway, with the mutual understanding that you'll have to say goodbye before things ever really begin.

"But the memories you make during your perfect pocket of time together will be there to hold on to and look back on for the rest of your life. You can pull out the moments and exchanges, gaze at them, smile, shake them up, use them to spark happiness, and daydream about your one that got away . . . when you need a daydream to keep you going.

"Because a snow-globe relationship never gets to leave the honeymoon stage of getting to know each other . . . it's perfect and hopeful in a way that a long-term relationship isn't. Because they always end poorly. Which is not something I necessarily believe, but . . ."

"Jamie does," Dawn finishes.

I nod. "The concept though, in its own pessimistic way, is kind of beautiful." I play with a strand of Dawn's hair, wrapping it and unwrapping it around my finger.

"That fantastic talented asshole of ours can be surprisingly poetic." Dawn wiggles closer on her side, until we're chest to chest.

I blink at her, emotion suddenly welling in my throat. "Thanks for giving me a snow globe to live in on all my un-perfect days."

Dawn's smile spreads up her cheeks. "Thank you for showing me so much kindness during a difficult time. It's been . . . a while since anyone made me feel so solid." She swallows. "And beautiful. I mean, I know I am. I know I'm a damn catch." She sighs. "But I struggled with self-esteem issues and feeling shitty about myself for a long time during my last relationship. I didn't even realize it was happening until I was in really deep with my ex."

"I'm so sorry that happened."

Dawn quirks up a shoulder. "Stronger now."

I catch her eyes. "You are absolutely intercoursing gorgeous."

She breaks into a rich laugh. I try to take this all in. Her smile and open heart. Her unclasped overalls. This room. This moment. I'm so content in this moment.

Dawn lifts her hand. Her pointer finger comes down on my bare shoulder. She traces lightly over my arm, the edge of my stomach, over my hip, down my thigh. It comes to a stop behind my knee. She inches forward and nips gently at my lips. I return the gesture, an eagerness rising in my chest.

"If you want, I think we have at least an hour left on that snow globe," she says.

"I have an hour," I whisper into her mouth. She wraps her fingers around my calf and hitches my leg around her hip.

Dawn walks me back to my dad's house around 10 p.m. I just had the most spectacular day of my life with this girl I met a little over forty-eight hours ago. I feel *free*. Like I can do no wrong. There are no eggshells to crack, just stable ground under my feet.

We stop along the side of the garage, out of the light. I glance down to where my foot has started drawing semicircles over the pavers.

Dawn's finger pulls my chin up gently. "So, what are the terms of this whole snow-globe thing? Is it closed? Is this a secret snow globe? Can we see each other before you go home? Do we never speak of this again? You spending the day with the fam tomorrow?"

I swallow. "It looks like I'll be with Grams and Dad tomorrow, but I'd love to at least say goodbye on Monday. I think it might be best for everyone if we keep our snow globe private, right? At least for right now? I don't think Jamie would want to know."

"Are you out?" she asks.

I nod. "To my mom and Papa." The garage rumbles and starts to open, so we stumble back farther along the side of the house. "But, I mean, Jamie never asked and it never came up."

Dawn's silent for a moment, looking down at our feet with a contemplative expression. "Well, I have absolutely zero exciting romantic dirt in my life, so I'm fine keeping this day between us if that's what you want." She sighs and meets my eyes again. "Ninety-five percent of the time Jamie does what Jamie wants and doesn't think about the consequences until someone points them out. I think we're allowed to have today and keep it to ourselves."

I nod, staring at her mouth now. "Can I kiss you again?" I ask.

Dawn winds her fingers into the straps of my overalls. This kiss is soft and light and leaves me feeling restless as she steps away, beaming. She backs away into the darkness, cutting through the backyard to her house.

"Talk tomorrow!" She sprints off.

For ten glorious minutes I don't think about all the anxiety and dread awaiting me in the next few interactions I'll have with my father or Jamie. I let myself revel in the endorphins spiraling through my limbs and careful-dance alone in the dark of the driveway.

I saunter into the living room fifteen minutes later and find my dad in the kitchen, standing near the table, sorting through a batch of mail.

I stop short as he looks up at me. "Hey, Jame, nice night?"

That's all it takes for everything in me to yank taut. "Yes? How are you?"

"I'm good. Glad we're having a nice family dinner tomorrow night."

"Good, me too." I turn toward the steps.

"Jamie, how long have you been emailing with your mother?" His voice is softer this time.

I pivot slowly to look at him again. "I haven't been emailing her, Dad. She, she emailed me one time, and I didn't respond because . . . I know how you feel about her." The words taste sour.

He squints at me. "Things between you and Dawn all good? After your week hiatus from the comedy group?"

Does Jamie talk to him about the comedy group?

I swallow, trying to work up the gumption to confront him further. This is an opening. He's listening. Point out how he's been gaslighting Jamie about Mara her entire life.

"Yeah, why wouldn't it be?" I answer.

"You know I love you," he says more quietly.

My lips start to wobble. I hate that he doesn't know who he's speaking to. I head up the stairs and lock myself in Jamie's room. I need to tell her how the gig went.

I'm dying to tell her how the gig went!

I pull out Gladys and punch in my own number. It goes straight to voice-mail. Three separate times.

"Jamie! Call me back! I have news and I want to tell you in person on the phone, not over an email!"

66. A Girl Is at a Rooftop Soiree

JAMIE
September 6, Sunday Evening
New York City

"Dude, you look hot!" I catcall from the middle of the street.

Zarar pivots in my direction, his face going blank for a moment as I step up onto the sidewalk.

His eyes flit down to my cleavage for half a second before they bounce back up to my eyes. "You." He runs his hand down the arm of my blazer. "You look like a sexy firework."

"Ah yes, the sexy firework. Exactly what I was going for."

"You're only five minutes late," Zarar compliments, placing a hand gently on my back and directing me down the block. "I was a little concerned when you didn't respond to my text this morning."

I grin. "That would be due to the fact that I'm off the grid. Left that piece of plastic at home and I'm living without its addictive pull. I tore apart Siri's room earlier and found a wristwatch." I hold up my arm. "A watch and a plan, it's all a girl really needs."

We step out of a taxi fifteen minutes later in front of a swanky hotel. A doorman pulls open the door as we walk through the entrance. Zarar leads me toward the elevator.

He's doing this smoldering thing with his eyes and I'm trying not to let it get to me, but it takes a conscious effort not to feel it in my loins.

We come to a stop in front of the lift.

"This place is chic, Mr. Intern. Look at you go." I smirk and reach out to tap his nose. He catches my hand midair and pulls it back down. The elevator dings open as he arches a brow at me. My breathing hitches as we step into the lift together. *Zarar.*

The doors slide closed and the car shoots upward. I slide my eyes sideways and wait for him to meet them. After a few seconds he does.

"Just so you know," I say, "I am so turned on right now."

His lip turns up. "Keep it in your pants, James, this is a business party."

I'm smiling my ass off when the doors open.

There's around thirty other people up here, chatting and drinking and being merry under the fairy lights strung over us all like a canopy of well-placed fireflies. Music slides among the guests, low enough that everyone can hear themselves talking, but loud enough that I can hear the song. Something soothing and calm that I don't recognize.

I look to Z for direction. "What shall we do first? Go meet your people? Mingle? Eat? I see food over there. Or drink, I see a bar."

"What would you like to do?"

I put my arm through his. "I would like to eat food and meet the people you work with. You need to network at these things, Zarar, not just hang out with me. Are they playing music the company produces?"

Zarar nods. "Yes, this is all from our artist list."

I nod approvingly. "So cool."

At the food table I load up on hummus dip, cucumbers, and sliders. The two of us huddle at a tiny standing table near the edge of the roof.

"So what is this for?" I ask as I stuff a hummus cucumber into my mouth.

"It's the company's anniversary; they hold a yearly rooftop party to celebrate. This is their ninth year in business, I think."

"Hey, Zarar, you made it," comes a warm voice behind me.

"Hey, Mr. Penn," Zarar greets politely. I spin around to find an attractive white dude in a plaid shirt and jeans, severely lacking any of the stylish ease of Zarar. This guy can't be the boss.

"Man, come on, we're on a first-name basis. We go way back, and I'm barely older than you," the guy replies.

"You're seven years older than me, Mr. Penn."

"Is this your boss?" I point to the guy and look at Zarar.

The guy looks at me. God, his eyes are freakishly sincere.

"I'm not his boss. I'm the guy he's working with."

"The guy that used to be in a band with his brother?" I ask. *Oof.* Something about the dude is familiar.

"That's the one," he confirms with a head bob.

"He's my boss," Zarar says through the side of his mouth with his equivalent of a smile.

I turn my smirk back on his boss. "How's he doing?" I point my thumb back at Z.

"Oh my gosh, Zarar!" A blond woman with wild curls appears next to Mr. Penn. "Nice to meet you! I've heard you're already doing such an amazing job."

Penn turns his gaze on the blond woman, and his neutral expression morphs into a smile. "This is my fiancée, and to answer your question, Zarar has been kicking ass—he's got the intern thing down to a T. I'm betting if you want, you can twist a job out of Frank, *the actual boss*, once your internship's done."

Zarar extends a hand to the blond lady. "Nice to meet you . . ."

"Shane," the woman fills in. She smiles broadly and shakes Zarar's hand before turning to me. "Who are you? Wow, your outfit is the coolest ever. And your braid is amazing. Wow." She waves her arms around. "I feel really—" She gestures to her black turtleneck and high-waisted bell-bottom jeans. She's wearing red lipstick to dress up the whole ensemble. "Underdressed."

"You look amazing." Penn watches her with googly eyes.

Siri would approve of her boring outfit.

I reach out my hand. "So nice to meet a fellow lady with a typical dude name. I'm Jamie. James, that is."

"Amazing." She beams and hops a little, like an excited rabbit. "Does your name have a story? I always ask my mom *Why Shane* and she has the most boring answer, she saw it in a baby book and *just liked it*?"

I snort. "You give off major Energizer bunny vibes and it's great."

Penn starts laughing and Shane smacks his arm with the back of her hand. He points from me to Zarar. "Are you two together or—?"

"Not quite," I start and glance at Zarar.

"First date," Zarar says.

Mr. Penn directs his attention at Zarar. "Where did you two meet?"

I turn to Shane. "My mom's a giant loser and named me after a problematic Game of Thrones character. She insists she just likes the name Jamie, and it's only my middle name that's Thrones-related, but I don't buy it."

Shane hesitates, wide-eyed, like she's choking on a laugh.

I nod. "Yeah. My middle name's George."

She snorts. "I'm so sorry, that's really funny."

I grin back at her. "Don't be, it's fucking hilarious." I glance over at Zarar. I missed what he told Penn about us meeting. My eyes flit back to Penn, and my memory suddenly clicks him into place.

I step back, my gaze darting between the two of them. "Holy shit, you're the 'Wrecking Ball' guy!" I point at him accusingly. "And you're that girl in the video." I blink dramatically. "Oh my god. I have to take a picture for Dawn. You guys don't even understand, we watched that video like five thousand times and belted that shit on the bus to school every day!"

Shane's eyes are about to pop out of her head as she turns to share a stupid grin with Penn.

Penn covers one of his eyes with a hand, but he's smiling. "No way, it only has like forty thousand views."

"What is this video?" Zarar asks.

"I'll pull it up for you. It's this semi-viral video from ancient YouTube times with the most ridiculous amazing lyrics."

"Okay, that's our cue to step away," Mr. Penn says shyly.

"I need a picture with you guys, hold on. Z, can you use your phone?"

Zarar digs his phone from his pocket, and I step in front of the couple, pointing at them with an expression of disbelief.

"This is ridiculous," Penn mumbles.

"Smirk for the damn camera, Pies."

"Got it." Zarar hands me his phone to inspect the picture.

"What do you do, Jamie?" Shane asks.

"She's a comedian," Zarar says. "She did an open mic set yesterday at QCZ, and I'll bet she does another in the next few weeks if you want to come."

I shoot him a look. "Zarar."

"She's really great. We could use some friendly faces in the audience next time."

Penn turns to Shane. "That could be fun."

Shane smiles at me. "We are so fudging there."

She and Siri would definitely get along.

"Do you guys laugh?" I ask. "You're only allowed to come if you laugh."

Shane holds her fingers up in some sort of salute. "I am super big on the laughing."

"What kind of question is that? Of course we laugh," Penn comments.

I point to Zarar. "This guy doesn't laugh; he just finds things internally funny."

Z side-smiles. "I open up to you about my weird thing, and this is what I get for it."

"You just invited your boss to my next set," I accuse cheerfully. "So, this is war."

"Zarar, make sure you let us know when that happens," Shane says as Penn puts a hand on her back and leads them away. "James, our laughter shall make up for the laughless one," she shouts.

I turn back to Zarar, scooting closer to him against the edge of the building. "We really maybe shouldn't call this a date. I'm leaving in two days."

Zarar holds my eyes. "But it is a date."

"I mean, it makes me twitchy when you say it out loud."

"You're too cool for the word 'date'?"

"Date implies more than one date will occur."

"Aren't you coming to meet my family tomorrow?"

"Yes, but—"

"But I think you're just going to have to get over your weird irrational fear of romance if you want to keep hanging out."

"I'm not afraid of romance. I'm afraid of hurting you."

Zarar shakes his head. "You're afraid of romance. You're afraid of the word 'boyfriend.'"

299

I flinch as he says it. His eyes spark in response.

I want him to tear my clothes off. I'd really love to lose myself in this patient, persistent, hot smart-ass that somehow got me here dressed up for him on a first date.

"You don't want to be my boyfriend. I'm an asshole," I say, a centimeter from his mouth.

"You don't get to decide what I want."

"I think you should mingle with some other women and make this feel less exclusive."

He cough-laughs.

I grin maniacally. "Say goodbye to laughing for the next year, Zarar. You're way over budget."

"Fine, introduce me to some other women if it'll make you feel better."

"Fine. Let's do it." I scan the roof. "There's a hot lady over there. We'll start with her."

"Okay." He gestures forward. "Lead the way."

I step in her direction. "I am leading the way."

Zarar and I taper off again to our own corner of the roof after engaging in small talk with three separate hot women, one of whom I got a number from for Zarar. It's scribbled down on a scrap of paper I ripped out of my comedy notebook.

The two of us lean up against the building's concrete wall with the beers we've acquired along the way.

"That was fun." I waggle my eyebrows at him. "Are you going to text that foxy lady that works in the other department?"

He shrugs, aiming his weird eye-smoldering thing at me and convincing 70 percent of my brain that it wants him to rip off my clothes right here and now. I almost tell him to knock it off, but I like it too much to actually voice the thought aloud.

"What, were my wing-woman skills not up to par, or something? I set you up with three meet-cute situations," I tell him. "Think of the story for the grandkids, crazed orange blazer lady introduced us randomly at a rooftop party? That's got spunk, Z. Do you need me to go find a stack of paper you can drop on her? Cuz I can do that."

Zarar reaches his arm out and rests it over my shoulders. I find myself leaning into it automatically. I shouldn't, I'm going to give him the wrong idea.

"I like just talking to you," he says.

I sigh. "It sucks that you're my favorite person to talk to on the East Coast."

"Why?"

I shift so I can look up at him. "Because I'm leaving and you're getting attached, and it's going to ultimately ruin this easy weird wonderful thing we have if you get too romantically involved."

"I don't think that's what's going to happen," he says confidently.

I scoff. "What *do* you think's going to happen?"

"I like to live in the now, so right now, I'm with you and I'm having a great time by your side."

I roll my eyes. "Let's stop talking about me for, like, a minute." I take a swig of beer.

"I'm an open book here, Jamie."

I swallow. "Okay, time for twenty first-date questions with Zarar."

"Shoot."

"What did you want to be when you grew up, back when you were five?"

He shrugs and sticks up a finger. "I don't think I've ever known. It's why I'm job-hopping right now." His lip tips upward.

"What's your favorite food?"

He raises a second finger, counting for me, I guess. "A dish my mom makes, chicken biryani with fresh raita and aloo shami."

"Favorite band?"

Three fingers. "*NSYNC," he says freely.

I almost do a spit take and glance around. "Zarar, shut up, don't say that so loud here. You'll get fired; they're way too pop."

"I always liked watching them dance."

"Have you tried dancing as a career too?"

Four. "I did dance classes growing up."

I shake my head, smiling. "Of course you did."

"What do you eat for breakfast in the morning?"

Five. "I'm an oatmeal guy."

"Bleh."

His forehead wrinkles up. "What do you eat for breakfast?"

"Here I eat Siri's Special K, which tastes like nothing. At home I grab a breakfast burrito down the street, or a granola bar."

"That sounds difficult. I like to go straight to the kitchen when I wake up."

"Favorite movie?"

Six. *"Jab We Met."*

"I've never heard of that."

"Well, you should watch it. It's on Amazon Prime."

I nod. "I will."

Seven. "Dream goal?"

Zarar leans back and takes a swig of his beer. "To settle down in the right job with the right person and find happiness."

I look down into my drink. "You are such a dweeb."

He shrugs. "That's the dream."

"Why did you and your last girlfriend break up?"

Eight. "She found someone else when we went to different states for college."

"Did she cheat on you?" I ask, appalled. "You are a precious flower of a human."

Nine. He quirks his head sideways, and my eyes dip to admire the muscles in his neck. "It happens. We weren't each other's lobsters."

My brows pull together. "And you're still such a sappy-ass romantic? How do you believe in that forever happy bullshit?"

Ten. "Because I do. It's real."

I roll my eyes, twisting to gaze out at the red lights of cars flowing down the veins of the city.

Zarar slides over till our legs touch and we're side by side. He's facing me and I'm facing outward.

He takes another sip of beer. "How exhausting is it to be *over* the entire idea of love?"

I shake my head. "You're so wrapped up in your romantic fantasies, you spew these statements that are so over the top. We've known each other for barely a second and you're so . . ." I search for the right word.

"We've known each other for a week and half, and we've talked every one of those days."

"I'm an asshole. I don't know how many times I have to tell you that for it to sink in."

"I don't think you are."

I stare him down for a long moment before chugging the rest of my beer. He looks so happy. And so sure.

"Can I see your apartment?" I ask.

He resets his fingers to one for question eleven. "Yeah, do you want to come by tomorrow before we head to my parents'?"

"Now," I tell him. "Can we go now?"

Twelve. Zarar searches my eyes. "Yes." He nods. "Yes, James, we can go now."

The wood creaks as we climb the narrow steps of Zarar's three-story apartment building.

He deftly unlocks a dark blue door right off of the staircase, flips on the light, and leads me into a small living room with a galley kitchen off to the left.

My mouth is dry.

I step past Zarar to do a lap around the room. There's a clean gray couch in front of a forty-inch TV and a small wood coffee table. He has some fishing poles against the wall in the far left corner of the room. There are minimal touches of decor here and there, and pictures. Zarar and a guy who looks a lot like him who must be his older brother, Javed, out in front of a tent among the trees. Zarar and his family at his graduation. Zarar and his mother on a couch.

Zarar walks toward a hallway off the living room so I follow. He leads me to the second door on the left and pushes it open.

"This is my room." He steps in and sits on his single bed. I lean against the doorframe.

It's very tiny. The walls are painted light gray, and his bedspread is a splotch of bold red among the neutral tones. There's a small narrow bookcase up against the far wall, full of what look like nonfiction or biography-esque novels. On top of the bookcase is another framed picture of him and his brother. He has a compact nightstand next to the bed. There's an Acting 101 book sitting on top of it.

"Is your roommate home?" I ask.

Zarar shakes his head. "At his boyfriend's."

I nod and walk back to the living room and sit on the couch.

Zarar follows.

"Very minimalist. I like it." I tell him.

"Thanks." He sits next to me. I stand. *I should just leave.*

Instead, I hold his eyes and play with the lapels of my orange sequined blazer. "So you like my outfit?" I smile and spin for him.

"I do. It's very Jamie. Sparkly and loud on the outside, dark and mysterious underneath."

"Help me take it off."

Zarar stares for a moment before he starts to get up. He doesn't break eye contact as I step forward and push him back down onto the couch.

He studies me for a second before shifting to get up again. I push him back down. Shake my head. When he starts to stand, I push him back a third time. "Tell me to leave, Z."

He shakes his head from the couch. "No."

"Tell me to stop and get the fuck out of here."

"I don't want you to stop, Jamie."

Zarar stands. He stuffs his hands under my blazer and shoves it off my shoulders. It clatters to the floor with the weight of all the sequins and beading.

"Yes?" He gazes down at me.

I step up onto the couch behind him and graze the back of his neck with my teeth as I work the leather jacket down over his shoulders. When I finally get the stubborn thing off he turns to look up at me with that damn jawline.

"Yes."

I push one of the jumpsuit straps off of my shoulder. Zarar reaches up and takes the other one. My heart thunders impatiently as he pulls it down. I shove my hands under his sweater vest and yank it over his head, ruffling his mass of dark hair. He slips his hands under the fabric of this tight-ass catsuit so they're against my skin, and slides them down over my breasts, stomach, thighs, slowly forcing it off. Heat blazes through me as he meets my eyes again.

I hop off the couch and circle around to push him down onto it one more time. He lets me do it, watching with the same hunger I feel coursing through my veins. He doesn't realize. He's a forest and I'm a fucking wildfire.

67. Angst and Ideas

SIRI
September 6, Sunday Morning
California

Someone is knocking on Jamie's bedroom door at 8 a.m. on a Sunday morning.

"What is it?" I grumble from my sleeping bag. My back is aching something fierce today. I moved in all sorts of different ways last night that I haven't in a long while. I need a hot shower and some ice.

"It's Grams. Get up, I'm taking you shopping today."

"Now?"

"Thirty minutes, I want to hit the road and get to the outlets before they get crowded."

"Fine, I'll be down in ten minutes," I whine.

"Good girl."

I freeze on my quest to rise from the floor, an idea taking shape. Eureka!

I know how I'm going to get my dad to Vegas on Tuesday!

I check Gladys for any sort of response or message from Jamie and come up empty, so I slap her computer keyboard a hundred times until it wakes up. I have an email.

Mara,

We made exactly the right decision. We were terrible together and
would have rained hell down around our children had we stayed on
the same coast, let alone tried to co-parent.

You're finally talking to Jamie? Why now? You can't handle your
own kid so you want to try to win the affection of mine?

Don't brainwash my daughter. I don't know what your angle is here
but I'm not buying it.

Stay in your lane.

—Grier

Another kind-hearted response from my father on the catfish account.
Nothing from Jamie.

Me [9:30am]: I'm shopping with Grams
 Me [10:07am]: Did you get my voicemail?
 Me [11:01am]: Jamie are you getting theses texts
 Me [11:38am]: Jamie FOR THE LOVE OF GOD RESPOND
 Me [12:00pm]: I'M ASSUMING YOU'RE ALIVE BUT YOU'RE STARTING
TO FREAK ME OUT
 Me [12:08 pm]: Grams bought you/me some new white sneakers.
Get pumped. Can we toss these excrement orange Converses?
 As time ticks by and I still don't hear from my sister, I start to imagine
that, somehow, she saw Dawn and me together yesterday and got so upset,
she decided to completely cut me out.
 At seven, Grams, my dad, and I sit down to eat the meal Grams and I
put together this afternoon: chicken saltimbocca with a Caesar salad made
from scratch, marinated roasted brussels sprouts, and twice-baked potatoes.

We spend the first five minutes of dinner eating in silence.

"How did the gig go yesterday?" Dad asks after he's devoured a portion of his plate.

I swallow what's in my mouth and dab my face with a napkin. "Really well, actually, and something exciting happened today. I was booked for another gig."

Grams jabs her fork in my direction. "What? Why didn't you tell me?"

"That's fantastic, Jame. Congratulations." Dad grins.

"When's the next gig, granddaughter?" Grams inquires as she cuts her second helping of chicken into meticulous pieces.

"It's on Tuesday."

"Oh wow—" Dad starts.

"It's in Vegas for a big open mic comedy night at MGM. I applied ages ago. Someone dropped out and they sent me an email invitation last minute." I look up at my father. "Dad, I was hoping you would road trip down with me, and we could spend some time together just the two of us . . . do some quality bonding. If you want, we can listen to that *Game of Thrones* podcast you like? You must be a little behind being so busy and all." I'm taking a gamble on that podcast prod—my mom listens to three of them.

Grams is staring daggers at Dad. Daggers that say, *You better not let this girl down.* If I've learned one thing this past week, it's that Dad listens to his mother. I smile innocently across the table.

"Tuesday, as in this Tuesday?" Dad clarifies.

"This Tuesday." I nod.

Dad glances between Grams and me. "Of course, Jame. I'll move some things around. Let's do it."

I grin, trying not to look too pleased with myself.

Grams smiles. "Good, that's settled, then."

The three of us are watching *Kill Bill* in the living room when Gladys starts buzzing in my pocket. I excuse myself and run up to Jamie's room.

It's Dawn.

"Have you heard from Jamie?" I ask. I texted Dawn earlier as my concern mounted.

"I'm worried," Dawn says. "I've been thinking a lot about that thing you *didn't* tell me yesterday, that you wanted to tell me. Can you possibly tell me now? I'm going to call her soon. I want to make sure I approach my opening statement the right way."

"Oh . . ." I mumble as I remember. I was going to fill her in on the piece of the puzzle she's missing. "Well, you were saying something about us being strong. I kind of never told you the most relevant details of my parents' split . . . You know Jamie left with my dad. I was super upset and sad, throwing tantrums . . . I was a four-year-old who couldn't figure out why my sister would leave me, and my mom told me that . . . Jamie was never real, she was an imaginary friend."

Dawn is silent on the other end of the line.

"She said that I was big enough to live without her and make real friends, and I was four and it worked. Kinda? We moved within that year to a place in New Jersey closer to my Papa. Papa got me into therapy, which kind of helped. But basically, I've thought Jamie wasn't real right up until we ran into each other at this retreat."

"So . . . Jamie, Jamie's over there with your mom who has been pretending for the last fourteen years that Jamie doesn't exist." Dawn's voice cracks.

"Yeah . . ." Shame rumbles in my gut.

Dawn heaves a long breath over the phone. "Okay, I'll call you back later. I have to try Jamie."

68. A Girl Is Conflicted

JAMIE
September 6, Sunday Night
New York City

"You can stay if you want," Zarar says softly from his single bed.

"Mara's going to be pissed enough as it is," I tell him as I pull on my boots. I'm sweaty and discombobulated. It was definitely a mistake to come back here. We had sex twice. Once on the couch. Once in his bedroom an hour later. Thrice if you count the stuff that happened in between. We had amazing sex. I stare blankly at the wall across from his bed.

I feel Zarar sit up behind me. "Can I have twenty questions before you run off?"

I shift, turning halfway to look at him. "Why?"

"Because this was a first date, and I didn't get the answers to some things I'd like to know." My stomach flutters with the steady intensity of his gaze.

I look up at the ceiling, batting my eyelashes and pulling a silly innocent expression as Z maneuvers closer. "You can have seven."

His hand slides from my waist down over my thigh. "You got twelve."

I exhale a slow breath, trying to keep a clear head as my insides reignite. "Eight, and that's my final offer."

Zarar's still shirtless. I underestimated what was under those layers. He said he was a personal trainer earlier this year. He carried me half the way to Terry's cabin last week. I should have been more prepared. I can't look directly at him or I'm going to jump his bones again.

I focus on those gentle eyes. "You promise to answer them all and answer honestly?" he asks.

"Yes," I huff.

He tilts his head thoughtfully. "Favorite movie?"

I hold up a finger like he did earlier. *Men in Black 2.*"

His forehead scrunches up. "What? Why?"

Two. "Will Smith, Aliens, weirdness, comedy."

"Longest sexual relationship?"

Three. "A month."

"Did you use the B word?"

Four. I shake my head. "No, we had a friends-with-benefits agreement."

"Do you like me as more than a friend?"

Five. I look away from him at the blood red comforter thrown haphazardly on the floor. "Yes."

"I thought so."

I whip my head back to shoot him an irritated look.

"Okay, is that it?" I raise my brows and pull on an over-the-top smile, pushing up off the mattress.

He grabs my hips before I can get away and pulls me back down onto him. As hard as I try not to laugh, a snort escapes me. I squirm and he gets me on my back, straddling me on his knees. He pins my arms at my sides, and I'm beaming, and I feel like my heart has been lit up from the inside and it's shining light through my every orifice and it's horrifying.

And now I'm looking directly at his naked torso again. What am I supposed to do with that?

He catches my gaze with a side smile. "Eyes up here, James."

I cackle under him.

"Is this okay?" he asks.

I believe he knows the answer to that. "That's six. You really shouldn't waste questions, Z."

He talks out the side of his mouth. "Answer the question, please."

"Yes, it's fucking amazing. You're really hot. I have an outstanding view. I'm very comfortable here. Is that what you want to hear?"

"Are you happy when we're around each other?" Seven.

I roll my eyes.

"Yes. But as much as I enjoy you, naked and otherwise, I've really got to go so Mara doesn't kill me."

"Will you turn on your phone and text me when you get home?" Eight.

I arch upward, curl my mouth up to his, and whisper, "I will text you when I get home, you giant dweeb," into his lips. He captures me in one last savage kiss before I push him away, roll off the bed, and stride out the door toward the living room, my body buzzing.

"Put on a shirt, please," I shout over my shoulder.

I hear him fumbling around behind me. "Can I walk you out?"

"No," I throw back cheerily as I scoop up my blazer and backpack and pull open his front door.

"Hey," he calls from the hall.

I turn to find him hopping around as he pulls on pants. "I care about you, canoe thief."

I bob my head from side to side and then nod.

"I'll see you tomorrow," he says.

I pivot and beeline down the stairs.

Mara's on the couch with a book when I get home at 2 a.m. She looks me up and down in my run-down party girl state, wearing the most judgmental expression I've ever seen. I raise my hands in rock-and-roll horns and stick out my tongue. She shakes her head. Her mouth pinches up into a tiny dot before she strides away to her room. I hear the door slam behind her.

Upstairs, I check my catfish email. I've got a message from Mara with her travel information for the interview in Vegas. She's booked a flight that gets in at 12 p.m. Time to book my ticket with Siri's only-for-groceries-and-emergencies credit card.

When I turn on Siri's iPhone, a thousand messages ping in asking if I'm alive. Plus some texts from Mara asking where I am. Plus a text from Zarar. Plus two voicemails? Jesus Christ.

Zarar: Did you get home safe?

I shoot him a quick reply, as promised.

Me: Yes.

He texts back immediately.

Zarar: Meet me at the train station at 5 tomorrow? We can head over to my parents' house together.

Me: You got it, dude. Can you send me that picture with your boss and his fiancée?

The picture pings in thirty seconds later. A wild rock-and-roll-looking Siri stands in the center of it, wearing my expression. Penn's face is red, and he's looking at his bubbly fiancée who's clearly amused. I can't wait to show Dawn. I tap out and dial Siri before she has a heart attack.

69. Angst and Storytime

SIRI
September 6, Sunday Night
California

"JAMIE?! What the hell is going on over there?" I yelp, closing the bedroom door, running into the closet, and closing that door as well. It's been two hours since my phone call with Dawn.

"What's wrong?" Jamie asks on the other end of the line.

"What's wrong?" I whisper-yell. "Your phone has been off for more than twenty-four hours! That's what's wrong! We haven't exchanged an update in like two days! We're supposed to be keeping in contact. Are you okay?"

"I'm fine. I just needed some time away from this thing."

"This thing being all means of communication?" I ask frantically.

"How did the gig go?" she says carefully.

I'm speechless for a moment. I can't believe she's going to blatantly brush this off. "Are you mad at me or something?"

"No. Tell me how it went," Jamie says quietly. It almost doesn't even sound like her.

I heave in a great breath, because I've been dying to tell Jamie how the gig went since the second I got off the stage.

I exhale, concentrating on letting go of my built-up frustration so I can fill her in with the enthusiasm yesterday deserves.

"Jamie, it went so well, like, better than I ever could have imagined! I was so anxious about starting a scene, but I started one about a girl rooming with her sister who's a professional villain in a New York apartment, and the words just flew out of me, and Dawn stepped out and played my sister, and she made it hilarious, and it just got better in the B and C and D beats. I don't know what happened. I, like, fell into it and let it happen instead of trying to consciously make it happen, and I can see why you love this so much because when things go well, they go so well! And everyone was laughing! Jamie, Timothée Chalamet and I had like, a fifteen-minute conversation afterward about Dad and Dad's movie and me—I mean you!" I correct. "And Duck Waterfall! And he took a picture with us for his Instagram, Jamie!!! He hasn't posted it yet, but if he does, it can blow up Dawn's Duck Waterfall Instagram! Dawn is so stoked, and I haven't felt so happy and relieved and energetic since my last ballet performance . . . so thank you for letting me do this. I needed it. Dawn and I went to this hipster ice cream place called Ulor's afterward to celebrate! I have Timothée's number, if you're interested in him in that way, or in a friendship way. I did my best to talk like you do, and I think I really nailed it, it's the most in character as you I've ever felt! It's in your phone when we switch back!"

I wait with bated breath for her reaction, leftover joy radiating in my chest.

"Jamie?" I ask. Did the line go dead?

I hear her inhale. "Dude, that's great. Good for you. You're a natural performer. Just like with ballet. You're funny too."

"Well, not funny like you," I tell her.

She doesn't respond.

"What's wrong? I thought you'd be happy. You sound . . ." She sounds like me before the switch. Angry. Inherently.

"Dawn took you to Ulor's," Jamie interrupts. "Dawn took you to number one on her top twenty Instagramable ice creams of SoCal list after knowing you for forty-eight hours?"

Top twenty Instagramable ice creams list? "Yeah? What have you been up to? I have Dad locked down for Tuesday."

"Mom's locked down too. I ordered us matching outfits off Amazon."

"Oh cool . . . when did you do that?"

"Just now when I bought my plane ticket."

"Okay . . ."

Why does this feel so uncomfortable? This is the opposite of how this conversation was supposed to go. "What is going on over there, Jamie?" I demand.

"I gotta go, it's late. I'll email you details and time stuff for Vegas," she says. The line goes dead.

70. A Girl Is Inferior

JAMIE
September 6, Sunday Night
New Jersey

My sister's a better me than I am.

71. Angst and Preparations

SIRI
September 7, Monday Evening
California

I spend the morning preparing for the road trip I'll take tomorrow with my dad. Jamie sends me an email detailing a play-by-play of her plan for Vegas tomorrow. I jot it down in my notebook along with the questions I'm going to ask Dad in the car, so I don't forget or chicken out.

Dawn doesn't get off work till eight today. Grams and I have spent the whole afternoon together cooking another meal entirely from scratch: chicken francaise with homemade pasta and a bruschetta appetizer. We've been having a great time making fun of the cheesy Netflix rom-coms Grams set to play in the background. She keeps commenting on the editing choices, and it's not till she references her own work that I realize Grams must have been an editor . . . for movies. In Hollywood. I'm so glad I got to meet this sassy old lady who happens to be my grandma, and I can't wait to re-meet her as myself when this magic wears off.

At 10 p.m. Dawn texts me that she's along the side of the house, much later than I thought I'd be seeing her. She's stopping by just to say goodbye because she has class early tomorrow morning.

Dawn's hair is pulled back in an impeccable high ponytail. She's wearing a hot pink skirt covered in subtle imprints of hearts, with matching pink heeled sneakers and a tight black top. She looks like a pop star.

Once I'm within three feet, she throws her arms around me in a hug, and I hug her back like my sanity depends on it.

"Sorry, I'm being awkward about hanging out on your last night here . . . I'm starting to feel weirder about furthering the snow globe if we're not going to tell Jamie," she babbles with her arms around me. She pulls back. "If you're ever in California for more than four days and you want more than a snow globe, I would love to explore that with you." She huffs a sad laugh. "I know if I come inside . . . the more we hang out now that we've . . . snow-globed, it'll be harder to say goodbye." She snorts. "I sound like such a loser."

I shake my head. "I am so thankful I met you."

She quirks her brows, gesticulating nervously. "We're going to meet again, you know. I'm excited to re-meet you when you come visit Jamie . . . and be friends, if you want to be. And like I said . . . I mean, I don't always find such a natural, easy . . . um, and if you wanted to try dating ever, you know where to find me . . . on Pizza Perfect."

I laugh. She smiles coyly at me and I grin hard back.

She nods again. "My point is, we could figure this out if you wanted to. Like eventually, when you feel more put together, and you ultimately realize that the East Coast is a dull freezing tundra compared to the glory that is SoCal."

Everything is so tangled up and confusing right now. I don't know what to say, so I pull her into another hug.

72. A Girl Meets a Family

JAMIE
September 7, Monday Evening
New York City

I'm only ten minutes late to meet Zarar as I sprint out of the train station. I spot him on the sidewalk, holding a bouquet of blood orange flowers.

A sense of relief floods through me at the sight of him—like falling onto the couch with some tea at the end of a long day *relief*. It's so hard to be in that house with Mara. Every interaction is stressful and strained.

"Hey, Z." I smile.

"Hey, James." He holds out half the flowers toward me. "These are for you. I'm glad you're coming today."

I take the flowers and bite my lip, looking down at them. "I hate flowers."

His eyes do this twinkly thing they do when he's amused but not laughing. "Of course you do."

We turn and start toward the subway.

"I do like the color, though."

"Good."

"But flowers are stupid."

He looks down at me, talking out the left side of his mouth, as we wind through hordes of New Yorkers during rush hour. "You're very welcome. I'll get you more next time."

I grin. "Next time I'd prefer cheese. Or a duck. Or a duck shaped out of cheese. Or pretzels. Or a cheese pretzel. Or pasta. Or a muffin. Or a burger."

We cross to the next block with a herd of humans. "So basically, any food," he comments.

"Yes, Jamie love food. Food good. Get her food." I floof my hair. "Who are the other flowers for?"

"My mom." His mouth turns up the slightest bit as we come up on the subway entrance. "She enjoys a good flower."

I grin, watching the pavement as we start down the stairs to the underground.

"Are you okay?" Zarar asks as we reach the rank-smelling landing. "You're giving off a sad vibe."

I shrug. "Torturing my mother isn't giving me the happy rewarding glow I thought it would, and Siri's kind of living it up in my place." I shake my head again. "I'm really glad I'm with you for the rest of the day."

Zarar presses his lips together as we step up to the edge of the platform. "They do always say that thing about revenge not being the answer."

I cross my arms. "It's not the answer, but it's fun. It was supposed to be fun."

Zarar's parents greet us together at the door to their gorgeous red brick sub-urban home like we're the king and queen of the world. Hugs and praises and compliments and offers of any beverage under the sun. They're both rather tall and slim, and I can see Zarar in their faces.

"Jamie, it's so nice to finally meet you. You look lovely!" I'm wearing a pair of Siri's black jeans and a blue blouse I stole from my mother's closet.

"We've heard so much about you!" Zarar's mother finishes as she fishes Siri's leather jacket from my arms.

We follow them through a marble-tiled foyer and into the living room where I stop dead in my tracks as I catch sight of Terry on the couch with another handsome brown man, Z's brother, Javed.

"Siri?" Terry balks.

I snatch Zarar's hand and rush him back out into the foyer. His parents who were slowly walking behind us, watch in confusion as I unlock the front door, open it, and step outside, dragging him along with me.

"Zarar!"

"Jamie."

"Is Terry your brother's fiancée?" I ask in disbelief.

"She is."

"Zarar!"

Zarar totally isn't registering why I'm freaking out. "What?" he answers calmly.

I gesture wildly with my hands. "Why didn't you tell me Terry was going to be here?"

He smiles. "I thought it'd be fun surprise to see another familiar face."

He's smiling for real with his teeth and entire mouth. I shake my head, grinning at him. "What the hell are you smiling about?"

He shrugs. "I like you."

I snort and roll my eyes. "Okay, I think you're forgetting a big piece of the puzzle right now—your family can't see me, they see Siri. Terry can't see me—she sees Siri and she knows us both."

Zarar's smile deflates. "Shit."

I nod. "Yes, this complicates things because it seems you told your parents about me."

"Of course I did, you're a part of my life."

I'm a part of his . . . We just . . . How does he blurt these things out with no regard for how ridiculous they may sound?

I close my eyes and exhale. "Terry's probably in there telling him my name is Siri and it's going to clash with what your parents know and it's all about to get very confusing."

Z presses his lips together. "I'm going to have to make up something about why you don't look like yourself. I don't want them to be baffled the next time they see you."

The next time? I'm leaving tomorrow.

Zarar mulls this over for a few minutes while I wander around him in a slow circle, worrying that I shouldn't have come. I probably shouldn't have come. It was selfish to come.

"Jamie, you should ask Terry about the happy haunted stuff," Zarar says suddenly.

I take a few steps backward. "Holy shit, you're right." How did my brain not jump to this immediately? I ram into the front door, throwing it open again. "Terry, darling!" I shout, "I'd love a word in private out here, please, stat!" I slam the door again.

I smile at Zarar while we wait for Terry. "Well, your parents are going to think I'm insane."

"No, I've told them you're a character."

"A character?" I say cynically.

"They know that you're eccentric in the most wonderful, unpredictable ways and have an amazing heart."

I squint at him. "What?" I ask, perplexed. "What else have you told them?"

"That we're dating." His barely there smile rears its head.

I bite my lip. "You wily bastard. We go out one time—"

The door opens behind me and we both look up at Terry.

"Terry, thank god." I slump.

"You were happy haunted?!" Terry screeches five minutes of explanation later. She's over the moon.

I grin at her. "Wow, could you look more thrilled about my distress? Were you happy haunted or do you happy haunt people? What's the deal, Terr?"

She reaches out and tries to touch what must be my phantom braid and steps back. "I— Wow. You don't know how nice it is to know for sure I'm not the only one this has happened to."

"What happened to you?!"

Terry takes a deep breath and settles her hands on her hips. "Six years ago, after my divorce—"

"You were divorced . . . at twenty-six? This is your second engagement? Terr, what the hell happened?"

She shoots me an exhausted look.

"Yeah, sorry, reflex. Irrelevant. Keep going."

"After the divorce, I went on a road trip by myself to see the country. I was looking for something in my life that I could call mine. Something I cared about. I didn't know exactly what that was. I was an art teacher already, and I loved that, but I had summers free and I had an entrepreneurial spirt bounding around inside me, so I hit the road.

"I was hoping to figure out what I wanted to do with that as I was hiking and renting cars and driving. I loved being out of touch with everything.

"Eventually I was out there in Colorado, and I swear I followed the trail out to the retreat area and it was just wilderness. No cabins, no head cabin. I found the signs for the trails that are out there behind the cafeteria with all the different mantras. I hiked Luck, thought about how nice it would be to have a retreat of sorts out here, how it could help people find the peace that I'm finding, how I'd love to help people start down their own journeys."

Terry pauses and blows out a breath. ". . . And I hiked back down and ran into this whole campground on the walk back to my car. There wasn't anyone around, so I headed to what was obviously the head cabin and registration area. The door was open so I walked in. On the kitchen table was a deed to the land and it was in my name."

I shift on my feet. "What?! The whole retreat was magicked to you? Your thing is completely different! That's ridiculous! Your story is ridiculous. I don't even know what to do with that. How many people have been affected by this?"

She shrugs. "I don't know. I've only known one other woman whom I suspected. She came back from a hike with long knee-length blond hair after going up with a short brown bob. I don't know what happened. She wouldn't share with me no matter how pointed my asks were, but I'm fairly sure she was happy haunted. Do you remember any sort of note?"

I nod. "Yes, there was a damn note; it was a riddle."

"And what did it say?"

"It had a timeline of four days and five nights, but I don't really remember the other details. We weren't expecting it to drastically shift the axis of our lives—and then we got glitter bombed and it was all sort of distracting."

She nods in understanding. "Ah, the glitter."

"Were you glittered?" I demand.

"Yeah. It wasn't in a cabin, though; it was from a box under a tree."

I cross my arms and shift backward to lean on my other hip. "I cannot believe this. Why didn't you share this story while we were at the retreat when you said it was happy haunted?!"

"Jamie, no one ever believes this story!"

I bark a humorless laugh.

Zarar butts in, "Ladies, I know this is fascinating and mysterious, but do you think we could discuss it at a time when my parents aren't anxiously waiting on the other side of the door to eat with us?"

We both turn to look at him in unison. "Of course," we chorus guiltily.

I turn back to Terry. "Don't forget to call me Jamie."

"I got it," she says curtly.

Z goes in first to explain away our weird exit and tell his parents about a "strict social experiment" I'm doing for comedy reasons where I cosplay my sister for a week. They apparently already know I'm a weirdo; what's a little more nonsense?

Terry and I head inside after counting to sixty together on the front steps. Z's brother jumps up to introduce himself, "Jamie, I'm Javed! You can call me Jay."

Z's mother pulls me aside to the corner of the living room and gives me a sweet smile. "Jamie, if you need the bathroom, it's down the hall and to the right."

I nod. "Thank you, Mrs. Jafri." I look over at Zarar, who's now enthusiastically chatting with Javed. They're so excited to talk to each other, it's pretty adorable. I catch his eye. "I'm going to head to the restroom real quick, Z."

He shoots me a discreet wink as I wander off. I guess he told them my behavior was bathroom-related.

When I return, everyone's taking seats at the Jafris' lavishly decorated table in the dining room. Z waves me over to the spot next to him. He and his brother are chatting about what Zarar's been working on his first week at the production place with Penn.

Mr. and Mrs. Jafri unveil a number of bronze dishes across the length of the gold table cloth.

Zarar leans over toward my ear and points to the bowls. "Chicken biryani," the brightly colored rice dish at the center of the table, "raita," a creamy yogurt-looking sauce, and "aloo shami," which look like fried potato patties. The air fills with the mouthwatering smell of spiced meat. His mother points to the food and in a warm voice says, "Bismillah karo beta, please begin!" After a moment we all dig in.

Zarar's dad turns to me from the head of the table as we're passing around the food. "So, Jamie! We saw your set the other day; you're so talented. When did you first get interested in comedy?"

I gawk at him for a moment before glancing at Zarar. He shrugs. "They wanted to come see you."

I turn back to Zarar's father, smiling bashfully. "I, wow, thanks for coming. You didn't have to."

"We're so glad we did!" Zarar's mother beams at me. "I've never been to a comedy show before. We had so much fun watching all you up-and-comers. We'd love to come to another!"

I huff, looking down at my partially full plate. "I've been dealing with some stage anxiety, so I'm sorry the set was cut off when you watched."

Zarar's father waves me off dismissively. "You'll get past it. It's like everything else."

"You were very funny," Zarar's mom says.

I huff again. "Well, thanks. If only I could make it ten minutes without losing my grip on my own material."

Mr. Jafri taps his fork against his plate lightly. "Did Z tell you we're anesthesiologists?""

I smile at him. "Wow, no. I knew you worked at a hospital but not what you specialized in."

Javed jumps in cheerily. "In med school, Dad couldn't stick anyone with a needle without fainting. The guy's a hack."

Zarar's father looks at Javed. "Hey, hey, I'm telling the story here," he says with mock annoyance. We all chuckle as he turns back to me. "My sons, they're so American, interrupting their father! I would never get away with that growing up!" He grins lovingly.

"Jay's not exaggerating, Jamie. I watched it happen at least seven times," his mother adds.

"I was a very manly fainter," his dad boasts.

"You two were in the same classes, then?" I smile at his mom.

"Every one." She beams at Z's father and passes along a bowl of fresh cucumber and onion salad to Terry, who's sitting to her right.

"I hit the floor so many times, my wife was jacked by the end of our first year from catching me every class."

His mom rolls her eyes and Zarar snorts.

I whip my head to serve him an incredulous look. *You just laughed at your father's pain,* I tell him through my eyes. He raises his brows happily.

"How'd you get past it?" I ask his dad.

"Same way you get past anything—you just keep trying to do it." He grins.

I nod appreciatively. "That's some grade-A perseverance," I tell him. "I can't believe you wanted to be a doctor in the first place."

"I can't believe it either," he replies.

I laugh. "How long have you been married?"

"Thirty-two years," his mom replies.

Terry pipes up. "Z, how's the first week of your acting course been? These new endeavors calling to you?"

"I don't think they're the ones, but I'm still learning a lot and having a great time."

"You have a great time at every job," Javed jokes.

"Except accounting," Terry adds.

I laugh.

"What's next on the job menu?" his father asks. "We can all start hunting down our connections."

"I'm thinking something with animals, a vet assistant or something at a zoo," Zarar explains.

His mom chuckles. "I love that; you always loved animals." She looks at me. "We could never have a pet when they were kids because I'm allergic, but Z begged us for one anyway, for years. He was obsessed with all his school friends' animals."

"He was so annoying, asking Dad every other day as an eight-year-old, coming up with lectures and written affidavits about how he would care for a cat or a parrot all on his own. No one would ever have to lift a finger." Jay scoffs.

"Remember that one time on the road trip to Florida when he made us pull over so he could pet that giant dog we were all afraid of?" Zarar's mom adds. They all laugh, and Terry smiles politely.

Zarar's father jumps into a story about a family road trip they had back in 2006. Jay reminisces about listening to Percy Jackson books on audio as a family during the ride and how funny they were. Zarar's mom tells me they used to play some sing-along game together when they weren't listening to audio books, but Javed would always push for a new title because he loves books so much.

Terry jumps in, smiling and cracking jokes about how their current apartment is so overloaded with books, they look like a couple of hoarders. Zarar asks how the wedding planning is going, and they all have a ball lightly making fun of Javed for being more into the decor part of planning than Terry is.

I listen to everything, smiling and struggling to process how close these people are. How they took road trips together. They were in the same car for hours at a time and they loved it. We eat our food and stay at the table long past finishing. Just talking. They talk about their neighbors, the TV shows they're all watching, movies, pop culture. They include me, asking specific questions to make sure I'm still a part of their conversations. There are no arguments. There are no long silences. They're genuinely happy to be around one another.

I didn't think these types of families were actually a thing. His parents are still in love. They watch each other with such kindness and care. Concern. They pay attention. They're all listening to one another. When I talk, they listen raptly to what I say. They comment and ask thoughtful follow-up questions. They're all so open. Zarar's parents knew everything he and I had done this past week.

Their love is so warm. Their support for Zarar is so palpable.

I feel heavy as Z and I ride the subway back into the city. It's 9:30 p.m. when we reach Penn Station. Zarar walks with me to the platform where I'll catch the train back to Jersey.

"So . . . your family's phenomenal," I tell him quietly.

Zarar is flushed with what I could only describe as an elated glow.

"Yeah, I love them," he says out of the side of his mouth. He reaches out and pushes my hair behind my ear. "Thank you for coming. I loved having you there with us. They loved you."

I pull up a small smile and grab his hand. "I had a great time. Thank you. Honestly, thank you for inviting me, Zarar. It's a super bummer that I'm leaving tomorrow."

I can't stop staring at him. He's smiling-smiling. It's kind of just like his non-smile smile; it's on one side of his face. But bigger and less subtle. It's really hot.

"You know what's great about the fact that you're leaving again for forever tomorrow?" he says.

I smirk. It's hard to do right now. I'm struggling to keep my breathing steady. "What?"

Zarar bounces his eyebrows. "This time I have your number."

I raise my brows. "Don't count your chickens. Who says I won't steal your phone and delete it before I leave?"

"You will not be able to pull that off in the next thirty seconds," he says confidently.

"Thirty seconds?" I turn to see the train coming in. I blow out another breath and turn back to him.

Zarar steps forward and leans down to meet my lips. It's a sweet, happy kiss, and when I pull away, he pops down for another quick peck.

The train doors slide open. "Thanks for being an amazing friend," I tell him.

"We'll see each other again, canoe thief," he insists. "We're going to keep in touch."

I step onto the train. He winks at me as the doors start to close. "You have Siri's number, hot shot, not mine," I blurt as they suction shut.

Z's eyebrows pull together, but he doesn't break eye contact through the window.

He holds my gaze as I stumble through the car, walking along the outside of it with me. I heave in slow, careful breaths, forcing myself to stay calm until my train has rumbled out of sight.

Then I fall apart.

Tears spill out of me like blood from a severed artery. I can't stop thinking about that dinner. About his family. The way they are together. I can't stop thinking about everything I didn't know I was missing and will never have.

73. A Girl Has Lost Control

JAMIE
September 7, Monday Evening
New Jersey

I'm still crying when I walk up to Mara's house and punch in the code to the garage. I can hardly make out the numbers through my waterlogged eyeballs. Where the fuck is all this water coming from? I should have gone dry thirty minutes ago.

I wander past the living room where Mara is reading, head straight up to Siri's room, and fall onto the bed.

Why did I think being an asshole back toward my asshole parents would make this better? I turn on Siri's phone that I left sitting on her nightstand. I have to check in with her before our flights tomorrow.

I don't know how long I've been lying in this puddle of a pillow when there's a knock on the door. I don't speak and I don't open it. After ten seconds, it opens by itself.

Oh joy, my mother's here.

Mara looks extremely uncomfortable. "Sorry, I—I was reading and I heard you get home, and decided after a while I should come check on you. Can I come in?"

I hastily sit up, wiping my face with my sleeves. "Why not?" I rasp.

Mara approaches the bed timidly, like I'm a wild animal. She puts her hand down first and then sits. She doesn't speak.

Why is it so hard for her to say anything? Why does she hold so much power over my mental state? Why does her every awkward statement, every rigid movement feel like a splinter pressing into my skin?

I need this confrontation to be over. "Mom, was Jamie really a figment of my imagination?"

I stare into her gold eyes. *Please just acknowledge the truth.* For a moment, a deep sadness shines through her features.

Then Mara looks down at her hands. "Siri" she says softly, "why are we still having this conversation? Of course she was."

"*Please, Mom,*" I sob.

She reaches out and rubs my back. "Siri, honey, stop dwelling on her. I am so, so sorry you're hurting. We have to be strong and move forward instead of looking back. You are going to get past all this sorrow. You are strong."

"You're saying Jamie for sure was not real," I repeat as robotically as I can manage.

"She was not real," Mara says.

I catch her eyes again, my face a mess of anguish and bodily fluid. "You never saw her."

She doubles down. "No, Siri."

Fresh hot tears sear down my cheeks.

"It's going to be okay." Mara shifts closer, pulling me into her arms.

This is the last place I want to be. But I let her do it anyway. I don't know why. I don't have the energy to do anything else.

74. A Girl Is a Hot Mess

JAMIE
September 7, Monday Evening
New Jersey

When Mara finally leaves an hour later, I reach over for the iPhone. Someone called during my sob fest.

Dawn.

I jolt upright and tap the video camera button next to her number.

The phone plays the little doo-doo-doo-doo-doo jingle that I've heard so many times in shows and movies. A lingering sob falls out of me as Dawn's face pixelates onto the screen.

"Jamie?!" Dawn looks fabulous as usual, with her hair in an Ariana Grande–esque ponytail with a hot pink scrunchie and black sweater.

I can see my Siri self in the tiny corner screen. I look like I just rolled out of a ditch.

"Lady Federov, whateth the helleth happened?" Her voice is heavy with concern.

"Can you see me, me or do you see Siri?" I gurgle.

"I see you, Jame. That shit doesn't work on me."

"Aces, thank the damn heavens." A hiccup pops out of me. "Lady Torres, I've missethed thou so freaketh much. I am so, so sorry, I hath been the biggest dicketh in the land." Hiccup. "I have taken you for granted so hard. I think you're a sensational writer, and I wish I included you in my set planning a long, long time ago. I'm sorry I didn't tell you about Siri. I'm a dumb dumbass and I thought you would think less of me. That's why I don't tell most people most things. I'm just starting to realize how much of a moron I've been. I love you. Please don't hate me forever. I need my best friend. I am such a stupid asshole sometimes."

Dawn's dimples pop onto her cheeks as I finish my monologue. "Bitch. I have waited so long to hear you say that." She sucks in a breath. "Wow, you are so gross when you cry." A single drop of water falls from her eye.

I snort through my unrelenting blubbering. "Shut up."

She wipes away her single tear. "I love you too, and I've missed you tremendously. Tell me everything. Every fucking detail of the last twelve days, and then and only then will I fill you in on anything that's happened on my end, got it?" She grins.

There's snot dripping down my face. I wipe it with the back of my hand. "Okay, should we start from today and work our way back? I met a guy's parents. Wait, also I had mind-blowing sex last night and it sucked not being able to tell you about it after. Oh shit, I cooked a meal for humans and it wasn't horrible. It was the worst, not being able to tell you every detail of everything right after everything!" I gasp. "Oh my god, I met the 'Wrecking Ball' YouTube guy last night!"

Dawn's face lights up. "No! 'I Came into the Dining Hall'?"

"Yes! I got a picture. Give me a second, I'm sending it over." I tap out of the call and throw the picture in a text thread. "Seriously, hold on to your ponytail because this is gonna be a wild roller coaster of shit. I haven't even gotten to tell you about my bomb."

"What bomb?" she says.

"The show I bombed so hard the week before the retreat that I went on the retreat."

"I called that." Her phone pings. She taps around and then gasps again. "And that's the girl!"

I nod triumphantly. "That's the girl!"

"Dude!! I wish I were there!"

"I wish you were here!"

"Get your ass back to California!"

"Should I do my set for you now or later? Because more than anything ever, I want your notes."

"Stop jumping around and start from the beginning!"

I sniffle and nod. "Okay," I say. "So it was September tenth, 1999, at ten fifteen a.m., when my mom triumphed in ejecting me from her vagina after fifteen hours of labor."

Dawn groans on the other end of the call and I'm still kinda crying, but I feel a thousand million times better than I did ten minutes ago.

PART 3

Better Together

75. Angst and Road Trips

It's Vegas Day. I open my eyes before Jamie's *Men in Black* alarm clock blares and flip it off. It's so jarring, my brain has resorted to clocking time on its own.

I clamber off the ground to where Gladys is plugged in.

Jamie: I'm at the airport. We're supposedly changing back to ourselves when we see each other so I'm thinking we do some matching fun statement makeup to mask our facial differences so we can freak the 'rents out harder once we're back to normal. You have my makeup so I'll leave that bit up to you.

"Wow . . . eccentric makeup choice," Dad greets as I come down wearing Jamie's backpack.

I've painted an orange glitter star over my right eye. I'm wearing a baggy sweatshirt over the overalls I threw on. Jamie has our matching outfits, so I have no obligations there.

"I'm trying out a new look for my set," I tell him as we walk out to his car.

I googled a new bunch of physical therapy exercises for my back and did them on the floor before I came downstairs because this four-hour car ride is going to be rough.

As we pull away from Beverly Hills, Dad presses play on an episode of *Ice and Firecast,* a *Game of Thrones* podcast I've heard my mother mention over the years. I sigh, settling in.

"You ready for some good old *Thrones* discussion?" he says enthusiastically. I nod.

The episode is an hour and a half long. It feels like two eternities. Dad laughs and talks along with the panel. Sometimes he interjects and tries to correct them.

"They can't hear you," I say at one point. He pretends like he can't hear me. Throughout the discussion, I'm rehearsing the questions I need to ask him, over and over in my head.

Right now, in this moment, I believe I can do this.

No matter what his response is, I'm going to be okay. Dawn was right. Being in touch with your emotions is not a weakness, it pushes you to confront your demons, and I'm ready to confront one of mine.

The second podcast ends, I reach out and turn off the radio. We're speeding down a blank, empty highway through a boundless span of desert. It looks like we've completely left civilized society. We pass the occasional sign for a wonky themed diner off in the middle of Nowheresville, but we have no plans to stop. We're going straight to Vegas. We'll eat when we get there.

"Nothing like a good *Thrones* breakdown, eh, Jame?" Dad muses again.

I exhale. "Yep, it was great, Dad."

"There's really so much in these books that we don't see until we put them under a microscope."

"Dad." Frustration leaks into the word.

"Yeah! What's up, you getting nervous for the show? You know I'm really proud of you getting this all by yourself. Who connected it? Someone from Laugh Drop?"

"Yeah, someone from Laugh Drop." I sigh, knowing I already told a story about how I applied for it online. I guess he just wasn't listening. "I want to talk about Mom."

I feel Dad's cheer blow out of him. "Not this again, Jame."

"I want to hear the story, of how you met and why you fell apart. Those days before we moved out here"—I swallow, trying to find the right words—"haunt me. To get past that, I have to understand what happened."

"What happened was your mother was stubborn and cold and didn't give a shit about anyone but herself."

Anger swells in my chest.

"I want to know something good about Mom," I say stiffly.

My dad has the nerve to laugh. "There's nothing good about Mom."

"There must have been or you wouldn't have married her!" I scream.

"Jesus Christ, Jamie," he bursts back. "Lower your voice."

"You stole me away from her, the least you could do is tell me what the *fuck* made you like her so much that you spent more than a week having sex with her!"

I blink, gazing out the windshield, a little taken aback by my own outburst. I just dropped the f-bomb for the first time since . . . I learned about the f-bomb.

Dad shudders. "I don't know, Jame! Your mother would always finish things and put them back in the refrigerator. She put too much ketchup on everything." He glances over at me. "She'd make that infuriating face that you're making when she was angry!"

"Tell me about when you first met. You two used to love each other, correct? Or did you get married for the hell of it?"

Dad's face is flushed as he stares straight out at the sand-colored nothingness surrounding the highway.

"Back then, everything was different. We were still in college." Each word comes short and clipped, like it's a struggle to get them out of his mouth. "She was a force of . . . nature. A captivating one. Graceful and full of life and ambition.

"Young Mara was going to be on Broadway and that was that. I had been in theater club since freshman year of college. She joined my senior year, her junior year, because she heard we were going to be doing a Game of Thrones musical production, back before there was a show, before it was mainstream at all, and she had to be a part of it.

"Thrones was fairly new then; popular, but nonreaders didn't know about it. We were waiting for book four to come out. The play was a comedic parody version of the first three books that I had written myself. All of us theater kids were obsessing over George's world."

Dad clears his throat. "I don't know what you want me to say. It was a whirlwind. I had no plans to be in New York my entire life, but once rehearsals started, we were flirting every day and going out for food all the time and then we were together. All the time. She was beautiful. I was attracted to her passion. Her . . . will. She's determined and she gets things done and she's confident about it. I didn't see the flaws that came alongside that."

I ignore that bit. "The theater part sounds romantic. Who did you play in the play?"

"I was the lead."

"Ned?" I ask. I don't know why I'm surprised.

My father smiles wistfully. "Yep."

"Who was Mom?"

"Cersei."

I choke on air. "Oh god."

"She was actually hilarious. Your mother used to have a great sense of humor. It slowly drained away as our marriage sucked the life out of us. It happened gradually, like erosion. We were really young; we didn't know what we were getting into. The more unhappy I became living in New York, the less open she was to hearing anything I wanted to say.

"She started to feel like an anchor on the career I'd dreamed of achieving my entire life."

I feel my face hardening. "So you just left."

"Your mother didn't love me anymore, James."

"You don't know that."

"Yes, I do."

Anger thumps in my chest. "So what, even if that's true—you still just left?"

"It felt like the only way."

I have to close my eyes. "What about Siri? You never talk about her. Why didn't we ever invite her out to visit?"

Dad lets go of an extended sigh. "It's complicated. We thought it'd be healthier to have a clean break, that way we wouldn't have to interact anymore. Our relationship was volatile. We fought *all the time*. It was always that way, but in the beginning the fights were smaller; we bickered about little things. It kind of made us more attracted to each other—I think because it'd always lead to—intense making up."

"TMI."

Dad has the audacity to laugh again.

"You wanted to hear about it . . . Anyway, the longer we were married, the less we'd make up and the more of a toll it was probably taking on you girls."

"And Siri?" I croak out.

"And Siri was so much like your mother. She looks just like her, was a natural dancer, you know."

I turn my face out toward the window. "I know, I remember."

I look back over when Dad remains silent. He's set his jaw.

"Just say it," I tell him.

"Your mother was shopping for a replacement while we were still married."

I couldn't have heard that right. "What—"

"Your mom was seeing another man for at least three weeks before I told her I was going to leave her. I hired a private investigator, because I couldn't believe that after all we'd been through, she was out spending her minimal free time toward the end of our relationship with a guy she danced with.

"The investigator got pictures, and when I pulled them out, she lost the ability to speak, as she often does. Your mother cannot admit when she's wrong. She likes to pretend she's a perfect human specimen.

"I had already started to talk to you about moving to California. I could tell you weren't happy with your mom's mandated ballet schedule. I told her that if she tried to stop me taking you, I would make a play for full custody of both of you and win. She wasn't around enough. She wasn't present enough. And she was cheating."

I'm internally gagging.

343

"So we split things fifty-fifty. Siri lives with her mother, you live with me. A clean break. A healthy break where you two didn't have to oscillate from coast to coast."

I am seething. I am seeing red. "You abandoned one of your daughters over there."

My dad makes a face like I'm being absurd. "I didn't abandon her. She's with her mother! We have it in writing, Jamie. We have an official divorce. We weren't to contact each other or our respective kids. A clean break."

He keeps repeating that phrase like it means something. Like it's applicable to human relationships.

"Your mother and I didn't agree on much, but miraculously, we both thought this was the easiest way to move forward."

I can't look at this man.

"Siri's not a kid anymore; she's almost nineteen now," I mutter.

"I hope she's doing well," Dad says.

"Are you going to reach out to her? Don't you love her?"

"Of course I love her, but I'm a stranger to her. Your mother has a new family, did you know that? Siri has a father figure. She doesn't need me."

"You should have tried to co-parent both of us," I whisper.

Dad shakes his head. "Jamie, you're not thinking about the logistics. I understand that hearing this now, you're thinking I'm a horrible person who stole you away, but I was just trying to find the path of least resistance for us to all be happy. You wanted to come with me."

A loose tear escapes my eye. I shoot out a finger to punch the stereo back on and stare out the window the rest of the ride.

76. A Girl Is Running on Fumes

JAMIE
September 8, Tuesday
New Jersey

I haven't slept. I went from yesterday straight to today. Dawn and I talked for two hours last night before she had to go. We didn't get to sift through everything to the extent I wanted. We barely got into her week. It really blows not living in the same state.

I'm at the airport. I don't know what it is about airports. They're full of people, but they're so lonely. And creatively stimulating. Something about the monotony of it all puts me in *the zone*. I want to write. I need to. Time to get Plan Parent Confrontation Trap–related words on paper.

I'm lonely.

Not something I saw coming when I planned this switcheroo revenge-parent-confrontation extravaganza. During every non-Zarar moment these past four days, I have felt extremely isolated.

My visit with the Jafris yesterday was so . . . delightful. But afterward I felt more alone than before. They're proof that so many of the relationship beliefs and bottom lines I've held

345

to be truth are in fact conjecture. That functional families are not a mirage to be sought after and never attained. They're attainable. They're real.

And I am not part of one in any way, shape, or form. Every aspect of my family life is a dumpster fire that I can't even begin to figure out how to douse because I'm a steaming pile of shit myself.

I have ten pages full of thoughts and musings from the past week and a half down by the time my plane boards.

Once I'm boarded, I study what I have and start to extract the highlights. The bits that relate to other aspects of daily life. The bits that can be juxtaposed against your everyday functional family. The bits that are so outlandish, I can't believe they actually happened. I organize them into columns and start rewriting.

The flight passes in a blur of seat belt announcements and flight attendants trying to give me drinks. When we touch down, I'm staring at the first draft of a new ten- to fifteen-minute set.

I hope I can get my shit together to perform it. I pull out the iPhone.

Me: Landed, ETA 30 minutes to hotel

Siri: We're at MGM, got keys to room 507. Dad is off to the casino for a bit. I told him to meet me in the room at 4

Me: Mom's set to land at 1:30, I'll email her from the catfish account about meeting at 4. See you soon

Siri: Keep a low profile, don't get seen by Dad.

Jamie: Don't worry, I'm sporting one of your many emo black sweatshirts feat. giant hood.

Zarar has texted me five separate times since I got home last night.

Zarar: Jamie, after all this, are you really going to leave without giving me your actual number?

Zarar: Good night! Good luck tomorrow. Let me know how it goes

Zarar: Good morning. Have a safe flight

Zarar: Did you get to Vegas?

Zarar: Jamie, I know you haven't switched back yet, you walked me through your timetable yesterday. Good luck.

I tap out of the texts.

I am stealth incarnate as I wind my way through the jungle of whirring noises and coin chatter that is MGM's casino floor. I keep my head down, my hand in my pocket, and my hood way up over my face as I drag Siri's roller bag behind me.

It's an enormous relief when the floor shifts from shitty color-speckled carpet to decadent white tile. I've reached the elevator bay. I stand straighter and throw back my hood. Peripheral vision reengaged.

Unfortunately, the nearest open elevator is already closing. It takes a second as I'm walking toward the call button for my eyes to register the old woman standing inside it. Her white hair is tied back in a neat bun and she's wearing a blue-and-white ascot.

"Grams?!" I blurt. She meets my eyes for a millisecond as the last sliver of the elevator seals shut.

Shit. Shit. Shit. I still look like Siri.

I stab repeatedly at the call button, and before my brain can register the transition, I'm banging on the door to room 507. Siri throws it open. Her eyes bulge.

Oh, this is so weird. We gape at each other . . . at ourselves, for fifteen seconds, both of us waiting for something to happen—for some sort of glitter mess to strike.

Siri breaks first.

"Why are you still me?" She puts a hand to her heart. "I miss my long hair."

She's painted an orange star over her right eye using my colorful eye shadow palette and some glitter. And her hair . . .

I take a step back, giving her a once-over. "Are you me? Or are you Geralt from *The Witcher* after a makeover from Claire's?"

Her brows furrow. "Who's that?"

I sigh. "Never mind. Your gray-blond hair is intense. Are you gonna invite me in, or should I set up camp in the hall?"

I don't like that we haven't switched back. *What the hell does this mean?* Are we doomed? Because that would be the cherry on top of a specular long weekend.

Siri stands aside and I step into the room, chucking the roller bag onto the closest bed and unzipping it. Trying to think. Trying to shift the plan for a scenario in which we haven't turned back into our normal selves. Trying not to panic.

"Jamie," Siri says as the door closes behind us. "We need to switch back for this to work. I want to be myself again."

No shit.

"Yes, dear sister," I respond as I sift through my supplies and pull out our matching outfits. "I, too, want to be myself again. Grams is here, Sier. Why is Grams here?" I lay our outfits on the bed.

"Grams?" Her forehead, which is mine right now, creases up. "She must have come to surprise me at my gig."

I zip up the bag and chuck it onto the floor. "You mean my gig."

Siri rolls her eyes. "Your gig, my gig, who cares, it's a fake gig." She plops onto one of the queen beds. I toss her a pair of black velvet overalls and a pink crop top and start changing.

"Jamie, what are you doing?" she asks as I'm popping my head through the neck of the crop top.

"I'm changing . . . ?" I sit on the edge of the bed across from her and belatedly finish craning my arms through the sleeves.

"We need to try to figure this out." She massages her temples. "I've been thinking about the note for the last hour to distract myself from the terrible conversation I had with Dad."

"What'd he—" I start.

"I'll tell you later; this first," she snaps. "I've been trying to jot it down in my Rediscover Yourself journal thing so we have it for reference. Clearly we're missing something."

She's right. I should have thought of this. Why haven't I done this?

77. Angst and Recall

SIRI
September 8, Tuesday
Nevada

We hunch over my notebook, side by side on the edge of the hotel bed.

> First Stanza
> Walk a mile in each other's shoes?
> Let me help pull off the ruse
> 4 days and 5 nights
> Tell just one they'll see the light
> On the 5th day reunite
>
> Second Stanza
> Something something feels
> Real?
>
> Third Stanza
> Or you've doomed?

Jamie taps on the last line of stanza one. "That's not right."
She presses her hands into her eyes, thinking. "I wish I had read this

aloud the first time. I feel like stanza three was the one that said reunite by the fifth day."

"Or in this state you're doomed to stay!" I yelp, my eyes going wide.

"Yes!" Jamie confirms. She holds her hand up for a high five, and I reach up and slap it excitedly.

I correct the draft.

Third Stanza
Reunite by the fifth day
Or in this state you're doomed to stay

"This stanza is pretty damning," Jamie mumbles.

I gnaw at my lip. "The second stanza has to be directions for the fifth day, about how we're supposed to switch back."

We stare at stanza two for another three minutes.

Jamie gets up and starts pacing. She recites the first stanza aloud, and then what I have on the paper. "Something something feels . . . real?"

I nod. "I remember *feels* rhyming with *real* and thinking the poem was mediocre and childish."

Jamie raises her/my brow sarcastically. "Ah, a critic. I'm sure the magical overlord of the universe is loving your feedback."

I hold up a finger. "Your counterpart feels . . . hold on, I've got it!" I stand, my eyes retreating into my head as I force my brain back to that moment. "Once you've discerned how your counterpart feels!"

Jamie nods from the other side of the room. "To come back to yourself . . ." she whispers.

"Just share something real!" I scream and throw my hands up in the air. "We need to share something real!"

Jamie opens and closes her mouth like a dying fish.

"We did it!" I throw my hands out.

"We didn't do anything," she says. "We're still not us."

I sit back down. "Come sit across from me on the other bed again," I instruct. "This should be easy; we just have to share something real."

Jamie throws herself onto the bed. "What the hell does that mean?"

"Share something that you felt during the switch!"

She settles herself crisscross applesauce. "You go first."

"Fine." I look directly at . . . myself who is Jamie and shake out my arms. "Okay . . . well I thought we were going to get closer by doing this, and that's why I agreed . . . but it made me feel further away from you, Jamie. No matter what happens today, I want to be sisters after this. Ever since I was little and lost you, I've dreamed about having a sister. And now I do . . . I want to be the kind of sisters who invite each other over, and talk on the phone for hours, and go on trips with their significant others together, and depend on each other when things are bad, and . . . who eventually have kids that are best cousin friends." I shrug. "I want loud, splashy Jamie sibling memories with you." I feel a sneeze coming on.

"That doesn't just happen over—" Jamie screams.

78. A Girl Is Having Trouble with This

JAMIE
September 8, Tuesday
Nevada

I fall backward as Siri sneezes and explodes into a cloud of sparkly particles.

I lunge forward off my bed, eyes burning, blindly flailing about. "Siri?!"

My hands land on a human. I fall into a squat, gripping what must be her elbows. She's coughing.

"Oh my god, Siri, you exploded! I watched my own self, who was you, explode into a dust cloud, and it basically gave me a heart attack. Can you hear me? That image is gonna be burned into my mind for the rest of time, so you better be okay. Are you okay? Are you?!"

"I can't see," she wheezes. "But I'm thinking it worked." She wheezes again.

I squint, trying to bat away the glitter in the air. I let go of one of her arms and drag her in the direction of the bathroom. We both come to a halt in front of the mirror when I flip on the light.

It did work. Siri is her actual self. Her hair has still been bleached gray-blond, but it's way less frizzy than it was when she was me. Glitter coats her skin and clothes, but she is her. She runs her hands over her face and chest and arms as she inspects herself in the mirror. My eyes slide over to my own reflection.

And I'm Siri as well. With a braid.

My chest tightens.

Siri turns to me, grabbing my arm. "Share something, Jamie, so we can get ready. We only have like an hour."

I don't know what to share. "I've been . . . talking to Zarar every day. And seeing him. Every day in New York."

Siri leads me to the toilet. "Sit down. Are you two going to continue seeing each other?"

I shake my head no, staring at my knees, an unbelievable sadness rushing through me. I hate all these feelings.

"Long distance doesn't work," I say flatly.

"How does that make you feel . . ." Siri prompts.

"I don't know, Sier." I throw up my hands and let them fall.

She sighs. "I'm trying to help you. How do you feel about you and me?" She walks out of the bathroom and comes back with my makeup kit.

The toilet is making my ass cold. It's cold in this hotel room.

"I'm looking forward to not being you anymore," I say. "I want my life back."

Siri starts painting makeup over my right eye. "I have an idea. You could read the miracle exercise we did that day at Rediscover with Donya."

"No, thanks," I snap.

"Do you *want* to be stuck like this forever?"

I blow out the most aggravated, annoying, Siri-esque sigh of my career, as she refreshes her brush and comes back toward my face with it. "Fine. You want to know how I feel about you?"

"Yes."

"I love you, but *I don't like you.* You're unstable and angry and irritatingly naive. I've always been jealous of your natural ability to be better than me at everything we do, and I hate how easily you slipped into my life the last four days. Growing up I did everything I could to differentiate myself from you! The real reason I wanted to leave with Dad fourteen years ago was so *I wouldn't have to live in your shadow!* Does that feel good? Is that what you want to hear?" My voice cracks. And then I sneeze.

79. Angst and Resolve

SIRI
September 8, Tuesday
Nevada

My ears are ringing from Jamie's explosion. We stay frozen in our positions as her cloud slowly settles on the floor of the bathroom. I'm holding a makeup brush aloft, standing in front of Jamie, who's sitting on the toilet. A new layer of glitter coats everything.

Jamie doesn't like me. Jamie proposed this switching plan with that in mind. Jamie wanted to put three thousand miles between us again. Jamie left because of me.

I throw the brush on the bathroom counter, trying not to tear up. "You're a jerk, Jamie."

She drops her head into her hands. "Surprise."

I walk out of the bathroom, stripping off my glitter-covered clothes so I can pull on the glitter-covered clothes on the bed that match Jamie's.

"I asked my big questions to Dad in the car on the way here, and it was not fun," I call from the bed.

Jamie sounds deflated. "What a coincidence, I asked my big question last night and it was super not fun as well."

"This is going to be a lot."

"It's going to be a shit show," Jamie corrects from the bathroom.

80. Angst and Confrontation

SIRI
September 8, Tuesday
Nevada

Jamie and I look as close to twins as we ever have. Matching makeup. Matching outfits. Matching cheekbones, matching eyes. Hers are bloodshot.

The scar on her forehead looks a little less fresh than last week. It's a thin inch-long curved pink line leading down to her brow.

You would think I'd be more crushed by what she said to me forty minutes ago, but I'm not. Because I'm finally starting to understand her. The blurry aloof cartoon that is Jamie Federov is finally coming into focus.

It's 3:55 p.m.

Five minutes till my greedy, selfish, abandoning jerk-and-a-half father returns to our hotel room. Jamie and I spent the last twenty minutes stiffly rehearsing and choreographing an outline of what we're going to say. We're sitting across from each other on the inner edges of the beds. Jamie's scribbling in her retreat notebook.

"It's three fifty-five," I tell her.

She grabs my iPhone from her pocket and sends out a text to my mother "from me" explaining that I've had some sort of emergency, that I'm in the hotel in Vegas, and I need her up in room 507. Her fake interview is scheduled to take place right now in the fourth-floor lounge.

My hands are shaking. I wring them together behind my back so Jamie can't see. I still don't know where I go from here. I brushed off the one job idea that sounded vaguely fun because it didn't feel like a real job. Cooking. *My old job was less of a real job than cooking.*

I don't know what I want to do and I don't want to decide yet. But how do I move forward without deciding? How does everyone make those sorts of decisions without thinking about them for years on end?

Right now, all I care about is salvaging my relationship with the girl across from me.

Jamie jolts at the sound of footsteps outside the hotel door. We make eye contact for a quick second. She closes her notebook, nods, and springs from the bed to hide in the bathroom.

I listen as my father pulls his key out from the door slot and the gadget unlocks. He pushes into the room.

I stand up for no apparent reason. "Dad," I blurt.

"Hey, Jame," he says casually. "Already blew two hundred bucks down there. You still mad at me or are you ready to run through your set?"

I resist the urge to roll my eyes. How obtuse, to think my anger with him is something that could dissipate in the span of four hours. Like I'm not holding onto fourteen years of repressed emotion, but riding out some menstrual cramps or a paper cut.

I don't respond as he kicks off his shoes and lays back on the far bed with his hands behind his head. I close my eyes, trying to cool the rousing monster in my chest.

"I want to get back down to the casino for a bit before we grab dinner and head to your show," he continues. "What club is it at?"

I sit down on the bed opposite of him. "Have a seat, Dad."

He sits up. "Weird ask when I'm already on the bed, what's up?"

"I have something really important to talk to you about."

He widens his eyes melodramatically. "More very important things to talk about. Is this about you and Dawn? I saw you two outside last night and I gotta say, I'm not surprised—"

I cut him off, "What, no! No, it's not about that—"

"Okay, but I'm fine with it, you know that, right—" Dad's squinting at me now.

"Dad, shut up, I don't want to talk about that right now!" I screech. *Excrement.*

He presses his lips together. "Don't tell me to shut up."

I exhale loudly.

"You look different, Jame." He studies me head-on.

I look down at the floor.

"Have you lost weight or something? Are you eating okay?"

We're interrupted by a knock at the door, thank god. I slip off the bed. As a precaution, I reach out and turn on the TV. It flips on to a menu channel. I fiddle with it frantically until a movie comes on and turn the volume up.

More knocks sound at the door. "Did you order room service?" Dad asks. He's already checking his phone again.

I use my body to block the view of the room as I open the door about thirty degrees.

"Siri?" My mother squeaks my name quietly, like the surprise of seeing me has strangled her. "What's happened, what's wrong, what are you doing here?! What did you do to your hair?" She continues to speak softly, like we're in danger of being overheard.

"It's a long story. Come in, Mom." I open the door a tiny bit more, still blocking the majority of the room from view. Gunshots from the TV drown out our dialogue, and I pat myself on the back for thinking on my feet with that.

"When did you get your hair done? I don't understand. I'm supposed to be . . ." She walks past me into the room and yelps at the sight of Dad.

"Grier?! What the fuck are you doing here?"

I gasp at the language. *It's not ladylike. It's extremely impolite. Trashy. No one likes a potty mouth.* My mother broke one of her own commandments.

"Intercourse!" I correct loudly from behind her.

She staggers into the wall next to the closet, looking from me to Dad.

Dad looks only at me, his eyes saucer-wide. I can see the cogs turning behind them.

"Jamie, what the hell are you doing?"

"Jamie?" my mother says.

I quickly turn off the TV.

"What are you doing here, Mara?" my father says calmly. "I'm here be-cause my daughter's performing a comedy set later. Were you invited as well?"

Mom's face twists up in confusion. She glances at me. "You're doing a comedy set?"

I shake my head. "I'm not."

Dad sits forward on the bed. "What do you mean you're not? We were literally about to run through your set."

Mom shoots laser beams at me through her eyeballs. "Siri Martine Maza, tell me what the hell is going on right now. Did you contact your father?"

"Jamie," Dad says from the bed.

Mom's eyes dart over to him.

"You're talking to Jamie, Mara." He sounds exhausted already, and she's been in the room for all of sixty seconds.

"I know my kid," Mom snaps venomously. "This is my daughter Siri, Grier."

"You're losing it, woman. Jamie, would you care to fill us in on whatever the hell you've gotten us into?"

I guess she never told Dad about the "Jamie is imaginary" lie. He probably would have brought blackmail back into the equation. *My dad was going to blackmail my mother out of her children.*

"Siri," Mom cries. "Explain!"

Mom's glaring at me, Dad's watching expectantly.

I . . . can't find the air to speak. I don't know which of them was more wrong. *Why do I feel the innate need to choose a side right now?* I feel betrayed in every way by these people who brought me into the world. I don't want to ever have to choose a parent. They shouldn't be making me choose. I'm supposed to start our dialogue. I brace my hand against the wall.

The bathroom door bursts open with loud dramatic flair, and Jamie strides into the room. Mom screams and bangs into the wall again. Dad makes a muffled, horrified noise, his face losing color. I push out the stagnant breath I've been holding for the last twenty seconds.

"Yeah, so I'm Jamie. I guess you haven't been following Siri on social media or you'd know we look a lot alike nowadays." She shrugs.

I frown, watching my mother slowly slide down to the floor. Her pointer finger wavers from Jamie to myself. I meet her eyes. "I found out about Jamie."

"Siri, you don't understand." Mom suddenly looks like a caged animal.

I don't like it. I don't like it at all.

Jamie walks up to me. "Save it, Mara. Take a seat on the bed; we're going to speak first."

Dad's wearing a flabbergasted expression. He looks to Jamie. "What did she do?"

Mom crawls over to the free queen bed and ambles onto it.

Jamie pulls on a smile as she turns to Dad. "Our mother here brainwashed young Siri into thinking that she never had a sister. She told her that I was an imaginary friend conjured due to extreme loneliness, moved to a new house, and got rid of any and all pictures I was in."

Mom's desperately shaking her head. "No, Jamie. Siri wasn't eating, she wasn't sleeping, she was wasting away. I had to do something to fix it, to help her move on."

I don't want to hear it right now. "What did she say about talking, Mom?" Mom's eyes flit back to me.

Jamie maneuvers herself so that her back is facing the wall opposite the beds, the lecture vantage point of the room. I move to stand next to her.

Jamie crosses her arms. "Long story short, you've both been horrible parents."

"You really do look so much alike," Dad says dreamily.

"Dad," Jamie continues, "manipulated me, a six-year-old, into leaving with him and convinced me it was in my best interest not to look back. He never spoke to his other daughter again." Jamie's overexcited expression makes her look almost . . . unhinged. She slow claps dramatically. "It sounds extra bad all laid out on the table."

I swallow nervously. *Jamie is not okay.*

"Now, we know everyone makes mistakes, everybody has those days. Pobody's nerfect!" Jamie paces the front of the room. "And we were hoping to find some closure by switching places for a bit."

Mom's mouth bobs open and closed.

"That's right, Mara." Jamie smiles wickedly. "You told me over and over again last night that I don't exist. Thanks for that. You've been with me for five days. Thanks for noticing. I was trying to find some way to absolve you of all this. If you told me last night that you had lied, when I genuinely was losing it, I would have told you who I was. I wanted nothing more than to be acknowledged by my mother."

Mom shakes her head. "No. Siri was acting strangely, but it was still Siri. I can tell the difference between my own daughters."

Pity rises in my throat. Mom holds my eyes, asking me to confirm her statement. I give the tiniest shake of my head.

"LOLOL except," Jamie explains gleefully, "we had been spelled with weird glitter magic this past week that made us look like each other. So, knowing what we look like wouldn't help you here, Mara."

"There's glitter everywhere." Dad is actually in shock, I think.

"Spelled?" Mom repeats.

"Yep, exactly how you're thinking, like that guy in your books with the face switching that somehow changes your entire appearance." Jamie gesticulates with spirit fingers. "The two of us met at that retreat and ran into some weird-ass magic that glamoured us as each other."

"The faceless men," Mom mumbles.

Dad's eyes dart to me. "You've been living in my house for a week?"

I nod. Wow. They're literally not even questioning the magic.

Jamie says what I'm thinking. "I love how you're not even questioning the *Freaky Friday* aspect of this, you giant nerds."

My parents look at each other for a moment. It's not an angry look; it's a look of wonder.

It's so not the time.

Dad points to me. "That's why cooking . . . and you performed with the group instead of a set at Tim's, and Dawn, oh my god . . ." His face falls into his hands for a moment, and then he looks back up. "Siri, I'm so sorry." There are tears in Dad's eyes.

Quiet tears make their way down my own cheeks. Jamie clasps her hands behind her back like a general.

"Mara claims you two divided us up for *us*." She rolls her head. "I think we can all agree that's bullshit. Y'all did this for you. You didn't want to deal with each other so you divided your assets the easiest way you could. *That's pretty shit.*

"We think we deserve some recompense, parents." Jamie claps. "Siri and I want to reconnect! We would appreciate that in the form of some financial support during a low-budget two-week sister road trip around the country, because we are both tight on cash but would like to do something special together to celebrate our reunion. On said venture, we shall start down the path of trying to forgive you."

Excrement. How did I not foresee how terribly this pitch would go over until right this very second? How privileged, self-righteous, and ridiculous it sounds. These two people are so not in the mood to be pitched a sisterly fun-cation by their mischievous estranged children. I can see it in Mom's face. She's going to lose it on us.

"Excuse me!" she cries, her eyes turned to the ceiling. "Someone explain what the underworld is going on! I'm here for an interview with the director of a Las Vegas production for—"

Her screeching spins the top off my anger. *"It's fake, Mom!"* I scream. "We catfished you to get you here because we knew you would never take this much time off work unless it was for even better work!"

Yeah, she's furious. Her face flushes scarlet. *"You what?"*

Dad raises his hand. "I'm sorry, does this mean Jamie's not performing tonight?"

Jamie winks at him and shoots him a finger gun. "No, but I would like to hear those notes," she chides.

Dad's hand falls to his thigh. "You're shitting me, Jamie. Do you know what I had to do to step away today? I had to reschedule five meetings."

Jamie continues to smile. "Yeah, I don't care."

I'm scared for Jamie. Or of Jamie.

Dad narrows his eyes. "Bold from someone you're asking to fund your little sister vacation."

I rub at my arms, trying to come in with some sort of logical assist. "Dad, we don't mean like an extravagant vacation—"

"Stop talking, Siri. You don't want anything from him. You sound like an entitled, spoiled child," Mom snaps.

Jamie turns to me. "They don't seem into it. We might just want to go super low budget and take a walk around the block together."

I groan.

"Mara, I can't believe you told our child that our other child doesn't exist," Dad bursts.

"Shut up, Grier." Mom looks to me. "Siri, I'm out busting my ass at work at all hours for you! To support us! You don't need his money!"

"Anymore," Jamie blurts with an amused flair.

I heave a breath. Logical. I have to be the logical one because Jamie has cracked.

"Mom, I'm not interacting with him because I want his money. I don't want anyone's money! I'm just tight on it because I had to quit my job—"

"Yeah, I understand that and I've been endlessly understanding, and in return, you've sent your sister to emotionally abuse me! Do you know what she's done this past week? She's been terrorizing me!"

87. A Girl Is Hanging with Her Family!

JAMIE
September 8, Tuesday
Nevada

Siri and Mara are *screaming* at each other. Dad turns his attention in my direction.

"What happened to your forehead?"

I touch my scar self-consciously. "A fishing boat–canoe hybrid flipped on me. Almost drowned."

"Jesus Christ, Jame. Okay, I'm glad you're okay . . ." He puts a hand to his forehead and blinks a million times like his brain is malfunctioning. "Do you know about your sister and Dawn?"

I bob my head. "Yes, I know of both their existences, thank you, Father, oh wise one."

Dad blows out an exhausted breath. "Ha-ha, I'm not talking about their existences." He puts on a silly Valley girl accent for that last word.

I shoot him a deadpan look. "What about them, Father?"

"She and Dawn, I think they're an item."

"An item?" I mimic him. Why have I resorted to mimicry? Shit, I'm tired. I glance over at Mara yelling and find Siri watching me with a worried expression.

"What?" I ask, grinning at her. My heartbeat grows louder. "Why are you looking at me like that?

I glance back at Dad who's now sheepishly frowning at the floor. I turn back to Siri. "Are you . . . and Dawn, what . . . like dating?" I slur. "It's only four days, I just talked to her . . ." I can't form a sentence.

I brace my hands against my knees, thinking of Zarar. How intense our connection feels; we've only been on one date and talking for a little over a week. My sister cannot be romantically interested in my best friend in the universe. She can't have her. That's against the woman code. They can't do that.

"We're not date . . . ing." The words trip slowly out of Siri's now-frightened mouth.

"No." I shake my head, feeling like my lungs have deflated.

Of course this would happen. Siri's better at being me than I am. She's probably better for Dawn. She's nicer. Even with her mood swings and angry outbursts, she cares so much about everything.

Dawn and I fixed things last night. She forgave me, didn't she? She didn't say anything about Siri. *Why wouldn't she have told me? She didn't even mention Siri. What if Siri moves in with Dad now?*

She'll want to join Duck Waterfall. What if she'll want to do stand-up too? And if they're involved and Dawn has to choose a side . . . I mean, she has to choose Siri's if they're together. She has to. Eventually I'm the odd man out of that equation. And when their relationship goes to shit like every relationship does, other than Z's damn parents, what happens then?

Do I have to choose a side?

I'd have to. Just like I have to choose now, just like I've had to choose my entire life. I've been with Dad. There's been no crossover; it's too messy for the separated parties. And when that happens, I'd have to choose my fucking sister. Isn't it written into my DNA? Dawn could easily need to distance herself from me by association.

This is a nightmare. I hate everything about this, and I have no one to blame but myself. I'm messed up. This is all messed up. Everything I've done is messed up.

I've backed myself into a corner without realizing it.

When I look up, everyone's watching like I'm a fragile vase that might fall over and break into a million pieces.

I meet Siri's eyes. "Were you . . . fucking my best friend while we were switched?" My voice is shaky and weak.

Siri's eyes go wide. "What?! No, Jamie!"

I feel the shift as the logical side of my brain completely flips off. My mouth barks words without running them by me in any capacity. "Answer the question."

"I just did!" Siri throws her hands up. "I said *no*! We just had a connection."

"You just had a connection," I repeat, lowering into a squat.

Jealousy. That bitch always finds me. She's a fist squeezing the air from my lungs. I don't want to share my best friend with my little sister.

"Sorry, bad time to bring it up," Dad says quietly.

"Shut up!" we both scream at him.

Siri's eyes flit to me as if we're in on some joke together; she thinks we're going to share a laugh. I glare at the floor.

"Can someone explain to me who Dawn is and how the hell all this happened?" Mara says.

"We ran into each other at the retreat, Mother," I hear Siri say.

"Ran into each other? By accident?" Grier chimes in.

There's frantic knocking at the door. We all look up at it. None of us moves. They knock again.

Mara gets up from the bed and opens the door. Grams and Papa stand there together in the hallway.

"What the actual intercourse?" Mom blurts.

"Language, Mara," Papa says cheerfully.

"Papa?" Siri says, voice laden with hope.

The room erupts into chaos. Everyone speaks over one another for a long ear-splitting minute until someone flips the lights on and off.

"SHUT YOUR TRAPS AND LET US TALK!" Grams booms.

82. A Girl's Head Is Spinning

JAMIE
September 8, Tuesday
Nevada

Grams steps forward. "We've been listening outside. This is our doing," she blusters. "We ran into each other on a trip three months ago, decided our children had been irresponsible parents, and have been plotting to get our grandchildren back in our lives ever since. We planted the idea of the retreat, and coordinated to get the girls there at the same time."

Papa glances at Siri and me. "I'm so sorry. We're both ashamed of the way our children have torn you two apart."

Grams puts her hands on her hips. "We didn't mean for things to get so twisted up. But it's high time we all took a step back, faced our faults, and moved past it as a family."

Dad glares at Grams. "Mom, it was not your place to meddle."

"Oh please, Grier." Grams waves him off.

Mara scolds her father, "You promised you would never betray my trust with this!"

"Come on, Mara. You told Siri one of our daughters wasn't real!" Grier yells.

The four of them get into it.

I feel like an astronaut. The conversation muffles through my own personal space suit as I float untethered outward into the nothing. Grams set

366

me up to attend the retreat? She was planning it for months? What does *coordinated* mean? Which bits of my downward spiral were manufactured?

These people raised me.

I really don't know . . . if I know what's right and what's wrong. I wonder if my gauge has always been completely off. Is what Siri and I did worse than what the parents did? What Grams did? What's justifiable? What is wrong with us? How can we ever move past all this? We're not just dysfunctional; we're a clusterfuck of molten garbage.

Siri fills my field of vision. She's squatting down in front of me.

"Jamie, you're crying."

She reaches out to touch my face, and I swat away her hand. "I'm not crying."

"Please," she begs. "Please don't be mad at me."

Why am I so mad? I'm usually so calm. I'm so collected. I can handle anything. Siri's done this to me. All her emotional bullshit has spread to me like a fungal infection. I hold a hand in front of my face like a third grader. *Talk to the hand.*

"No, I'm talking to you! We're speaking about this," she insists. When did she get so confident? "We have to talk. We have to work this out. I want our sister trip, no matter how pathetic and low budget it is. We're going to have a relationship."

I can't meet her eyes. "I don't want it!" I blurt with all the force built up inside me. "You've taken my one real friend and made her *yours*. You've turned me into this!"

"I haven't *taken* anything. I haven't *turned* you into anything! Wake up! You're a real person with feelings and that's normal and okay," she bellows back. A yelling match from the other four people in the room rages behind us.

"Fuck off," I tell her. "I can't believe you did this after everything you went through with your backstabbing friend from the ballet company."

Siri stands up, so she's looking down at me. "That was so different, I can't even begin to go into it. Intercourse you, Jamie. I see through your bullshit. You can stop throwing it at me because I'm not going to entertain it any-more. You're being a selfish ass. The things you do, the choices you make, the words that come out of *your* mouth—they have a profound effect on the people around you.

"You use Dawn as an emotional crutch, Jamie. She gives you all of her and she has a tiny piece of you. And now you're doing the same thing with Zarar."

"What does that even mean?" I feel myself rise off the ground, but I don't remember actually giving my body the order to do it. "You don't know what you're—"

"Your best friend didn't know why you were at the retreat, Jamie. Your best friend didn't know you had a sister. She thought your mom had died."

"That doesn't mean—" My words are a slur.

"How many times has Zarar asked you out, Jamie? When was the last time? How many times have you said no and still deemed it okay to monopolize his time—"

I shake my head. "You have no idea what's going on there."

She steps closer to me, her dark eyebrows lifting and falling to the rhythm of her words. "No, I see you now. You're so scared of the people around you that you don't form real relationships with *anyone*. You've always got one foot out the door. Relationships are about *give* and take, Jamie.

"You don't give yourself to anyone. Not Dawn. Not your dad, your grandma, definitely not me. If you want to keep the people who love you in your life, you have to let them be a part of it." Siri's tears sparkle down her cheeks. "You think real love doesn't exist, but it's all around you, and you're too busy being afraid of it to notice. Guess what, Jamie?" She comes right up in my face. "You're being a giant asshole, but I still love you and *like you*. I'm your fucking little sister and I want to be a part of your life. Stop going out of your way to make it so hard."

"I'm making it hard?! Did I start dating your only friend?!" My face feels like the surface of the sun. Am I melting?

"I don't have a friend! You're the closest thing I've ever had to a real friend!"

I don't know what shifted in my face, but Siri nods, wiping her nose. "I know, pathetic, right?" She shakes her head. "I'm so over this right now. Congratulations, you're just like Dad."

I bob my head. "I'm going back with Mara," I tell her.

"So am I," Siri challenges, her face inches away.

"Go back to your new girlfriend," I whisper.

"No," she says simply.

"Fine, then I'm going home with Dad."

"Fine, then so am I," Siri insists.

A growl rips out of me, and I push her backward. I instantly regret it, staring at my hands like they've betrayed me. Siri trips into the lone hotel lounger chair. The wooden armrest goes straight into her lower back. She emits a piercing scream.

The room goes silent. Mara is on the floor in a millisecond, helping Siri up slowly. She can move. Thank god.

I can't.

What is wrong with me?

When did I become a monster?

Siri's breathing is labored as she heaves through whatever pain she's experiencing.

And then I throw up. I manage to aim it at the foot of the bed, away from my panting sister.

"Jesus, Jamie." Dad sighs.

Siri catches my eye as Mara helps her to her feet. "You're a terrible sister. I don't know why I was so obsessed with you growing up."

I suck in a rattling breath and look across the room at Papa.

"Papa, can I go back with you? Do you have a spare room?" My voice is a weak whisper.

He glances over at my parents and back at me. "Of course, sweetheart."

Dad looks at me, incredulous. "Really, Jame?"

"I'll come back when I'm ready," I gurgle. Grams comes over and drops a towel over my pile of vomit. She rubs my back. I move away from her, struggling to catch my breath.

"Let's go home, Siri," Mom urges.

"We're not finished discussing this," Siri heaves out to Mara. "And that's the only reason I'm going back with you."

Siri takes her iPhone and leaves Gladys on the nightstand.

"Sier, I'd love for you to come stay with me for a bit," Grier throws out belatedly.

"I've been there for the last five days, Dad."

"But I didn't know. I'd like to spend some time with you. The real you."

Wow. Dad would like to "spend some time" with the daughter he abandoned. He says it as if he hasn't seen her in a couple of weeks rather than a decade.

Papa and Grams exchange a heartfelt hug. Siri watches me as she exits with our mother.

Dad gets up.

"Send me those notes," I say suddenly.

He nods. He looks worried. I've never seen him look so worried. "Jame, you should come home."

"I'm fine, Grier."

He closes his eyes and opens them slowly. "I'll email you the notes . . . You know, I knew something weird was afoot. I didn't *not* notice you weren't yourself."

"Sure you didn't."

"Jamie." He steps closer. "I knew something was very different. I could never have guessed that something as wild as you're describing actually happened. Do you think your grandparents actually wrapped their brains around that tidbit, because they have yet to comment."

I glance over to where Grams and Papa are huddled near the door. "Doesn't matter. It's over."

"What's over?"

I shake my head. "I don't know . . . everything." I grab my shit and stagger over to Papa.

Things that are over: my dream career, my best friend, my belief that parental recompense would make me feel less hollow inside, my thing with Zarar, the fragile bond I formed with my sister, me. I am canceled.

83. A Girl Ruined Everything

JAMIE
September 9, Late Tuesday Night/
Early Wednesday Morning
New Jersey

Papa's extra room is tiny. I stretch the mint-green sheet he gave me across the frameless full-size bed and try to smoosh the fitted bit over the corner that's up against the wall.

Apparently, this was Mara's room. There are a few pieces of old furniture, a dresser, and a mirror, but they're covered in odds and ends. Papers. There are boxes along the floor and stacked against the walls.

Papa appears in the doorway. "Here's a pillow, sweetie." He hands me a pillow and disappears again. "And here's a clean blanket." He reappears with a thick, soft, green blanket.

"Thank you," I tell him.

He lingers in the doorway. "Jamie."

I look up from where I'm spreading the blanket over the sheets. "Yeah?"

"I am so sorry for the part I played in your mother's lie. I love you. I was trying to honor your mother's wishes. I thought that was where my duty lay as a father, but I wasn't thinking about the big picture. About my duty as a grandfather. It is the greatest failure of my life, and I am truly sorry."

I focus on a piece of lint stuck to the blanket as my eyes well up with unwelcome tears.

Papa bobs his head. "Good night. I'll be up for another hour or so if you want to chat or play a round of rummy."

I nod and he closes the door softly behind him.

When I finish making the bed I shuffle out of the room toward Papa's round little kitchen table. He's waiting there, reading his paper with a deck of cards out. He looks up and grins.

"You shuffle. I'll deal," I tell him. He cracks the cards around through bridges and different shuffling measures before handing them to me. I dole them out, seven cards apiece, and we enter a round of gin rummy.

"Papa," I start. And stop immediately. This is so hard.

He waits, eyebrows raised.

I exhale a forced breath. "I am a walking, talking human manifestation of failure."

"Jamie," Papa sighs.

I shake my head. "No, let me have this, I am. I don't mean to hurt everyone around me," I mumble. "But I do. All the time. I say things, and I do things for laugh value, and I don't register the collateral damage until . . . I've done it. Siri is right. I'm a selfish shit stick—"

He winces at my curse.

"All I've been able to bring myself to do in the last five hours on the plane and at the airport is scribble down more jokes about all this crap, so I can use it in the future to make other people laugh." I pause, serving him a look. "That's messed up. I haven't apologized to anyone. I haven't attempted to talk it through. I've been here exploiting the drama I'm still waist-deep in." I stare unseeing at my cards. "It's how my brain has always sifted through things. And it's messed up."

I pick a card from the draw pile, compare it to my hand, and discard.

Papa draws a card. "I don't know why you're getting so down on yourself for wanting to make people laugh. It sounds like you're feeling guilty for having a passion. If comedy is how you process life, then that's how you process life. People need laughter, it's what keeps us going through life's roughest moments. And you need to process what's happening around you before you can go about trying to fix it."

I fiddle with the clasps of my overalls. "I'm *jealous* of Siri, Papa." I stick out my tongue and make a dying zombie noise. "I hate it. I hate how jealous I am of her." I get up from the table and shake out my limbs. "Woof, I said it out loud." I sit back down. "It's irrational and immature, but having her in California without me was driving me insane. I felt the hooks of it creeping up around me all week, and they got me today . . . I was horrible." My voice squeaks. It's unpleasant.

"It's your turn," Papa reminds me. I mindlessly yank up a card.

"I shouldn't be reacting this way to the idea that Siri and Dawn might like each other. It's gross. But I have these relentless, nasty possessive feelings weeding through me all the same." I glance up at Papa's kind expression and immediately feel ill. I drop my head into my free hand. "I shouldn't have told you that. What am I doing right now?"

"Your discard," Papa says softly.

I put down a card without looking at it, and I stare through my fingers at the discard pile. Papa picks it up.

"James. Everyone has flaws. We all make mistakes. We all have horrible thoughts sometimes. You are not a human manifestation of failure. Failure is human."

"I want to be an alien," I tell the table. Papa discards.

"Jamie, there is strength in recognizing when you're in the wrong. There's strength in acknowledging your faults and working to be better. That's something your mother still struggles with."

I pick up a card and look him in the eye again. Papa smiles at me. "Part of being successful in anything you're looking to accomplish is knowing when to ask for help. Discerning when you need it and taking the initiative to find it."

I discard.

Papa picks it up and lays down his hand. "Gin."

84. Angst and Intervention

SIRI
September 9, Wednesday Early Morning
New Jersey

We take a red-eye home. My back is in spasm and it makes for a horrible flight. I watch *Frozen* on the tiny six-inch screen embedded into the chair in front of me and cry.

The familiarity of being back in my own house is a massive comfort. I drop my stuff and head straight for the shower.

Hot water chases away the tension in my chest and eases the pain in my back. I missed this shower.

Our stupid plan backfired in so many different ways. Jamie thought this was going to give us some kind of closure, but if anything, it's opened more wounds.

My cornerstone self-esteem questions are back monopolizing my every thought: *What could I have done to make Dad think I was worthy of sticking around for? Without dance, where is my value to Mom?*

I want to move forward from this excrement. I know they're irrational questions. But I still have them. I don't want them. And I don't want to keep harkening back to my anger. It's not worth my time! It's not worth the recurring angst. I want to be present. I want more snow globe–worthy moments. I want to be happy.

I don't want to see Dr. Sparrow. But I don't know how to let all of this go! I clearly can't do it on my own.

When I head into the kitchen around 9 a.m. for a fresh ice pack, I dig into my mother's purse. She's been in her room since we got home. I slip out her insurance card, snap a picture, head upstairs, and dial the number on the back.

After tapping through a bunch of menus, I speak with a human. At the end of our conversation, the insurance company emails me a list of therapists that are in our network.

I pull open my laptop and scroll through the email, pulling out the women and pasting them into a doc. My eyes stop on one name in particular: Dr. Donya Wendell. I pull up a new window and google her name.

A familiar face pops up.

85. A Girl Is Not Sure How to Proceed

JAMIE
September 9, Wednesday
New Jersey

Papa leaves the house early to go to church, despite how late we were up last night. Once he's gone, I head down the hall to the tiny old pink-tiled bathroom and glare at my reflection in the mirror. My hair is dark and bleh. I'm paler than ever. I'm literally transitioning into a shadow.

Okay, not literally.

I'm . . . drowning in a well of self-pity. Gag.

I dress in the overalls from yesterday—I'm never wearing another pair of black leggings if I can help it.

There's a salon I passed multiple times near QCZ last week—that's where I'm heading today.

As I walk through the city, I take note of a NOW HIRING window at an independent movie theater. I purse my lips, looking up at the CINEMA LAND sign across the top of the marquee. That could be fun.

86. Angst and Support

"I am so glad you reached out, Siri," Donya says with genuine enthusiasm after I've spent forty-five minutes letting all my problems spill out of me. Today, she's in a maroon sweater and dark jeans with her hair down. She has an office in the city, and when I called, she said she would fit me in today.

I nod, staring down at the white sneakers Grams got me.

"The way I see it, there are a couple of options you have moving forward, and neither is inherently right or wrong. It's all up to you and what will make you the happiest."

I stay quiet, listening intently. I'm sitting on a warm purple velvet couch and the wall behind her is covered in books and trinkets. The other wall has a couple of framed yoga posters with different inspirational sayings on them.

"The first option would be to distance yourself from the people who have brought on this pain and strife in your life. You could stay with your grandfather and Jamie for a while if it's too hard to be around your mom. Try to get a job and work toward getting your own place. But that doesn't sound like what you want."

I've been shaking my head no from the beginning of her proposal. "No, I—I want my family to be my family. How do I fix us?"

"Your family has hurt you in so many different ways, and clearly you've

377

been holding on to that anger for a very long time. If you truly want to move forward, I think you need to ask yourself if you have the capacity to forgive them. And then you have to figure out what you need from them moving forward to ensure your trust is won back."

I look up from the floor and meet her eyes.

"I know this is going to be difficult. But we can work through it together. And you know . . . it would be helpful to have Jamie here too. I'm sure she's dealing with some very similar struggles right now."

"She has some weird aversion to therapy; there's no way she'll want to come."

"Would you like her to come?" Donya asks.

I nod.

"Tell her that. She can be your first letter. See if you can forgive her. Lay out everything she's done that has hurt you. And tell her what you would like moving forward. See what happens. You're allowed to ask for what you need, Siri. That's the only way for people to know that you need it. If someone can't respect what you need from a relationship, then they're probably not worth having around."

I swipe at the tears dripping out of me and nod.

"Have you spoken to Dawn since you left?"

I shake my head vigorously.

"Why not?"

"I don't want to make Jamie more upset, and . . . I told Dawn it was a snow globe and that's it, and then I'll be gone and we can just look back at our perfect day."

"But you really like her."

I nod.

"And you'd like to keep in touch with her."

I nod.

"So why did you propose this snow globe?"

"It's something Jamie told me she was doing with Zarar . . . Jamie says some stupid excrement, but sometimes, when you think about the stuff hard enough, it starts to seem reasonable and kind of lovely in a broken sort of way."

Donya nods. "I would write your letter to Jamie. Explain how you feel. What you need from her. Give her some time to digest her anger about you and Dawn. Go from there. You can contact Dawn if you want to. You've formed a caring, supportive relationship with her, and you don't have many of those. You don't have to isolate yourself."

I bite my lip.

"We can meet again tomorrow if that works, Siri. Talk to Jamie tonight. You can do it."

87. A Girl Has Some Work to Do

JAMIE
September 9, Wednesday Evening
New Jersey

I got a job here! I start on Monday. That's pretty cool.

When the stylist (Maggie, originally from Kansas, but moved out to New York to get a taste of city life and hone her craft) peels away the black salon cape, I finally look like myself.

Outside, strolling the streets of New York alongside the hustlers and the blaring horns, I *feel like* myself again. Confident. Grounded. Like I might have the power to turn this shit show around. Maggie has faith in me. She laughed at my jokes quite a bit too.

It's bizarre how something as simple as a haircut and color can catapult you into a new mindset. *Yes,* it is indeed used to drive the protagonist forward in *every movie ever,* and it's become a laughable cliché, but it's a cliché for a reason. It's real. It's kind of like that feeling you have at the start of a new year. The illusion of a fresh start. Like you hit the reset button on *you,* and you've earned permission to be better.

I thought of five more potential set joke ideas while my hair was soaking, so I use the train ride home to draw them out of my brain and into my notebook.

I walk home to Papa's from the train station. He told me last night I'm welcome to stay as long as I want, and gave me a copy of his key. The man really is the sweetest, and it's a damn shame I haven't been able to get to know him till now. His car is in the driveway.

"Hey, Pops!" I greet, pushing open the front door.

I don't know why I'm so shocked to see Siri in the kitchen with him, but I freeze up like there's a bear in the room. She's making dinner . . . and it smells amazing. Like, brie macaroni and cheese?

Siri spins toward me in a black feather-patterned apron. "You're home." She points at me with a wooden spoon. "I'm making your favorite: weird brie mac and cheese and grilled-apple sandwiches."

I blink at her. "Um . . . yesterday I screamed at you, and then assaulted you, correct?"

Siri nods and turns back to the stove. "Um, yeah, I was hoping we could talk. I wrote you a letter, if you're willing to listen."

Papa's eyes vacillate between us.

I pull out a seat at the table. "Okay . . . Can we talk after we eat? That smells way too good to delay."

Siri smiles at me now. She usually projects a dark witch goddess aura with her slight pout . . . but smiling changes her entire aesthetic. She's giving off such optimistic vibes. What's happening?

"We definitely can, and I like your hair!" she says. "The new shade of orange without your gross grown-out roots looks great."

I bob my head hesitantly. "Thank you?"

Siri serves us beautifully staged plates of Mom's macaroni grilled cheese sandwiches. Shit, I thought I did a good job with this, but Siri's version tastes a zillion times better. The bread is thick and toasted to precision. The macaroni is packed to the tenth degree with flavor. The apples are more neatly cut up and evenly distributed. Plus, she made some damn good roasted broccoli to go on the side.

Papa and I help Siri clean after we feast. Of course she's one of those weirdos who loves doing dishes and refuses to use the dishwasher. As Siri's wrapping up at the sink, Papa disappears from the vicinity into his bedroom at the end of the hall.

Siri makes her way over to the tiny living room couch/TV area with a piece of paper in her hand.

She motions with her head. "Can you come sit down?"

"Are you giving . . . a presentation?" I ask.

"Sit down," she repeats.

I walk over skeptically and sit on the couch.

Siri clears her throat.

"Should I turn on the TV?" I ask. Her eyes flit up to glare at me. I smile.

"Okay." She blows out a long breath and starts to read.

"Jamie. You've been an asshole." She pauses.

I nod in agreement from the couch, but she doesn't look up to see.

"Most recently you pushed me, but I've caused you physical pain too. The whole canoe thing was pretty bad and I'm sorry. Thanks for being so cool about it. I can't promise it will never happen again because you're annoying and my sister, but I'll try really hard to be better. Starting with forgiving you. For everything. Because . . . truth be told, I'm still holding a bit of a grudge against six-year-old Jamie. And I know that little girl was misled and she's not here anymore.

"You ignore me sometimes. You almost, like, subconsciously manipulate conversations away from yourself. You're problematically obsessed with independence. You actively drive people away." She shrugs. *"I'm not afraid of that anymore. I know you're human. I'm going to hammer at your stupid walls until I get through because that's what you need. And I need you.*

"All I ever wanted growing up was for you to be real. All I remembered was how much better things were when you were around. I had the coolest friend-slash-sister in the world, who always made me laugh. Finding out that you were real and realizing you aren't the perfect person I've always imagined, it was hard to get over the initial shock of that.

"It took the other day in the hotel room for me to really see that you're just as broken as I am. Don't interrupt me because I know you're already dying to deny it." Siri doesn't look at me, just holds strong to staring at the paper, but I smile.

"But you can't deny it to me. We're part of each other, and I can see through your cracks, James George Federov.

"I lied the other day with whatever mean thing I said after you pushed me. All I ever wanted was to be was like you. I'm eighteen now and it's still true. I love how confident you are about any and every stupid thing you spout to anyone around you. How you can approach anyone at any given moment and say what's on your

mind. I watched you do it all the time at Rediscover. I don't think you realize how hard that is for some of us. How it holds a lot of us back from . . . everything." Her face turns red. *"It's really admirable. And everyone always wants to talk to you. They're drawn to you. You have that thing. I don't want to be you, Jamie. I don't want to steal your identity. I want to learn to be more like you. If you'll let me, I'd like to be the Anna to your Elsa."*

She clears her throat. *"I think we went about this Parental Confrontation thing all wrong. I know you had kind of good intentions? Like barely good intentions."* Siri grins. *"I know, in the deepest secret part of you, what you really needed and wanted was to confront Mom and Dad about what they've put us through. We can't understand our broken parts without understanding how they came to be. But I think we're both so broken, you know, we could never have been expected to do that alone.*

"We gave your way a go. So, I think it's only fair we try mine now. I'm here to propose a new plan where we stick together. Because I need you with me to do this confrontation thing right. And I think you need me too. We are stronger, smarter, better together." She stops talking and shakily takes the paper away from her face.

I press my lips together. They're wobbling and it's humiliating. "Damn you for being fucking sweet and evolved."

88. Angst and Progress

I'm working on my letter to Dad when I hear Mom clattering around downstairs in the kitchen. It's 11:30 at night. What the underworld is she doing? I put my pen down.

It smells like cake. She's in the kitchen, icing a cake?

"What are you doing?" I ask abrasively.

Mom looks up at me, stark fear in her eyes. "Um, it's James's birthday at midnight . . . I, I know it's probably a stupid idea, but I wanted to . . . I was going to bring this over to Papa's."

Mara is not all bad. Mara is damaged. Mara has made terrible mistakes. But Mara never stops trying. When she puts her efforts toward something, she accomplishes it. I hope she turns her efforts on us. I don't want to discount all the kind things she's ever done because of the bad things.

Moving forward with her is going to be difficult, and I'm going to lose my patience, but right now, watching her smear icing on a cake at 11:30 p.m. to surprise Jamie for her birthday that I didn't know about—I can't bring myself to hug her, but I love her.

89. A Girl Isn't Tired

JAMIE
September 10, Late Wednesday Night/
Early Thursday Morning
New Jersey

This bed isn't very comfortable itself, but something about being in this tiny room and knowing it's where my mom spent her childhood makes it comforting. It has history. I like imagining a young Mara in here getting ready for school. I wonder what she was like: probably a stuck-up know-it-all type who tattled on the kid next to her when she caught them doing something vaguely scandalous.

I'm voluntarily going to therapy with Siri tomorrow. Donya is her new therapist. Who would have thunk Donya also lives in New York. The whole Rediscover crew is out here. I guess it makes sense because it's Terry's retreat and she lives here.

There's a soft knock at the door.

"Yeah?"

"Can you come out to the kitchen, Jamie?" Papa says through the door.

"Sure, Pops, in a second." I roll off the bed and pad out into the hallway. All the lights are off.

I creep toward the kitchen, my hand trailing along the wall until I'm in the vicinity of the table.

"What are you playing at, Papa?" My hand falls on the switch. I flip it up.

385

Mara's sitting at the table with a cake full of unlit candles.

"Gah!" I jump back. "Jesus Christ."

"Scary, right?" Mara comments. She starts lighting the candles. "I couldn't resist."

Papa chuckles from where he is over on the couch. Siri's smiling over in the corner near him like a creepy lurker.

I turn around as Mara starts singing "Happy Birthday." Papa chimes in to say cha-cha-cha on the right beats. With everything going on, I didn't even take note of the date, or the fact that we're turning over onto my birthday. *Is it midnight?*

Firelight dances over Mara's face as she finishes singing. Her mouth is set in a tiny little smile.

I don't feel happy like I want to. Sadness sloshes around in me. It's so hard not to think about the fact that this woman's been pretending I never happened for my last million birthdays.

I heave in a breath and knock out the candles in one swift blow. Siri claps from the corner. She's letting Mara have the spotlight. This must have been Mom's idea; I doubt Siri even knows my birthday.

I pull on a gloomy smile. "Thanks for the cake and acknowledgment of my birth."

Mara sighs as Papa walks over to the kitchen drawers and shuffles around for plates and silverware.

"I'm here for a truce," Mara says.

I pull out a chair and sit down. "This half of the family is really into using food as a weapon."

Siri snorts. Papa hands Mara some small plates and a knife. She slices a piece for me. I take a forkful and stuff it in my mouth. "I'm listening," I say around my cake.

Mara cuts three more pieces. Once she's distributed them, she pokes at her own. "I usually celebrate your birthday alone with one of those brie macaroni sandwiches," she says quietly. "I take it up to my room and eat it by myself. I try to imagine what you might be doing. What you might look like. Be like."

I exhale a disgruntled huff.

"Vegas was a lot in the moment. I'm very disappointed in myself," she whispers. "It's hard to confront your missteps and weaknesses by having them laid out in front of you by your kids."

I swallow another bite of cake and look up at her. "Okay," I say flatly.

Mara looks down, directing her words at my plate. "I'm not saying I should be excused for anything. I just, I'd like to get to know you, spend time with you this week. Whenever you want to. Tell me when and I'll take off work. I promise I'm not completely terrible. I'm . . . stubborn and impulsive sometimes when I'm trying to get things done, and I mess up. And I like to be right, and it's hard for me to come to terms with how extensively fallible I am."

Looks like I got some of my most annoying traits from my mother.

I stare at her finger that's drawing circles on the table. "I'm done terrorizing you, Mara. You don't have to worry about that."

She meets my eyes. There's a spark of hope there that almost hurts my heart.

"Don't get too excited," I tell her.

"Could we do something together this week? For your birthday? For all the missed birthdays?"

90. Angst and Birthdays

I want Jamie to be able to interact with Mom without me there to distract. But I also want to be here because, well, it's her birthday and I want to be around for my sister's birthday. I want her to be around for my birthday.

Mom waved me over for cake, but I grabbed my piece and retreated back to the corner to eat it. Papa seems to be taking my cue; he's eating his at the coffee table in front of the couch.

"Could we do something together this week. For your birthday? For all the missed birthdays?" Mom asks.

Jamie looks over *at me*. I pause with my fork hovering close to my mouth.

"Sier, will you come with us if we do something for my birthday this week?"

My heart grows three sizes as I stare back at her.

I wouldn't go anywhere with Mom by myself right now, but I would love to go to support Jamie. I nod.

Jamie turns to my mother. "Would you be down to do the whole mother-daughter, shopping, nails, go home, drink wine, and watch a movie on the couch thing?"

Mom nods with her mouth closed. If I didn't know better, I'd say she's close to tears. Mom and Jamie are much more alike than Jamie probably knows. Mom just hides behind a different kind of wall.

We agree to celebrate on Friday. I don't know how long it would have taken me to agree to spend any time with Mom if Jamie weren't here.

I wasn't expecting forgiving Jamie so quickly to feel this good. I was expecting it to . . . I don't know, be a relief. Things still feel a bit one-sided because Jamie hasn't apologized. And she hasn't said anything about Dawn. But I think she wants to. I can hear it in the way she phrases the things she's said to me since then. She needs time.

If that's what it takes to figure out how we can fit together, I can give her time.

97. A Girl Is Voluntarily Here

"I did it, Donya! I talked to Jamie and she's here. I think I deserve a certificate of excellence!" Siri extends her arms toward me in a flourish. The two of us are side by side on Donya's purple couch.

Donya meets my eyes and laughs. "I can see that and I'm really proud of you."

Who knew Siri could be adorable? She had headphones in the entire train ride here, listening to the most hardcore emo stuff I've ever heard. She let me pop in a bud, and I tapped out after a minute.

"What do you think?" she asked hopefully.

I nodded. "Intense. Not for me, but I love that you love it."

"I know it's hard to hear the lyrics and feel the music at first," she explained. "It's kind of like learning a new dialect—the more you listen to it, the more you hear. I love that it's kind of like poetry; there's a lot of layers to analyze."

"Dang, watch out, ballet, I think Siri's found something else she's passionate about. Angst Lord mode activated."

Siri rolled her eyes and popped her second earbud back in, smiling.

She's smiling so much more since she got back from California. Is that because of something Dawn helped her through?

Dawn sent me a happy birthday text last night: Happy birthday, Jame. I miss you. <3 Excited to celebrate after we work through all the shit we're tangled up in. I don't know if you've talked to Siri about things, but I don't want to come between you two. Siri stuff . . . that wasn't to hurt you. Nothing was done to hurt you. I hope we can talk-talk soon. These last 2 weeks have felt like an eternity without you in them to latch onto in all my free moments.

It would have been in character for a selfish asshole like me to think Dawn put the moves on my sister to hurt me, but that thought didn't ever cross my mind because Dawn is the best person in the universe and I know she would never do that.

How could Siri resist the charms of the best, most caring person in the universe? And Siri cares so much about things. In ways that, I guess, I don't. I don't know. Siri's nice. Dawn could use someone like that in her life.

I don't know who to be upset with when it comes to my best friend kissing my sister. Is it anyone's fault? Is it my fault? Is it a fault? I just know that I'm upset . . . It probably has nothing to do with them. It's my own issue. And I'm not ready to talk it through with Siri yet. I'll get upset, and I don't want to be upset right now. I want to be on the same team. I want to try things her way.

I rub my hands together and smile at Donya. "So, what are we in for today, Don?"

"We wanted to have a team chat about talking to your mom and dad."

That wasn't terrible. It felt like talking through a problem with a friend who's really good at giving advice. No exercises and no reading aloud. It's the first time I've successfully made it through an entire therapy session. That's a victory in itself.

"What'd you think?" Siri asks as we stroll out onto the city sidewalk.

I shrug and bite back a smile. "Donya's pretty cool."

"You're going to write your own letters, right?" she asks earnestly. "You'll do it with me?"

When Donya suggested this letter thing, my gut reaction was *eh*.

I don't know why I've had such an aversion to advice over the years. I have a special high-grade disregard for Grams's and my father's suggestions. Their advice feels like control. It feels like there's an ulterior motive. And to be honest, I like the triumph of figuring something out all on my own.

But that's not working. And part of succeeding is . . . *knowing when to ask for help.*

And I mean, I think they're going to make a difference, because fuck if Siri's letter yesterday didn't turn things around in less than an hour.

I nod to her. "Yeah, I'll do the letters."

"For real?" She stares sideways at me.

I glance up at the sky. "Yeah, sis, I'm on it."

"Thank you!" She claps her hands together excitedly. "Okay! Well, I think I'm going to meet you at home. I have something I want to do before I head back."

I shoot her a dubious look. "Your weirdly happy demeanor is throwing me off my axis. It's so off brand. What the excrement happened to you?"

She giggles. "It would be *what the intercourse.*"

"You giggle now?" I burst. "Are you someone else wearing Siri's skin? Did you get glitter bombed again? Were you like this before the accident? Was Angst Lord Siri a phase?"

Siri rolls her eyes, walking backward away from me. "She wasn't a phase."

"Okay, where are you going?" I ask.

"To the ballet studio. I have to run this errand by myself."

"Okay, well, be careful," I shout, worry creeping into my gut like I'm dropping my child off at school. "Make good choices!!"

She spins with another grin and runs off down the street.

"Don't run! You're going to hurt your back!" I watch her immediately slow down. She sticks an arm up and waves at me, using the other arm to brace her lower back as she power walks. Excited dummy.

"SIRI 2.0, PERK LORD OF YORK," I shout after her.

I stop and take in my surroundings. There's a familiar-looking food truck parked down the street. I think I have some things I want to do too.

92. A Girl Wants to Make It Better

JAMIE
September 10, Thursday Afternoon
New York City

It takes me three separate tries, but I finally manage to walk through the doors of QCZ. It's Thursday, so I think he should be here . . . his improv class should have just ended.

The door is open but no one's behind the desk.

I knock on the wood. "Hello?"

There's a fumbling crashing noise from the room behind the desk, and then Zarar's standing behind the counter.

I hold up a grilled cheese sandwich. "I brought a peace offering."

He blinks at me. "Your hair is orange again."

I nod. "How did you know?"

"I just have this feeling."

I snort.

"I like this shade." He sighs. "What are you doing here?"

"I'm, um, here for the time being."

"What does that mean?"

I shrug. "I'm not sure."

"Okay, well, if you're here to use me for sex and stimulating conversation for a couple of days and then ghost me again . . . I'm not here for that."

"That's fair," I concede after an extended silence. "I didn't think I'd be back."

He studies me for a moment. "Is that it?" He's holding something in his left hand. A script.

I swallow. Crap. Is that it? He hasn't taken my sandwich offering. Maybe I need to write him a letter too.

"Do you need something?" he asks.

"Um, I had a random thought. Can I ask you something?"

He shrugs. "Obviously you can."

"Can you get me a meeting with that Penn music guy you work for?"

Zarar raises a brow. "You know he's engaged."

"Oh, come on, not for that. He's not my type."

"What's your type?"

"I type eighty-five words a minute." I serve him finger guns.

Zarar stares at me. "That was not funny."

"Harsh." I frown at my feet. "Can you get me a meeting or no?"

He pulls a flyer from a pile behind him and starts writing something down. "I'll give you his number. I'll let him know to expect a call from you. You can set it up yourself."

He hands me the paper. I'm still holding his food. "Um, do you want this grilled cheese?"

He shakes his head. "No, thanks. That's not what I'm looking for."

"Wha—" I frown. Shit. What have I done here? I legitimately like this man. "I didn't mean to ever . . . I'm trying to. Crap bucket damnit."

I spin around and walk out. I obviously can't make a romantic gesture to save my life. I don't know how to do relationships! I drop the sandwich in the trash.

I *do* know how to work a meeting. I punch the number Zarar wrote on the flyer into Gladys.

93. Angst and Letting Go

SIRI
September 10, Thursday
New York City

Two weeks ago, I thought to myself, if I can't dance here, I never want to see it again.

But here I am. Voluntarily. That's unbelievable.

I hold my arms to my chest, watching through the window to the studio as my fellow company members rehearse, waiting patiently for the end of whatever routine they're running. Bran and Celia dance next to each other now.

When the formation disperses, hands drop to hips and wipe noses, foreheads. That's when Celia glances this way and catches my eye. Her brows shoot up.

I mouth *Can we talk?* through the window.

Celia looks around until she finds Bran and angles her head in my direction. After a moment, they both stride out of the studio.

I heave out a breath, my back seeming to throb along with my heartbeat. I feel a little woozy as they step into the room where I'm waiting. As they make their way toward me, my mind flashes to them fornicating. Celia's dead expression. I close my eyes and shake the image away. This isn't about them.

Celia stops a foot away from me, and Bran stops behind her.

"Hi, Siri," she says hesitantly. "Are you—are you back?"

I shake my head. "No, I'm never coming back. I'm just here to say good-bye." I look up at Bran. He won't make eye contact with me.

"Oh," Celia says.

"I wanted to tell you that, uh, you were my first real friends. Celia, I thought you were the coolest, most interesting person, and Bran, you were so handsome and talented. What y'all did really hurt, but I'm working on forgiving you. *I'm going to forgive you.* I don't want to think of you as enemies. It's a waste of brain space. I wish you had told me how you were feeling."

They stare at me awkwardly.

I shrug. "Phew! Well, I don't want anything from you, so that's it!" I smile at them. "I forgive you! Have a good life."

I pivot and walk out the door feeling like gravity has loosened her grip the tiniest bit, and it makes all the difference.

94. A Girl Works a Meeting

JAMIE
September 10, Thursday
New York City

"Penn!" I wave Z's boss over to where I'm waiting at the coffee place next to his office. It's another one of these minimalist places where they've tried to make the inside look like an outdoor patio by putting fake vines on the wall.

Penn sits across from me looking extremely confused. "Jamie?"

"Yep."

"You cut off your super long hair."

"Oh yeah, yep. I did that."

"And dyed it orange." He squints at me.

"Yep."

"And got a nose ring."

"Yeah."

"And a . . . fresh scar over your eyebrow. All in the last four days."

"Yep."

"Did you decide comedy's not for you and join a band? Is this . . . like, do you need a producer? That was fast."

"No, Penn."

"What happened?"

"I fell out of a canoe. A fishing boat hybrid that's not technically a canoe, but they call them canoes—you know what, it's not important. I was wearing makeup over it the other day."

He squints at me. "My name's actually Pilot. Penn's my last name."

"Can I call you Penn?" I almost tell him Pilot's a ridiculous non-name and I won't say it aloud, but I don't because I want a favor out of this guy.

He shrugs. "Why not."

I get up, order us fancy coffee, and bring it back to the table. "Okay, I'll get straight to it here. Does this production company make more than indie-pop mellow stuff?"

"Uh, well, we're a branch of a bigger company that has other genres attached."

"Emo music? Angry music like . . . metal?" I ask hopefully.

He narrows his eyes. "Yeah."

"Do you think you could arrange an internship for someone who's really passionate about that stuff? I think she might really enjoy it."

He raises his eyebrows. "Is 'someone' you?"

"No, Penn, believe it or not, I don't much care about music. I'm asking for a friend."

He nods pensively. "I have to make some calls, but I think we can at least get her an interview."

I feel my face light up. "Oh snap, really?"

"Yes, really." He grins.

"Thanks, dude."

He sips his cappuccino. "No problem. Any friend of Zarar's is a friend of mine. He's a good guy."

"He is." I take a sip of my coffee. "You're a weird boss."

"I'm not the boss. I'm the guy he's interning for."

"Question. Did he invite you to his acting thing?"

"He did." Penn smiles. "Shane and I are going. See you there on Saturday?"

"You two are quite the social butterflies."

Penn snorts. "We like to support cool people chasing after cool careers."

I raise an eyebrow. "Zarar is cool?"

Penn bobs his chin up and down with his eyes closed. "The coolest."

"When and where is it?"

Before I head home, I stop by QCZ one more time. They're gearing up for their first real show of the evening and a handful of other people are around. Zarar's not currently at the front desk; a woman's standing there. I take advantage of the absence.

"Can I sign up for an open mic night two weeks from now?" I ask.

She pulls out a clipboard.

95. Angst and Wine

SIRI
September 11, Friday
New York City

Mom, Jamie, and I are sitting in a fancy restaurant after a day full of shopping when conversation shifts to Gladys, Jamie's thirteen-year-old Chocolate cell phone. Mom pronounces it absolutely unacceptable. Jamie puts up a hilarious defense.

Sitting here, watching her bicker with Mom about such a mundane mother-daughter thing, I don't know, it makes me feel really full. I finally speak up and take Mom's side on this debate.

Who knows where Jamie will end up living in a month? I want to be able to FaceTime with her. I know she won't be good at keeping in touch long distance. She'll retreat back into emotional hermit-hood. Mom already proposed this FaceTiming argument with her, but it's my two cents that puts Jamie over the line.

"*Fine.*" Jamie deflates. "Fine. Fine, but I'm taking the day with Gladys. We're not turning an iPhone on till tomorrow. I need time to say goodbye."

Mom interrogated us last night to figure out what kind of restaurant to bring us to. Jamie had no preference. I want to start dabbling in some Filipino recipes, so I made us reservations at one of the highest-rated Filipino restaurants I could find on Yelp.

Jamie's sipping a peach cucumber martini when her Chocolate buzzes.

She's been paying special attention to it for the last couple of hours. She snatches it up now.

"Sier," she gushes immediately.

I swallow my mouthful of chicken adobo. "What?"

Jamie lets go of a long breath. "How would you feel about interning for a recording studio where they produce metal albums and emo music and all that shit you're into?"

The forkful of rice I've been prepping slides back onto my dish.

"I . . . wow, I . . . um . . . that sounds really cool, actually."

"You have an interview at Metal Stone next Tuesday. I'll text over the info."

I put down my fork. "An interview? How?"

"I know a guy."

"How did you even . . . when did you even think of this? I haven't even thought of, I didn't even think . . ."

Jamie grins. "I noticed it's a thing you like, and you're trying to figure out what you want to do. I wanted to help if I could."

And then I start to cry.

96. A Girl Is Enjoying Herself

JAMIE
September 11, Friday
New York City

Both Mom and Siri have yet to see *Men in Black 2*. This is a crime.

"You girls don't want to binge a *Thrones* season—" Mom starts as she brings over a bottle of wine and three glasses.

"No." We both cut her off at the same time. Siri and I break into laughter, and after a second Mara joins in.

"It's *Men in Black 2* or nothing!" I declare.

Mara smiles. "Where did I go wrong with you two and *Thrones*?"

"I think it was when you middle named us George and Martine?" I say with mock-thoughtfulness as she pours me a glass. Siri giggles.

This feels too good to be true. This day is too good to be true. I can't believe we're laughing with our mother. Together.

I can't believe *I* am. Like I'm part of this family.

I know this is a moment I'm going to hold on to for . . . ever.

Siri and I have written our letters and we're doing them later, after the movie. We discussed it via text and we don't want to ruin what's been a really nice day.

We're all good and tipsy when Mara pauses the movie during the climactic scene.

402

"Before we get any further into the wine, and I can't articulate my thoughts as clearly, I need to give you your present." Mara gets off the couch and fumbles into the kitchen.

"You already got me an iPhone, Mara," I call out. I glance over at Siri. She's lying flat on her back with her feet in my lap. She finally explained that she can only sit bolt upright or flat on her back at this point.

"I love this," she tells me. Her face is beet red from the wine she insisted she wasn't going to like. A girl thought she didn't like wine, but that girl hadn't tried Moscato.

"I told you you would like *MIB 2*. No one appreciates this amazing masterpiece."

She rolls her eyes. "Not *Men in Black 2*, you weirdo. This."

"Your gross ballet feet in my lap?"

"My feet are talented," she slurs.

"Talented and shredded all the same."

She shakes her head. "I love being a family," she whispers. "Even if we're super messed up."

I squeeze her nasty feet as Mom returns with two big, thin, wrapped rectangles.

"Did you buy me art to go with my iPhone?" I snort.

Mara shakes her head and hands me one of the gifts. Siri takes her feet off my thighs and sits up so I can put it in my lap.

I tear off the wrapping eagerly at first, but I stop when I see my face under the paper I ripped away. I slowly knead off the rest and swallow at the knot rising in my throat.

When Dad and I left, we left without pictures.

I'm holding a framed 8 × 10 of little me and tiny Siri. It's a close-up on our faces and we're hugging in our dance recital outfits.

"Thank you, Mara," I mumble, trying not to get emotional. I'm not as good at silent crying as Siri is. It takes a lot of effort for me, and I'm a little too drunk to really pull it off.

I suck in a watery garble. "What's the other one?"

Mara pulls the second frame up on her lap, another 8 × 10. "This one's for me." She unwraps it so it's facing her, not Siri and me.

After a moment, she spins it around. It's a young Mara. She looks like she can't be much older than I am now. She's at the beach buried in the sand. Toddler Siri's holding a shovel and sitting pretzel-style next to Mara's head, and I'm in the left foreground doing a split with my hands up, shovel in the air.

Siri gasps next to me.

I snort. "Oh my god. Wow."

Mara puts it on the couch next to her and shakes out her hands before looking up at me. She slides off the couch and gets down on one knee.

"Mara, are you proposing to me? Because I'm not interested in you that way," I say instinctively.

Her head falls forward, and I hear her laughing through what sound like tears. Are we all crying right now? I glance over at Siri to share a look with her. Of course there are streams flowing down her face. She's like a faucet, that one.

"Don't make me laugh, James. I want to say something." Mara shakes her head, stretching out her mouth. "Okay, I'm not good at this. I'm sorry if I stumble or something."

"Just say it, Mom," Siri says.

Mara exhales. "Jamie . . . I was a coward letting you go that day fourteen years ago. It broke my heart when you said you didn't want to live with me. I shouldn't have let it affect me the way I did. You were a child, but it broke me.

"I didn't act like an adult. I was still in my twenties and I was really stupid sometimes. I'm still really stupid sometimes. I didn't know what to do. Your father had seen me having dinner with this other guy. We already were on rocky ground, and he had pictures . . . I thought if I put up any sort of fuss, he would be able to take both of you away. I didn't have the willpower or the courage to deal with lawyers and the fighting, and I let you slip away from both of us. It's not a good excuse. It's not an excuse. But it's the truth, and I hope someday you can forgive me."

My jaw tightens. "I hope someday I can too."

Siri stands up at this. She does a little sidestep as she tilts to the right. "Ma, we actually prepared something to say to you, if you could get back on the couch, please."

Mara's jaw pops open. "Of course, Siri."

I don't really want to do this right now. But I promised Siri. I get up to stand beside her. She pulls a folded piece of paper out of her bra. I pull mine from my front overall pocket. I've read mine so many times, I'm off book. But I have it on me for Siri. I want her to know I wrote it.

Siri goes first, spilling her heart out to Mara about all her hopes and dreams of being a mother-daughter ballet duo and how she feels like she's never enough to hold her attention. How sad she is about all Mara's lies. How she wants Mara to keep being the mom she looks up to, but she also needs her to try to be better. To be more present even when things aren't bad.

And then I go. I'm actually glad I wrote it down once I start speaking because these words are so vulnerable . . . I don't think I'd actually be able to spit them out with Mara looking at me. The paper gives me something to stare at.

When we finish, it feels like I've let go of a darkness that's been taking up residence in my chest. I blow out a long sigh.

"Don't respond right now, Mara. You're emotional and kind of drunk, and so am I. I think I should go. Let's let everything marinate and talk about it some other time next week."

Mara nods, wiping stray tears.

97. Angst and Bridges

SIRI
September 11, Friday
New York City

Jamie went back to Papa's.

After reading my mom letter, I feel overwhelmed and heavy with emotions rather than light and relieved. This letter was way more complicated and convoluted than the one to Jamie. It was a hundred times harder to stand up there and say these words to my mother, the woman who raised me, than to forgive Bran and Celia.

But I said them. I could say them because I knew Jamie was there to defend me if I needed her to.

It was heartbreaking hearing Jamie's letter. Mara sat stone-still for the ten minutes it took us to finish talking, her usual inscrutable expression marred with shame. She didn't know what to do when we were done, but I know she wanted to do something.

I'm glad Jamie told her to sit with it. I'm glad Jamie left and gave me the out to leave the room.

Today was wonderful, but that doesn't make everything that's happened disappear. We have to have discussions like these in order to have more days like this.

During our session with Donya together yesterday, Jamie and I made plans to visit Dad next weekend. I volunteered to get in contact with him and see if he'd fly us out there.

Me: Jamie and I would like to come and talk to you next weekend. Can you fly us out and make plans to spend the day with us?

Dad: Done. I'll have my assistant get the tickets and send you over confirmations. When do you want to fly out and what's your email, Siri?

Me: Friday night, please. Out of EWR. AskSiriAboutBallet11@gmail.com. We'd like to fly back here Sunday on the red-eye.

Dad: Looking forward to it, Siri

I check in with Jamie Saturday morning to let her know about Dad. She's on her way out to Staples when I text her, and she asks me if I want to join.

Jamie is inviting me places with her!

Five minutes later, she pulls up in front of Mom's house in Papa's white Honda Accord.

I smile as Jamie rolls down the window. "Pop's hip is acting up today, so we're picking him up some groceries on the way home. Hop in, woman."

At Staples, I help Jamie print pages and pages of words as she fills me in on her plans for the day. After grabbing groceries, we head back to Papa's together. I help her cut papers and prep for the evening. She makes fun of my precise way of organizing the table while we work, and I am smitten with the growing proof that we are friends. Jamie and I are going to be friends.

Jamie's trying really hard to be better in all the ways that count, and I am really stupidly proud.

98. A Girl Is Going for It

JAMIE
September 12, Saturday
New York City

I stop in at Duane Reade to grab one last thing on my way to the theater. I'm wearing a new pair of overalls I found shopping with Mara yesterday, and I've done my eyes up in shades of orange and gold.

It's 6:50 p.m. when I skitter up to the tiny theater Zarar's performing in tonight with his acting class. I pay the five bucks for a ticket and make my way to a seat. It's a small room; there's only like fifteen people in the audience.

"Jamie!" someone calls as I head toward the front. Penn's bubbly fiancée is waving at me from the third row. Penn raises a hand in greeting from the seat next to her.

"You're welcome to sit with us," he calls.

I shuffle down and scoot into the seat next to Shane. "Can you guys watch my stuff while I go do some recon? I want to figure out where the actors come out after the show."

"Of course." Shane grins.

I wander around the foyer area until I stumble upon some steps leading down to a door that must lead to the backstage area. Yahtzee! My heart's beating more aggressively as I race back to my seat. Maybe I should have done this before the show, so I wouldn't be nervous the entire time. We're three minutes from curtain.

As I settle in, I turn to Penn and Shane for distraction. "How did you two meet, then?"

"England." Penn grins.

I wait a second for him to elaborate, but he doesn't.

I arch a brow. "Wow, what a tale. Tell it again."

Shane snickers. She opens her mouth like she's about to go into more detail, but she's cut off as the lights dim and the show starts.

Each student duo is doing a five-minute scene from a well-known film. Before each performance, a student dressed all in black walks out and tells us blah-blah and blah-blah will be performing a selection from insert movie here.

I'm having some trouble paying attention to the other budding actors. Penn and his fiancée keep whispering and smiling at each other disgustingly between scenes. I am a third wheel and my gut reaction is to analyze them, figure out when and how they'll end up breaking up.

Why do I do that?

Why do I constantly project worst-case scenarios on people? I think of myself as a fairly happy-go-lucky person. Love isn't logical, and it can't be measured properly with a statistic, and it's not black and white, and I don't know why I ever thought breakup shit was funny.

Penn and Shane snort together again as a new group comes onto the stage. I should have sat by myself in the front row.

After what feels like an hour, but has to have only been twenty minutes, the narrator student announces Zarar and a woman named Patty performing a selection from *Titanic*. Zarar's wearing a cream-colored long-sleeve shirt and tan pants with suspenders. I am here for it.

Of course Zarar would choose to do a scene from *Titanic*. Zarar and a woman in her forties start the scene where Jack and Rose walk around the ship and Rose looks through Jack's drawings. Zarar is decent! But I keep having to cover my mouth with my hand, trying not to laugh.

When they wrap the scene, the two of them bow and we applaud. I don't want to make my presence known yet, so I don't stand and cheer obnoxiously like I want to. As soon as he clears the stage, I grab my backpack and race out.

I wait in a nook down the stairs, in the narrow hallway that leads backstage. I brace myself when the stage door opens, but it's the forty-something woman, not Z. I blow out a breath and step back as she walks by.

When the door opens again thirty seconds later, I'm all in. I bend my knees, brace, and leap out from the nook, colliding directly into Zarar.

"Oh excuse me, sir!" I squeak frantically.

He yelps as all the tiny papers I'm holding go flying. I give them a little chuck for extra effect as I trip sideways into the wall.

They're neon orange today. And they look quite nice as they all flutter to the ground around us.

Zarar stumbles back, his face breaking out in a signature left-side-of-his-mouth smile.

"Jamie?" he huffs.

I collapse, playing at trying to pick them all up. "Oh gosh, crap, crap, crap. I'm not good at this holding-stuff thing." I glance up at him with my most over-the-top klutzy lady look. "I'm so sorry. I seem to have dropped my fifty million papers. Would you mind getting your ass down here to help me pick them up?"

He crouches down, and picks one up. "Will you go out with me?" he reads in amused disbelief.

He meets my gaze, his gorgeous brown eyes lighting up. There are about twenty of those. I wanted to make sure he saw it.

He picks up another. "I think you're pretty freaking great, and in more than a friendly way."

And another. "Tootsie Pops are prime."

And another. "Canoe thief has a thing for you."

And another. "Here's my actual number, call me."

And another. "I'm really freaking sorry for ghosting your amazing ass (and winning personality)."

He locks eyes with me again. His are smug now as both of us squat here on the floor like dumbasses. My heart's beating so fucking fast, it really feels like I'm either going to throw up out of embarrassment or explode.

With a slightly shaky hand, I pull a bouquet of Tootsie Pops from my backpack. I find the correct paper lying on the floor and hand it to him.

"Will you accept this label?" he reads carefully.

I bite my tongue, trying not to die as I hold out the Tootsie Pop bouquet with a big HELLO MY NAME IS: BOYFRIEND sticker taped onto it.

He stares at it for the longest five seconds of my life.

"Oh my god, I feel like such a loser. How the hell do you do this? You best decide what you're doing right now or else."

He cough-laughs, plucks the sticker from the bouquet, and slaps it onto his chest. "I accept this label with pride."

I glance up at the ceiling and blow out a sigh of immense relief. "Thank you, universe." I take the GIRLFRIEND name tag I have prepped out of my pocket and slap it front and center on my chest. "I've gone down like a thousand cool points."

"You are the most uncool now." Zarar's eyes crinkle with humor. "Like maybe public hand-holding level of loserdom."

I snicker, starting to pick up the papers and stuff them into my backpack. "Just uncool enough to be your girlfriend, you hot weirdo."

"I thought you'd never ask," he says.

I roll my eyes. "You thought I'd never ask . . . what?" I repeat sarcastically. "You are a walking cliché, that didn't even make conversational sen—" He cuts me off, stepping forward onto his knee to kiss me like the world's ending.

Excrement.

I would drag him out of here and back to his apartment if I didn't know Penn and Shane were waiting to talk to him outside. Lord help me, why am I using the word "excrement" unironically?

99. Angst and Los Angeles

SIRI
September 19, Saturday
California

Grams is waiting for us at LAX when we arrive at midnight Pacific time.

Jamie yells down to her as we're descending on the escalator. "Grams, Papa sold you out! You paid off my landlord? I literally can't believe you got me kicked out of my apartment, what the hell?!"

"It was a bit of a shithole." Grams smiles as we step off onto ground level. She starts toward the exit and we fall into step.

"It was my shithole!" Jamie argues.

"Well, I'm sorry, I thought it was for the greater good."

Jamie rolls her eyes. "Congratulations, Olenna Tyrell, you did it. We're here together."

I laugh.

"That reference is wasted on me, granddaughter."

"Well, Siri got it."

"Does this mean I'm forgiven?"

"Probably."

"You love me."

"Yeah, whatever, Grams, you wily fox."

Dad's not around when we get to the house. We're exhausted, so we head straight to Jamie's room and get ready for bed.

Jamie slips under her comforter, and I get cozy in her sleeping bag on the floor next to her. She flips off the light.

"Siri," Jamie says into the dark.

"Yeah," I answer quietly.

"I'm going to drop down a piece of paper, but don't read it right now."

"Okay . . ." A folded-up square lands on the floor next to me.

"I'm sorry I pushed you into Plan Parent Confrontation Trap, and that we're not getting an official sister trip," Jamie says.

I turn toward the bed. "Thank you. And, well, we're kind of having our sister trip now. It's been really cool hanging out with you all week."

". . . I'm also sorry about how I reacted about you and Dawn. She's wonderful and you're wonderful. She'd be lucky to have a girlfriend as generous as you are."

A knot in my chest loosens, and I smile in her direction. "I know how close you two are . . . I should have talked to you as soon as I started feeling something. Which was immediately because she's a goddess and you gave me no warning."

"I didn't realize you were bi . . . Are you? Or are you not into labels?"

"I'm bi," I tell her. "I had crushes all across the spectrum growing up. But I'm not good at flirting. Or dating, or anything romantic."

"You and me both. *Thanks, Grier and Mara*," she squawks in a goofy British voice.

I laugh. "Didn't you just woo Zarar into being your boyfriend?"

"Indeed, I did," she says in a Southern belle accent. "We had really phenomenal sex afterward too. Who knew commitment could make things even hotter."

I can't believe she just shared that with me. "I think we all knew. That's a thing people say all the time."

"Yeah, but I always said that was an urban legend to shame us and quash our zest for carefree sexual escapades."

I cringe. "Okay, I don't know if I'm ready to hear any more about your sexual life."

She laughs.

After a quiet minute she says, "But seriously, about Dawn. If that's ever something that happens, I'll be okay with it. We'll be fine. Me and you, and me and her. I might be weird for a bit, but I'll get over it eventually, I promise."

My lips wobble as a wave of emotion takes the wheel. I know how hard it must have been for her to say that. Only a week ago, she had a full-blown meltdown.

"That's really nice of you," I say very quietly.

"Have you had any more thoughts about what you want to do? I know I set up that internship and kind of sprung it on you. And you said the interview went well, but if you felt like you had to say that, like . . . I can always get you out of it, you don't have to do it."

"It's strange hearing you be all sensitive."

Jamie huffs and shifts so that she's leaning over the side of the bed, looking down at me. "I'm feeling sentimental, and I'm trying to be less emotionally repressed!" She smiles. "Do you want the internship?"

"Jamie, you hit the nail on the head with that idea. I want the internship."

She falls back onto her pillow. "Thank god. You haven't mentioned it since, and I thought I pushed you into another thing you didn't want to do and I was inadvertently a steamrolling asshole again. Can you let me know ASAP when I'm being a steamrolling asshole, instead of being polite?"

I nod. "I can try. I don't realize it sometimes."

"Okay, but whenever you do, spit it at me, hollaback girl."

I giggle. "Okay. I might want to work in music, but I'm also thinking about something else."

Jamie takes a few seconds to respond. "It's not comedy, is it?"

I roll my eyes.

"It's okay if it is. I'll get over it," she says quickly.

"It's not comedy," I insist. "I think I might want to do the internship and then do culinary school and see which feels more right."

"Culinary school?" Jamie wiggles around like a rabid worm, hanging over the edge again. "Sier! Look at you figuring shit out. I was going to suggest that option fifty years ago, but it seems so obvious, I thought you had already nixed it."

"I don't know if I'd ever want to run a kitchen. That feels . . . daunting, it's too loud, but maybe something in food science or something?"

"Food science! You are so cool."

"Not as cool as you."

"You're right. I'm pretty fucking awesome."

I smack her bed with my hand. "What are you doing about your future?" I challenge.

"I'm gonna do that thing successful people do—get up and try the hell again."

"What's that mean?" I smile.

"I'm grooming a new set."

"Is it about me?" I squeak.

"It's about you and all of us."

Excitement buzzes through me. "Can I hear it?'

"Right now, it's a rough draft. It needs to be edited."

"When can I hear it?"

"I signed up for open mic night at QCZ next Saturday, so I have a hot second to pull shit together. And if it goes well, I might sign up for as many open mic slots as I can find in the New York City places."

I sit up to a kneeling position so I can lean against the bed and push her shoulder. "*Jamie!* You're doing a gig with a new set and I'm invited? I'm so coming!"

She turns away to face the other side of the bed. "Okay, pipe down, you're welcome. Good night."

When it sounds like Jamie has fallen asleep, I duck into my sleeping bag with my phone flashlight and open the folded square. It's a ripped page from the Rediscover Yourself journal.

ZE OVERNIGHT MIRACLE

Honestly, if an overnight miracle came in to fix my life, I'd be waking up fourteen years ago. Mr. Miracle would give me the chance to fix this shit myself, instead of doing all the work for me overnight. That's how we grow, folks.

He'd throw me back to the day my dad decided he was leaving.

I wouldn't leave with my fucking dad. I'd stay in New York with my mom and Siri where I belonged. More than that, where I was needed. Siri needed me. Siri still needs me. I don't know what happened to her, but if I was there, maybe I could have stopped it. I don't know how, but I know I would have fought for that girl's happiness. I want to fight for it now. She needs a change. She doesn't want to go home to Mom. Maybe it would be best to invite her back to Dad's?

My mom needed my help. If I was there, she could never have ruined herself with this lie. She would never need to pretend I didn't exist. She'd want me to exist in her life no matter what.

My dad didn't need me. He still doesn't need me.

Siri and I would grow up alongside each other. We'd bicker, but we'd be a team when it came down to it. I wouldn't grow up thinking my dad was right. Thinking his mannerisms were dickish, but his ideas were well-founded. I would know how to care about people the right way.

I want to. I swear I do. But I can't manage to go more than a week before I fuck something up for someone. Ruin someone's day. Cause an argument. Make someone cry. Say the wrong thing. I wouldn't be a constant liability. In Miracle Land, I'd figure out how to separate myself from my own bullshit.

100. Angst and Hope

SIRI
September 19, Saturday
California

I sneak out of Jamie's room early. She's still on her stomach, drooling, when I head downstairs in a black sweatshirt and leggings.

It's Saturday so Dawn might not be awake, but I feel like I need to talk to her. Now that Jamie and I have talked, I need to at least check in.

I ring the doorbell and wait, anxiously doing rond de jambes with my left foot on her doorstep.

"Siri?" I spin to find a sweaty Dawn walking up her driveway in light pink shorts and a tight matching athletic zip-up. She pulls headphones out of her ears.

"Hi." I look at my feet, embarrassed. "Sorry, I didn't mean to drop by unannounced. I felt like I needed, I owed you a . . . something . . . a talk or I don't know."

"You want to come in? My mom's at work; she had an early surgery."

I nod and follow her into the house.

"It's nice to see you again so soon!" She smiles. "You don't owe me an anything. I wasn't going to tell Jamie. Your dad came around to tell me what happened. I'm sorry she found out the way she did." She grabs a water bottle out of the refrigerator.

"Well, um, I wanted to tell you I think you're great, and I . . . I have an internship lined up in New York, but I'd love to keep in touch, no strings attached or anything. If you want to keep in touch, that is. I think I plan on coming back here eventually. I don't think I want to live in New York forever."

Dawn puts down the water she's swigging from. "Really?"

"Really."

"How's Jamie?"

"Much better. She agreed to come to therapy with me once a week. I've been going like every other day." I shake my head. "TMI, sorry."

Dawn shakes her head. "Siri, if your therapist is helping you and you're going through the shit, why not see her more than once a week."

I smile weakly.

"So, Jamie's not freaking out about us anymore?" she asks.

I shake my head. "She's working through it. But I kinda don't think I'm ready for anything relationship-y right now. I have to find my footing again in all the other aspects of my life." I huff a sad laugh.

Dawn nods.

"Can I show you something?" she says softly.

I blow out a relieved breath. "Of course."

"Don't make fun of me, okay?"

"I would never."

Dawn leads me into her dreamy room and opens the top drawer of her nightstand. She pulls out a snow globe, her hands clasped over it.

"So, after you left, I was looking through the pictures we took and . . . um, well, I did a thing."

She takes her hand off the snow globe and puts it in my outstretched palm. Our ice cream–covered faces are pressed cheek to cheek in the picture at the center. I'm not Jamie in it anymore . . . I'm me.

Dawn spins the globe in my hand. The stand that holds the picture allows for another on the back. In the back picture, we're kissing.

I suck in a sharp breath. I didn't even know she snapped that. "You made us a real snow globe."

She smiles shyly. "I know it's cheesy and stupid. I didn't think you'd be back so soon, and I didn't know how seriously you wanted to take the idea of never seeing each other again. But I don't have many perfect days. I wanted to make sure I could never lose this one."

I look up at her with watery eyes. "This is the most beautiful thing I've ever seen."

She steps closer and puts her forehead against mine. "Good thing it was a two-for-one snow globe deal at Walmart then."

"Is it a bad idea to kiss you again?" I ask.

"I think that train has left the station."

Dawn and I make out for five glorious minutes on her bed before I leave with my new most prized possession.

101. A Girl Has One More Letter

JAMIE
September 19, Saturday
California

Now that we've done this once before with Mom and things ended so somberly, we're taking a different approach. We're going to start with our letters in the morning and get them over with, before we spend the day with Dad.

Siri and I meet him in the living room at 10 a.m. Siri's plan is to make breakfast for the three of us as a sort of pick-me-up when we're done.

Dad sits on the couch, and we stand in front of him like we're about to give a movie pitch.

Siri clears her throat. "Dad." Her voice cracks on the first word. I reach over, take her hand, and squeeze it. She doesn't pull away; she holds on.

"Dad," Siri starts again.

She opens with a list of daydreams she's had about Grier coming to reunite with her throughout the years. It's gut-punch sad. By the end of it, I can't even look up at Dad.

"*. . . your leaving has sculpted me as a person. I'm overly emotional. I have self-esteem issues. I'm angry. I don't want those things to define me anymore. I don't want what you've done to be the dominant thing rumbling around inside me through everything I do for the rest of my life. So, I'm here to wave a white flag. I'm here . . . because I want to forgive you.*" She closes her eyes. "*I do*

420

forgive you for leaving. I will never forget. But I will let you try to be a part of my life if you would like to be."

Siri lowers her paper. I raise my letter and jump right in before I lose my nerve.

"Hey, Dad, it took a week wearing a glitter-dust mirage and extensive conversations with a hurt and broken Siri to realize you've been gaslighting me my entire life."

I dig into the sad epiphanies I had at Rediscover. How his love feels conditional on my decisions aligning with his wishes.

". . . You made me feel like cutting them out was okay. That it was more than okay, that I deserved my own separate life so I could follow my own ever-important dreams. And yeah, having dreams and goals are important and great, but some things have to be more important. Moms. Sisters. Daughters. Family, Dad. You don't cut off your people so that you can fly. You find a way to bring them with you. To make it work. And if you can't make it work with them in the picture, you choose them, not the dream.

"You chose your dream over your daughter, Dad. Can you see that? Do you understand that? You and Mom both.

"I am so messed up. I chase things, and I leave people bruised and broken along the way. That's how you've molded me. And I hate it.

"I'm going to evolve if it's the last goddamn thing I do. I'd like to open that opportunity to you too. Take it or leave it.

"If you leave it, then I'm not going to be able to be around much. And I hate that, because I love you. But I can't erase all this. I see you and I feel like I'm being controlled. You use me when you need me. You push me to look a certain way." I shrug. *"I need to make my own decisions and live my own life, and I need you to be okay with that. We need you to love and support us and do it for free. And I know you think you already do. You're wrong."*

I gesture to Siri. "Exhibit fucking A." I take a breath. *"You can't blow this off as a one-and-done fix. You need to do the work. It'll take time, and it'll be inconvenient for you. But I need you to do it anyway."*

Water drips down onto my boobs. I'm crying. Dad's crying too. So much crying. I don't want to cry again for at least another ten years. "Siri, get those damn pancakes going, please."

102. A Girl Is Trying Again

JAMIE
September 26, Saturday
New York City

Z and I have been practicing every day for the past six days. He interrupts me. He fake-laughs. He throws me off. Jeers. He's brought me into QCZ when no one was around so I could practice on the stage. We've had Dawn on FaceTime three times, jeering along with him. I've done it sitting, standing, dancing, and lying flat on my back.

They've both given me three rounds of feedback on three different versions of this new ten-minute set.

I'm on in five minutes.

Zarar is back here in the green room, giving me assurance after assurance. Siri's going to be in the audience. There's so much in the set about her, and I haven't worked up the courage to give her any sort of preview. Zarar is going to tape the performance so we can send it to Dawn.

"You've got this," Zarar insists for the fifteenth time in the last thirty minutes. "I'll be out there. If you need me, look at me."

I lean forward to kiss him. "Okay, I've got this. Leave me."

He shoots me a sideways smile and disappears out the door.

The audience is dark. The spotlight hits me as I take the microphone.

"Hey hey hey, I'm Jamie Federov, hello." I wave. "Good day, sea of darkness, I hope you're having a pleasant evening thus far.

"So FYI." I lunge-step, lunge-step, lunge-step across the stage, making stupid faces. "I have intense stage anxiety, so if I collapse, run off screaming, or stare blankly into the distance at any time during this performance, that's perfectly normal. Don't be alarmed. We're good." I stop abruptly and stare into the distance with wide dead eyes for a good ten seconds. Some people start to laugh. I unfreeze. "Ah! That was a practice test and you passed. Good work. Normal comedians take a sip of water, I hyperventilate, we all have our quirks.

"So I've just come off of a pretty gnarly social experiment." I pace the stage. "You know that show *Love Island*?" I freeze, looking around, nodding, watching interest spark in the few faces I can make out in the front.

"It wasn't like that at all. Sorry you got excited for nothing. HEHE." I do a weird jig and then go still, abruptly neutralizing my expression. "*You guys.* I successfully executed an impossible feat. Last week, I pulled off an actual *Parent Trap* scenario with my eighteen-year-old sister."

I pause, gazing around. "Yeah, I see that interest cropping up again. You heard right, I'm not fucking kidding . . . I'm twenty-one and I can pass for eighteen, can you believe it?" A number of people snort.

"So, our parents are divorced. How many of you have divorced parents?" A sea of hands go up. "Relax, that was a rhetorical question. I know they're all divorced.

"*The Parent Trap* sounds pretty innocent, so let me paint you a better picture here. We weren't out to set our parents back up. We were two almost grown-ass women, out for like, Regina George–takedown, *Mean Girls*–level blood . . ." I switch to my Valley girl voice. "Because yo, um, that divorce really fucked us up," I whine.

I get into it. Talking about Siri, and her emo angry ways, how our various issues complement each other. I weave in how our parents met and their overzealous obsession with Game of Thrones.

"Yeah, okay, with that in mind, let's circle back to my name." I take a few quiet steps. "I don't know if you remember. But it's Jamie. That's my name. And my sister, her name's Siri." I take another few steps and blink excessively.

"I mean, are you hearing it, is it ringing any—Jamie and Siri, Jamie and Siri, does it sound, I don't know, a little like"—I stomp aggressively across the stage—"JAIME AND CERSEI?!"

The crowd erupts in laughter.

"MY SISTER AND I ARE NAMED AFTER JAIME AND CERSEI?!" I pause. "THE INCESTUOUS ASSHOLES FROM GAME OF THRONES? Jaime and Cersei are an incestuous brother-sister duo!"

"Yeah." I pause, nodding with an over-the-top expression. "*They did that.* I had to have that revelation as a twelve-year-old girl." I smile at the crowd. "Our dysfunction was"—I put on a robotic romantic voice—"written in the stars."

I wander to the other side of the stage. "Don't even get me started on our middle names. Honest to god, they're George and Martine."

People are laughing. The material has all been hitting.

Seven minutes in I'm riding so high, beaming so hard: and then it all goes quiet when a joke about Timothée Chalamet's house falls flat. My throat jerks shut.

Shit. Bucket. Shit. We debated whether or not he was a well-known-enough reference to keep in, but we ultimately decided it was okay.

I go silent, staring off into the distance with a glazed-over expression.

And slowly, people start to chuckle. The longer I hold it, the more people start to laugh. I accidentally start to smile as my eyes land on Zarar in the front row. This bit is working.

I take a step to the side like we've been practicing. Get stuck, step to the side. Talk more.

I lunge-step, lunge-step like a weird monster across the stage before lifting the microphone back to my lips. "So that's how I walk when I'm pretending to be my sister—she's got a pretty distinctive gait. It was a great week for my thighs." A bunch more people burst into laughter. It's a little rocky, but it hits.

I start up again, veering to some material from my first set about my dad and LA, his Botox and my quest for his attention. And I end with the story about how I met Siri, fourteen years after we last saw each other, by literally running into each other naked in a shower in the middle of nowhere, Colorado. It hits hard. I am fucking glowing.

Then I'm done and I'm saying *Goodbye, you've been a delightful audience.* This is the closest I've ever gotten to a perfect set.

The spotlight fades as I take my bow, and suddenly I can see the crowd. And two rows behind Zarar are Siri and Papa? Mom. Grams. And Dawn? My breath catches. And Dad. And . . . Terry? And Javed and Zarar's parents. And Penn and Shane. They're all standing up and . . . whooping their asses off.

103. Angst and Pride

SIRI
September 26, Saturday
New York City

I've cried a lot this month, but not like this. I'm in tears because Jamie is killing it. My sister is on a stage in front of a hundred people in here, slaying.

And I'm in the audience with my entire family.

I've dreamed about a moment like this. Being in one place, together, with all of them. They're not arguing, they're not screaming, they're united in laughter and love for Jamie on the stage.

I have to tamp down the urge to stand up and scream, "That's my sister up there, and she's intercoursing killing it!" Of course, I'd never risk throwing her off her game right now. But I don't usually have urges like that!

The awestruck look of happiness and surprise on Jamie's face when the lights come up is worth all the hours of trouble it took to organize getting all these hooligans here at 11 p.m. on a Saturday night without her finding out.

When Jamie comes out to the tiny lobby where we're waiting, she beelines straight for me. "Did you invite all these fools to the first performance of a new set I've never tested on an audience before?" she says seriously.

I look down at my feet. Is this about to backfire?

And then I feel her arms around me. Jamie's hugging me. Hugging me like I made her year. I wrap my arms around her to squeeze her back.

She pulls away and nods with a tight expression. "I love you, Sier."

She moves on to hugging Dawn. I start crying again.

104. A Girl Is Freaking Flying

JAMIE
September 26, Saturday
New York City

"Thank you, thank you, okay, I know I was great. Save your praise for later when the imposter syndrome strikes back," I jeer.

I've just endured five minutes straight of hugs and positivity on the sidewalk outside the theater with almost everyone I care about. I feel like I'm in a fever dream.

I meet Z's eyes across my mini entourage. He shoots me a brilliant side smile and I serve one right back. He's been giving me space to talk to everyone from the other coast.

Grams and Papa pull Siri and me aside as those of us who can continue the celebrations start moving toward a restaurant for food and drinks. They hand us two envelopes.

Siri and I exchange a look before opening them. In one we find an Amex, and in the other, two plane tickets for Spain.

"What the—"

Grams interrupts me. "We want you to have your sister trip, have some drama-free fun together. Start in Spain and buy a Europass. Siri, study some fabulous foreign dishes. Jamie, see how your set fares in other areas of the world."

I shake my head, thunderstruck. "Oh, Grams, I can't accept this. I don't want your money."

Grams puts on her stern face. "James Federov, you will use this Amex. I cannot take it with me. I am not your father, stop trying to defy me."

Papa nods, a small smile on his face. "We triggered this sister-switch disaster; we feel very responsible for the fallout. We're old. Let us have this."

Siri spins to look at me with pure, undiluted joy. I feel so incredibly fucking lucky she rammed her way back into my life.

Epilogue

I'm no longer human as I walk over to Dawn's. I am a collection of chaotic bees in girl form.

Dawn and I texted consistently the first six months after the switch. Then at least once a week. Then we checked in every couple of months. Now, we haven't talked since Christmas. It's March.

I flew out from New York with Jamie and Zarar last night.

It's exactly 11 a.m. as I knock on the front door.

I blow out a grounding breath as someone pulls it open.

Dawn looks exquisite in an oversized yellow jacket over high-waisted yellow pants and a cropped yellow tank. Her hair is pulled back into an elaborate braid today. I've never seen her style it like that. It's beautiful.

Her mouth pops open. "Siri?"

My cheeks stretch wider than I thought possible. "Hi."

I've left my hair down and tried to curl it. The further I've gotten from the dance world, the less I've felt the need to tie it back and keep it one color. It's a kind of reverse ombré now, gray-blond from the roots to around my chin, where it goes pitch-black.

"Hi!" Dawn rushes forward and engulfs me in a hug. I nuzzle a bit into her hair since I can't wrap my arms properly around her. I've got bags in both hands. She pulls away.

431

"Your hair is stunning! What are you doing here? Are you only here for the day?! Shit, I'm supposed to be hosting a Duck Waterfall meeting all afternoon."

My face heats. "I actually had Jamie set that up as a decoy so you would be free . . . you look stunning too. You always do."

Dawn blinks at me. I've been keeping tabs on her through Jamie. She was just hired on for a writer's assistant job she applied for at a new Netflix show called *Upside Down Adulting*.

"Is Jamie coming?" Dawn asks tentatively.

I shake my head. "She has plans with Zarar."

Dawn gapes, hovering in the doorway. "She has plans—?"

"—I kind of have some news," I blurt.

Her brows shoot up. "Do tell."

"I'm going to culinary school."

Dawn does an adorable little hop. "Ah! Siri!"

I grin. "In Napa."

She does a double take, looking behind her and then back at me. "As in California Napa?"

I nod, laughing now.

"As in same time zone, I can drive there within a day, Napa?"

I nod again, more eagerly this time. "Mom, Jamie, and I are headed up there together to check out the area tomorrow afternoon."

We stare at each other for a long moment, smiling.

"Um," I start, "I was wondering . . . I haven't seen it on your Instagram, have you hunted down that chicken adobo pizza?"

Her eyes flit to the ground for a moment. "I kind of gradually stopped looking for it because I've maybe been holding out hope I'd get to make it with you."

The bees in my torso tornado excitedly. I hold up my bags. "Are you hungry? I've kind of been working on this recipe for like, a year and six months."

Dawn's eyes sparkle as she waves me into the house. "Get the intercourse in here, Siri Martine."

JAMIE

Z and I follow yet another dude through another condo complex. He unlocks the front door of the vacant unit and lets us head in to take a look.

This might be the one. It's bright, the rent is in our budget, and it's halfway between Burbank and the veterinary school Zarar will be starting at this fall.

It took him all of three days shadowing a vet at a clinic to realize that was it. The guy knows what he wants when he finds it.

I let Z drag me through the place by the hand. He's brimming with enthusiasm about this move. I am too.

A talent manager adopted me as her client about eight months ago. Since then, I've gotten a few paid comedy gigs opening up for rising comics around New York and Los Angeles, I booked a cheeky commercial with the major cell phone company Sprintal, and yesterday I auditioned for a new Netflix stand-up competition. I've got my fingers crossed.

Zarar leads me into the bedroom. It has a high ceiling, hardwood floors, a nice walk-in closet, a big window. I can see us here.

"Janu." Z fully side-smiles at me. "I think this is it."

I smirk back at him. I asked his brother what Janu meant a couple of months back when he first used it. It's apparently super cheesy and romantic. It comes out to something like sweetheart, darling, *forever lover*: an incredibly intimate sentiment to match my incredibly starry-eyed boyfriend. "Stop calling me that. Jay says it's embarrassing."

Zarar smolders at me. "You love it."

I squint at him, "You're lucky you're extremely good looking."

He gestures to the room around us. "Thoughts?"

I nod in agreement. "I mean, it's pretty perfect."

"It is." I follow Z as he casually backs up toward the walk-in closet. "And it has a great closet."

And, we're in the closet.

He smolders at me.

I cock a brow. "We're not going to get this place if they catch us in here."

He tilts his head. "What are you, the closet police?"

I poke his chest and he grabs my hand, pressing it to his heart.

"I am a bad influence on you," I chide.

His lopsided grin kicks up. "We've made it this far. I really think the universe is on our side."

We have made it pretty far. I've thrown my fair share of shit at our relationship, and we're still here. Together. And thrilled about it.

I push the door closed.

We gaze at each other for a beat before I grab his perfect chin and crush his lips with mine.

We've had a number of spontaneous sexual escapades over the past two years. They're always my favorite. Every time we're together, I feel like a human supernova.

We're chaotically de-clothing as he breaks away. "Marry me, canoe thief?"

"Are you shitting me?" I yank off his belt. "This again?"

I hold tight to the bar hanging along the border of the little room, catching my breath as he peels off my fitted flare overalls.

"I'm not shitting you, James," Zarar breathes as he works his way from the floor back up to my face.

I grin as he meets my eyes. "Damnit, Z, no. We're moving in together. Give it a second."

This is his second proposal. The first was on our one-year anniversary.

He laughs as I pull him against me. "Why am I not surprised?" he murmurs against my lips.

"I fucking love you," I whisper into his face.

We're so pleased with ourselves when we slip out five minutes later without reprimand. Z pulls out his iPhone and FaceTimes Siri as we leave the place with an application.

"What's the verdict?" she says as soon as she picks up the phone. She's in Dawn's kitchen. Those two are smitten, and they haven't even started dating yet.

Z laughs. "She said no. You owe me fifty bucks!"

I gawk at him as he points the phone in my direction.

"Excrement! Jamie!" Siri complains.

I loose a disbelieving huff. "Excuse me, gluteus maximus trench, you bet on yes?"

I have plans to propose myself, when I'm good and ready.

A girl has to draw this out so our love story is epic enough for Future Zarar to woo his damn grandkids.

DR. DONYA WENDELL

CHECK IN: Do you feel like you've made progress? What has changed? What hasn't?

The whole family healing thing is a roller coaster. We're all trying, but it's really hard. It takes so much patience and effort not to shut down when Dad's an ass. Especially when it's just me and him. I think Siri would agree—we have some wonderful days with our parents, and we have the occasional terrible ones. But Siri and I are in this shit together, and it makes all the difference.

DR. DONYA WENDELL

CHECK IN: Do you feel like you've made progress? What has changed? What hasn't?

EVERYTHING HAS CHANGED. I LOVE YOU, DONYA, you're a spectacular therapist. Thanks for making us do this exercise so I can see where Jamie's head is at on the subject.

I go to dinner with my dad and Jamie once a month.

436

Mom, Jamie, and I have a monthly FaceTime together.

Mom's seeing a therapist, and I can really feel the difference in the way she approaches our relationship.

Dad's dating his therapist? His girlfriend is a therapist so he's using that as his excuse not to actually have to go to therapy. Papa and I have scheduled a weekly phone call time for when I move to California.

I'm kind of blowing up on food ClikClok.

I'm going to culinary school.

I'm dating the girl of my dreams.

Jamie is my best friend.

Acknowledgments

I *actually* can't believe I'm already writing the acknowledgments for my second novel. This feels so strange. I didn't know what to expect going into book two. I subconsciously assumed it would be similar to writing my first book, but it's been such a completely separate, different experience in almost every way. Writing *Again, but Better* was this invigorating, thrilling, bubbly journey, and writing *Better Together* was this challenging struggle that had its fun wonderful moments, but was filled with so much AnGsT. All of the dumpster fire 2020 angst! But it made finishing all the more rewarding! I am so grateful for all the brilliant, understanding people I've had behind me throughout this process.

I have to thank my family, without whom I wouldn't be a person capable of writing this book. I wouldn't find so much catharsis and joy from family dramas, sister stories, and heartwarming sibling moments, and that would be a damn shame. Madre and Padre, thank you for giving me two younger siblings! Thank you for nurturing my bossy, ambitious, first-child spirit!

Thank you to my amazing, supportive, kick-ass super-agent, JL, for everything you've done for me and this book. Thank you for your enthusiasm. Thank you for believing in me so hard!

A ginormous thank-you to the entire team at New Leaf! Thank you, Suzie Townsend, for your integral feedback during the outline stage of this book.

Thank you to my sensational editor, Eileen, for making this book *happen* in all the ways! Thank you to the spectacular team at Wednesday Books for being so encouraging and collaborative. Thank you to DJ, Mary, Tiffany, and Kerri for all the amazing work you do.

Kat O'Keeffe! Thank you for being the first person to read the *Better Together* outline (and first full draft) in its raw AF form. Thank you for helping me steer it in the right direction. I'm always so grateful for your feedback and support.

Thank you, Dr. Kait McCormick-Huhn, for reading this book in its raw, super-long second-draft form! Thank you for encouraging me over the phone whenever I got neurotic and anxious about any aspect of this story, every step of the way. Your light and positivity pulled me out of so many spirals during this process. I'm so lucky to have the most amazing soul sister best friend in the universe.

Thank you to my wonderful cousin Holly Springhorn for reading this in its early form! Your feedback means so much to me. All your commentary was so helpful, heartwarming, and reassuring. I love you! Thank you so much.

Julia Friley! Thank you for helping me sort through this plot before I ever put pen to paper. Thank you for reading act one multiple times and giving me amazingly detailed notes once you finished the draft. The book did not feel complete until I got your two cents!

Thank you to Umer Durrani, Mina Divinagracia, Morgan Paige, Tiernan Bertrand-Essington, and Emma Giordano for providing such insightful, critical feedback and guidance during the drafting process!

Thank you to Jenna Presto, Jesse George, Kristina Marjieh, and Natasha Polis for your endless support, kindness, and patience throughout this long, intense year of drafting. Thank you for previewing parts of this story and sharing your thoughts and feels!

Thank you, Alex Ling, for sharing behind-the-scenes info about that ballet company auditioning life! Juan, thank you for the encouragement and love during all the intense, chaotic late nights of writing! Thanks for staying up to the wee hours to be there to celebrate with me when I finished.

Thank you, Mom and Nana, for the ocean of love and support you've so generously shared during my most intense moments of anxiety and self-doubt.

To my siblings Paul and Olivia, did you finish this one? Do you know that acknowledgments exist? Did you ever read the *Again, but Better* ones? XD Thanks for being here now (if you're here). Thanks for inspiring various aspects of these characters' personalities, likes, and dislikes. I love y'all. I live for the moments when the three of us are all on the same team.

Papa, I put you in this book. I miss you. It was really nice to pretend to be able to talk to you again. Thank you for teaching me so many things, one of which was how to play all the card games and lose them gracefully. Thanks for always being such a loving, dependable, calm presence in my life.

To my Booktube, Bookternet family: I'm currently in 2020 and we haven't been able to see each other this year. I miss you all so much! Here's hoping that in 2021 I get to see all your beautiful faces in person again. Thank you for all the support, virtual love, and encouragement over social and in my comments. You inspire me daily. Thank you for being amazing friends. I'm so incredibly lucky to have you in my life.

To my subscribers/viewers. I know I said this in my last acknowledgment blurb, but THANK YOU. Thank you for being here. Thank you for sticking with me. For believing in me. For preordering my books. For commenting and making my day. For making the time I put into making things feel important. Thank you for sharing your hearts with me. Thank you for all the messages and tweets. Thank you for reading and fangirling with me throughout the years. I appreciate you all more than you could ever know.

Reader! Hey! I am so happy you're here. Thank you so much for picking up this book and supporting my writing endeavors. I hope it brought you joy! I hope it made you feel a thing. If this is our first time talking, hi! My name's Christine. I like books and oatmeal. I'd love to keep in touch. I'm on the YouTubes as polandbananasBOOKS if you want to chat some more.

xoxo Christine
2020

Turn the page for an exclusive
bonus chapter!

I squint at the audience as I step onto the stage between Chandler Laruso and Paul Plowman. We all match in our steel-toed shoes, black pants, white chef coats, and tall white hats.

Jamie's hair burns bright amongst the sea of family and friends waiting in the maroon, upholstered theater seats. Zarar's on her right, chatting with our mom on his right. Jamie catches my eye and grins. She shoots out both arms in a double thumbs-up. I smile back meekly, trying my best to ignore the knot of sadness at the base of my throat.

I don't want to be sad today. *Today is not sad! My entire family is here!*

Jamie looks so . . . healthy? She's kind of glowing. She's been working on a project with Dad of all people. They're collaborating on some sort of reality TV show that Jamie thought up and Dad's producing. They've been secretive about the specifics because Jamie's convinced explaining it in detail to anyone who doesn't *have to know* said details will jinx it out of existence. (Jamie still has some trust issues.) This past week the two of them pitched it to a whole batch of different networks. Don't ask me how they went, she won't talk about it—the jinxing thing again.

Dad and Jamie working together was something Donya brought up during a family session a few months back. I can't believe it's actually happening. I can't believe how happy it's making Jamie.

Dad's sitting on Jamie's left, and his pregnant girlfriend, Ronnie, is next to him. I have a half sibling coming in around three months. That's going to be weird, but as silly as this sounds for an almost twenty-three-year-old to say—I'm excited to be a big sister. Ronnie's been really good for Dad. I love her. She's calls him out on all his excrement, and they work it out before things get too dire.

Next to Ronnie are Papa and Grams, chatting away themselves. And next to them is an empty seat. Looking at it makes my heart do an uncomfortable fishlike flop in my chest.

Dawn couldn't be here. Can't be here.

She's been pouring her heart and soul into her own dramedy show pitch for Netflix. She's written the first five episodes and mapped out the first *five seasons*. She and Jamie are so in sync, they both ended up getting meetings to pitch their dream projects the same week.

Of course the time slot Dawn received to pitch is today. Her meeting is really soon. Before I shuffled onto the stage, I shot her a good-luck text. I understand why she can't be here. Her dream career is right there, she can reach out and brush it with her fingertips. I would never, ever want to pull her away from that!

But this morning, I spent a good forty-five minutes pining, staring at the floating shelf above my desk—home to my growing collection of snow globes. I have four now. All from Dawn. For different days we've had together. It's become a thing we do. Snow globe different days for each other. We've been dating long distance for two years.

Our entire relationship has been long distance. Our entire relationship has been building to this moment, this day, this crescendo, when I graduate and can finally relocate to Los Angeles. When we can finally live in the same city! We've been counting down to today through our entire official relationship. Today isn't just my graduation. Today marks the beginning of a new era in our relationship, and she won't be here to commemorate it.

I'm moving out of my Napa apartment tomorrow. Jamie and Zarar have a guest room, and they're letting me move in with them until I figure out my LA living situation. I can't wait to be close to them all again.

Dawn and I have fallen into a routine these past two years, traveling to see each other every other weekend. (My dad surprised me with a barely used Prius when I moved out to California. Talk about a guilt purchase.) Once a month, I drive down to LA for a long weekend. Two weeks later, Dawn drives up here to Napa. Then the cycle starts again, texting, calling, and FaceTiming in between.

Our first six months together were exhilarating. The second six months were excruciating.

When she's not here, I miss her lips and her smell and the feel of her skin. I miss the way her eyelashes brush against my cheek. I miss the compassion I can feel in her fingertips when she rubs my back. I miss the warmth of her voice in the crook of my neck. Constantly chasing every brief reunion, only to part ways, sometimes after less than forty-eight hours together, to be apart for another fourteen days—it starts to feel like a repetitive kick to the gut.

I complain to Jamie about how hard it all is on a regular basis, and to her credit, she's never said *I told you so*. Instead, she keeps me updated on how Dawn is doing through her eyes. They see each other at Duck Waterfall performances, of course, but now they also cohost a weekly comedy relationship advice podcast. I listen religiously on Mondays as I walk to and from class. I can almost trick myself into thinking I'm in the room with them.

This second year of long distance has been rough. The longer I love her, the harder it is to be okay with the extended time apart. Dawn's schedule has only become more chaotic and LA-based. My classes have remained steady, holding me here consistently. This is a two-year expedited program with no summer break.

Lately we've cut down our phone calls, so she can make it to meetings or get to bed early enough for work. Dawn had to cancel her most recent trip up here (two weeks ago) because of an emergency writing deadline for *Upside Down Adulting*. She apologized profusely, but that didn't make it hurt any less. We haven't seen each other in twenty-eight days.

There are nights when I spiral out, convinced she's slipping away. The same way my mother did. Through success. Last night was one of them.

Today just feels *important*. I blink at the empty seat, pressure building behind my eyes. This whole thought spiral feels disgustingly selfish. I want the people I love to succeed! I want them to achieve all their goals! But it hurts to continually feel like the sacrifice they need to make to get there. I always end up being the first sandbag to be sliced. The first box thrown to slow a sinking ship. The thing left behind when the house is on fire.

I've been channeling my neurotic long-distance relationship feels into cooking. And cooking ClikCloks. I've actually acquired a pretty sizable audience, which never stops being surprising.

I blink back to reality as my phone vibrates in my pocket. The ceremony has started. Dean Windchair is at the podium speaking about our food journeys and impending futures in fine dining. I slip out my iPhone.

Jamie: You okay? You look emo. We're soups proud of you out here, sis. Can't wait to have you around. Will you cook for us every night? WE HEREBY OFFICIALLY VOLUNTEER TO TASTE TEST ANY AND EVERYTHING YOU CONJURE.

I look up at Jamie in the audience. She waggles her eyebrows and dances stupidly in her seat. Zarar dances alongside of her, both of them widening their eyes at me. I crack a grin and slip the phone back in my pocket as the dean starts calling out names.

When I'm called, I step forward, a stupid grin making its way onto my face. My area of the auditorium applauds enthusiastically.

"FUCK YEAH! That's my sister, she's already a famous chef with 200,000 followers on ClikClok. Go follow her!"

I dip my head, cheeks burning as I return to my spot.

After Olivia Zeele settles back into her seat, the dean congratulates the class of 2024. Someone tosses their chef's hat up toward the ceiling, and everyone follows suit. I throw mine into the mix, a hopeful, anxious, untethered feeling blooming in my chest as it soars up into the air with the others. In a way, it's been comforting to be back in school. Now life is open-ended again. Exciting, scary, and unknown, like after my accident.

My eyes find Dawn's empty seat. *Stop looking at it!*

I can't *not* look at it. I have too many feelings. I hope to god she still wants me when I'm not long distance. I hope to god she's not slowly ghosting away. I hope today is the beginning of a new era and not the beginning of the end.

My family is waiting for me in a little huddle outside on the grass. Jamie runs up and hugs me. I talked about hugs in one of our Donya sessions. Since then, she's greeted me with obnoxious overbearing embraces.

Mom pulls me in next. We hug now too. It would be weird if she didn't now with everyone else around her doing it. Papa comes in next, then Dad, Grams, Zarar, and Ronnie, all telling me how proud they are. How much they liked my latest easy ClikClok recipe. How great I look in a chef's uniform. I grin at them all. So much has changed in past three years. *How can I be sad right now, when I'm so lucky.*

"I think we have reservations at some place your mother found online?" Dad says with his arm around Ronnie.

"Yes!" Mom asserts. "We should get going." Our group starts toward the parking lot.

"Wait." Jamie grabs my arm and pulls me aside.

"What?"

"Dude, I forgot a jacket."

I give her a once-over. She's wearing a vintage sleeveless emerald-green turtleneck jumpsuit with a neon-green, thick high-waisted belt. She looks cute. "Jame. You always forget a jacket."

"Look at me. I'm wearing a sleeveless turtle neck! It's fall—"

"It's August," I inject.

"I need a jacket, we'll be outside!"

"It's sixty degrees."

"Yeah, it's sixty degrees!" she says pointedly. "Let me borrow one of yours. Please! I love you." She bats her eyelashes at me.

"My apartment's a ten-minute walk."

"Great, I'll go with you! I'm cold. Can I wear your chef's hat?"

I roll my eyes, picking it off my head and handing it to her as I glance over at everyone else. With the exception of Zarar, who hung back, the elders are now at least fifty feet away. "Are we going to make everyone wait because you were too careless to bring a jacket?"

Jamie settles my hat on her head and waves dismissively. "Z and I drove ourselves. We'll meet them there. I'll text Dad to go ahead without us."

I blow out a sigh.

Jamie clicks away at her iPhone for thirty seconds. "'Tis done!" She loops an arm through mine and waves Zarar over.

Jamie fills me in on Zarar's latest attempt to propose as the three of us meander down the sidewalk toward my building. Zarar watches Jamie adoringly with a glint of amusement in his eyes. He interjects every so often to tease Jamie. It makes me miss Dawn even more than I already do.

I lead the way up the steps to my studio apartment. Jamie and Z are fifteen feet behind me now, flirting like they only met an hour ago. My chef's hat is now on Zarar. I huff out a flustered breath and unlock my door.

I fumble inside and hastily shove off my clunky chef shoes. As soon as I look up, my forehead knocks into a foreign object. I grapevine anxiously into the wall. "What the—?"

It's a piece of paper hanging from my ceiling. A paper snowflake. A glittery paper snowflake, slowly rotating on a clear string, sparkling green in the afternoon light. *The ceiling.* There are glittery paper snowflakes hanging from the ceiling across the *entire apartment.* I take another step inside, and the heavy door falls shut behind me. Each snowflake is strung from a different length of string, making the overall aesthetic all the more enchanting.

Across the room, my dark comforter has been covered with a giant fluffy white blanket. The place looks like a sparkly winter wonderland. It looks like . . . *the inside of a snow globe.*

"Hi."

I whip to my left. Dawn is sitting up against the wall on my tiny kitchen counter three feet away. She pulls at something, a party popper, and blue confetti erupts over my head.

"Congratulations," she says softly.

Dawn's dressed all in white. Tight ripped white jeans. White platform sneakers. White cowl neck blouse. Pearl drop earrings. Her hair is loose; the curled ends spiral down over her collarbone. Her dimples hit full force as she smiles.

She's stunning. She's always stunning. How is she here? I'm crying before the confetti from her party popper has made its way to the ground.

"You're here?" I gurgle.

"I'm here."

I gape at her for a moment. "But the pitch! You didn't miss the pitch?"

Dawn hops off the counter and steps toward me. "I didn't miss the pitch. I managed to reschedule for yesterday."

"Yesterday? You didn't say anything," I squeak.

She laughs and takes my hands in hers. "Yeah, I wanted to surprise you!"

I glance around, taking in more of the decor. She's artistically placed fake snow all over the place. It looks beautiful. "You did this?"

"I did." She swings our hands side to side. "I've been busy and over-whelmed and . . . I feel like I haven't been prioritizing *us* these past few months. I hate that I canceled my last Napa trip. I should have come anyway. You are just as important as any deadline. It was our last Napa weekend. It was our last long-distance visit! I know you had something special planned. I should have just worked up here and been with you. I'm sorry."

I did have something special planned. "It was okay," I mumble.

She shakes her head. "No, it wasn't. I've missed you so much, and I know the way I canceled made you feel shitty. I never want to be the thing making you feel shitty."

I squeeze her hands and nod, water still dribbling down my face. I love her so much.

"Thank you." I am a mess. "How . . . how did the pitch go?"

Dawn swipes a tear from my cheek. "I think well."

"I'm so glad you're here. How did you even get in?" I whisper.

She smiles, leaning her forehead against mine. "I got a copy of your key made last time I was here and you were in class."

I hiccup a small gasp. "That was mischievous."

"I grew up with your sister."

I snort. My nose is all clogged so it sounds gross. But Dawn leans forward and kisses me.

Everything goes gold. My heart throws itself into a grand pirouette, spin-ning relentlessly, gaining momentum with every rotation. Kissing Dawn is always joyous. There is no gravity. There are no limits. When we're together, I can fly.

She pulls back a millimeter. "I can't believe my endlessly talented gorgeous girlfriend is a certified gourmet chef, and I get to have her back in LA."

I glance down as my cheeks flush. "I can't believe you transformed my apartment into a real physical snow globe."

Dawn runs a finger up my neck and gently lifts my chin. "I wanted to finish earlier." She smiles. "I planned on making it to the ceremony. I'm a little late because I found a new apartment this week, and I had to pick up the keys this morning before gunning it up here."

A new apartment? Dawn lives with a roommate ten minutes away from Dad's house. She moved out of her mom's a year and a half ago and into a two-bedroom with Jess from Duck Waterfall. *She hasn't said anything about a new apartment.*

"You're moving?"

She reaches into her back pocket and pulls out a weathered key on a chef's hat keychain. "I was hoping maybe you'd move with me."

"I—" I choke on oxygen. Sparks of warmth soar through me as I stare at the gold key pinched between her beautifully smudgy, white-painted fingernails. I might still be crying.

"I probably should have told you." She squirms. "I'm sorry. I found this place with a great kitchen and decided to go for it. I was being super picky; it had to have a spacious countertop so you could cook with—"

I close the space between us, catching her lips in mine and sliding my hands into her hair. She giggles against my mouth before twisting her arms around my neck. The key jangles against my back. My lips part with hers, a warm static building in my chest. We slowly sidestep, making our way toward the fluffy blanket on my bed.

I break away abruptly as my butt hits the mattress. "Are you sure? It's not too soon?"

She beams down at me, humor sparking in her eyes. "Really? Too soon?"

I shrug nervously. "Well, we've never been around each other for long periods of time. We've been long distance since we met."

Dawn shifts forward, maneuvering herself over me on the bed until I'm lying flat on my back against the soft blanket. Her hair falls around my face. Paper snowflakes drift and glitter over her head.

"Siri, I'm very aware of how much distance we've been dealing with." She lowers herself against me and my insides ignite. "I'm so intercoursing tired of not being able to touch you every day."

How many times am I going to be rendered speechless today? I've died and gone to long-distance relationship heaven. I run my finger down her cheek. Trace over her dimple. Say the only thing I can think right now: "I love you."

"I love you too."

I grab her hips and roll us over, so I'm hovering above her smiling face. "We're about to be in an extremely short-distance relationship."

Dawn's hands glide up my thighs. "There's nothing I want more than to be in a short-distance relationship with you."

Someone pounds on the door. I bristle like a startled cat, flailing off of Dawn.

"Did you find me a jacket!?"

"Intercourse!" I scramble to my feet. "Jamie and Zarar are in the hallway!"

Dawn snorts, casually straightening her clothes. "They knew I was in here."

I look toward the door and back at her. "They . . . you . . ." I narrow my eyes. "She doesn't even need a jacket, does she?"

More knocking. "I do need a jacket! Put a pin in it love-bitches, we're on a schedule!" Jamie yells from the hall.

I throw open the door to reveal Jamie's smirking face.

"You set me up."

Jamie does a little jig. "You're welcome. But wait, there's more." She sticks a hand in her pocket and yanks out four ticketlike things to wave in my face. "Happy graduation! I got us Billie Eilish tickets!"

I blink at her, still giddy and drunk on Dawn. "Wha . . . you got us Billie Eilish tickets?"

"I did."

"You got me a graduation gift?!"

"Obviously we got you a graduation gift," Jamie says.

Zarar, who's been standing behind her, laughs. He takes off my chef's hat and plops it back onto my head.

"And that gift is tickets for us all to see Billie?"

"Yeah, pick your jaw up off the ground, stanch the waterworks, and grab your sneakers. We gotta move. We have to be in San Francisco in an hour if we want to eat dinner before the show."

A door creaks open behind me, and I turn to see Dawn rummaging through my closet.

I blink some more before turning back to Jamie. "Tickets for tonight?! What about everyone else?"

She scoffs. "Sier, everyone already knows. They'll still be around to help you move tomorrow. Did you grab me a jacket?"

"I'm grabbing you a fucking jacket, Jame," Dawn calls.

"I—I . . . thank you!" I look down at my chef's outfit. "I can't believe this. I have to change!"

"I'm grabbing you clothes," Dawn sings.

Zarar puts an arm around Jamie. "I always keep a jacket for you in the back of the car. You know that, right?"

"Yeah, but I wanted to steal one of Siri's. That's what sisters are for."

Dawn sidles up next to me and holds my black jean jacket out to Jamie.

Jamie snatches the garment. "Thanks, D, Sier. Let's roll." She pivots, grabbing Zarar's hand and leading him back down the hall.

Slung over Dawn's elbow is my leather jacket and a plain black V-neck top she knows I like. She shoves the door closed and starts to help me out of my chef's uniform.

I laugh, feeling completely caught off guard in every possible way. *How long has Jamie been planning the concert? When did they discuss Dawn surprising me? Decorating the apartment? Does Jamie know Dawn was going to ask me to move in with her? Was she humoring me?*

Once I'm free of the chef jacket, I pull on the clothes Dawn stole out of my closet. She stands a foot away, brazenly staring as I re-dress. When I'm clothed, I pull her close, sliding my arms around her waist. "I can't properly verbalize or process the happiness I'm feeling right now. I've gone into happiness shock."

She tilts her chin so our lips are a breath apart. "I can't wait till we get back so we can properly celebrate the beginning our short-distance relationship."

My head's whirring and my skin is pulsing as we meet Z and Jamie at the end of the corridor. *We're going to see Billie Eilish!*

Jamie's babbling about how great our seats are as we push open the foyer doors and step back out into the afternoon. Her iPhone buzzes mid-soliloquy, and she offhandedly brings it up to her eye line. "You're going to be able to see the damn sweat dripping off her fa—"

She comes to an abrupt verbal and physical halt as she focuses on her screen. Then she pivots and whips the iPhone over her shoulder at my building.

"Jamieee!!!" I screech as it hits the brick and falls to the ground. "Excrement! I hope Mom got her insurance on that. What the underworld?!"

"Did someone send you a gif of the ring girl again?" Dawn chides.

Zarar has moved to stand in front of Jamie. "What's wrong, James?"

"That was my dad," she whispers loudly.

When she doesn't continue, I bulge my eyes expectantly. "And?"

"CTS wants to buy our show," she wheezes. "The show that Dad and I are working on. They're going to make the show, we're going to make the show—"

Dawn starts excitedly screaming. Zarar pulls Jamie into a hug. My eyes predictably well up with more tears.

Jamie pushes away from Zarar to scream with Dawn, "They want to buy my fucking show!"

"Fucketh yeah, they want your fucking show! YOU'RE AMAZING, I KNEW THEY WOULD!" Dawn belts back.

Jamie explodes into a run before throwing herself into cartwheels down the sidewalk. I giggle, watching Dawn sprint down the walkway cheering alongside her.

Z and I share an amused look before grabbing Jamie's cracked phone. We start after them in comfortable silence.

I've done so much preparing in my life. In this year. This month. This week. Today, I prepared to graduate. To be jobless. To move in with my sister. To see my family. To be sad about Dawn. I forgot that life can be so delightfully unpredictable.